ECHOES OF
VALOR II

Tor books by Karl Edward Wagner
Echoes of Valor (ed.)
Echoes of Valor II (ed.)
Why Not You and I?

ECHOES OF VALOR II

Edited by
Karl Edward Wagner

TOR
fantasy

A TOM DOHERTY ASSOCIATES BOOK
NEW YORK

This book is a work of fiction. All the characters and events portrayed
in it are fictional, and any resemblance to real people or incidents is
purely coincidental.

ECHOES OF VALOR II

Copyright © 1989 by Karl Edward Wagner

A TOR Book
Published by Tom Doherty Associates, Inc.
49 West 24th Street
New York, N.Y. 10010

Printed in the United States of America

First edition: August 1989

0 9 8 7 6 5 4 3 2 1

ACKNOWLEDGMENTS

"The Frost King's Daughter" by Robert E. Howard. First published as "Gods of the North" in *The Fantasy Fan,* March 1934. Reprinted by permission of Glenn Lord, Agent for the Estate of Robert E. Howard.

"The Frost-Giant's Daughter" by Robert E. Howard. Copyright ©1976 by Glenn Lord for *Rogues in the House.* Reprinted by permission of Glenn Lord, Agent for the Estate of Robert E. Howard; and of Conan Properties, Inc.

"An Autobiographical Sketch of C. L. Moore" by C. L. Moore. First published in *Fantasy Magazine,* June 1936. Copyright © 1936; renewed 1964 by C. L. Moore. Reprinted by permission of Don Congdon Associates, Inc., Agents for the Estate of C. L. Moore.

"Quest of the Starstone" by C. L. Moore and Henry Kuttner. Copyright © 1937 by The Popular Fiction Publishing Company for *Weird Tales,* November 1937; renewed 1965. Reprinted by permission of Don Congdon Associates, Inc., Agents for the Estates of C. L. Moore and Henry Kuttner.

"Nymph of Darkness" by C. L. Moore and Forrest J Ackerman. First published in *Fantasy Magazine,* April 1935. Copyright © 1935: renewed 1963. Reprinted by permission of Don Congdon Associates, Inc., Agents for the Estate of C. L. Moore, and by permission of Forrest J Ackerman.

The Editor wishes to express his special gratitude to those who generously helped to assemble this book: Forrest J Ackerman, Ray Bradbury, David Drake, Glenn Lord, Richard Minter, Sam Moskowitz, Virgil Utter, and Frances Wellman.

To C. L. Moore

Flesh is transient,
Dreams are Eternal—

TABLE OF CONTENTS

I.

ROBERT E. HOWARD

INTRODUCTION

Wait! Stop! *Read this part first!*

The following two short stories are virtually the same—"The Frost-Giant's Daughter" being a later version of "The Frost King's Daughter," revised by Robert E. Howard into a Conan story. So if you're a casual reader, skip the first version and just read "The Frost-Giant's Daughter." But if you're a serious fan of heroic fantasy, keep on reading from here. This gets curiouser and curiouser.

Born January 22, 1906 in Peaster, Texas, Robert E. Howard grew up moving across Texas from one small town to another before his father and mother settled in Cross Plains. There Howard worked furiously to make a living as a writer. His first sale, a short story about primitive man entitled "Spear and Fang," was published in the July 1925 issue of *Weird Tales*. Although Howard tried to write in various genres, sales were extremely slow until the start of the 1930s. By this time his work was beginning to attract attention in *Weird Tales,* and he had started to sell to other, better paying markets. While his western and adventure

stories paid the bills, Howard devoted the most energy and
affection to his work for *Weird Tales*—creating there such
memorable characters as Solomon Kane, a Puritan adventurer
in the age of Elizabeth; Bran Mak Morn, a Pictish king in the
early years of third-century Roman Britain; King Kull, a
savage who became king in the age of lost Atlantis; Conan, a
barbarian from Cimmeria who roved, reaved, and ruled
across the fabled Hyborian Age. While heroic fantasy is as old
as the human race itself, one may accurately argue that it was
Howard's fusion of myth, imagination, and pulp adventure
that crystallized heroic fantasy into the genre's modern form.
Unfortunately, Robert E. Howard never lived to see this
legacy or even to achieve his peak as a writer. On June 11,
1936 he put a bullet through his brain.

By far Howard's most famous creation is Conan. Between early 1932 and July of 1935 Howard would write and
complete twenty-one tales of Conan, their lengths ranging
from 3500 to 75,000 words. Of these, seventeen were
published in *Weird Tales*. The remaining four were rejected
by editor Farnsworth Wright and did not see publication
until many years after Howard's death. One of these four was
"The Black Stranger," published for the first time in its
original form in *Echoes of Valor I;* a second of these is "The
Frost-Giant's Daughter"—published here in its original
form for the first time in a mass market edition.

Correction: in its original *forms*.

Howard was wont to say that Conan had simply leapt
forth from his imagination and onto the page like the
proverbial bolt out of the blue. For example, in a short
autobiographical sketch in the July 1935 issue of *Fantasy
Magazine*, Howard wrote: "Conan simply grew up in my
mind a few years ago when I was stopping in a little border
town on the lower Rio Grande. I did not create him by any
conscious process. He simply stalked full grown out of
oblivion and set me at work recording the saga of his
adventures."

This isn't strictly true, however. While Conan certainly
was the fictional extension of the author's idealized self-

image, as such Conan was also a refinement of many of Howard's earlier characters. The first two Conan stories Howard wrote were revisions of unsold stories utilizing other characters. These stories were "The Phoenix on the Sword," a rewrite of the King Kull story, "By This Axe I Rule!" and "The Frost-Giant's Daughter," a rewrite of "The Frost King's Daughter" featuring Amra of Akbitana. Howard fans will remember that Conan is sometimes known as Amra.

Howard submitted both of these stories to *Weird Tales* and received the following letter, dated March 10, 1932, from editor Farnsworth Wright:

I am returning THE FROST-GIANT'S DAUGHTER in a separate envelope, as I do not much care for it.

But THE PHOENIX OF THE SWORD has points of real excellence. I hope you will see your way clear to touch it up and resubmit it. It is the first two chapters that do not click. The story opens rather uninterestingly, it seems to me, and the reader has difficulty in orienting himself. The first chapter ends well, and the second chapter begins superbly; but after King Conan's personality is well established, the chapter sags from too much writing. I think the very last page of the whole story might be re-written with advantage; because it seems a little weak after the stupendous events that precede it."

"The Phoenix on the Sword" appeared in the December 1932 issue of *Weird Tales,* and Conan's career was launched. While certainly one of Howard's best stories, "The Frost-Giant's Daughter" was decidedly too risqué for the puritanical Wright, who saw Conan as a noble barbarian out to perform deeds of chivalrous heroism. And so, "The Frost-Giant's Daughter" passed into limbo. Sort of. This gets complicated.

In a letter dated November 10, 1933, Howard submitted "The Frost King's Daughter" to Charles Hornig, editor of the amateur magazine, *The Fantasy Fan:*

Here is a short story, "The Frost King's Daughter" which I thought you might find suitable for The Fantasy Fan.

This story was subsequently published in the March 1934 issue of *The Fantasy Fan* under the new title, "Gods of the North." The obscure reprints of this version have retained this retitling. The version published here is taken from its original appearance in *The Fantasy Fan* and for the first time restores Howard's original title.

Meanwhile, the Conan version, "The Frost-Giant's Daughter," remained lost for twenty years, until being discovered in a batch of Howard's unpublished stories in the early 1950s. Thus, "The Frost-Giant's Daughter" finally saw print in the August 1953 issue of *Fantasy Fiction*. Only—not *quite*.

The version, as then published, of "The Frost-Giant's Daughter" was extensively rewritten by L. Sprague de Camp, despite the fact that this was indeed a polished, complete draft. Regrettably, virtually all subsequent reprintings of "The Frost-Giant's Daughter" have been the de Camp revision—the sole exception being in an expensive limited edition of *Rogues in the House* (Donald M. Grant: 1976). This latter text was printed from Robert E. Howard's original manuscript of "The Frost-Giant's Daughter," as is the version of the story presented here. This is the first mass market appearance of "The Frost-Giant's Daughter" *exactly* as Howard himself wrote it.

So here you have them, published together for the first time: "The Frost King's Daughter" and "The Frost-Giant's Daughter"—the former text taken from its original amateur magazine appearance, the latter text taken directly from Howard's original manuscript. For serious students of heroic fantasy, here's a chance to compare the two texts and to witness the genesis of Conan the Cimmerian. And for casual fans of the genre, either version makes for a damn fine read.

THE FROST KING'S DAUGHTER

by Robert E. Howard

The clangor of the swords had died away, the shouting of the slaughter was hushed; silence lay on the red-stained snow. The pale bleak sun that glittered so blindingly from the ice-fields and the snow-covered plains struck sheens of silver from rent corselet and broken blade, where the dead lay in heaps. The nerveless hand yet gripped the broken hilt; helmeted heads, back-drawn in the death throes, tilted red beards and golden beards grimly upward, as if in last invocation to Ymir the frost-giant.

Across the red drifts and mail-clad forms, two figures approached one another. In that utter desolation only they moved. The frosty sky was over them, the white illimitable plain around them, the dead men at their feet. Slowly through the corpses they came, as ghosts might come to a tryst through the shambles of a world.

Their shields were gone, their corselets dinted. Blood smeared their mail; their swords were red. Their horned helmets showed the marks of fierce strokes.

One spoke, he whose locks and beard were red as the blood on the sunlit snow.

"Man of the raven locks," said he, "tell me your name, so that my brothers in Vanaheim may know who was the last of Wulfhere's band to fall before the sword of Heimdul."

"This is my answer," replied the black-haired warrior: "Not in Vanaheim, but in Valhalla will you tell your brothers the name of Amra of Akbitana."

Heimdul roared and sprang, and his sword swung in a mighty arc. Amra staggered and his vision was filled with red sparks as the blade shivered into bits of blue fire on his helmet. But as he reeled he thrust with all the power of his great shoulders. The sharp point drove through brass scales and bones and heart, and the red-haired warrior died at Amra's feet.

Amra stood swaying, trailing his sword, a sudden sick weariness assailing him. The glare of the sun on the snow cut his eyes like a knife and the sky seemed shrunken and strangely far. He turned away from the trampled expanse where yellow-bearded warriors lay locked with red-haired slayers in the embrace of death. A few steps he took, and the glare of the snow fields was suddenly dimmed. A rushing wave of blindness engulfed him, and he sank down into the snow, supporting himself on one mailed arm, seeking to shake the blindness out of his eyes as a lion might shake his mane.

A silvery laugh cut through his dizziness, and his sight cleared slowly. There was a strangeness about all the landscape that he could not place or define—an unfamiliar tinge to earth and sky. But he did not think long of this. Before him, swaying like a sapling in the wind, stood a woman. Her body was like ivory, and save for a veil of gossamer, she was naked as the day. Her slender bare feet were whiter than the snow they spurned. She laughed, and her laughter was sweeter than the rippling of silvery fountains, and poisonous with cruel mockery.

"Who are you?" demanded the warrior.

"What matter?" Her voice was more musical than a silver-stringed harp, but it was edged with cruelty.

"Call up your men," he growled, grasping his sword.

"Though my strength fail me, yet they shall not take me alive. I see that you are of the Vanir."

"Have I said so?"

He looked again at her unruly locks, which he had thought to be red. Now he saw that they were neither red nor yellow, but a glorious compound of both colors. He gazed spell-bound. Her hair was like elfin-gold, striking which, the sun dazzled him. Her eyes were neither wholly blue nor wholly grey, but of shifting colors and dancing lights and clouds of colors he could not recognize. Her full red lips smiled, and from her slim feet to the blinding crown of her billowy hair, her ivory body was as perfect as the dream of a god. Amra's pulse hammered in his temples.

"I can not tell," said he, "whether you are of Vanaheim and mine enemy, or of Asgard and my friend. Far have I wandered, from Zingara to the Sea of Vilayet, in Stygia and Kush, and the country of the Hyrkanians; but a woman like you I have never seen. Your locks blind me with their brightness. Not even among the fairest daughters of the Aesir have I seen such hair, by Ymir!"

"Who are you to swear by Ymir?" she mocked. "What know you of the gods of ice and snow, you who have come up from the south to adventure among strangers?"

"By the dark gods of my own race!" he cried in anger. "Have I been backward in the sword-play, stranger or no? This day I have seen four score warriors fall, and I alone survive the field where Wulfhere's reavers met the men of Bragi. Tell me, woman, have you caught the flash of mail across the snow-plains, or seen armed men moving upon the ice?"

"I have seen the hoar-frost glittering in the sun," she answered. "I have heard the wind whispering across the everlasting snows."

He shook his head.

"Niord should have come up with us before the battle joined. I fear he and his warriors have been ambushed. Wulfhere lies dead with all his weapon-men.

"I had thought there was no village within many leagues of this spot, for the war carried us far, but you can have come no great distance over these snows, naked as you are. Lead me to your tribe, if you are of Asgard, for I am faint with the weariness of strife."

"My dwelling place is further than you can walk, Amra of Akbitana!" she laughed. Spreading wide her arms she swayed before him, her golden head lolling wantonly, her scintillant eyes shadowed beneath long silken lashes. "Am I not beautiful, man?"

"Like Dawn running naked on the snows," he muttered, his eyes burning like those of a wolf.

"Then why do you not rise and follow me? Who is the strong warrior who falls down before me?" she chanted in maddening mockery. "Lie down and die in the snow with the other fools, Amra of the black hair. You can not follow where I would lead."

With an oath the man heaved himself upon his feet, his blue eyes blazing, his dark scarred face convulsed. Rage shook his soul, but desire for the taunting figure before him hammered at his temples and drove his wild blood riotously through his veins. Passion fierce as physical agony flooded his whole being so that earth and sky swam red to his dizzy gaze, and weariness and faintness were swept from him in madness.

He spoke no word as he drove at her fingers hooked like talons. With a shriek of laughter she leaped back and ran, laughing at him over her white shoulder. With a low growl Amra followed. He had forgotten the fight, forgotten the mailed warriors who lay in their blood, forgotten Niord's belated reavers. He had thought only for the slender white shape which seemed to float rather than run before him.

Out across the white blinding plain she led him. The trampled red field fell out of sight behind him, but still Amra kept on with the silent tenacity of his race. His mailed feet broke through the frozen crust; he sank deep in the drifts and forged through them by sheer strength. But the girl danced across the snow as light as a feather floating across a pool; her naked feet scarcely left their imprint on the hoar-frost. In spite of the fire in his veins, the cold bit through the warrior's mail and furs; but the girl in her gossamer veil ran as lightly and as gaily as if she danced through the palms and rose gardens of Poitain.

Black curses drooled through the warrior's parched lips. The great veins swelled and throbbed in his temples, and his teeth gnashed spasmodically.

"You cannot escape me!" he roared. "Lead me into a trap and I'll pile the heads of your kinsmen at your feet. Hide from me and I'll tear apart the mountains to find you! I'll follow you to hell and beyond hell!"

Her maddening laughter floated back to him, and foam flew from the warrior's lips. Further and further into the wastes she led him, till he saw the wide plains give way to low hills, marching upward in broken ranges. Far to the north he caught a glimpse of towering mountains, blue with the distance, or white with the eternal snows. Above these mountains shone the flaring rays of the borealis. They spread fan-wise into the sky, frosty blades of cold flaming light, changing in color, growing and brightening.

Above him the skies glowed and crackled with strange lights and gleams. The snow shone weirdly, now frosty blue, now icy crimson, now cold silver. Through a shimmering icy realm of enchantment Amra plunged doggedly onward, in a crystalline maze where the only reality was the white body dancing across the glittering snow beyond his reach—ever beyond his reach.

Yet he did not wonder at the necromantic strangeness of it all, not even when two gigantic figures rose up to bar his way. The scales of their mail were white with hoar-frost; their helmets and their axes were sneathed in ice. Snow sprinkled their locks; in their beards were spikes of icicles; their eyes were cold as the lights that streamed above them.

"Brothers!" cried the girl, dancing between them. "Look who follows! I have brought you a man for the feasting! Take his heart that we may lay it smoking on our father's board!"

The giants answered with roars like the grinding of icebergs on a frozen shore, and heaved up their shining axes as the maddened Akbitanan hurled himself upon them. A frosty blade flashed before his eyes, blinding him with its brightness, and he gave back a terrible stroke that sheared through his foe's thigh. With a groan the victim fell, and at the instant Amra was dashed into the snow, his left shoulder numb from the blow of the survivor, from which the warrior's mail had barely saved his life. Amra saw the remaining giant looming above him like a colossus carved of ice, etched against the glowing sky. The axe fell, to sink through the snow and deep into the frozen earth as Amra hurled himself aside and leaped to his feet. The giant roared and wrenched the axe-head free, but even as he did so, Amra's sword sang down. The giant's knees bent and he sank slowly into the snow which turned crimson with the blood that gushed from his half-severed neck.

Amra wheeled, to see the girl standing a short distance away, staring in wide-eyed horror, all mockery gone from her face. He cried out fiercely and the blood-drops flew from his sword as his hand shook in the intensity of his passion.

"Call the rest of your brothers!" he roared. "Call the dogs! I'll give their hearts to the wolves!"

With a cry of fright she turned and fled. She did not laugh now, nor mock him over her shoulder. She ran as for her life, and though he strained every nerve and thew, until his temples were like to burst and the snow swam red to his gaze, she drew away from him, dwindling in the witch-fire of the skies, until she was a figure no bigger than a child, then a dancing white flame on the snow, then a dim blur in the distance. But grinding his teeth until the blood started from his gums, he reeled on, and he saw the blur grow to a dancing white flame, and the flame to a figure big as a child; and then she was running less than a hundred paces ahead of him, and slowly the space narrowed, foot by foot.

She was running with effort now, her golden locks blowing free; he heard the quick panting of her breath, and saw a flash of fear in the look she cast over her alabaster shoulder. The grim endurance of the warrior had served him well. The speed ebbed from her flashing white legs; she reeled in her gait. In his untamed soul flamed up the fires of hell she had fanned so well. With an inhuman roar he closed in on her, just as she wheeled with a haunting cry and flung out her arms to fend him off.

His sword fell into the snow as he crushed her to him. Her supple body bent backward as she fought with desperate frenzy in his iron arms. Her golden hair blew about his face, blinding him with its sheen; the feel of her slender figure twisting in his mailed arms drove him to blinder madness. His strong fingers sank deep into her smooth flesh, and that flesh was cold as ice. It was as if he embraced not a woman of human flesh and blood, but a woman of flaming ice. She writhed her golden head aside, striving to avoid the savage kisses that bruised her red lips.

"You are cold as the snows," he mumbled dazedly. "I will warm you with the fire in my own blood—"

With a desperate wrench she twisted from his arms, leaving her single gossamer garment in his grasp. She sprang back and faced him, her golden locks in wild disarray, her white bosom heaving, her beautiful eyes blazing with terror. For an instant he stood frozen, awed by her terrible beauty as she posed naked against the snows.

And in that instant she flung her arms toward the lights that glowed in the skies above her and cried out in a voice that rang in Amra's ears for ever after:

"Ymir! Oh, my father, save me!"

Amra was leaping forward, arms spread to seize her, when with a crack like the breaking of an ice mountain, the whole skies leaped into icy fire. The girl's ivory body was suddenly enveloped in a cold blue flame so blinding that the warrior threw up his hands to shield his eyes. A fleeting instant, skies and snowy hills were bathed in crackling white flames, blue darts of icy light, and frozen crimson fires. Then Amra staggered and cried out. The girl was gone. The glowing snow lay empty and bare; high above him the witch-lights flashed and played in a frosty sky gone mad, and among the distant blue mountains there sounded a rolling thunder as of a gigantic war-chariot rushing behind steeds whose frantic hoofs struck lightning from the snows and echoes from the skies.

Then suddenly the borealis, the snowy hills and the

blazing heavens reeled drunkenly to Amra's sight; thousands of fireballs burst with showers of sparks, and the sky itself became a titanic wheel which rained stars as it spun. Under his feet the snowy hills heaved up like a wave, and the Akbitanan crumpled into the snows to lie motionless.

In a cold dark universe, whose sun was extinguished eons ago, Amra felt the movement of life, alien and unguessed. An earthquake had him in its grip and was shaking him to and fro, at the same time chafing his hands and feet until he yelled in pain and fury and groped for his sword.

"He's coming to, Horsa," grunted a voice. "Haste—we must rub the frost out of his limbs, if he's ever to wield sword again."

"He won't open his left hand," growled another, his voice indicating muscular strain. "He's clutching something—"

Amra opened his eyes and stared into the bearded faces that bent over him. He was surrounded by tall golden-haired warriors in mail and furs.

"Amra! You live!"

"By Crom, Niord," gasped he, "am I alive, or are we all dead and in Valhalla?"

"We live," grunted the Aesir, busy over Amra's half-frozen feet. "We had to fight our way through an ambush, else we had come up with you before the battle was joined. The corpses were scarce cold when we came upon the field. We did not find you among the dead, so we followed your spoor. In Ymir's name, Amra, why did you wander off into the wastes of the north? We have followed your tracks in the snow for hours. Had a blizzard come up and hidden them, we had never found you, by Ymir!"

"Swear not so often by Ymir," muttered a warrior, glancing at the distant mountains. "This is his land and the god bides among yonder mountains, the legends say."

"I followed a woman," Amra answered hazily. "We met Bragi's men in the plains. I know not how long we fought. I alone lived. I was dizzy and faint. The land lay like a dream before me. Only now do all things seem natural and familiar.

The woman came and taunted me. She was beautiful as a frozen flame from hell. When I looked at her I was as one mad, and forgot all else in the world. I followed her. Did you not find her tracks. Or the giants in icy mail I slew?"

Niord shook his head.

"We found only your tracks in the snow, Amra."

"Then it may be I was mad," said Amra dazedly. "Yet you yourself are no more real to me than was the golden-haired witch who fled naked across the snows before me. Yet from my very hands she vanished in icy flame."

"He's delirious," whispered a warrior.

"Not so!" cried an older man, whose eyes were wild and weird. "It was Atali, the daughter of Ymir, the frost-giant! To fields of the dead she comes, and shows herself to the dying! Myself when a boy I saw her, when I lay half-slain on the bloody field of Wolraven. I saw her walk among the dead in the snows, her naked body gleaming like ivory and her golden hair like a blinding flame in the moonlight. I lay and howled like a dying dog because I could not crawl after her. She lures men from stricken fields into the wastelands to be slain by her brothers, the ice-giants, who lay men's red hearts smoking on Ymir's board. Amra has seen Atali, the frost-giant's daughter!"

"Bah!" grunted Horsa. "Old Gorm's mind was turned in his youth by a sword cut on the head. Amra was delirious with the fury of battle. Look how his helmet is dinted. Any of those blows might have addled his brain. It was an hallucination he followed into the wastes. He is from the south; what does he know of Atali?"

"You speak truth, perhaps," muttered Amra. "It was all strange and weird—by Crom!"

He broke off, glaring at the object that still dangled from his clenched left fist; the others gaped silently at the veil he held up—a wisp of gossamer that was never spun by human distaff.

THE FROST-GIANT'S DAUGHTER

by Robert E. Howard

The clangor of the swords had died away, the shouting of the slaughter was hushed; silence lay on the red-stained snow. The bleak pale sun that glittered so blindingly from the ice-fields and the snow-covered plains struck sheens of silver from rent corselet and broken blade, where the dead lay as they had fallen. The nerveless hand yet gripped the broken hilt; helmeted heads, back-drawn in the death throes, tilted red beards and golden beards grimly upward, as if in last invocation to Ymir the frost-giant, god of a warrior-race.

Across the red drifts and mail-clad forms, two figures glared at each other. In that utter desolation only they moved. The frosty sky was over them, the white illimitable plain around them, the dead men at their feet. Slowly through the corpses they came, as ghosts might come to a tryst through the shambles of a dead world. In the brooding silence they stood face to face.

Both were tall men, built like tigers. Their shields were gone, their corselets battered and dented. Blood dried on their mail; their swords were stained red. Their horned helmets showed the marks of fierce strokes. One was beard-less and black-maned. The locks and beard of the other were red as the blood on the sunlit snow.

"Man," said he, "tell me your name, so that my brothers in Vanaheim may know who was the last of Wulfhere's band to fall before the sword of Heimdul."

"Not in Vanaheim," growled the black-haired warrior, "but in Valhalla will you tell your brothers that you met Conan of Cimmeria."

Heimdul roared and leaped, and his sword flashed in deathly arc. Conan staggered and his vision was filled with red sparks as the singing blade crashed on his helmet, shivering into bits of blue fire. But as he reeled he thrust with all the power of his broad shoulders behind the humming blade. The sharp point tore through brass scales and bones and heart, and the red-haired warrior died at Conan's feet.

The Cimmerian stood upright, trailing his sword, a sudden sick weariness assailing him. The glare of the sun on the snow cut his eyes like a knife and the sky seemed shrunken and strangely apart. He turned away from the trampled expanses where yellow-bearded warriors lay locked with red-haired slayers in the embrace of death. A few steps he took, and the glare of the snow fields was suddenly dimmed. A rushing wave of blindness engulfed him and he sank down into the snow, supporting himself on one mailed arm, seeking to shake the blindness out of his eyes as a lion might shake his mane.

A silvery laugh cut through his dizziness, and his sight cleared slowly. He looked up; there was a strangeness about all the landscape that he could not place or define—an unfamiliar tinge to earth and sky. But he did not think long of this. Before him, swaying like a sapling in the wind, stood a woman. Her body was like ivory to his dazed eyes, and save for a light veil of gossamer, she was naked as the day. Her slender bare feet were whiter than the snow they spurned. She laughed down at the bewildered warrior. Her laughter was sweeter than the rippling of silvery fountains, and poisonous with cruel mockery.

"Who are you?" asked the Cimmerian. "Whence come you?"

"What matter?" Her voice was more musical than a silver-stringed harp, but it was edged with cruelty.

"Call up your men," said he, grasping his sword. "Yet though my strength fail me, they shall not take me alive. I see that you are of the Vanir."

"Have I said so?"

His gaze went again to her unruly locks, which at first glance he had thought to be red. Now he saw that they were neither red nor yellow, but a glorious compound of both colors. He gazed spell-bound. Her hair was like elfin-gold; the sun struck it so dazzlingly that he could scarcely bear to look upon it. Her eyes were likewise neither wholly blue nor wholly grey, but of shifting colors and dancing lights and clouds of colors he could not define. Her full red lips smiled, and from her slender feet to the blinding crown of her billowy hair, her ivory body was as perfect as the dream of a god. Conan's pulse hammered in his temples.

"I cannot tell," said he, "whether you are of Vanaheim and mine enemy, or of Asgard and my friend. Far have I wandered, but a woman like you I have never seen. Your locks blind me with their brightness. Never have I seen such hair, not even among the fairest daughters of the AEsir. By Ymir—"

"Who are you to swear by Ymir?" she mocked. "What know you of the gods of ice and snow, you who have come up from the south to adventure among an alien people?"

"By the dark gods of my own race!" he cried in anger. "Though I am not of the golden-haired AEsir, none has been more forward in sword-play! This day I have seen four score men fall, and I alone have survived the field where Wulfhere's reavers met the wolves of Bragi. Tell me, woman, have you seen the flash of mail out across the snow-plains, or seen armed men moving upon the ice?"

"I have seen the hoar-frost glittering in the sun," she answered. "I have heard the wind whispering across the everlasting snows."

He shook his head with a sigh.

"Niord should have come up with us before the battle joined. I fear he and his fighting-men have been ambushed. Wulfhere and his warriors lie dead.

"I had thought there was no village within many leagues of this spot, for the war carried us far, but you cannot have come a great distance over these snows, naked as you are. Lead me to your tribe, if you are of Asgard, for I am faint with blows and the weariness of strife."

"My village is further than you can walk, Conan of Cimmeria," she laughed. Spreading her arms wide, she swayed before him, her golden head lolling sensuously, her scintillant eyes half shadowed beneath their long silken lashes. "Am I not beautiful, oh man?"

"Like Dawn running naked on the snows," he muttered, his eyes burning like those of a wolf.

"Then why do you not rise and follow me? Who is the strong warrior who falls down before me?" she chanted in maddening mockery. "Lie down and die in the snow with the other fools, Conan of the black hair. You cannot follow where I would lead."

With an oath the Cimmerian heaved himself up on his feet, his blue eyes blazing, his dark scarred face contorted. Rage shook his soul, but desire for the taunting figure before him hammered at his temples and drove his wild blood fiercely through his veins. Passion fierce as physical agony flooded his whole being, so that earth and sky swam red to his dizzy gaze. In the madness that swept upon him, weariness and faintness were swept away.

He spoke no word as he drove at her, fingers spread to grip her soft flesh. With a shriek of laughter she leaped back and ran, laughing at him over her white shoulder. With a low growl Conan followed. He had forgotten the fight, forgotten the mailed warriors who lay in their blood, forgotten Niord and the reavers who had failed to reach the fight. He had thought only for the slender white shape which seemed to float rather than run before him.

Out across the white blinding plain the chase led. The

trampled red field fell out of sight behind him, but still Conan kept on with the silent tenacity of his race. His mailed feet broke through the frozen crust; he sank deep in the drifts and forged through them by sheer strength. But the girl danced across the snow light as a feather floating across a pool; her naked feet barely left their imprint on the hoar-frost that overlaid the crust. In spite of the fire in his veins, the cold bit through the warrior's mail and fur-lined tunic; but the girl in her gossamer veil ran as lightly and as gaily as if she danced through the palm and rose gardens of Poitain.

On and on she led, and Conan followed. Black curses drooled through the Cimmerian's parched lips. The great veins in his temples swelled and throbbed and his teeth gnashed.

"You cannot escape me!" he roared. "Lead me into a trap and I'll pile the heads of your kinsmen at your feet! Hide from me and I'll tear apart the mountains to find you! I'll follow you to hell!"

Her maddening laughter floated back to him, and foam flew from the barbarian's lips. Further and further into the wastes she led him. The land changed; the wide plains gave way to low hills, marching upward in broken ranges. Far to the north he caught a glimpse of towering mountains, blue with the distance, or white with the eternal snows. Above these mountains shone the flaring rays of the borealis. They spread fan-wise into the sky, frosty blades of cold flaming light, changing in color, growing and brightening.

Above him the skies glowed and crackled with strange lights and gleams. The snow shone weirdly, now frosty blue, now icy crimson, now cold silver. Through a shimmering icy realm of enchantment Conan plunged doggedly onward, in a crystalline maze where the only reality was the white body dancing across the glittering snow beyond his reach—ever beyond his reach.

He did not wonder at the strangeness of it all, not even when two gigantic figures rose up to bar his way. The scales of their mail were white with hoar-frost; their helmets and their axes were covered with ice. Snow sprinkled their locks; in their beards were spikes of icicles; their eyes were cold as the lights that streamed above them.

"Brothers!" cried the girl, dancing between them. "Look who follows! I have brought you a man to slay! Take his heart that we may lay it smoking on our father's board!"

The giants answered with roars like the grinding of icebergs on a frozen shore and heaved up their shining axes as the maddened Cimmerian hurled himself upon them. A frosty blade flashed before his eyes, blinding him with its brightness, and he gave back a terrible stroke that sheared through his foe's thigh. With a groan the victim fell, and at the instant Conan was dashed into the snow, his left shoulder numb from the blow of the survivor, from which the Cimmerian's mail had barely saved his life. Conan saw the remaining giant looming high above him like a colossus carved of ice, etched against the cold glowing sky. The axe fell, to sink through the snow and deep into the frozen earth as Conan hurled himself aside and leaped to his feet. The giant roared and wrenched his axe free, but even as he did, Conan's sword sang down. The giant's knees bent and he sank slowly into the snow, which turned crimson with the blood that gushed from his half-severed neck.

Conan wheeled, to see the girl standing a short distance away, staring at him in wide-eyed horror, all the mockery gone from her face. He cried out fiercely and the blood-drops flew from his sword as his hand shook in the intensity of his passion.

"Call the rest of your brothers!" he cried. "I'll give their hearts to the wolves! You cannot escape me—"

With a cry of fright she turned and ran fleetly. She did not laugh now, nor mock him over her white shoulder. She ran as for her life, and though he strained every nerve and thew until his temples were like to burst and the snow swam red to his gaze, she drew away from him, dwindling in the witch-fire of the skies, until she was a figure no bigger than a child, then a dancing white flame on the snow, then a dim blur in the distance. But grinding his teeth until the blood started from his gums, he reeled on, and he saw the blur grow to a dancing white flame, and the flame to a figure big as a child; and then she was running less than a hundred paces ahead of him, and slowly the space narrowed, foot by foot.

She was running with effort now, her golden locks blowing free; he heard the quick panting of her breath, and saw a flash of fear in the look she cast over her white shoulder. The grim endurance of the barbarian had served him well. The speed ebbed from her flashing white legs; she reeled in her gait. In his untamed soul leaped up the fires of hell she had fanned so well. With an inhuman roar he closed in on her, just as she wheeled with a haunting cry and flung out her arms to fend him off.

His sword fell into the snow as he crushed her to him. Her lithe body bent backward as she fought with desperate frenzy in his iron arms. Her golden hair blew about his face, blinding him with its sheen; the feel of her slender body twisting in his mailed arms drove him to blinder madness. His strong fingers sank deep into her smooth flesh; and that flesh was cold as ice. It was as if he embraced not a woman of human flesh and blood, but a woman of flaming ice. She writhed her golden head aside, striving to avoid the fierce kisses that bruised her red lips.

"You are cold as the snows," he mumbled dazedly. "I will warm you with the fire in my own blood—"

With a scream and a desperate wrench she slipped from his arms, leaving her single gossamer garment in his grasp. She sprang back and faced him, her golden locks in wild disarray, her white bosom heaving, her beautiful eyes blazing with terror. For an instant he stood frozen, awed by her terrible beauty as she posed naked against the snows.

And in that instant she flung her arms toward the lights that glowed in the skies above her and cried out in a voice that rang in Conan's ears forever after: "Ymir! Oh, my father, save me!"

Conan was leaping forward, arms spread to seize her, when with a crack like the breaking of an ice mountain, the whole sky leaped into icy fire. The girl's ivory body was suddenly enveloped in a cold blue flame so blinding that the

Cimmerian threw up his hands to shield his eyes from the intolerable blaze. A fleeting instant, sky and snowy hills were bathed in crackling white flames, blue darts of icy light, and frozen crimson fires. Then Conan staggered and cried out. The girl was gone. The glowing snow lay empty and bare; high above his head the witch-lights flashed and played in a frosty sky gone mad, and among the distant blue mountains there sounded a rolling thunder as of a gigantic war-chariot rushing behind steeds whose frantic hoofs struck lightning from the snows and echoes from the skies.

Then suddenly the borealis, the snow-clad hills and the blazing heavens reeled drunkenly to Conan's sight; thousands of fire-balls burst with showers of sparks, and the sky itself became a titanic wheel which rained stars as it spun. Under his feet the snowy hills heaved up like a wave, and the Cimmerian crumpled into the snows to lie motionless.

In a cold dark universe, whose sun was extinguished eons ago, Conan felt the movement of life, alien and unguessed. An earthquake had him in its grip and was shaking him to and fro, at the same time chafing his hands and feet until he yelled in pain and fury and groped for his sword.

"He's coming to, Horsa," said a voice. "Haste—we must rub the frost out of his limbs if he's ever to wield sword again."

"He won't open his left hand," growled another. "He's clutching something—"

Conan opened his eyes and stared into the bearded faces that bent over him. He was surrounded by tall golden-haired warriors in mail and furs.

"Conan! You live!"

"By Crom, Niord," gasped the Cimmerian. "Am I alive, or are we all dead and in Valhalla?"

"We live," grunted the AEsir, busy over Conan's half-frozen feet. "We had to fight our way through an ambush, or we had come up with you before the battle was joined. The corpses were scarce cold when we came upon the field. We did not find you among the dead, so we followed your spoor. In Ymir's name, Conan, why did you wander off into the

wastes of the north? We have followed your tracks in the snow
for hours. Had a blizzard come up and hidden them, we had
never found you, by Ymir!"

"Swear not so often by Ymir," uneasily muttered a
warrior, glancing at the distant mountains. "This is his land
and the god bides among yonder mountains the legends say."

"I saw a woman," Conan answered hazily. "We met
Bragi's men in the plains. I know not how long we fought. I
alone lived. I was dizzy and faint. The land lay like a dream
before me. Only now do all things seem natural and familiar.
The woman came and taunted me. She was beautiful as a
frozen flame from hell. A strange madness fell upon me when
I looked at her, so I forgot all else in the world. I followed
her. Did you not find her tracks? Or the giants in icy mail I
slew?"

Niord shook his head.

"We found only your tracks in the snow, Conan."

"Then it may be I am mad," said Conan dazedly. "Yet
you yourself are no more real to me than was the golden-
locked witch who fled naked across the snows before me. Yet
from under my very hands she vanished in icy flame."

"He is delirious," whispered a warrior.

"Not so!" cried an older man, whose eyes were wild and
weird. "It was Atali, the daughter of Ymir, the frost-giant! To
fields of the dead she comes, and shows herself to the dying!
Myself when a boy I saw her, when I lay half-slain on the
bloody field of Wolraven. I saw her walk among the dead in
the snows, her naked body gleaming like ivory and her
golden hair unbearably bright in the moonlight. I lay and
howled like a dying dog because I could not crawl after her.
She lures men from stricken fields into the wastelands to be
slain by her brothers, the ice-giants, who lay men's red hearts
smoking on Ymir's board. The Cimmerian has seen Atali, the
frost-giant's daughter!"

"Bah!" grunted Horsa. "Old Gorm's mind was touched
in his youth by a sword cut on the head. Conan was delirious
from the fury of battle—look how his helmet is dented. Any
of those blows might have addled his brain. It was an

hallucination he followed into the wastes. He is from the south; what does he know of Atali?"

"You speak truth, perhaps," muttered Conan. "It was all strange and weird—by Crom!"

He broke off, glaring at the object that still dangled from his clenched left fist; the others gaped silently at the veil he held up—a wisp of gossamer that was never spun by human distaff.

II.

C. L. MOORE

INTRODUCTION

In his introduction to "Werewoman" in his anthology, *Horrors Unknown,* Sam Moskowitz declared: "C. L. Moore is probably the most talented woman writer of science fiction to appear on the scene since Mary Wollstonecraft Shelley wrote *Frankenstein.*" While from 1818 to 1933 (when Moore's first story, "Shambleau," was published) is a pretty fair stretch of time, the judgment is valid—not so much because science fiction as a genre didn't really get rolling until the latter part of the nineteenth century, nor because the genre was largely the province of male writers until long after World War II, but rather because C. L. Moore was one of those immensely talented writers who come among us rarely and leave an indelible mark upon the field. Sadly for us, such writers as often as not are not with us long enough.

Born in Indianapolis, Indiana on January 24, 1911, Catherine Lucille Moore left college during the Depression to work as a secretary at the Fletcher Trust Company in her home town. Like her contemporary, Robert E. Howard, Moore was seriously ill as a child and devoted much of her time to reading fantastic literature—Edgar Rice Burroughs was a favorite—and to creating adventures within her own imagination. She practiced her typing skills by writing down some of these adventures and submitting them for publication to the pulp markets. This wasn't a bad idea, since her first sale netted her a neat $100.00—equal to a month's salary at the bank. This story was "Shambleau," published in the November 1933 issue of *Weird Tales* (just eleven months following the first appearance of Robert E. Howard's Conan in that magazine), and C. L. Moore became a star in *Weird Tales* from that moment.

"Shambleau" was the first in a series of thirteen stories about Northwest Smith, a hunted outlaw/adventurer who roamed the future spaceways of a decidedly Edgar Rice Burroughs planetary system, where Venus was swampy and Mars was dried canals and red desert and danger lurked in every shadowy ruin and waterfront dive. Pure space opera, but with a difference. Moore welded elements of supernatural fantasy, intensely surreal imagery, and fully developed characterizations onto the framework of pulp-style adventure— and left her readers in awe. It was a blend of science fiction and fantasy—a coexistence of dark magic and super-science, of steel blades and rayguns—that falls into a subgenre known as science-fantasy, best exemplified by the works of A. Merritt, and sometimes today given the awkward designation "sword-and-planet." Moore's interpretation of science-fantasy was a dark, moody vision—usually downbeat and nihilistic for all its atmospheric richness—far better suited to the weird/fantasy markets than to the science fiction pulps. And, indeed, the former markets proved receptive to Moore's work. Here there is some controversy.

Sam Moskowitz states in *Horrors Unknown* (Walker and Company: 1971): "Moore's first love was science fiction and she unsuccessfully tried to sell stories to *Amazing Stories* and *Wonder Stories;* when they rejected them because of an atmosphere of near fantasy and grim horror of the themes, she tried *Weird Tales* magazine with 'Shambleau.'"

However, Moore denies this in her afterword to *The Best of C. L. Moore* (Nelson Doubleday, Inc.: 1975): "One last comment on 'Shambleau.' This is as good a time as any to clear up a misconception which has long crept about unchallenged. This story was *not* rejected by every magazine in the field before it crept humbly to the doorstep of *Weird Tales*. My own perfectly clear memory tells me that I sent it first to *WT* because that was the only magazine of the type I knew well, and that an answering acceptance and a check for the (then) fabulous amount of $100.00 arrived almost by return mail."

There is tragic irony in her assertion, and perhaps Moore's own autobiographical sketch from 1936 (reprinted here) may shed more light on the matter. The significant point is that Moore did find a market for her stories in *Weird Tales*—and not only for Northwest Smith. The October 1934 issue of *Weird Tales* marked the debut of Jirel of Joiry in "The Black God's Kiss"—the first in a series of six stories featuring this medieval swordswoman.

Jirel of Joiry was to a later generation of sword-wielding female warriors what Conan was to an innumerable progeny of furjockstrap-clad barbarian warriors. As with Conan, the prototype is not easily surpassed. Jirel's adventures were set in an imaginary sort of medieval France—calling to mind Clark Ashton Smith's Averoigne series, then running in *Weird Tales*. Like her creator, Jirel was a red-haired beauty and fiercely independent—arguably one of the genre's first liberated heroines. Jirel was not simply Conan in a brass bra. Moore portrayed Jirel with a depth of characterization and a sure grasp of feminine feeling that placed Jirel generations beyond the rest of the pulp field.

Both Northwest Smith and Jirel of Joiry proved enormously popular in *Weird Tales,* and fans wondered whether the medieval swordswoman and the space-roving outlaw might somehow meet one another. They did, finally, in "Quest of the Starstone" *(Weird Tales,* November 1937) written in collaboration with Moore's future husband, fellow *Weird Tales* author Henry Kuttner. Even if you're a veteran C. L. Moore fan, you probably haven't had a chance to read this story. Now you have that chance, and herein hangs a tangled tale.

There are four "orphan" stories between the two series.

There are eighteen stories total in the two series together (counting only once "Quest of the Starstone," which combines both series). Of these stories, fourteen were collected into two hardcover volumes: *Shambleau and Others* (Gnome Press: 1953) and *Northwest of Earth* (Gnome Press: 1954). The contents of these original two volumes were reshuffled variously for later collections, some of which include a fifteenth story, "Song in a Minor Key." The remaining three stories have never been included in any of the series collections.

Counting "Song in a Minor Key," these four orphan stories are (in order of first publication):

"Nymph of Darkness" (in collaboration with Forrest J Ackerman) from *Fantasy Magazine,* April 1935.

"Quest of the Starstone" (in collaboration with Henry Kuttner) from *Weird Tales,* November 1937.

"Werewoman" from *Leaves II,* Winter 1938/1939.

"Song in a Minor Key" from *Scienti-Snaps,* February 1940.

With the exception of "Quest of the Starstone," these were all published in amateur magazines. "Nymph of Darkness" was later reprinted—in an expurgated version—in *Weird Tales,* December 1939. For reasons never entirely clear, these four stories (with the later exception of "Song in a Minor Key") were excluded from Moore's other collections. It may be that Moore later lacked access to some of these stories, due to the obscurity of their publication (see Moskowitz's foreword to "Werewoman"). Perhaps she objected to including collaborations, although she and Kuttner collaborated on most of their writing following their marriage in 1940. The usual explanation is that C. L. Moore simply did not consider these four stories up to the standards of the other fourteen. While respecting the author's judgment, each story does have its strong points, and each is in its own way unique within a series (or pair of series) unusual for its period—or for any period.

"Quest of the Starstone" accomplishes the formidable task of bringing together a woman of the mythical past and a man from an imaginary future—rather like Red Sonja teaming up with Flash Gordon. The story was a through-the-mail collaboration with her future husband (who in 1936 had written her a fan letter addressed to Mr. C. L. Moore), and as such it displays much more attention to straightforward action and structured plot than was Moore's wont.

"Nymph of Darkness" arose from one of those good-natured fannish collaborations that were far more common then than now—when aspiring stars and gosh-wow fans were young and enthusiastic and swept up in the joyous wonder of a new genre. Science fiction was *fun* back then. The story is the closest thematically to Moore's other stories in the two series. The text presented here is the original, unexpurgated version of the story.

"Werewoman" is a curious piece—and it is *not* about a transsexual, despite the title. The novelette is atypical of the rest of the series in being unabashed supernatural horror, without any trappings of space opera. Its structure is basically an extended hallucinogenic vision, written in an extravagant style far more lush even than Moore's customarily rich prose. "Werewoman" is clearly a very early work, and, after reading Sam Moskowitz's foreword to the story, one might well speculate that "Werewoman" was an unfinished draft which R. H. Barlow undertook to revise and complete. Its prose is certainly reminiscent of Barlow's story, "The Night Ocean," supposedly touched by H. P. Lovecraft.

"Song in a Minor Key" gives us about all we ever learn about Northwest Smith's early life and how he became a hunted outlaw and exile. It is also perhaps as tightly written a piece as Moore ever created, and its 750 words pack a punch that Bruce Lee would have envied.

These four orphan stories are presented here together for the first time ever. Add this as a third volume to any of the other two-volume collections, and you will have a complete set of the Northwest Smith and Jirel of Joiry series. To insure a definitive text, all four stories are taken from their original magazine publication, and most of these are amateur publications of extreme rarity.

In addition to these stories, presented here is a short autobiographical sketch written by a youthful C. L. Moore for the June 1936 issue of *Fantasy Magazine*, reprinted for the first time.

And there's more. Two of the field's most knowledgeable fans and historians, Forrest J Ackerman (born November 24, 1916) and Sam Moskowitz (born June 30, 1920), both men friends of C. L. Moore from the pulp days, have contributed firsthand in-depth commentary upon these stories. Ackerman, who collaborated with Moore on "Nymph of Darkness," contributes the story-behind-the-story of their collaboration with "The 'NYMPH' o' ManiAck," first published in the January–February 1948 issue of *Shangri-LA*. The text presented here is taken from a photocopy of that rare fanzine. 4SJ or 4e, as Ackerman is known to other fans, has also included a newly written introduction to this earlier piece disclosing that he was also an uncredited collaborator on another Northwest Smith story, "Yvala" *(Weird Tales, February 1936)*. Sam Moskowitz has not only been good enough to provide photocopies of the texts of "Werewoman" and "Song in a Minor Key" from his personal copies of the fragile and priceless magazines, but he also took pains to write informative forewords to these two stories.

C. L. Moore's career began brilliantly, fulfilled its early potential—then ended prematurely in tragedy, even as tragedy closed her own final years.

In 1940 C. L. Moore and Henry Kuttner were married, and their marriage was one of those rare and marvelous successes wherein two writers merge both their mutual talents and their love for each other. Born in Los Angeles on April 7, 1915, Kuttner broke into *Weird Tales* only a few years after Moore had made her debut there. By the time of their marriage, Kuttner was a thoroughly established and tremendously prolific pulp writer, working under an assortment of pseudonyms in addition to his own name. Kuttner hit virtually all the pulp markets, although he is best remembered for his successes in the science fiction, fantasy, and horror genres. His heroic fantasy novella, "Wet Magic," was reprinted in *Echoes of Valor I*.

After their marriage, the couple lived in New York, where Kuttner's writing career continued to zoom and, slowly, to gain the respect of his peers. Moore now wrote very little under her solo byline, and, while she and Kuttner shared bylines on some of their work, the fact is that virtually everything that appeared under Kuttner's name (or pseudonym) alone following their marriage was to some degree a collaboration. Reportedly one writer simply took over for the other as needed—fatigue, writer's block, time for lunch, whatever—so that there was a total fusion of their dissimilar talents into a sort of symbiotic artistic entity.

Then, on February 3, 1958, Kuttner died of a sudden heart attack. Moore effectively vanished from the science fiction field and, indeed, ceased writing fiction altogether. As Catherine Kuttner, she wrote teleplays for television series until 1963, and for a while she taught writing and literature at the University of Southern California (the couple had moved to Los Angeles not long before Kuttner's death). In 1963 she remarried and abandoned writing entirely.

For years Moore seemed to have disappeared. In the early 1970s she made a few guest appearances at conventions, granted a few interviews, received a few belated awards. Still a beautiful and gracious lady, she appeared increasingly frail and confused. The horrendous truth soon became apparent: C. L. Moore was suffering from Alzheimer's disease—a slow and incurable deterioration of the brain, resulting in loss of memory and cognitive function. In her last years she lay in a coma, until death mercifully came on April 4, 1987.

So detached had she become from the science fiction/ fantasy field, that it was not until February 1988 that her fans learned of her death. Indeed, neither Forrest J Ackerman nor Sam Moskowitz knew of her death at the time they were writing their commentaries herewith presented. Nor was I aware of her death during the process of acquiring rights to reprint these stories through her agent. I wonder whether her agent even knew: evidently not.

Read her stories and remember her.

AN AUTOBIOGRAPHICAL SKETCH OF C. L. MOORE

by C. L. Moore

They found me under a cabbage plant in Indianapolis on the 24th of January, 1911, and I was reared on a diet of Greek mythology, Oz books and Edgar Rice Burroughs, so you can see I never had a chance. In case anyone's interested, about five years ago I started out ambitiously to acquire an education at the State University, with art school and business college filling in summer vacations, but along came the Depression and I abandoned the pursuit of knowledge to work in a bank, which abode of Mammon I still brighten with the sunshine of my presence, and will probably continue to do so for the next ninety years.

As soon as I could talk I began telling long, obscure tales to everyone I could corner. When I learned to write I wrote them, and have been at it ever since. Incidentally I think practice like this is the only way to acquire smoothness and fluency in writing. I've been at it fifteen years and there's room for improvement yet.

Nothing used to daunt my infant ambition. I wrote about cowboys and kings, Robin Hoods and Lancelots and Tarzans thinly disguised under other names. This went on for years and years, until one rainy afternoon in 1931 when I succumbed to a lifelong temptation and bought a magazine called *Amazing Stories* whose cover portrayed six-armed men in a battle to the death. From that moment on I was a convert. A whole new field of literature opened out before my admiring gaze, and the urge to imitate it was irresistible.

Not until Northwest Smith gradually assumed reality, however, did I think of writing for publication. Heaven only knows how he evolved. I am perfectly helpless in the hands of my characters, as I suppose all authors are, and they develop quite independently of their creators. I have remote glimmers of memory about a wild, wild Western that never went beyond the idea that there ought to be a One-Eyed Jack, (possibly of hearts) and a Northwest Smith on a ranch called the Bar-Nothing. Thence the name, but whence the character no one knows, least of all myself. When I first began to consider him as a space-ranger I was guilty of a saga which started out,

> *Northwest Smith was a hard-boiled guy*
> *With an iron fist and a roving eye—*

of which the less is said the better. It has been pointed out to me that "Northwest" is a singularly inappropriate name for a traveler of the spaceways, but I can only plead complete irresponsibility.

Jirel grew up just as mysteriously, out of the everywhere into the here. Long, long ago I had thoughts of a beligerent dame who must have been her progenitor, and went so far as to begin a story which went something like this: "The noise of battle beating up around the walls of Arazon castle rang sweetly in the ears of Arazon's warrior lady." And I think it went no farther. So far as I know she stands there yet listening to the tumult of an eternal battle. Back to her Jirel of Joiry no doubt traces her ancestry.

Jirel's Guillaume whom I so ruthlessly slew in the first of her stories, yet whom I can't quite let die, was patterned after the drawing of Pav of Romne with which I illustrated her latest story, "The Dark Land" in *Weird Tales*. I made that drawing somewhere in the remote past, and have cherished it all these years in the confidence that someday it would come in handy. I meant to use it to illustrate "The Black God's Kiss," first of the Jirel tales, but somehow the story got out of hand, and I've never since been able to introduce a situation it would fit until "The Dark Land."

If you want to know how NOT to write, let me tell you about my method. I just begin. Something like this: "Northwest Smith hitched his gun forward a little and stepped out into the motley crowd that jostled down the streets of— Blank." I know if I leave him alone for a few minutes something will happen, and sure enough, in a short while a mysterious beauty will stumble into his arms gasping of nameless perils, or a stranger from the drylands of Mars or the Venusian swamps will offer him a fabulous sum to perform some desperate deed. Whereupon my troubles begin. Before I know it I'll be involved in such a mess of circumstances that there seems no possible way out. I live in constant terror of the day when I'll have to let him be extinguished as the only conceivable solution. Until then I'll go on agonizing through story after story, never knowing what's coming next, always remembering that though heaven has sent me a solution in the last desperate moments of all my past tales, yet this time how *can* it? And then, after my last hope has died, something clicks and everything falls into place, villainy is foiled again, virtue triumphs and Smith makes another hairbreadth escape.

Curiously, Jirel's stories run more smoothly. But for the adventures of neither character do I deserve either credit or blame, for silly as it sounds I really have very little to do with the stories I write. All I do is start them off, and then urge them along until everything is tangled into knots of insolvable dilemma, and then bang! the plot gets the bit in its teeth and gallops off at a furious pace with me hanging on behind trying to keep up with it. No one is more surprised than I when the whole thing ends.

About me, aside from my stories, there's very little to say, and much as I'd like to talk about myself all I can think of to offer is the information that I love chow mein, formal dances, the heavenly taste of peach brandy and the writings of Messrs. Lovecraft and Howard, and despise spinach, Al Jolson and codliver oil. And that seems to cover the subject pretty thoroughly.

Thanks for listenin'.

QUEST OF THE STARSTONE

by C. L. Moore and Henry Kuttner

*Jirel of Joiry is riding down with a score of men at her
    back,*
*For none is safe in the outer lands from Jirel's outlaw
    pack;*
*The vaults of the wizard are over-full, and locked with
    golden key,*
*And Jirel says, "If he hath so much, then he shall share
    with me!"*
*And fires flame high on the altar fane in the lair of the
    wizard folk,*
*And magic crackles and Jirel's name goes whispering
    through the smoke.*
*But magic fails in the stronger spell that the Joiry
    outlaws own:*
*The splintering crash of a broadsword blade that
    shivers against the bone,*
*And blood that bursts through a warlock's teeth can
    strangle a half-voiced spell*
*Though it rises hot from the blistering coals on the
    red-hot floor of Hell!*

The rivet-studded oaken door crashed open, splintering from the assault of pike-butts whose thunderous echoes still rolled around the walls of the tiny stone room revealed beyond the wreck of the shattered door. Jirel, the warrior-maid of Joiry, leaped in through the splintered ruins, dashing the red hair from her eyes, grinning with exertion, gripping her two-edged sword. But in the ruin of the door she paused. The mail-clad men at her heels surged around her in the doorway like a wave of blue-bright steel, and then paused too, staring.

For Franga the warlock was kneeling in his chapel, and to see Franga on his knees was like watching the devil recite a paternoster. But it was no holy altar before which the wizard bent. The black stone of it bulked huge in this tiny, bare room echoing still with the thunder of battle, and in the split second between the door's fall and Jirel's crashing entry through its ruins Franga had crouched in a last desperate effort at—at what?

His bony shoulders beneath their rich black robe heaved with frantic motion as he fingered the small jet bosses that girdled the altar's block. A slab in the side of it fell open abruptly as the wizard, realizing that his enemy was almost within sword's reach, whirled and crouched like a feral thing. Blazing light, cold and unearthly, streamed out from the gap in the altar.

"So that's where you've hidden it!" said Jirel with a savage softness.

Over his shoulder Franga snarled at her, pale lips writhed back from discolored teeth. Physically he was terrified of her, and his terror paralyzed him. She saw him hesitate, evidently between his desire to snatch into safety what was hidden in the altar and his panic fear of her sword that dripped blood upon the stones.

Jirel settled his indecision.

"You black devil!" she blazed, and lunged like lightning, the dripping blade whistling as it sheared the air.

Franga screamed hoarsely, flinging himself sidewise beneath the sword. It struck the altar with a shivering shock that numbed Jirel's arm, and as she gasped a sound that was

half a sob of pain and fury, half a blistering curse, he scurried
crabwise into a corner, his long robe giving him a curiously
amorphous look. Recovering herself, Jirel stalked after him,
rubbing her numbed arm but gripping that great wet sword
fast, the highlights of murder still blazing in her yellow eyes.

The warlock flattened himself against the wall, skinny
arms outstretched.

"*Werhi-yu-io!*" he screamed desperately. "*Werhi!
Werhi-yu!*"

"What devil's gibberish is that, you dog?" demanded
Jirel angrily. "I'll—"

Her voice silenced abruptly, the red lips parted. She
stared at the wall behind the wizard, and something like awe
was filming the blood-lust of her eyes. For over that corner in
which Franga crouched a shadow had been drawn as one
draws a curtain.

"*Werhi!*" screamed the warlock again, in a cracked and
strained voice, and—how could she not have seen before that
door against whose panels he pressed, one hand behind him
pushing it open upon darkness beyond? Here was black
magic, devil's work.

Doubtfully Jirel stared, her sword lowering. She did not
know it, but her free hand rose to sign her breast with the
church's guard against evil. The door creaked a little, then
swung wide. The blackness within was blinding as too much
light is blinding—a dark from which she blinked and turned
her eyes away. One last glimpse she had of the gaunt, pale face
of Franga, grinning, contorted with hate. The door creaked
shut.

The trance that had gripped Jirel broke with the sound.
Fury flooded back in the wake of awe. Choking on hot
soldier-curses she sprang for the door, swinging up her sword
in both hands, spitting hatred and bracing herself for the
crash of the heavy blade through those oaken panels so
mysteriously veiled in the shadow that clung about that
corner.

The blade clanged shiveringly against stone. For the
second time, the agonizing shock of steel swung hard against
solid rock shuddered up the blade and racked Jirel's shoul-

ders. The door had vanished utterly. She dropped the sword from nerveless hands and reeled back from the empty corner, sobbing with fury and pain.

"C-coward!" she flung at the unanswering stone. "H-hide in your hole, then, you fiend-begotten runaway, and watch me take the Starstone!"

And she whirled to the altar.

Her men had shrunk back in a huddle beyond the broken door, their magic-dazzled eyes following her in fascinated dread.

"You womanish knaves!" she flared at them over her shoulder as she knelt where the wizard had knelt. "Womanish, did I say? Ha! You don't deserve the flattery! Must I go the whole way alone? Look then—here it is!"

She plunged her bare hand into the opening in the altar from which streamed that pale, unearthly light, gasped a little, involuntarily, and then drew out what looked like a block of living flame.

In her bare hand as she knelt she held it, and for minutes no one moved. It was pale, this Starstone, cold with unearthly fire, many-faceted yet not glittering. Jirel thought of twilight above the ocean, when the land is darkening and the smooth water gathers into its surface all the glimmering light of sea and sky. So this great stone gleamed, gathering the chapel's light into its pale surface so that the room seemed dark by contrast, reflecting it again transmuted into that cold, unwavering brilliance.

She peered into the translucent depths of it so near her face. She could see her own fingers cradling the gem distorted as if seen through water—and yet somehow there was a motion between her hand and the upper surface of the jewel. It was like looking down into water in whose depths a shadow stirred—a living shadow—a restlessly moving shape that beat against the prisoning walls and sent a flicker through the light's cold blue-white gleaming. It was—

No, it was the Starstone, nothing more. But to have the Starstone! To hold it here in her hands at last, after weeks of siege, weeks of desperate battle! It was triumph itself she cradled in her palm. Her throat choked with sudden ecstatic laughter as she sprang to her feet, brandishing the great gem toward that empty corner through whose wall the wizard had vanished.

"Ha, behold it!" she screamed to the unanswering stone. "Son of a fiend, behold it! The luck of the Starstone is mine, now a better man has wrested it from you! Confess Joiry your master, you devil-deluder! Dare you show your face? Dare you?"

Over that empty corner the shadow swept again, awesomely from nowhere. Out of the sudden darkness creaked a door's hinges, and the wizard's voice called in a choke of fury,

"Bel's curse on you, Joiry! Never think you've triumphed over me! I'll have it back if I—if I—"

"If you—what? D'ye think I fear you, you hell-spawned warlock? If you—what?"

"Me you may not fear, Joiry," the wizard's voice quavered with fury, "but by Set and Bubastis, I'll find one who'll tame you if I must go to the ends of space to find him—to the ends of time itself! And then—beware!"

"Bring on your champion!" Jirel's laughter was hot with scorn. "Search hell itself and bring out the chiefest devil! I'll lift the head from his shoulders as I'd have lifted yours, with one sweep, had you not fled."

But she got for answer only the creak of a closing door in the depths of that shadow. And now the shadow faded again, and once more empty stone walls stared at her enigmatically.

Clutching the Starstone that—so legend had it—carried luck and wealth beyond imagination for its possessor, she shrugged and swung round to her soldiers.

"Well, what are you gaping at?" she flared. "Before heaven, I'm the best man here! Out—out—pillage the castle—there's rich loot of that devil's servant, Franga! What are you waiting for?" and with the flat of her sword she drove them from the chapel.

"By Pharol, Smith, have you lost your taste for *segir*? I'd as soon have expected old Marnak here to sprout legs!"

Yarol's cherubic face was puzzled as he nodded toward

the waiter who was moving quickly about the little private drinking booth of polished steel in the back of the Martian tavern, placing fresh drinks before the two men, regardless of his artificial limbs—lost, some said, during an illicit amorous visit to the forbidden dens of the spider women.

Northwest Smith frowned moodily, pushing the glass away. His scarred dark face, lighted with the pallor of steel-colored eyes, was morose. He drew deeply on the brown Martian cigarette that smoked between his fingers.

"I'm getting rusty, Yarol," he said. "I'm sick of this whole business. Why can't something really worth the effort turn up? Smuggling—gun-running—I'm sick of it, I tell you! Even *segir* doesn't taste the same."

"That's old age creeping up," Yarol advised him owlishly above the rim of his glass. "Tell you what you need, N.W., a snort of the green Mingo liquer old Marnak keeps on his top shelf. It's distilled from *pani*-berries, and one shot of it will have you prancing like a pup. Wait a minute, I'll see what I can do."

Smith hunched over his folded arms and stared at the shining steel wall behind Yarol's vacant chair as the little Venusian slid out of the booth. Hours like these were the penalty of the exiled and the outlaw. Even the toughest of them knew times when the home planet called almost intolerably across the long voids of the spaceways, and all other places seemed flat and dull. Homesickness he would not have admitted to anyone alive, but as he sat there alone, morosely facing his dim reflection in the steel wall, he found himself humming that old sweet song of all Earth's exiled people, *The Green Hills of Earth:*

> *Across the seas of darkness*
> *The good green Earth is bright—*
> *Oh, star that was my homeland*
> *Shine down on me tonight . . .*

Words and tune were banal, but somehow about them had gathered such a halo of association that the voices which sang them went sweeter and softer as they lingered over the well-remembered phrases, the well-remembered scenes of home. Smith's surprisingly good baritone took on undernotes of a homesick sweetness which he would have died rather than admit:

> *My heart turns home in longing*
> *Across the voids between,*
> *To know beyond the spaceways*
> *The hills of Earth are green . . .*

What wouldn't he give just now, to be free to go home again? Home without a price on his head, freedom to rove the blue seas of Earth, the warm garden continents of the Sun's loveliest planet? He hummed very softly to himself,

> *—and count the losses worth*
> *To see across the darkness*
> *The green hills of Earth . . .*

and then let the words die on his lips unnoticed as he narrowed steel-colored eyes at the polished wall in which a moment before his dim reflection had faced him. It was darkening now, a shadow quivering across the bright surfaces, thickening, clouding his mirrored face. And the wall—was it metal, or—or stone? The shadow was too thick to tell, and unconsciously he rose to his feet, bending across the table, one hand hovering back toward the heat-gun on his thigh. A door creaked open in the dimness—a heavy door, half seen, opening upon darkness beyond too black to gaze on—darkness, and a face.

"Are your services for hire, stranger?" quavered a cracked voice speaking in a tongue that despite himself sent Smith's pulses quickening in recognition. French, Earth's French, archaic and scarcely intelligible, but unquestionably a voice from home.

"For a price," he admitted, his fingers closing definitely on his gun. "Who are you and why do you ask? And how in the name of—"

"It will reward you to ask no questions," said the

cracked quaver. "I seek a fighting-man of a temper strong enough for my purpose, and I think you are he. Look, does this tempt you?"

A claw-like hand extended itself out of the shadow, dangling a double rope of such blue-white pearls as Smith had never dreamed of. "Worth a king's ransom," croaked the voice. "And all for the taking. Will you come with me?"

"Come where?"

"To the planet Earth—to the land of France—to the year of 1500."

Smith gripped the table-edge with one frantic hand, wondering if the *segir* he had drunk could somehow have sent him into paroxysms of dream. By no stretch of imagination could he really be standing here, in this drinking-booth in a Martian tavern, while out of a door that opened upon darkness a cracked voice beckoned him into the past. He was dreaming, of course, and in a dream it could do no harm to push back his chair, skirt the table, step closer to that incredible door thick-hung with shadows, take the out-stretched hand over whose wrist the luminous pearls hung gleaming . . .

The room staggered and whirled into darkness. From somewhere far away he heard Yarol's voice shouting frantically, "N.W.! Wait! N.W., where're you going—" And then night too black to gaze on blinded his dark-dazzled eyes and cold unthinkable flamed through his brain, and—and—

He stood on a green hilltop whose gentle slope rolled downward to a meadow where a brook wound with a sound of rippling water. Beyond, on a high upthrust of craggy rock, a great gray castle loomed. The sky was blessedly blue, the air fresh in his nostrils with the sweetness of green growing things. And all about him rolled grassy uplands. He took a deep, deep breath. "The Green Hills of Earth!"

"N.W., what in—by Pharol, I—hell's blazes, man, what's happened?" Yarol's spluttering amazement jolted him out of his delight.

Smith turned. The little Venusian stood on the soft grass

beside him, two small glasses full of pale green liquid in his hands and a look of almost idiotic bewilderment on his good-looking, cherubic face. "I come back into the booth with the *pani*-juice," he was muttering dazedly, "and there you are stepping through a door that—damn it!—that wasn't there when I left! And when I try to pull you back I—I—well, what *did* happen?"

"You stumbled through the Gateway—uninvited," said a cracked voice ominously behind them.

Both men whirled, hands dropping to their guns. For a dazed moment Smith had forgotten the voice that had lured him into the past. Now for the first time he saw his host—a small man, wizened, dark, stooping under his robe of rich black velvet as if the evil reflected on his seamed face were too heavy to bear upright. Dark wisdom glinted in the eyes that stared malevolently at Yarol.

"What's he saying, N.W.?" demanded the little Venusian.

"French—he's speaking French," muttered Smith distractedly, his gaze on the lined and evil face of their host. And then to the warlock, *"Qui êtes-vous, m'sieur? Pourquoi—"*

"I am Franga," interrupted the old man impatiently. "Franga, the warlock. And I am displeased with this blundering stranger who followed us through the door. His speech is as uncouth as his manners. Were it not for my magic I could not guess his meaning. Has he never learned a civilized tongue? Well, no matter—no matter.

"Listen, now. I have brought you here to avenge my defeat at the hands of the lady of Joiry whose castle you see on yonder hilltop. She stole my magical jewel, the Starstone, and I have vowed to find a man who could tame her if I had to search outside my own world and time to do it. I am too old myself, too feeble now. Once when I was as young and lusty as you I won the jewel from a rival as it must be won, bloodily in battle, or its magic is void to the possessor. Too, it may be given freely and maintain its power. But by neither method can I take it from Joiry, and so you must go up to the castle and in your own way win the stone.

"I can help you—a little. This much I can do—I can

put you beyond the reach of the pikes and swords of Joiry's men."

Smith lifted an eyebrow and laid his hand lightly on his heat-gun, a blast of whose deadly violence could have mowed down a charging army like wheat ripe for the scythe.

"I'm armed," he said shortly.

Franga frowned. "Your arms would not avail you against a dagger in the back. No, you must do as I say. I have my reasons. You must go—beyond the Gateway."

Cold, pale eyes met the wizard's veiled stare for a moment. Then Smith nodded.

"It doesn't matter—my gun burns as straight in any land. What's your plan?"

"You must get the lady of Joiry through the Gateway—that same Gateway by which you came hither. But it will take you into another land, where—where"—he hesitated—"where there are—powers—favorable to me, and therefore to you. Make no mistake; it will not be easy to wrest the Starstone from Joiry. She has learned much of the dark lore."

"How shall we open the Gateway?"

Franga's left hand rose in a swift, strangely archaic gesture. "By this sign—learn it well—thus, and thus."

Smith's gun-callused brown hand imitated the queer motion. "Thus?"

"Yes—and the spell must be learned as well." Franga mouthed something queer and garbled, Smith echoing him with twisted tongue, for the words were as strange as he had ever spoken.

"Good." The warlock nodded, and again the strange syllables came incoherently from his thin lips, again his hand moved, giving the gestures an oddly cadenced rhythm. "When you voice the spell again the Gateway will open for you—as it opens now for me!"

Silently a shadow swept down upon them, dimming the sunlit hill. In its midst a blacker oblong darkened, the creak of a door sounded faintly as if from enormous distances.

"Bring Joiry through the Gateway," the wizard whispered, vicious lights crawling in his cold eyes, "and follow. Then you may seize the Starstone, for the powers in this—

this other land will fight with you. But not here, not in Joiry. You must follow me . . . As for this little man who blundered through my door of darkness—"

"He is my friend," said Smith hastily. "He will help me."

"Eh—well, let his life be hostage then to your success. Win me the stone, and I stay my wrath at his stupid interference. But remember—the sword of my magic hovers at your throat . . ."

A shadow quivered over the wizard's black-robed form. His image quivered with it as a reflection in troubled water shakes, and abruptly shadow and man were gone.

"By great Pharol," articulated Yarol in measured syllables, "will you tell me what this is all about? Drink this—you look as though you need it. As for me"—he thrust a small glass into Smith's hand, and drained his own drink at a gulp—"if all this is a dream, I hope there's liquor in it. Will you kindly explain—"

Smith threw back his head and tossed the *pani*-spirits down his grateful throat. In crisp sentences he outlined the situation, but though his words were brisk his eyes lingered like a caress over the warm, sweet-scented hills of home.

"Um-m," said 'Yarol, when he had finished. "Well, why are we waiting? Who knows, there may be a wine-cellar in that cozy-looking castle over there." He licked his lips reflectively, tasting the last of the green liqueur. "Let's get going. The sooner we meet the woman the sooner she'll offer us a drink."

So they went down the long hill, Earth's green grass springing under their spaceman's boots, Earth's warm June breezes caressing their Mars-burned faces.

The gray heights of Joiry loomed above the two before life stirred anywhere in the sunny midday silences of this lost century. Then high in the buttresses a man shouted, and presently, with a rattling of hooves and a jangle of accouterments, two horsemen came thundering across the lowered drawbridge. Yarol's hand went to his heat-gun, and a smile of ineffable innocence hovered on his face. The Venusian never looked so much like a Raphael cherub as when death was trembling on his trigger finger. But Smith laid a restraining hand on his arm.

"Not yet."

The horsemen bore down on them, vizors lowered. For a moment Smith thought they would trample them down, and his hand hovered ever so lightly over his gun, but the men reined to a halt beside the two and one of them, glaring down through his helmet bars, roared a threatening question.

"We're strangers," Smith told him haltingly at first, and then more easily as long-forgotten French flowed back into his memory. "From another land. We come in peace."

"Few come in peace to Joiry," snapped the man, fingering his sword-hilt, "and we do not love strangers here. Have you, perhaps"—a covetous gleam brightened the eyes half hidden by the vizor—"gold? Or gems?"

"Your lady can judge of that, fellow." Smith's voice was as cold as the steel-gray eyes that caught the man's gaze in a stare of sudden savagery. "Take us to her."

The man hesitated for an instant, uncertainty eloquent in the eyes behind the vizor. Here was a dusty stranger, afoot, swordless, unarmed, such a fellow as Joiry's men might ride down on the highway and never notice twice. But his eyes were the eyes of—of—he had never seen such eyes. And command spoke in his cold, clipped voice. The soldier shrugged inside his mail and spat through the bars of the helmet.

"There's always room in Joiry's dungeons for one more varlet, if our lady doesn't fancy you," he said philosophically. "Follow me, then."

Yarol, plodding across the drawbridge, murmured, "Was he speaking a language, N. W.—or merely howling like a wolf?"

"Shut up," muttered Smith. "I'm trying to think. We've got to have a good story ready for this—this Amazon."

"Some brawny wench with a face like a side of beef," speculated Yarol.

So they entered Joiry, over the drawbridge, under the spiked portcullis, into the high-vaulted, smoke-blackened banquet hall where Jirel sat at midday table. Blinking in the dimness Smith looked up to the dais at the head of the great T-shaped board where the lady of Joiry sat. Her red mouth glistened with the grease of a mutton-bone she had been gnawing, and the bright hair fell flaming on her shoulders.

She looked into Smith's eyes.

Clear and pale and cold as steel they were, and Joiry's yellow gaze met them with a flash like the spark of meeting blades. For a long moment there was silence between them, and a curious violence flamed in the silent stare. A great mastiff loped to Smith's knee, fangs bared, a growl rumbling in its furry throat. Without looking down, Smith's hand found the beast's head and the dog sniffed for a moment and let the man rough its shaggy fur. Then Jirel broke the silence.

"Tigre—ici!" Her voice was strong and suddenly deeper in timbre, as if emotions she would not acknowledge were stirring in her. The mastiff went to her chair and lay down, finding a well-gnawed bone to crack. But Jirel's eyes were still fast on Smith's, and a slow flush was mounting her face.

"Pierre—Voisin," she said. "Who is he?"

"I bring you news of treasure," said Smith before they could speak. "My name is Smith, and I come from a—a far land."

"Smeet," she murmured. "Smeet. . . . Well, what of this treasure?"

"I would speak to you alone of that," he said guardedly. "There are jewels and gold, guarded by thieves but ripe for the harvesting. And I think Joiry—harvests well."

"C'est vrai. With the luck of the Starstone—" She hesitated, wiping her mouth on the back of a narrow hand. "Are you lying to me? You who come so curiously clad, who speak our language so strangely—always before I have seen the lie in the eyes of the man who tells it. But you—"

Suddenly, and so quickly that despite himself Smith blinked, she had flung herself across the table, leaning there on one knee while the slender blade of her dagger flickered in the air. She laid the point of it against Smith's bare brown throat, just where a strong pulse stirred beneath sunburnt flesh. He watched her without a quiver of expression, without a twitch of muscle.

"I cannot read your eyes—Smeet . . . Smeet. . . . But if you are lying to me"—the point dented the full swell of his muscular throat—"if you are, I'll strip the skin from your carcass in Joiry's dungeons. Know that!"

The blade fell to her side. Something wet trickled stickily down Smith's neck inside the leather collar. So keen was that blade he had not known himself scratched. He said coldly,

"Why should I lie? I can't get the treasure alone—you can help me win it. I came to you for aid."

Unsmilingly she bent toward him across the table, sheathing her dagger. Her body was one sweep of flowing grace, of flowing strength, slim as a sword-blade, as she half knelt among the broken meats upon the board. Her yellow eyes were cloudy with doubt.

"I think there is something more," she said softly, "something you have left untold. And I have a memory now of a yelling warlock who fled from my blade, with certain—threats. . . ."

The yellow eyes were cold as polar seas. She shrugged at last and stood up, her gaze sweeping down over the long table where men and women divided their time between feasting and fascinated staring at the tableau by the tablehead.

"Bring him up to my apartment," she said to Smith's captors. "I'd learn more of this—treasure."

"Shall we stay to guard him?"

Jirel's lips curled scornfully.

"Is there a man here who can best me with steel—or anything else?" she demanded. "Guard yourselves, you cravens! If you brought him in without getting a poniard in the belly, I can safely talk with him in the heart of Joiry's stronghold. Well, don't stand there gaping—go!"

Smith shrugged off the heavy hand laid on his shoulder.

"Wait!" he said crisply. "This man goes with me."

Jirel's eyes dwelt on Yarol with a velvety, menacing appraisal. Yarol's sidelong black stare met hers eloquently.

"Brawny wench, did I say?" he murmured in the liquid cadences of High Venusian. "*Aie*—the Minga maidens were not more luscious. I'll kiss that pretty mouth of yours before I go back to my own time, lady! I'll—"

"What is he saying—he gurgles like a brook!" Jirel broke in impatiently. "He is your friend? Take them both, then, Voisin."

Jirel's apartment lay in the top of the highest tower of Joiry, at the head of a winding stone stairway. Lofty-roofed, hung with rich tapestries, carpeted with furs, the place seemed to Smith at once alien and yet dearly familiar with a strange, heart-warming familiarity. Separated from his own time by dusty centuries, yet it was earth-sprung, earth-born, reared on the green hills of his home planet.

"What I need," said Yarol carefully, "is some more Minga-liqueur. Did you see how that hell-cat looked me over? Black Pharol, I don't know if I'd sooner kiss her or kill her! Why, the damned witch would run her sword through my gullet on a whim—for the sheer deviltry of it!"

Smith chuckled deep in his throat. "She's dangerous. She—"

Jirel's voice behind him said confidently,

"Wait beyond the door, Voisin. These two strangers may visit our dungeons, after all. This little one—how are you named?"

"He's called Yarol," Smith said curtly.

"Yes—Yarol. Well, we may find means to make you a taller man, Yarol. You would like that, eh? We have a little device—a ladder which I got from the Count of Görz when he visited me last summer—and the Count is clever in these things."

"He does not speak your tongue," Smith interrupted.

"No? It is not strange—he looks as though he came from a far land indeed. I have never seen a man like him." Her eyes were puzzled. She half turned her shoulder to them, toying with a sword that lay on a table at her side, and said without looking up, "Well, your story. Let's have it. And— yes, I'll give you one more chance at living—if you're lying, go now. None will stop you. You are strangers. You do not know Joiry—or Joiry's vengeance."

Over her shoulder she slanted into Smith's eyes a level glance that burnt like the stab of lightnings. Hell-fires flickered in it, and despite himself Smith knew a sudden crawl of unease. Yarol, though he did not understand the words, whistled between his teeth. For a heartbeat no one spoke. Then very softly in Smith's ear a voice murmured,

"She has the Starstone. Say the spell of the Gateway!"

Startled, he glanced around. Jirel did not stir. Her lion-yellow eyes were still brooding on him with a gaze that smoldered. Yarol was watching her in fascination. And Smith realized abruptly that he alone had heard the cracked quaver of command in—yes, in Franga's voice! Franga, the warlock, whispering through some half-opened door into infinity. Without glancing aside at Yarol he said in the ripples of High Venusian, "Get ready—watch the door and don't let her out."

Jirel's face changed. She swung round from the table, her brows a straight line of menace. "What are you muttering? What devil's work are you at?"

Smith ignored her. Almost involuntarily his left hand was moving in the queer, quick gesture of the spell. Phrases in the unearthly tongue that Franga had taught him burned on his lips with all the ease of his mother-tongue. Magic was all about him, guiding his lips and hands.

Alarm blazed up in Jirel's yellow eyes. An oath smoked on her lips as she lunged forward, the sword she had been toying with a gleam in her fist. Yarol grinned. The heat-gun danced in his hand, and a white-hot blast traced a trail of fire on the rug at Jirel's feet. She shut her red lips on a word half uttered, and twisted in midair, flinging herself back in swift terror from this sudden gush of hell-flame. Behind her the door burst open and men in armor clanged into the room, shouting, dragging at their swords.

And then—down swept the shadow over the noisy room. Cloudy as the sweep of the death-angel's wings it darkened the sunny air so that the ray from Yarol's gun blazed out in dazzling splendor through the gloom. As if in the

misted depths of a mirror Smith saw the men in the door
shrink back, mouths agape, swords clattering from their
hands. He scarcely heeded them, for in the far wall where a
moment before a tall, narrow window had opened upon
sunlight and the green hills of Earth—was a door. Very
slowly, very quietly it was swinging open, and the black of
utter infinity lay beyond its threshold.

"Hai—s'lelei—Smith!" Yarol's warning voice yelled in
the darkness, and Smith threw himself back in a great leap as
he felt a sword-blade prick his shoulder. Jirel sobbed a furious
curse and plunged forward, her sword and sword-arm a single
straight bar. In the dimness Yarol's gun hand moved, and a
thin beam of incandescence burned bright. Jirel's sword
hissed in midair, glowed blindingly and then dripped in a
shower of white-hot drops to the stone floor. Her momen-
tum carried her forward with a hilt and a foot of twisted steel
still gripped in her stabbing hand, so that she lunged against
Smith's broad chest thrusting with the stump of the ruined
sword.

His arms prisoned her, a writhing fury that sobbed wild
oaths and twisted like a tiger against him. He grinned and
tightened his arms until the breath rushed out of her crushed
lungs and he felt her ribs give a little against his chest.

Then vertigo was upon him. Dimly he realized that the
girl's arms had gone round his neck in a frantic grip as the
room swayed—tilted dizzily, amazingly, revolving as though
on a giant axis—or as if the black depths of the Gateway were
opening under him . . . he could not tell, nor was he ever to
understand, just what happened in that fantastic instant
when nature's laws were warped by strange magic. The floor
was no longer solid beneath his feet. He saw Yarol twisting
like a small sleek cat as he stumbled and fell—fell into
oblivion with his gun hand upflung. He was falling himself,
plunging downward through abysses of dark, clasping a
frightened girl whose red hair streamed wildly in the wind of
their falling.

Stars were swirling about them. They were dropping
slowly through stars while the air danced and dazzled all
around them. Smith had time to catch his breath and flex the

muscles of his gun thigh to be sure the comforting weight pressed there before a spongy ground received them softly. They fell like people in a nightmare, slowly and easily, with no jar, upon the strange dim surface of the land beyond the Gateway.

Yarol landed on his feet like the cat he was, gun still gripped and ready, black eyes blinking in the starry dark. Smith, hampered by the terrified Jirel, sank with nightmare ease to the ground and rebounded a little from its sponginess. The impact knocked the stump of sword from the girl's hand, and he pitched it away into the blinding shimmer of the star-bright dark before he helped her to her feet.

For once Joiry was completely subdued. The shock of having her sword melted by hell-fire in her very grasp, the dizzying succession of manhandling and vertigo and falling into infinity had temporarily knocked all violence out of her, and she could only gasp and stare about this incredible starlit darkness, her red lips parted in amazement.

As far as they could see the mist of stars quivered and thickened the dim air, tiny points of light that danced all around them as if thousands of fireflies were winking all at once. Half blinded by that queer, shimmering dazzle, they could make out no familiar topography of hills or valleys, only that spongy dark ground beneath them, that quiver of stars blinding the dim air.

Motion swirled the shimmer a little distance away, and Jirel snarled as Franga's dark-robed form came shouldering through the stars, spinning them behind him in the folds of his cloak as he moved forward. His withered features grimaced into a grin when he saw the dazed three.

"Ah—you have her!" he rasped. "Well, what are you waiting for? Take the stone! She carries it on her."

Smith's pale eyes met the warlock's through the star-shimmer, and his firm lips tightened. Something was wrong. He sensed it unmistakably—danger whispered in the air. For why should Franga have brought them here if the problem was no more complex than the mere wresting of a jewel from a woman? No—there must be some other reason for plung-

ing them into this starry dimness. What had Franga hinted—
powers here that were favorable to him? Some dark, nameless
god dwelling among the stars?

The warlock's eyes flared at Jirel in a flash of pure
murder, and suddenly Smith understood a part of the puzzle.
She was to die, then, when the jewel could no longer protect
her. Here Franga could wreak vengeance unhampered, once
the Starstone was in his hands. Here Joiry was alone and
helpless—and the flame of hatred in the wizard's eyes could
be quenched by no less than the red flood of her bloody
death.

Smith glanced back at Jirel, white and shaken with recent
terror, but snarling feebly at the warlock in invincible savagery that somehow went to his heart as no helplessness could
have done. And suddenly he knew he could not surrender her
up to Franga's hatred. The shift of scene had shifted their
relations, too, so that the three mortals—he could not think
of Franga as wholly human—stood together against Franga
and his malice and his magic. No, he could not betray Jirel.

His gaze flicked Yarol's with a lightning message more
eloquent than a warning shout. It sent a joyous quiver of
tautening along the little Venusian's body, and both men's
gun hands dropped to their sides with simultaneous casual-
ness.

Smith said: "Return us to Joiry and I'll get the stone for
you: Here—no."

That black glare of murder shifted from Jirel to Smith,
bathing him in hatred.

"Take it from her now—or die!"

A smothered sound like the snarl of an angry beast
halted Smith's reflexive snatch at his gun. Past him Jirel
lunged, her red hair streaming with stars, her fingers flexed
into claws as she leaped bare-handed at the warlock. Rage had
drowned out her momentary terror, and soldier's curses
tumbled blistering from her lips as she sprang.

Franga stepped back; his hand moved intricately and
between him and the charging fury the starlight thickened—
solidified into a sheet like heavy glass. Jirel dashed herself

against it and was hurled back as if she had plunged into a stone wall. The silvery mist of the barrier dissolved as she reeled back, gasping with rage, and Franga laughed thinly.

"I am in my own place now, vixen," he told her. "I do not fear you or any man here. It is death to refuse me—bloody death. Give me the stone."

"I'll tear you to rags with my bare nails!" sobbed Joiry. "I'll have the eyes out of your head, you devil! Ha—even here you fear me! Come out from behind your rampart and let me slay you!"

"Give me the stone." The wizard's voice was calm.

"Return us all to Joiry and I think she'll promise to let you have it." Smith fixed a meaning stare upon Jirel's blazing yellow eyes. She shrugged off the implied advice furiously.

"Never! Yah—wait!" She leaped to Yarol's side and, as he shied nervously away, his eyes mistrustfully on her pointed nails, snatched from his belt the small knife he carried. She set the blade against the full, high swell of her bosom and laughed in Franga's face. "Now—kill me if you can!" she taunted, her face a blaze of defiance. "Make one move to slay me—and I slay myself! And the jewel is lost to you for ever!"

Franga bit his lip and stared at her through the mist of stars, fury glaring in his eyes. There was no hesitancy in her, and he knew it. She would do as she threatened, and—

"The stone had no virtue if not taken by violence or given freely," he admitted. "Lifted from a suicide's corpse, it would lose all value to anyone. I will bargain with you then, Joiry."

"You'll not! You'll set me free or lose the jewel for ever."

Franga turned goaded eyes on Smith. "Either way I lose it, for once in her own land Joiry would die before surrendering it, even as she would here. You! Fulfill your bargain—get me the Starstone!"

Smith shrugged. "Your meddling's spoiled everything now. There's little I can do."

The angry black eyes searched his for a long moment, evil crawling in their deeps. They flicked to Yarol. Both men stood on the spongy ground with feet braced, bodies balanced in the easy tautness which characterizes the gunman, hands light on their weapons, eyes very steady, very deadly. They were two very dangerous men, and Smith realized that even here Franga was taking no chances with their strange weapons. Behind them Jirel snarled like an angry cat, her fingers flexing themselves involuntarily. And suddenly the wizard shrugged.

"Stay here then, and rot!" he snapped, swinging his cloak so that the stars swirled about him in a blinding shower. "Stay here and starve and thirst until you'll surrender. I'll not bargain with you longer."

They blinked in the sudden eddy of that starry mist, and when their vision cleared the bent black figure had vanished. Blankly they looked at one another through the drifting stars.

"Now what?" said Yarol. "*Shar,* but I could drink! Why did he have to mention thirst?"

Smith blinked about him in the swirling brightness. For once he was utterly at a loss. The wizard had every advantage over them in this dim, blinding outland where his god reigned supreme.

"Well, what have we to lose?" he shrugged at last. "He's not through with us, but there's nothing we can do. I'm for exploring a bit, anyhow."

Yarol raked the starry dark with a dubious gaze. "We couldn't be worse off," he admitted.

"*Comment?*" demanded Jirel, suspicious eyes shifting from one to the other. Smith said briefly.

"We're going to explore. Franga's got some trick in mind, we think. We'd be fools to wait here for him to come back. We—oh, wait!" He snapped his fingers involuntarily and turned a startled face on the surprised two. The Gateway! He knew the spell that opened it—Franga had taught him that. Why not voice the invocation now and see what happened? He drew a quick breath and opened his mouth to speak—and then faltered with the remembered words fading from his very tongue-tip. His fingers rose halfheartedly in the intricate gestures of the spell, groping after the vanished memory as if it could be plucked out of the starmisted air. No use. His mind was as blank of the magical remembrance as if it had never been. Franga's magic worked well indeed.

"Are you crazy?" demanded Yarol, regarding his hesitating ally with an amazed gaze. Smith grinned ruefully.

"I thought I had an idea," he admitted. "But it's no good. Come on."

The spongy ground was wicked to walk on. They stumbled against one another, swearing in a variety of tongues at the blinding air they groped through, the hard going under foot, the wretched uncertainty that kept their eyes scanning the dazzle as they walked.

It was Jirel who first caught sight of the shrunken brown thing. Indeed, she almost stumbled over it, a mummified body, curled up on its side so that its bony knees nearly touched the brown fleshless forehead. Smith turned at her little gasp, saw the thing, and paused to bend over it wonderingly.

It was not pleasant to see. The skin, stretched tightly over the bony frame, was parchment-brown, hideously rough in texture, almost as if the hide of some great lizard had been stretched over the skeleton of a man. The face was hidden, but the hands were slender claws, whitish in places where the granulated skin had been stripped from the bone. Wisps of straw-like hair still clung to the wrinkled scalp.

"Well, come along," said Yarol impatiently. "Certainly *he* can't help us, or harm us either."

Silently assenting, Smith swung on his heel. But some instinct—the little tingling danger-note that whispers in the back of a spaceman's head—made him turn. The position of the recumbent figure had changed. Its head was lifted, and it was staring at him with swollen, glazed eyes.

Now the thing should have been dead. Smith knew that, somehow, with a dreadful certainty. The face was a brown skull-mask, with a vaguely canine cast, and the nose, although ragged and eaten away in places, protruded with a shocking resemblance to a beast's muzzle.

The limbs of the horror twitched and moved slowly, and the skeletal, tattered body arose. It dragged itself forward among the whirling star-motes, and instinctively Smith recoiled. There was something so unutterably dreary about it, despite the dreadful attitude of hunger that thrust its beast's head forward, that he sickened a little as he stared. From Jirel came a little cry of repugnance, quickly muffled.

"We'd better get out of here," said Smith harshly.

Yarol did not speak for a moment. Then he murmured, "There are more of the things, N. W. See?"

Hidden by the starry mists close to the ground, the ghastly things must have been closing in upon them with that hideous dreary slowness for the past several minutes. They came on, scores of them veiled in stars, moving with a dreadful deliberation, and none of them stood upright. From all sides they were converging, and the dancing motes lent them a curious air of nightmare unreality, like carven gargoyles seen through a fog.

For the most part they came on hands and knees, withered brown skull-faces and glaring bulbous eyes staring blindly at the three. For it seemed to Smith that the beings were blind; the swollen eyes were quite whitish and pupilless. There was nothing about them that savored of the breathing flesh which they so hideously caricatured save the terrible hunger of their approach, made doubly hideous by the fact that those rotting jaws and parchment-dry bellies could never satisfy it by any normal means.

The deformed muzzles of some of them were twitching, and Smith realized abruptly what instinct had led them here. They hunted, apparently, by scent. And their circle was closing in, so that the three humans, recoiling before that creeping, dryly rustling approach, stood very close together now, shoulder to shoulder. Smith felt the girl shudder against him, and then give him a swift sidelong glance, hot with anger that she should have betrayed weakness even for a moment.

A little hesitantly he drew his heat-gun. There was something a bit incongruous about the very thought of shooting at these already dead things. But they were coming closer, and the prospect of contact with those brown, scaling bodies was so repulsive that his finger pressed the trigger almost of its own volition.

One of the approaching horrors toppled over, the left arm completely burned from its body. Then it regained its balance and crawled onward with a crab-like sidewise motion, the severed arm forgotten behind it, although the skeleton fingers writhed and clawed convulsively. The creature made no outcry, and no blood flowed from the wound.

"Shar!" breathed Yarol. "Can't they—die?" His gun jarred and bucked in his hand. The head of the nearest horror became a blackened, cindery stub, but the thing betrayed no pain. It crawled on slowly, the nimbus of swirling stars like a malefic halo about the burned remnant of a head.

"Yarol!" said Smith sharply. "Double strength—we'll cut a path through them. Follow us, Jirel." Without waiting for an acknowledgment he flicked over a lever on his heat-gun's muzzle, and sent the searing ray flaming through the dark.

The stars danced more swiftly, troubled. Smith sensed a quick, intangible menace in their aroused motion. It was as though something, drowsy and dreaming, had awakened suddenly from slumber to confront the intruders in this strange land. Yet nothing happened; the stars raced back from the heat-ray's beam, but the crawling monsters paid it no attention, even though they blackened into cinders as they crept. The dry, rustling hordes of them advanced straight into the heat-gun's path, and crisped into ruin—and crunched under the feet of their destroyers into fragments that twitched and squirmed with unquenchable animation too hideous to be called life.

Yarol and Smith and Jirel moved forward over brittle black things that still moved and crunched and crept beneath their feet. The two heat-guns hissed softly, mowing a path. Jirel's yellow eyes dwelt speculatively on Smith's brawny back, and once she touched Yarol's dagger sheathed at her side. But she made no hostile move.

So they won free at last from the withered brown horrors, although until the thickening star-mist hid them Smith could see the nightmare horde crawling behind them, slowly, inexorably. And ever the stars danced and swung in their oddly patterned orbits, seeming to watch with detached and sardonic amusement as the three moved on.

The misty brilliance thickened about them sometimes until they could not see each other's faces; sometimes it thinned so that distances were visible, long corridors of emptiness stretched through the stars. Along one of these aisles at last they caught a glimpse of rising ground, and turned toward it in some hopeless hope of escape.

The spongy earth became firmer as they advanced, until by the time they reached the upland they were walking on black, splintered rock from which a sort of star-veiled mountain rose into the misty upper air. Here the stars thickened about them again, so that they could see nothing, but they stumbled up the jagged slope blindly, clutching at the rock with slipping fingers as they helped one another from ledge to ledge.

In Smith, as he mounted the difficult slopes, a fever of exploration had begun to burn so hotly that their danger retired to the back of his mind. What lay ahead, what unimaginable heights rearing among the stars, what lands beyond the mountain? He was not to know, then or ever.

The slope had grown steeper and more rugged at every step. There was no progress save by painful climbing. And now, as Smith braced his back against a rocky outcropping, straining upward to his full height as he supported Yarol's scrambling boots which a moment before had left his shoulders, his arms encountered a queer, thick obstruction in the starry mist overhead. Full of the desire to know what lay ahead, his mind intent on helping Yarol to a foothold above, he scarcely heeded it until the obstruction had thickened until he could hardly move his hands.

Then the shock of memory jarred him sickeningly awake as he recalled the wall of mist that had solidified between Franga and Jirel. He moved with whiplash swiftness to jerk his arms down, but not quite swiftly enough. That thickening mist had turned to strong steel about his wrists, and after a moment of surging struggle against it, while the veins stood out on his forehead and the blood thundered in his ears, he relaxed against the stone, stretched painfully to full height so that he almost swung from his prisoned wrists, and blinked about him in the dazzling dim air, searching for Franga.

He knew now, with a sick regretfulness, that danger had never been farther from them in the mist than they had been from one another. Franga must have moved invisibly at their sides, waiting patiently for the men's hands to stretch far enough from their guns so that his shackles could prison them before they could reach the weapons. Well, he had them now.

From above, Yarol's voice, muffled in the starry mist, spoke passionately of gods and devils. Smith heard boots thrashing upon the rock and realized that the little Venusian must be struggling with bonds like his own. As for himself, he stood spread-eagled with his back to the mountain and his face to the starry void, boots braced on a long slope of rising stone.

He saw Jirel's back as she loitered below them on the slope, waiting for their call that the next highest ledge had been reached. He said quietly, "Joiry!" and met her gaze with a small, rueful grin.

"Well—what?" She was at his side before the question was out of her mouth, a blaze smoldering in her yellow eyes as she saw what had happened. Then she said viciously, "Good! This comes of trafficking with warlocks! May you hang there till you rot!"

"Heh!" came a dry chuckle from behind her. "He'll do just that, Joiry, if he doesn't obey my commands!" Franga came shuffling up the slope, emerging from the stars as from a thick fog, his malice-bright eyes gloating on the prisoned men. From above, Yarol's voice poured smoking Venusian curses upon the wizard's unheeding head.

Jirel matched his fervor with a hot French oath and spun toward Franga purposefully. He smiled crookedly and stepped back, his hands weaving in the air between them. And once more the cloudy barrier thickened in the dimness. Through it, in a triumphant voice, Franga called to Smith,

"Now will you fulfill your bargain and wrest the jewel from Jirel?"

Smith pressed his head back against the stone and said wearily,

"Not until you return us to Joiry."

The warlock's eyes were on his, and in the baffled fury glaring there he thought he read suddenly the full reason why they had been brought here. Franga had no thought of paying the debt he had contracted, nor of letting any of the three escape alive. Once the stone was surrendered they would die here, in some unimaginable way, and their bones would whiten until Judgment Day in the darkness at the mountain's foot. Their only hope of salvation lay in their ability to bargain with Franga over the Starstone. So he shut his lips on the refusal and shifted his shoulders to ease his already aching arms. The weight of the gun on his leg was a tantalization almost unbearable, so near and yet so hopelessly far from his shackled hands.

Franga said: "I think I can change your mind."

His hands behind the barrier moved cryptically, and there came a stirring in the stars that danced between him and Smith. They moved as if fireflies were swarming there, moved toward Smith and swirled about him dizzyingly, blindingly, so that the eye despaired of following their motion. They turned into streaks of flame spinning about him, and now the nearest brushed across his cheek.

At the touch he started involuntarily, jerking back his head from the flame. For it was hot with a heat that sent pain stabbing deeper than a ray-burn through his flesh. Above him he heard Yarol's sharply caught breath, and knew that the hot pain was upon him too. He set his teeth and stared through the swirl at the warlock, his eyes pale and deadly. The spinning flames closed in, brushing his body with scores of tiny tongues, and at every touch the white-hot pain of their torment leaped through him until it seemed to him that every inch of his body flamed with deep-running agony.

Through the blinding pain and the blinding shimmer Franga's voice rasped, "Will you do my bidding?"

Stubbornly Smith shook his head, clinging even in the hot torture of the flames to the desperate hope which was all that remained to him—that so long as Franga had not the Starstone he dared not kill them. Smith had endured pain before; he could endure it now long enough to hold Franga to his bargain. And Yarol must endure it with him for a while. The Venusian had a shameless sort of bravery against physical pain for the simple reason that he could not endure it, quietly fainted and was out of it if called upon to suffer long. Smith hoped he reached that point soon. He said, "No," shortly, between clenched teeth, and pressed his head back against the rock, feeling sweat gather on his forehead as the flashing streaks of flame seared by him, every touch sending deep agony flaming through his flesh.

Franga laughed in a brief, hard cackle and gestured with one hand. And the star-swirls began to flash like knives before Smith's eyes. If they had flamed before, now they dazzled too blindingly to follow. The deep, hot torture of their flickering roared over him in a storm of agony, so that the torment wiped out all thought of Franga or Jirel or Yarol or anything but his own racked flesh flaming with ray-hot pain. He did not know that his fists were clenched above the shackles, or that the muscles stood out in ridges along his jaws as he fought to keep the agony voiceless behind his teeth. The world was a hell of unbearable torment that swept him on a white-hot tide of pain deep into blazing oblivion. He did not even feel the drag on his wrists as his knees gave way beneath him.

Jirel had been watching with mingling emotions as the stars began to swirl into flames about her tall enemy. Triumph was foremost among them, as resentment and fury were foremost among her thoughts just then. But somehow, she who had looked hardily on torture many times before now felt a queer, hot weakness rising in her as the stars became brushing flames and she saw the sweat beading Smith's forehead and his fists clench against the rock.

Then Franga's hateful voice demanded that he rob her by

violence of her jewel and she had tensed herself involuntarily to the struggle before she heard Smith's tortured but resolute "No." She stared at him then half in amazement, her mind whirling with wonder at his motives. And a small, reluctant admiration was coloring her resentment of him as she watched. Jirel was a connoisseur of torture, and she could not remember a man who had endured it more resolutely than Smith. Nor was there a sound from Yarol, half hidden in the starry mist above them, though the small flames streaked the dimness even there.

Then she saw the tenseness melting from Smith's racked body as his long legs buckled at the knees, saw him collapse against the mountainside, swinging by his wrists from the shackles. And a sudden fury of sympathy and hot emotion rushed over her, a sudden gust of pain in his pain. Without realizing how it had happened she found herself beating with clenched fists against the barrier that parted her from Franga, heard her own voice crying,

"Stop it! Stop! Let him go free—I give you the Starstone!"

In the deeps of his pain-flaming oblivion Smith heard that high, passionate cry. The significance of it jolted him back into the memory that a world existed outside the burning circle of his agony, and with infinite effort he lifted his sagging head, found a footing on the rocky slope once more, struggled back into consciousness and flaming anguish. He called in a voice as hoarse as if it had screamed itself raw,

"Jirel! Jirel, you fool, don't do it! He'll kill us all! Jirel!"

If she heard him she did not heed. She was wrenching with both hands at the doeskin tunic buckled at her throat, and Franga, the barrier dissolving, leaned eagerly forward with clawed hands outstretched.

"Don't—Jirel, don't!" yelled Smith despairingly through the dazzle of the flames as the leather parted and suddenly, blindingly, the Starstone flamed in her hands.

Even his own hot pain was blotted for a moment from Smith's mind as he stared. Franga bent forward, breath sucked in, eyes riveted upon the great pale glory of the jewel.

There was utter silence in that strange, dim place as the Starstone blazed through the dusk, its cold, still pallor burning in Jirel's fingers like a block of frozen flame. Looking down, she saw again her own fingers distorted through its translucency, saw again that queer, moving flicker as if a shadow stirred in the deeps of the stone.

For a moment it seemed to her as if these smooth, cool surfaces against her hands enclosed a space as vast as the heavens. In a moment of sudden vertigo she might have been staring deep into an infinity through whose silences moved a something that filled it from edge to edge. Was it a world she held here, as vast in its own dimensions as space itself, even though her narrow hands cradled it between them? And was there not a Dweller in that vast, glowing place—a moving shadow that—

"Jirel!" Smith's pain-hoarse voice startled her out of her dreaming daze. She lifted her head and moved toward him, half visible in the swirl of his torture, holding the jewel like a lamp in her hands. "Don't—don't do it!" begged Smith, gripping hard at his ebbing consciousness as the flames stabbed through him.

"Free him!" she commanded Franga, feeling her own throat constrict inexplicably as she saw the pain etched upon Smith's scarred face.

"You surrender the stone willingly?" The warlock's eyes were ravenous upon her hands.

"Yes—yes, only free him!"

Smith choked on his own desperation as he saw her holding out the jewel. At any cost he knew he must keep it from Franga's clutches, and to his pain-dazed brain there seemed only one way for that. How it would help he did not stop to think, but he put all his weight on his prisoned wrists, swinging his long body through the burning stars in an arc as he kicked the jewel from Jirel's outstretched hands.

She gasped; Franga screamed in a thin, high note that quivered with terror as the Starstone was dashed from her hands against the jagged rock of the mountainside. There was a cracking sound that tinkled like broken glass, and then—

And then a pale, bright glory rolled up in their faces as if the light that dwelt in the jewel were pouring out of its shattered prison. The winking stars were swallowed up in its splendor, the dim air glowed and brightened, the whole mountainside was bathed in the calm, still glory that a moment before had blazed in the Starstone's deeps.

Franga was muttering frantically, twisting his hands in spells that accomplished nothing, gabbling in a cracked voice incantations that evoked no magic. It was as if all his power had melted with the melting stars, the vanished dimness, and he stood unprotected in the full glow of this alien light.

Smith was scarcely heeding it. For as the great pale glory billowed up about him the flashing torment of the stars vanished as their flames vanished, and the utter bliss of peace after pain left him so weak with relief that as the shackles dissolved about his wrists he could only reel back against the rock while waves of near-oblivion washed over him.

A rattling and scuffling sounded above him, and Yarol's small form slid to the ground at his feet in the complete relaxation of unconsciousness. There was a silence while Smith breathed deeply and slowly, gathering strength again, while Yarol stirred in the beginnings of awakening and Franga and Jirel stared about them in the broadening light from the Starstone.

Then down about them swept a thing that can be called only a shadow of light—a deeper brilliance in the glory of the pale day about them. Smith found himself staring directly into its blazing heart, unblinded, although he could make out no more than the shadowy outlines of a being that hung above them inhuman, utterly alien—but not terrible, not menacing. A presence as tangible as flame—and as intangible.

And somehow he sensed a cool and impersonal regard, an aloof, probing gaze that seemed to search the depths of his mind and soul. He strained his eyes, staring into the heart of the white blaze, trying to make out the nature of the being that regarded him. It was like the graceful whorl of a nautilus—and yet he sensed that his eyes could not fully comprehend the unearthly curves and spirals that followed a fantastic, non-Euclidean system of some alien geometry. But the beauty of the thing he could recognize, and there was a deep awe within him, and a feeling of fathomless delight in the wonder and beauty of the being he gazed on.

Franga was screaming thinly and hoarsely, falling to his knees to hide his eyes from the deep splendor. The air quivered, the shadow of brilliance quivered, and a thought without words quivered too through the minds of the three at the mountain's foot.

"For this release We are grateful," said a voiceless voice as deep and still and somehow flaming as the light that made it manifest. "We Whom strong magic prisoned in the Starstone ages ago would grant one last favor before We return to Our own place again. Ask it of Us."

"Oh, return us home again!" gasped Jirel before Smith could speak. "Take us out of this terrible place and send us home!"

Abruptly, almost instantaneously, the shadow of light enveloped them, swept blindingly about them all. The mountain dropped away underfoot, the glory-bright air swept sidewise into nothingness. It was as if the walls of space and time opened up all around them.

Smith heard Franga's shriek of utter despair—saw Jirel's face whirled by him with a sudden, desperate message blazing in her yellow eyes, the red hair streaming like a banner in the wind—and then that dazzle all about him was the dulled gleam of steel walls, and a cold steel surface was smooth against his cheek.

He lifted his head heavily and stared into silence into Yarol's eyes across the table in the little Martian drinking-booth he had left an eon ago. In silence the Venusian returned that long stare.

Then Yarol leaned back in his chair and called, "Marnak! Liquor—quick!" and swung round and began to laugh softly, crazily.

Smith groped for the glass of *segir*-whisky he had pushed away when he rose from this table, ages past. He threw back his head and tossed the liquid down his throat with a quick, stiff-wristed gesture, closing his eyes as the familiar warmth burned through him. Behind the closed lids flashed the remembrance of a keen, pale face whose eyes blazed with some sudden violence of emotion, some message he would never know—whose red streaming hair was a banner on the wind. The face of a girl dead two thousand years in time, light-years of space away, whose very dust was long lost upon the bright winds of earth.

Smith shrugged and drained his glass.

NYMPH OF DARKNESS

by C. L. Moore and Forrest J Ackerman

The thick Venusian dark of the Ednes waterfront in the hours before dawn is breathless and tense with a nameless awareness, a crouching danger. The shapes that move murkily thru its blackness are not daylight shapes. Sun has never shone upon some of those misshapen figures, and what happens in the dark is better left untold. Not even the Patrol ventures there after the lights are out, and the hours between midnight and dawn are outside the law. If dark things happen there the Patrol never knows of them, or desires to know. Powers move thru the darkness along the waterfront to which even the Patrol bows low.

Thru that breathless blackness, along a street beneath which the breathing waters whispered, Northwest Smith strolled slowly. No prudent man ventures out after midnight along the waterfront of Ednes unless he has urgent business abroad, but from the leisurely gait that carried Smith soundlessly thru the dark he might have been some casual sightseer. He was no stranger to the Ednes waterfront. He knew the danger thru which he strolled so slowly, and under narrowed lids his colorless eyes were like keen steel probes that searched the dark. Now and then he passed a shapeless shadow that dodged aside to give him way. It might have been no more than a shadow. His no-colored eyes did not waver. He went on, alert and wary.

He was passing between two high warehouses that shut out even the faint reflection of light from the city beyond when he first heard that sound of bare, running feet which so surprised him. The patter of frantically fleeing steps is not uncommon along the waterfront, but these were—he listened closer—yes, certainly the feet of a woman or a young boy. Light and quick and desperate. His ears were keen enough to be sure of that. They were coming nearer swiftly. In the blackness even his pale eyes could see nothing, and he drew back against the wall, one hand dropping to the ray gun that hung low on his thigh. He had no desire to meet whatever it was which pursued this fugitive.

But his brows knit as the footsteps turned into the street that led between the warehouses. No woman, of whatever class or kind, ventures into this quarter by night. And he became certain as he listened that those feet were a woman's. There was a measured rhythm about them that suggested the Venusian woman's lovely, swaying gait. He pressed flat against the wall, holding his breath. He wanted no sound to indicate his own presence to the terror from which the woman fled. Ten years before he might have dashed out to her—but ten years along the spaceways teaches a man prudence. Gallantry can be foolhardy sometimes, particularly along the waterfront, where any of a score of things might be in close pursuit. At the thought of what some of those things might be the hair prickled faintly along his neck.

The frantic footsteps came storming down the dark street. He heard the rush of breath thru unseen nostrils, the gasp of laboring lungs. Then those desperate feet stumbled a bit, faltered, turned aside. Out of the dark a hurtling figure plunged full-tilt against him. His startled arms closed about a woman—a girl—a young girl, beautifully made, muscular and firmly curved under his startled hands—and quite naked.

He released her rather quickly.

"Earthman!" she gasped in an agony of breathlessness. "Oh, hide me, hide me! Quick!"

There was no time to wonder how she knew his origin or to ask from what she fled, for before the words had left her lips a queer, greenish glow appeared around the corner of the warehouse. It revealed a pile of barrels at Smith's elbow, and he shoved the exhausted girl behind them in one quick motion, drawing his gun and flattening himself still further against the wall.

Yet it was no nameless monster which appeared around the corner of the building. A man's dark shape came into view. A squat figure, broad and misshapen. The light radiated from a flash-tube in his hand, and it was an oddly diffused and indirect light, not like an ordinary flash's clear beam, for it lighted the man behind it as well as what lay before the tube, as if a greenish, luminous fog were spreading sluggishly from the lens.

The man came forward with a queer, shuffling gait. Something about him made Smith's flesh crawl unaccountably. What it was he could not be sure, for the green glow of the tube did not give a clear light, and the man was little more than a squat shadow moving unevenly behind the light-tube's luminance.

He must have seen Smith almost immediately, for he came straight across the street to where the Earthman stood against the wall, gun in hand. Behind the glowing tube-mouth Smith could make out a pale blur of face with two dark splotches for eyes. It was a fat face, unseemly in its puffy palor, like some grub that has fed too long upon corruption. No expression crossed it at the sight of the tall spaceman in his leather garb, leaning against the wall and fingering a ready gun. Indeed, there was nothing to arouse surprise in the Earthman's attitude against the wall, or in his drawn gun. It was what any nightfarer along the waterfront would have done at the appearance of such a green, unearthly glow in the perilous dark.

Neither spoke. After a single long glance at the silent Smith, the newcomer began to switch his diffused light to and fro about the street in obvious search. Smith listened, but the girl had stilled her sobbing breath and no sound betrayed her hiding place. The sluggish searcher went on slowly down the street, casting his foggy light before him. Its luminance faded by degrees as he receded from view, a black, misshapen shadow haloed in unholy radiance.

When utter dark had descended once more Smith holstered his gun and called to the girl in a low voice. The all but soundless murmur of bare feet on the pavement heralded her approach, the hurrying of still unruly breath.

"Thank you," she said softly. "I—I hope you need never know what horror you have saved me from."

"Who are you?" he demanded. "How did you know me?"

"They call me Nyusa. I did not know you, save that I think you are of Earth, and perhaps—trustworthy. Great Shar must have guided my flight along the streets tonight, for I think your kind is rare by the sea edge, after dark."

"But—can you see me?"

"No. But a Martian, or one of my own countrymen, would not so quickly have released a girl who dashed into his arms by night—as I am."

In the dark Smith grinned. It had been purely reflexive, that release of her when his hand realized her nudity. But he might as well take credit for it.

"You had better go quickly now," she went on, "there is such danger here that—"

Abruptly the low voice broke off. Smith could hear nothing, but he sensed a tensing of the girl by his side, a strained listening. And presently he caught a far away sound, a curious muffled wheezing, as if something shortwinded and heavy were making laborious haste. It was growing nearer. The girl's caught breath was loud in the stillness at his elbow.

"Quick!" she gasped. "Oh, hurry!"

Her hand on his arm tugged him on in the direction the squat black searcher had taken. "Faster!" And her anxious hands pulled him into a run. Feeling a little ridiculous, he loped thru the dark beside her with long, easy strides, hearing nothing but the soft fall of his own boots and the scurrying of the girl's bare feet, and far behind the distant wheezing breath, growing fainter.

Twice she turned him with a gentle push into some new byway. Then they paused while she tugged at an unseen door, and after that they ran down an alley so narrow that Smith's broad shoulders brushed its walls. The place smelled of fish and decayed wood and the salt of the seas. The pavement rose in broad, shallow steps, and they went thru another door, and the girl pulled at his arm with a breathed,

"We're safe now. Wait."

He heard the door close behind them, and light feet pattered on boards.

"Lift me," she said after a moment. "I can't reach the light."

Cool, firm fingers touched his neck. Gingerly in the dark he found her waist and swung her aloft at arm's length. Between his hands that waist was supple and smoothly muscled and slim as a reed. He heard the fumble of uncertain fingers overhead. Then in an abrupt dazzle light sprang up about him.

He swore in a choked undertone and sprang back, dropping his hands. For he had looked to see a girl's body close to his face, and he saw nothing. His hands had gripped—nothing. He had been holding aloft a smooth and supple—nothingness.

He heard the fall of a material body on the floor, and a gasp and cry of pain, but still he could see nothing, and he fell back another step, lifting an uncertain hand to his eyes and muttering a dazed Martian oath. For look tho he would, he could see no one but himself in the little bare room the light had revealed. Yet the girl's voice was speaking from empty air.

"What—why did—Oh, I see!" and a little ripple of laughter. "You have never heard of Nyusa?"

The repetition of the name struck a chord of remote

memory in the Earthman's mind. Somewhere lately he had heard that word spoken. Where and by whom he could not recall, but it aroused in his memory a nebulous chord of night peril and the unknown. He was suddenly glad of the gun at his side, and a keener awareness was in the pale gaze he sent around the tiny room.

"No," he said. "I have never heard the name before now."

"I am Nyusa."

"But—where are you?"

She laughed again, a soft ripple of mirth honey sweet with the Venusian woman's traditionally lovely voice.

"Here. I am not visible to men's eyes. I was born so. I was born—" Here the rippling voice sobered, and a tinge of solemnity crept in. "—I was born of a strange mating, Earthman. My mother was a Venusian, but my father—my father was Darkness. I can't explain . . . But because of that strain of Dark in me, I am invisible. And because of it I—I am not free."

"Why? Who holds you captive? How could anyone imprison an invisibility?"

"The—Nov." Her voice was the faintest breath of sound, and again, at the strange word, a prickle of nameless unease ran thru Smith's memory. Somewhere he had heard that name before, and the remembrance it roused was too nebulous to put into words, but it was ominous. Nyusa's breathing whisper went on very softly at his shoulder. It was a queer, unreal feeling, that, to be standing alone in a bare room and a girl's sweet, muted murmur in his ears from empty air.

"The Nov—they dwell underground. They are the last remnant of a very old race. And they are the priests who worship That which was my father. The Darkness. They prison me for purposes of their own.

"You see, my heritage from the lady who bore me was her own lovely human shape, but the Thing which was my father bequeathed to his child stranger things than invisibility. I am of a color outside the range of human eyes. And I have entry into—into other lands than this. Strange lands, lovely and far—Oh, but so damnably near! If I could only pass by the bars the Nov have set to shut me away. For they need me in their dark worship, and here I must stay, prisoned in the hot, muddy world which is all they themselves can ever know. They have a light—you saw it, the green glow in the hands of the Nov who pursued me thru the dark tonight—which makes me visible to human eyes. Something in its color combines with that strange color which is mine to produce a hue that falls within man's range of vision. If he had found me I would have been—punished—severely, because I fled tonight. And the Nov's punishments are—not nice.

"To make sure that I shall not escape them, they have set a guardian to dog my footsteps—the thing that wheezed on my track tonight—Dolf. He sprang from some frightful union of material and immaterial. He is partly elemental, partly animal. I can't tell you fully. And he is cloudy, nebulous—but very real, as you would have discovered had he caught us just now. He has a taste for human blood which makes him invaluable, tho I am safe, for I am only half human, and the Nov—well, they are not wholly human either. They—"

She broke off suddenly. Outside the door Smith's keen ears had caught a shuffle of vague feet upon the ground, and thru the cracks came very clearly the snuffle of wheezing breath. Nyusa's bare feet pattered swiftly across the boards, and from near the door came a series of low, sibilant hissings and whistlings in a clearer tone than the sounds the great Dolf made. The queer noise crescendoed to a sharp command, and he heard a subdued snuffling and shuffling outside and the sound of great, shapeless feet moving off over flagstones. At his shoulder Nyusa sighed.

"It worked that time," she said. "Sometimes I can command him, by virtue of my father's strength in me. The Nov do not know that. Queer, isn't it—they never seem to remember that I might have inherited more from their god than my invisibility and my access to other worlds. They punish me and prison me and command me to their service like some temple dancing girl—me, the half divine! I think—yes, I think that someday the doors will open at my own command, and I shall go out into those other worlds. I wonder—could I do it now?"

The voice faded to a murmurous undertone. Smith realized that she had all but forgotten his presence at the realization of her own potentialities. And again that prickle of unease went over him. She was half human, but half only. Who could say what strange qualities were rooted in her, springing from no human seed? Qualities that might some-day blossom into—into—well, he had no words for what he was thinking of, but he hoped not to be there on the day the Nov tried her too far.

Hesitant footsteps beside him called back his attention sharply. She was moving away, a step at a time. He could hear the sound of her bare feet on the boards. They had almost reached the opposite wall now, one slow step after another. And then suddenly those hesitating footfalls were running, faster, faster, diminishing in distance. No door opened, no aperture in the walls, but Nyusa's bare feet pattered eagerly away. He was aware briefly of the vastnesses of dimensions beyond our paltry three, distances down which a girl's bare feet could go storming in scornful violation of the laws that held him fast. From far away he heard those steps falter. He thought he heard the sound of fists beating against resistance, the very remote echo of a sob. Then slowly the patter of bare feet returned. Almost he could see a dragging head and hopelessly slumped shoulders as the reluctant footfalls drew nearer, nearer, entered the room again. At his shoulder she said in a subdued voice,

"Not yet. I have never gone so far before, but the way is still barred. The Nov are too strong—for a while. But I know, now. I know! I am a god's daughter, and strong too. Not again shall I flee before the Nov's pursuit, or fear because Dolf follows. I am the child of Darkness, and they shall know it! They—"

Sharply into her exultant voice broke a moment of blackness that cut off her words with the abruptness of a knife stroke. It was of an instant's duration only, and as the light came on again a queer wash of rosy luminance spread thru the room and faded again, as if a ripple of color had flowed past. Nyusa sighed.

"That is what I fled," she confided. "I am not afraid now—but I do not like it. You had best go—or no, for Dolf still watches the door I entered by. Wait—let me think."

Silence for a moment, while the last flush of rose faded from the air, to be followed by a ripple of fresh color that faded in turn. Three times Smith saw the tide of red flow thru the room and die away before Nyusa's hand fell upon his arm and her voice murmured from emptiness,

"Come. I must hide you somewhere while I perform my ritual. That color is the signal that the rites are to begin—the Nov's command for my presence. There is no escape for you until they call Dolf away, for I could not guide you to a door without having him sense my presence there and follow. No, you must hide—hide and watch me dance. Would you like that? A sight which no eyes that are wholly human have ever seen before! Come."

Invisible hands pushed open the door in the opposite wall and pulled him thru. Stumbling a little at the newness of being guided by an unseen creature, Smith followed down a corridor thru which waves of rosy light flowed and faded. The way twisted many times, but no doors opened from it nor did they meet anyone in the five minutes or so that elapsed as they went down the hallway thru the pulsing color of the air.

At the end a great barred door blocked their passage. Nyusa released him for an instant, and he heard her feet whisper on the floor, her unseen hands fumble with something metallic. Then a section of the floor sank. He was looking down a shaft around which narrow stairs spiraled, very steeply. It was typically a Venusian structure, and very ancient. He had descended other spiraled shafts before now, to strange destinations. Wondering what lay in store for him at the foot of this, he yielded to the girl's clinging hands and went down slowly, gripping the rail.

He had gone a long way before the small, invisible hands plucked at his arm again and drew him thru an opening in the rock thru which the shaft sank. A short corridor led into darkness. At its end they paused, Smith blinking in the queer, pale darkness which veiled the great cavern that lay before them.

"Wait here," whispered Nyusa. "You should be safe enough in the dark. No one ever uses this passage but myself. I will return after the ceremony."

Hands brushed his briefly, and she was gone. Smith pressed back against the wall and drew his gun, flicking the catch experimentally to be sure it would answer any sudden need. Then he settled back to watch.

Before him a vast domed chamber stretched. He could see only a little of it in the strange dark pallor of the place. The floor shone with the deep sheen of marble, black as quiet water underground. And as the minutes passed he became aware of motion and life in the pale dark. Voices murmured, feet shuffled softly, forms moved thru the distance. The Nov were taking their places for the ceremony. He could see the dim outlines of their mass, far off in the dark.

After a while a deep, sonorous chanting began from nowhere and everywhere, swelling and filling the cavern and echoing from the domed ceiling in reverberant monotones. There were other sounds whose meaning he could not fathom, queer pipings and whistlings like the voice in which Nyusa had commanded Dolf, but invested with a solemnity that gave them depth and power. He could feel fervor building up around the dome of the cavern, the queer, wild fervor and ecstasy of an unknown cult for a nameless god. He gripped his gun and waited.

Now, distantly and very vaguely, a luminance was forming in the center of the arched roof. It strengthened and deepened and began to rain downward toward the darkly shining floor in long streamers like webs of tangible light. In the mirrored floor replicas of light reached upward, mistily reflecting. It was a sight of such weird and enchanting loveliness that Smith held his breath, watching. And now green began to flush the streaming webs, a strange, foggy green like the light the Nov had flashed thru the waterfront streets in pursuit of Nyusa. Recognizing the color, he was not surprised when a shape began to dawn in the midst of that raining light. A girl's shape, half transparent, slim and lovely and unreal.

In the dark pallor of the cavern, under the green luminance of the circling light, she lifted her arms in a long, slow, sweeping motion, lighter than smoke, and moved on tiptoe, very delicately. Then the light shimmered, and she was dancing. Smith leaned forward breathlessly, gun hanging forgotten in his hand, watching her dance. It was so lovely that afterward he could never be sure he had not dreamed.

She was so nebulous in the streaming radiance of the light, so utterly unreal, so fragile, so exquisitely colored in the strangest tints of violet and blue and frosty silver, and queerly translucent, like a moonstone. She was more unreal now, when she was visible, than she had ever seemed before his eyes beheld her. Then his hands had told him of her firm and slender roundness—now she was a wraith, transparent, dream-like, dancing soundlessly in a rain of lunar color.

She wove magic with her dancing body as she moved, and the dance was more intricate and symbolic and sinuous than any wholly human creature could have trod. She scarcely touched the floor, moving above her reflection in the polished stone like a lovely moonlight ghost floating in mid-darkness while green moon-fire rained all about her.

With difficulty Smith wrenched his eyes away from that nebulous creature treading her own reflection as she danced. He was searching for the sources of those voices he had heard, and in the green, revealing light he saw them ringing the cavern in numbers greater than he had dreamed. The Nov, intent as one man upon the shimmering figure before them. And at what he saw he was glad he could not see them clearly. He remembered Nyusa's words, "—the Nov are not wholly human either." Veiled tho they were in the misty radiance and the pallor of the dark, he could see that it was so. He had seen it, unrealizing, in the face of that squat pursuer who had passed him in the street.

They were all thick, shapeless, all darkly robed and white-faced as slugs are white. Their formless features, intent and emotionless, had a soft, unstable quality, not shaped with any human certainty. He did not stare too long at any one face, for fear he might make out its queer lack of contour, or understand the portent of that slug-white instability of feature.

Nyusa's dance ended in a long, floating whirl of unhuman lightness. She sank to the floor in deep obeisance, prostrate upon her own reflection. From the front ranks of the assembled Nov a dark figure stepped with upraised arms. Obediently Nyusa rose. From that dark form, from the slug-like, unfeatured face, a twittering whistle broke, and Nyusa's voice echoed the sounds unerringly, her voice blending with the other's in a chant without words.

Smith was so intent upon watching that he was not aware of the soft shuffling in the dark behind him until the wheeze of labored breath sounded almost upon his neck. The thing was all but on him before that sixth sense which had saved him so often before now shrieked a warning and he whirled with a choked oath of surprise and shock, swinging up his gun and confronting a dim, shapeless immensity out of which a dull glow of greenish light stared at him. His gun spat blue flame, and from the imponderable thing a whistling scream rang quaveringly, echoing across the cavern and cutting short that wordless chant between the Nov and the girl.

Then the dark bulk of Dolf lurched forward and fell smotheringly upon Smith. It bore him to the floor under an engulfing weight which was only half real, but chokingly thick in his nostrils. He seemed almost to be breathing Dolf's substance, like heavy mist. Blinded and gasping, he fought the curiously nebulous thing that was smothering him, knowing he must win free in a few seconds' time, for Dolf's scream must bring the Nov upon him at any moment now. But for all his efforts he could not break away, and something indescribable and nauseous was fumbling for his throat. When he felt its blind searching his struggles redoubled convulsively, and after a frantic moment he staggered free, gulping in clean air and staring into the dark with wide eyes, trying to make out what manner of horror he had grappled with. He could see nothing but that dull flare, as of a single eye, glowing upon him from an imponderable bulk which blended with the dark.

Dolf was coming at him again. He heard great feet shuffling, and the wheezing breath came fast. From behind the shouts of the Nov rose loud, and the noise of running men, and above all the high, clear call of Nyusa, screaming something in a language without words. Dolf was upon him. That revolting, unseen member fumbled again at his throat. He thrust hard against the yielding bulk and his gun flared again, blue-hot in the dark, full into the midst of Dolf's unstable blackness.

He felt the mass of the half-seen monster jerk convulsively. A high, whistling scream rang out, shrill and agonized, and the sucking organ dropped from his throat. The dim glow of vision dulled in the shape's cloudy midst. Then it flickered, went out. Somehow there was a puff of blackness that dissolved into misty nothing all about him, and the dark shape that had been Dolf was gone. Half elemental, he had gone back into nothingness as he died.

Smith drew a deep breath and swung round to front the first of the oncoming Nov. They were almost upon him, and their numbers were overwhelming, but his flame-gun swung its long arc of destruction as they swarmed in and almost a dozen of the squat, dark figures must have fallen to that deadly scythe before he went down under the weight of them. Pudgily soft fingers wrenched the gun from his hand, and he did not fight hard to retain it, for he remembered the blunt-nosed little flame-thrower in its holster under his arm and was not minded that they should discover it in any body-to-body fight.

Then he was jerked to his feet and thrust forward toward the pale radiance that still held Nyusa in its heart, like a translucent prisoner in a cage of light. A little dazed by the swiftness of events, Smith went on unsteadily in their midst. He towered head and shoulders above them, and his eyes were averted. He tried not to flinch from the soft, fish-white hands urging him forward, not to look too closely into the faces of the squat things swarming so near. No, they were not men. He knew that more surely than ever from this close sight of the puffy, featureless faces ringing him round.

At the brink of the raining light which housed Nyusa the Nov who had led the chanting stood apart, watching impassively as the tall prisoner came forward in his swarm of captors. There was command about this Nov, an air of regality and calm, and he was white as death, luminous as a corpse in the lunar reflections of the light.

They halted Smith before him. After one glance into that moveless, unfeatured face, slug pale, the Earthman did not look again. His eyes strayed to Nyusa, beyond the Nov who fronted him, and at what he saw took faint hope again. There was no trace of fear in her poise. She stood straight and quiet, watching, and he sensed a powerful reserve about her. She looked the god's daughter she was, standing there in the showering luminance, translucent as some immortal.

Said the leader Nov, in a voice that came deeply from somewhere within him, tho his unfeatured face did not stir.

"How came you here?"

"I brought him," Nyusa's voice sounded steadily across the space that parted them.

The Nov swung round, amazement in every line of his squatness.

"You?" he exclaimed. "You brought an alien to witness the worship of the god I serve? How dared—"

"I brought one who had befriended me to witness my dance before my father," said Nyusa in so ominously gentle a tone that the Nov did not realize for a moment the significance of her words. He spluttered Venusian blasphemy in a choked voice.

"You shall die!" he yelled thickly. "Both of you shall die by such torment—"

"S-s-s-zt!"

Nyusa's whistling hiss was only a sibilance to Smith, but it cut the Nov's furious flow abruptly short. He went dead quiet, and Smith thought he saw a sicker pallor than before spreading over the slug face turned to Nyusa.

"Had you forgotten?" she queried gently. "Forgotten

that my father is That which you worship? Dare you raise your voice to threaten Its daughter? Dare you, little worm-man?"

A gasp ran over the throng behind Smith. Greenish anger suffused the pallid face of the priest. He spluttered wordlessly and surged forward, short arms clawing toward the taunting girl. Smith's hand, darting inside his coat, was quicker than the clutch of his captors. The blue flare of his flame-thrower leaped out in a tongue of dazzling heat to lick at the plunging Nov. He spun round dizzily and screamed once, high and shrill, and sank in a dark, puddly heap to the floor.

There was a moment of the deepest quiet. The shapeless faces of the Nov were turned in one stricken stare to that oddly fluid lump upon the floor which had been their leader. Then in the pack behind Smith a low rumble began to rise, the mutter of many voices. He had heard that sound before—the dawning roar of a fanatic mob. He knew that it meant death. Setting his teeth, he spun to face them, hand closing firmer about the butt of his flame-thrower.

The mutter grew deeper, louder. Someone yelled, "Kill! Kill!" and a forward surge in the thick crowd of faces swayed the mass toward him. Then above that rising clamor Nyusa's voice rang clear.

"Stop!" she called. In sheer surprise the murderous mob paused, eyes turning toward the unreal figure in her cage of radiance. Even Smith darted a glance over his shoulder, flame gun poised in mid-air, his finger hesitating upon the catch. And at what they saw the crowd fell silent, the Earthman froze into stunned immobility as he watched what was happening under the rain of light.

Nyusa's translucent arms were lifted, her head thrown back. Like a figure of triumph carved out of moonstone she stood poised, while all about her in the misty, lunar colors of the light a darkness was forming like fog that clung to her outstretched arms and swathed her half real body. And it was darkness not like any night that Smith had ever seen before. No words in any tongue could describe it, for it was not a darkness made for any vocal creature to see. It was a blasphemy and an outrage against the eyes, against all that man hopes and believes and is. The darkness of the incredible, the utterly alien and opposed.

Smith's gun fell from shaking fingers. He pressed both hands to his eyes to shut out that indescribably awful sight, and all about him heard a long, soft sighing as the Nov sank to their faces upon the shining floor. In that deathly hush Nyusa spoke again, vibrant with conscious godhood and underrun with a queer, tingling ripple of inhumanity. It was the voice of one to whom the unknown lies open, to whom that utterly alien and dreadful blackness is akin.

"By the Darkness I command you," she said coldly. "Let this man go free. I leave you now, and I shall never return. Give thanks that a worse punishment than this is not visited upon you who paid no homage to the daughter of Darkness."

Then for a swift instant something indescribable happened. Remotely Smith was aware that the Blackness which had shrouded Nyusa was spreading thru him, permeating him with the chill of that blasphemous dark, a hideous pervasion of his innermost being. For that instant he was drowned in a darkness which made his very atoms shudder to its touch. And if it was dreadful to him, the voiceless shriek that rose simultaneously from all about him gave evidence how much more dreadfully their god's touch fell upon the Nov. Not with his ears, but with some nameless sense quickened by that moment of alien blackness, he was aware of the scream of intolerable anguish, the writhing of extra human torment which the Nov underwent in that one timeless moment.

Out of his tense awareness, out of the spreading black, he was roused by a touch that startled him into forgetfulness of that dreadful dark. The touch of a girl's mouth upon his, a tingling pressure of sweet parted lips that stirred delicately against his own. He stood tense, not moving a muscle, while Nyusa's mouth clung to his in a long, close kiss like no kiss he had ever taken before. There was a coldness in it, a chill as alien as the dark that had gathered about her translucency under the light, a shuddering cold that struck thru him in one long, deep-rooted shock of frigid revulsion. And there was warmth in it, headily stirring the pulse which that cold had congealed.

In the instant while those clinging lips melted to his mouth, he was a battleground for emotions as alien as light and dark. The cold touch of Darkness, the hot touch of love. Alienity's shuddering, frozen stab, and humanity's blood stirring throb of answer to the warm mouth's challenge. It was a mingling of such utter opposites that for an instant he was racked by forces that sent his senses reeling. There was danger in the conflict, the threat of madness in such irreconcilable forces that his brain blurred with the effort of compassing them.

Just in time the clinging lips dropped away. He stood alone in the reeling dark, that perilous kiss burning upon his memory as the world steadied about him. In that dizzy instant he heard what the rest, in their oblivious agony, could not have realized. He heard a girl's bare feet pattering softly along some incline, up and up, faster and faster. Now they were above his head. He did not look up. He knew he would have seen nothing. He knew Nyusa walked a way that no sense of his could perceive. He heard her feet break into an eager little run. He heard her laugh once, lightly, and the laugh cut off by the sound of a closing door. Then quiet.

Without warning, on the heels of that sound, he felt a tremendous release all about him. The darkness had lifted. He opened his eyes upon a dimly lighted cavern from which that rain of light had vanished. The Nov lay in quivering windows, about his feet, their shapeless faces hidden. Otherwise the whole vast place was empty as far as his eyes could pierce the dark.

Smith bent and picked up his fallen gun. He kicked the nearest Nov ungently.

"Show me the way out of this place," he ordered, sheathing the flame-thrower under his arm.

Obediently the sluggish creature stumbled to his feet.

THE GENESIS OF AN INVISIBLE VENUSIENNE

Afterword to *Nymph of Darkness*
by Forrest J Ackerman

There is an apocryphal story that the California town of Azusa was so named because when a nomenclature for it was sought it seemed that everything had already been appropriated from A to Z in the USA.

There is no truth to the rumor that Nyusa was initially known as NY, USA; like Wendayne (my wife's naturalized citizen name when she came to Earth from somewhere beyond Infinity), Nyusa burgeoned in my brain in the same manner as Tarzan in Edgar Rice Burroughs's: the result of many mental gymnastics with quixotic sound combinations till the satisfactory amalgamation materialized. En passant, it is a virtually forgotten fact—except by Sharane Yvala Dewey, a woman I knew as a little girl, who was so named by her science fiction author father G. Gordon Dewey, who was captivated by the name of A. Merritt's heroine in *The Ship of Ishtar* and the Yvala of Catherine Moore's Northwest Smith adventure of the same name—it is a practically unknown fact that I created the character (pronounced Ee-*vah*-lah). I hope it's not unchivalrous to suggest it, with dear Catherine so mentally decimated by Alzheimer's disease that she has not known me or herself or what she wrote for two years or more, but reflecting on the origin of the story it occurs to me I might retroactively be entitled to a byline on "Yvala" because in retrospect I feel I contributed about as much inspiration and plot gimmick to it as I did to "Nymph." I will not belabor the point, however, since Catherine's memory is a blank book and she is in no position to agree or disagree with my observation. (Incidentally, Gordon Dewey gave his other daughter a Catherine character name: Judai.)

The January–February 1948 club organ of the Los Angeles Science Fantasy Society, *Shangri-LA,* featured the following article by me on the story behind the story on "Nymph of Darkness."

THE "NYMPH" O' MANIACK

by Forrest J Ackerman

This is the story behind the story of a collaboration in which I was honored to have my name linked some years ago with the lovely and talented Catherine Moore, now the wife of an old friend—sensational Henry Kuttner. As I am composing this article a few hours before midnite, New Year's Eve, I believe it would be apropos to preface it with a quotation from a New Year letter from Catherine which I ran across in searching for the material for the following.

1936: "Dear Forrie: Happy New Year. And by the way, if you heard a new year's horn blowing extra loudly just at midnight, your time, and couldn't locate it—that was me. I blew a special blast for you at about 2:00 a.m. or thereabouts, as nearly as I can remember now—of New Year's morning just as the radio announced that it was at that moment midnight in Los Angeles. I never quite believe things like that—different times, I mean. Of course, know that you lose a day going round the world, and all that—but somehow can't quite believe it anyway. I read a story somewhere once in which someone in New York phoned someone in London, and over the wire "the late afternoon New York traffic vibrated weirdly in the stillness of the London night." It seems so impossible, if you see what I mean."

Catherine Moore—puzzled by geo-chronological paradoxes!

But about NYMPH OF DARKNESS by CLMoore and FJAckerman, whose chief claim to fame was that it was among the titles which vied for third place as best fantasy of the year in a poll taken among the "Auslanders"—the Australian fans, down under. (Also, it was one of the earliest stories illustrated by Hannes Bok, a new artist whom a young fan named Ray Bradbury had personally persuaded the late Farnsworth Wright to try.)

Here is the original outline I sent to Catherine when she was living in Indianapolis and working in a bank vault:

THE NYUSA NYMPH—One short and exciting experience in the adventure-filled life of Northwest Smith . . . Of a fleeing figure in the nite that bumped into NW at the Venusian waterfront—an *unseen* form—that of Nyusa, the girl who was born *invisible!* Further details: The business of the squat creature who came swiftly slinking thru the street, short on the heels of the figure in NW's arms, with the strange lite-tube in its hands flashing from side to side (it would have caused Nyusa to become visible, you know—the lite from the tube) . . . and of Nyusa, whose abnormally high body-temperature kept her comfortable free from clothing; so that invisible she remained, as born—And from what she fled, and how NW was of service to her, etc.—I will leave to you.

MOORE to Ackerman: I think I know why the pursuer's flash made Nyusa visible. Did you ever notice the peculiar colors one's skin turns under different lights? A violet-ray machine turns lips and nails—as I remember—a sickly green, and the blue lights they use in photographers shops, sometimes, make you purple. I once figured out why, but can't remember and haven't time now to go into it. Something about complementary colors and mixing yellow and blue, and whatnot. Well, you remember in Bierce's THE DAMNED THING his invisible monster was a color outside our range of perception. Couldn't this flash-light be of some shade which, combined with Nyusa's peculiar skin-tone, produced a visible color? * And Venus is the Hot Planet anyhow, so no need to increase her body temperature above normal to make it possible for her to run about in the altogether. * Smith had met her in the absolutely black dark of the starless Venusian night. She came tearing down the street and bumped into him, and, tho considerably astonished to find his arms full of scared and quite unadorned girl, he of course didn't realize her invisibility then. Afterward came this squat, dark pursuer, flashing his greenishly glowing ray to and fro. When he'd gone by she heard another sound—origin yet unknown, to me or anyone else—which so alarmed her that she pulled Smith into a run and guided him at top speed thru [the spellings "thru" & "tho" are Catherine's] devious byways and into an unlighted room. "Lift me up," said she, "so I can reach the light." And when it goes on he realizes that he is holding in midair a beautifully muscular, firmly curved armful of nothingness. He had just dropped her onto the floor and staggered back, doubting his sanity. What happens next I don't know. * If you have any more ideas, they'll be welcome. This is the stage of a story when I usually sweat blood for several days, racking an absolutely sterile brain for ideas. Then something takes fire and the whole story just gallops, with me flying along behind trying to keep up with it. Very strenuous. * Think hard and see if you can find any possible reasons, sane or insane, as to what the noise was she had heard, why it alarmed her so, whether she is invisible just by a freak of nature or whether by some mysterious mastermind's intent. I suspect she is in the power of some insidious villain, but don't know yet. * All thru the preface of the story I've made such veiled hints about the nameless horrors which stalk by night along the water-front of Ednes, that said villain might be almost anything —some horror out of the ages before man, or some super-brain of the far advanced races we know nothing of, or an unhappy medium like the Alendar. (That reminds me—Vaudir is the infinitive of—as I remember my college days—the French verb *wish*. I presume Nyusa is purely original with you, so you deserve more credit than I, for it's a grand name.) ["Thank you kindly, ma'am," said the 18-year-old lad. "There is no truth to the rumor that I made it up from the initials of our major metropolis, N.Y., U.S.A."]

ACKERMAN to Moore—[This is the point where I was supposed to come in for my big hunk of egoboo, quoting my share in the development of the plot, but I can't find the vital letter!] What I wrote must be imagined from the mirror of Catherine's reply.

MOORE to Ackerman: Thanks for the further sugges-tions. I had already gone on past my stopping point when I wrote you, so can't use all your ideas, but have incorporated Dolf and the dancing-girl idea. It seems Nyusa is—sorry— really innately invisible, being the daughter of a Venusian woman and a Darkness which is worshiped by a queer race of slug-like, half-human beings which dwell under the Venusian city of Ednes. (Incidentally, Ednes, the city where in the Minga stood, is simply lifted bodily out of the middle of W*ednes*day.) Anyhow, Nyusa is forced by the priests to dance in their ritual worship under a peculiar light which renders her visible in a dim, translucent way. And because of her mixed breed she has access into other worlds from which her masters bar her out by their own strange mental powers because she'd never return to dance for them if she once got away. Dolf guards her for the same reason. I think now that Nyusa's captors drive her too far sometime, and she realizes that after all she is half divine, and calls upon the strain of Darkness within her to burst the bonds they have imposed. Smith, attacked by Dolf as he hides in their temple watching the ritual dance, fights with the worshippers and kills the high priest, whereupon their power over Nyusa is weakened and she exerts her demi-divinity to escape. Thus, tho Smith doesn't get the fortune you suggested, he at least is spared the expense of buying her any clothes, which was a very practical idea on your part.

ACKERMAN to Moore: I have a suggestion about the ending. Shambleau stunned Smith; to this day he has probably not forgotten "it." Sweet, was the girl of the Scarlet Dream. While in the Black Thirst, he gazed upon beauty incredible. But Shambleau was to be shunned; and the girl of the Dream . . . Vaudir dissolved. So, let the Nymph—Nyusa—just before she escapes . . . couldn't she—kiss Smith? A kiss never to be forgotten: a kiss . . . so cool, with a depth drawn out of Darkness. And yet, a kiss of fire—from her Venusian strain—hot, alive, searing Northwest's lips. A kiss, of delicious demi-divinity . . . a fond caress of frozen flame. Making it, under your care, Catherine, a kiss smothering with extra-mundane emotion, leaving the readers gasping. Smith's reward, the kiss that becomes famous and concludes the story.

MOORE to Ackerman: I do wish I had had your suggestion about the parting kiss before I finished. I wasn't able to expand the idea as fully as I'd have liked to, both because of the space-saving necessity and because to give it the attention it deserved I'd have had to write the story toward it from the beginning. It was a grand idea and would have given the story just the punch it needed at the end. Oh well, no story of mine is complete unless I leave out some major point until too late. I meant to make Shambleau's eyes shine in the dark, and to play up the idea of the Guardians in BLACK THIRST.

*   *   *

"Nymph of Darkness" was first published in the printed fan magazine *Fantasy Magazine,* in the April 1935 issue, and professionally published, in an expurgated form, in the Dec. 1939 *Weird Tales*.

FOREWORD

by Sam Moskowitz

The genesis, logic, and submission history of C. L. Moore's "Werewoman" has never been clarified, not even by her when she was asked to do so in a direct question. In a letter dated April 2, 1962, Moore said: "I believe Wright bounced my second attempt, but bought everything else I submitted to him." Even though "Werewoman" was under discussion in that same letter she never singled it out as the rejected story. At the time I was selecting reprints for *Fantastic* and asked for reprint rights. She was reluctant to grant them and in my letter of May 20, 1962, in the hope of changing her mind, I gave her my opinion of the story: "I can understand your hesitance about its further publication, since it is atypical of the other Northwest Smith stories. Northwest Smith is a character in the story but he is an accessory, not a necessity; and any other strong male figure would have done. The story is also different inasmuch as it is a pure weird-fantasy with almost no leverage in time or space such as the planets Mars and Venus give the other Northwest Smith stories. Nevertheless, there is also a great deal to be said for it. The writing, evaluated against the style you were writing in at the period, is excellent, at points evocatively poetic. Once accepting the fact that the story will not be in the traditional Northwest Smith pattern, the writing carries you along easily, enthrallingly, colorfully, and with the sense of special experience.

"I think that had it been published at the time the Northwest Smith sagas were in vogue, or at the time the collected volumes were turned out—Gnome Press—it would have struck a jarring note. But I think today's audience would accept it without preconceived notions of what a Northwest Smith story should be like and I feel confident that it would be very popular."

Henry Kuttner had written me October 4, 1956, some years earlier from Santa Monica, California, the following: "What I wanted to ask you about was whether or not you had a record of publication for a story by C. L. Moore about Northwest Smith called 'Werewoman.' It was unfinished, written in the late thirties, I think, and Catherine doesn't remember its being published anywhere. But we keep running across references to it, and there's a possibility it may have been given to some fan mag which Catherine has forgotten about. Since you're about the only one who'd really have complete records of this sort of thing, I'm wondering if you happen to recall any publication data on this yarn. If you do and could let us know, we'd be very grateful.

I informed him that "Werewoman" had been published in the second (1938) issue of *Leaves,* edited and stenciled by R. H. Barlow and mimeographed and bound by Claire P. Beck, at that time the publisher of a leading fan magazine *The Science Fiction Critic* out of Lakeport, California.

R. H. Barlow was a precociously talented teenager who was a very close friend of H. P. Lovecraft. In every sense *Leaves* was a fan magazine aimed at the Lovecraft circle and filled with contributions from them, including a number by Lovecraft himself. The first issue dated Summer 1937 was made up of eighty letter-sized mimeographed pages and sold for thirty-five cents. It ran fiction and poetry by A. Merritt, Donald Wandrei, Frank Belknap Long, August W. Derleth, Clark Ashton Smith among others, both original and reprint.

It editorially stated it was intended to replace *The Recluse* published by W. Paul Cook in 1927. It was financed by Ernest Edkins, one of the leading lights of amateur journalism and one hundred copies were run off.

The second issue, which featured "Werewoman" by C. L. Moore, appeared no earlier than December 1938. It was stenciled by R. H. Barlow in Mexico City, Kansas City, and Lakeport, California, and ran sixty-six pages and sold for fifty cents. In the last city he was a guest at the home of Claire P. Beck, who presumably did the mimeographing on his own equipment. Unlike the first, all the material in the second issue—except a story by Henry S. Whitehead "The Tree-Man"—was original and that story was heavily revised for the *Leaves* printing. The issue was weighted on material by the Lovecraft circle—including fiction by Donald Wandrei and Samuel Loveman, three prose poems, an article, "In Defense of Dagon," an excerpt from a letter by H. P. Lovecraft, and contributions from R. H. Barlow and Vrest Orten. It also ran Fritz Leiber, Jr.'s lengthy poem "The Demons of the Upper Air" which had previously been submitted to H. P. Lovecraft for criticism and which was one of Leiber's earliest published efforts. Barlow states that sixty copies of this issue were offered for sale, indicating that there may have been a few more printed.

I suggested to Kuttner that he write to Clyde Beck, one of the brothers of Claire Beck, who I knew was still resident in Lakeport, and see if he had retained an extra copy of *Leaves* II that he might wish to sell. He was successful, writing to me January 9, 1957: "We did get in touch with Clyde Beck, who had one copy of the issue. We certainly didn't expect him to present it to Catherine, but that's what he did, a hell of a nice gesture."

It seems likely that R. H. Barlow solicited the contribution from Moore with the aid of an endorsement from H. P. Lovecraft. It was obviously something she didn't think she was going to be able to sell. She was later to misplace the copy that Clyde Beck sent her, so it is quite possible she also misplaced the original author's copy or copies she should have received from Barlow.

In interviews in the latter part of the seventies, C. L. Moore had published a number of statements that flatly contradicted information—some under her own byline—published in the period 1933 to 1936, much closer to the events involved than her recollections more than forty years later. Her motives appeared puzzling until several years ago Forrest Ackerman reported that she had been institutionalized with Alzheimer's Disease, a condition with a slow onset that eventually results in the individual even forgetting the identities of their beloved ones. Consequently, we will never get further information on the origin of "Werewoman" from C. L. Moore. Possibly some light may be thrown on it from her diary, if she ever kept one; from letters or publication records. In the interim, the story is well worth preserving.

WEREWOMAN

by C. L. Moore

With the noise of battle fading behind him down the wind, Northwest Smith staggered into the west and the twilight, stumbling as he went. Blood spattered brightly behind him on the rocks, leaving a clear trail to track him by, but he knew he would not be followed far. He was headed into the salt wastelands to the westward, and they would not follow him there.

He urged his reluctant feet faster, for he knew that he must be out of sight in the grey waste before the first of the scavengers came to loot the dead. They would follow—that trail of blood and staggering footsteps would draw them like wolves on his track, hot in the hope of further spoils—but they would not come far. He grinned a little wryly at the thought, for he was going into no safety here, though he left certain death behind. He was stumbling, slow step by step, into almost as certain a death, of fever and thirst and hunger in the wastelands, if no worse death caught him first. They told tales of this grey salt desert. . . .

He had never before come even this far into the cold waste during all the weeks of their encampment. He was too old an adventurer not to know that when people shun a place completely and talk of it in whispers and tell little half-finished, fearful stories of it over campfires, that place is better left alone. Some might have been spurred by that very reticence into investigation, but Northwest Smith had seen too many strange things in his checkered career to doubt the basis of fact behind folktales or care to rush in heedlessly where others had learned by experience not to tread.

The sound of battle had dwindled to a faint murmur on the evening breeze. He lifted his head painfully and stared into the gathering dark ahead with narrowed eyes the no-colour of pale steel. The wind touched his keen, scarred face with a breath of utter loneliness and desolation. No man-smell of smoke or byre or farmstead tainted it, blowing clear across miles beyond miles of wastelands. Smith's nostrils quivered to that scent of unhumanity. He saw the greyness stretching before him, flat and featureless, melting into the dark. There was a sparse grass growing, and low shrub and a few stunted trees, and brackish water in deep, still pools dotted the place at far intervals. He found himself listening. . . .

Once in very long-ago ages, so campfire whispers had told him, a forgotten city stood here. Who dwelt in it, or what, no man knew. It was a great city spreading over miles of land, rich and powerful enough to wake enmity, for a mighty foe had come at last out of the lowlands and in a series of tremendous battles razed it to the ground. What grievance they had against the dwellers in the city no one will ever know now, but it must have been dreadful, for when the last tower was laid to earth and the last stone toppled from its foundation they had sown the land with salt, so that for generations no living thing grew in all the miles of desolation. And not content with this, they had laid a curse upon the very earth wherein the city had its roots, so that even today man shun the place without understanding why.

It was very long past, that battle, and history forgot the very name of the city, and victor and vanquished alike sank together into the limbo of the forgotten. In time the salt-sown lands gained a measure of life again and the sparse vegetation that now clothed it struggled up through the barren soil. But men still shunned the place.

They said, in whispers, that there were dwellers yet in the salt-lands. Wolves came out by night sometimes and carried off children straying late; sometimes a new-made grave was found open and empty in the morning, and people breathed of ghouls. . . . Late travellers had heard voices wailing from the wastes by night, and those daring hunters who ventured in search of the wild game that ran through the underbrush spoke fearfully of naked werewomen that howled in the distances. No one knew what became of the adventurous souls who travelled too far alone into the desolation of the place. It was accursed for human feet to travel, and those who dwelt there, said the legends, must be less than human.

Smith discounted much of this when he turned from the bloody shambles of that battle into the wastelands beyond. Legends grow, he knew. But a basis for the tales he did not doubt, and he glanced ruefully down at the empty holsters hanging low on his legs. He was completely unarmed, perhaps for the first time in more years than he liked to remember; for his path had run for the most part well outside the law, and such men do not go unarmed anywhere—even to bed.

Well, no help for it now. He shrugged a little, and then grimaced and caught his breath painfully, for that slash in the shoulder was deep, and blood still dripped to the ground, though not so freely as before. The wound was closing. He had lost much blood—the whole side of his leather garments was stiff with it, and the bright stain spattering behind him told of still greater losses. The pain of his shoulder stabbed at him yet, but it was being swallowed up now in a vast, heaving greyness. . . .

He drove his feet on stubbornly over the uneven ground, though the whole dimming landscape was wavering before him like a sea—swelling monstrously—receding into vague distances. . . . The ground floated up to meet him with surprising gentleness.

He opened his eyes presently to a grey twilight, and after

a while staggered up and went on. No more blood flowed, but the shoulder was stiff and throbbing, and the wasteland heaved still like a rolling sea about him. The singing in his ears grew loud, and he was not sure whether the faint echoes of sound he heard came over grey distances or rang in his own head—long, faint howls like wolves wailing their hunger to the stars. When he fell the second time he did not know it, and was surprised to open his eyes upon full dark with stars looking down on him and the grass tickling his cheek.

He went on. There was no great need of it now—he was well beyond pursuit, but the dim urge to keep moving dinned in his weary brain. He was sure now that the long howls were coming to him over the waste stretches; coming nearer. By instinct his hand dropped to clutch futilely at the empty holster.

There were queer little voices going by overhead in the wind. Thin, shrill. With immense effort he slanted a glance upward and thought he could see, with the clarity of exhaustion, the long, clean lines of the wind streaming across the sky. He saw no more than that, but the small voices shrilled thinly in his ears. Presently he was aware of motion beside him—life of some nebulous sort moving parallel to his course, invisible in the starlight. He was aware of it through the thrill of evil that prickled at the roots of his hair, pulsing from the dimness at his side—though he could see nothing. But with that clarity of inner vision he felt the vast and shadowy shape lurching, formlessly through the grass at his side. He did not turn his head again, but the hackles of his neck bristled. The howls were nearing, too. He set his teeth and drove on, unevenly.

He fell for the third time by a clump of stunted trees, and lay for a while breathing heavily while long, slow waves of oblivion washed over him and receded like waves over sand. In the intervals of lucidity he knew that those howls were coming closer and closer over the greyness of the salt-lands.

He went on. The illusion of that formless walker-in-the-dark still haunted him through the grass, but he was scarcely heeding it now. The howls had changed to short, sharp yaps, crisp in the starlight, and he knew that the wolves had struck his trail. Again, instinctively, his hand flashed downward toward his gun, and a spasm of pain crossed his face. Death he did not mind—he had kept pace with it too many years to fear that familiar visage—but death under fangs, unarmed . . . He staggered on a little faster, and the breath whistled through his clenched teeth.

Dark forms were circling his, slipping shadowily through the grass. They were wary, these beasts of the outlands. They did not draw near enough for him to see them save as shadows gliding among the shadows, patient and watching. He cursed them futilely with his failing breath, for he knew now that he dared not fall again. The grey waves washed upward, and he shouted something hoarse in his throat and called upon a last reservoir of strength to bear him up. The dark forms started at his voice.

So he went on, wading through oblivion that rose waist-high, shoulder-high, chin-high—and receded again before the indomitable onward drive that dared not let him rest. Something was wrong with his eyes now—the pale-steel eyes that had never failed him before—for among the dark forms he was thinking he saw white ones, slipping and gliding wraithlike in the shadow. . . .

For an endless while he stumbled on under the chilly stars while the earth heaved gently beneath his feet and the greyness was a sea that rose and fell in blind waves, and white figures weaved about his through the hollow dark.

Quite suddenly he knew that the end of his strength had come. He knew it surely, and in the last moment of lucidity left to him he saw a low tree outlined against the stars and staggered to it—setting his broad back against the trunk, fronting the dark watchers with lowered head and pale eyes that glared defiance. For that one moment he faced them resolutely—then the tree-trunk was sliding upward past him—the ground was rising— He gripped the sparse grass with both hands, and swore as he fell.

When he opened his eyes again he stared into a face straight out of hell. A woman's face, twisted into a diabolical smile, stooped over him—glare-eyed in the dark. White fangs slavered as she bent to his throat.

Smith choked back a strangled sound that was half-oath, half-prayer, and struggled to his feet. She started back with a soundless leap that set her wild hair flying, and stood staring him in the face with wide slant eyes that glared greenly from the pallor of her face. Through the dark her body was white as a sickle moon half-veiled in the long, wild hair.

She glared with hungry fangs a-drip. Beyond her he sensed other forms, dark and white, circling restlessly through the shadows—and he began to understand dimly, and knew that there was no hope in life for him, but he spread his long legs wide and gave back glare for glare, pale-eyed and savage.

The pack circled him, dim blurs in the dark, the green glare of eyes shining alike from white shapes and black. And to his dizzied eyes it seemed that the forms were not stable; shifting from dark to light and back again with only the green-glowing eyes holding the same glare through all the changing. They were closing in now, the soft snarls rising and sharp yaps impatiently breaking through the guttural undernotes, and he saw the gleam of teeth, white under the stars.

He had no weapon, and the wasteland reeled about him and the earth heaved underfoot, but he squared his shoulders savagely and fronted them in hopeless defiance, waiting for the wave of darkness and hunger to come breaking over him in an overwhelming tide. He met the green desire of the woman's wild eyes as she stooped forward, gathering herself for the lunge, and suddenly something about the fierceness of her struck a savage chord within him, and—facing death as he was—he barked a short, wild laugh at her, and yelled into the rising wind. "Come on, werewoman! Call your pack!"

She stared for the briefest instant, half poised for leaping —while something like a spark seemed to flash between them, savageness calling to savageness across the barriers of everything alive—and suddenly she flung up her arms, the black hair whirling, and tossed back her head and bayed to the stars; a wild, long, ululating yell that held nothing of humanity, a triumphant bay of fierce delight echoing down the wind. All about her in the dark, hoarse throats caught up the yell and tossed it from voice to voice across the salt-lands until the very stars shivered at the wild, exultant baying.

And as the long yell trembled into silence something inexplicable happened to Smith. Something quivered in answer within him, agonisingly, the grey oblivion he had been fighting so long swallowed him up at a gulp—and then he leaped within himself in a sudden, ecstatic rush; and while one part of him slumped to its knees and then to its face in the grass, the living vital being that was Smith sprang free into the cold air that stung like sharp wine.

The wolf-pack rushed clamorously about him, the wild, high yells shivering delightfully along every nerve of his suddenly awakened body. And it was as if a muffling darkness had lifted from his senses, for the night opened up in all directions to his new eyes, and his nostrils caught fresh, exciting odours on the streaming wind, and in his ears a thousand tiny sounds took on sudden new clarity and meaning.

The pack that had surged so clamorously about him was a swirl of dark bodies for an instant—then in a blur and a flash they were dark no longer—rose on hind legs and cast off the darkness as they rose—and slim, white, naked werewomen swirled around him in a tangle of flashing limbs and streaming hair.

He stood half dazed at the transition, for even the wide salt moor was no longer dark and empty, but pale grey under the stars and peopled with nebulous, unstable beings that wavered away from the white wolf-pack which ringed him, and above the clamour of wild voices that thin, shrill chattering went streaming down the wind overhead.

Out of the circling pack a white figure broke suddenly, and he felt cold arms about his neck and a cold, thin body pressing his. Then the white whirl parted violently and another figure thrust through—the fierce-eyed woman who had called him across the barriers of flesh into this half-land of her own. Her green-glaring eyes stabbed at the sister wolf whose arms twined Smith's neck, and the growl that broke from her lips was a wolf's guttural. The woman fell away from Smith's embrace, crouching at bay, as the other, with a

toss of wild hair, bared her fangs and launched herself straight
at the throat of the interloper. They went down in a tangle of
white and tossing dark, and the pack fell still so that the only
sound was the heavy breathing of the fighters and the low,
choked snarls that rippled from their throats. Then over the
struggle of white and black burst a sudden torrent of scarlet.
Smith's nostrils flared to the odour that had a new, fascinat-
ing sweetness now—and the werewoman rose, bloody-
mouthed, from the body of her rival. The green-glowing eyes
met his, and a savage exultation flowing from them met as
savage a delight wakening in him, and her keen, moon-white
face broke into a smile of hellish joy.

She flung up her head again and bayed a long, triumphant cry to the stars, and the pack about her took up the yell,
and Smith found his own face turned to the sky and his own
throat shouting a fierce challenge to the dark.

Then they were running—jostling one another in savage
play, flying over the coarse grass on feet that scarcely brushed
the ground. It was like the rush of the wind, that effortless
racing, as the earth flowed backward under their spurning feet
and the wind streamed in their nostrils with a thousand
tingling odours. The white werewoman raced at his side, her
long hair flying behind her like a banner, her shoulder
brushing his.

They ran through strange places. The trees and the grass
had taken on new shapes and meanings, and in a vague,
half-realised way he was aware of curious forms looming
round him—buildings, towers, walls, high turrets shining in
the starlight, yet so nebulous that they did not impede their
flight. He could see these shadows of a city very clearly
sometimes—sometimes he ran down marble streets, and it
seemed to him that his feet rang in golden sandals on the
pavement and rich garments whipped behind him in the
wind of his speed, and a sword clanked at his side. He
thought the woman beside him fled in bright-coloured
sandals too, and her long skirts rippled away from her flying
limbs and the streaming hair was twined with jewels—yet he
knew he ran naked beside a moon-bare wolf-woman over
coarse grass that rustled to his tread.

And sometimes, too, it seemed to him that he fled on four legs, not two—fleetly as the wind, thrusting a pointed muzzle into the breeze and lolling a red tongue over dripping fangs. . . .

Dim shapes fled from their sweeping onward rush—great, blurred, formless things; dark beings with eyes; thin wraiths wavering backward from their path. The great moor teemed with these half-seen monstrosities; fierce-eyed, some of them, breathing out menace, and evil, angry shapes that gave way reluctantly before the were-pack's sweep. But they gave way. There were terrible things in that wasteland, but the most terrible of all were the werewomen, and all the dreadful, unreal beings made way at the bay of those savage voices. All this he knew intuitively. Only the thin chattering that streamed down the wind did not hush when the were-voices howled.

There were many odours on the wind that night, sharp and sweet and acrid, wild odours of wild, desolate lands and the dwellers therein. And then, quite suddenly on a vagrant breeze, lashing their nostrils like a whip—the harsh, rich, blood-tingling scent of man. Smith flung up his head to the cold stars and bayed long and shudderingly, and the wild wolf-yell rang from throat to throat through the pack until the whole band of them was shaking the very air to that savage chorus. They loped down the wind-stream, nostrils flaring to that full, rich scent.

Smith ran at the forefront, shoulder to shoulder with the wild white creature who had fought for him. The man-smell was sweet in his nostrils, and hunger wrenched at him as the smell grew stronger and faint atavistic stirrings of anticipation rose in his memory. . . . Then they saw them.

A little band of hunters was crossing the moorland, crashing through the underbrush, guns on their shoulders. Blindly they walked, stumbling over hummocks that were clear to Smith's new eyes. And all about them the vague denizens of the place were gathering unseen. Great, nebulous, cloudy shapes dogged their footsteps through the grass, lurching along formlessly. Dark things with eyes flitted by, turning a hungry glare unseen upon the hunters. White shapes wavered from their path and closed in behind. The men did not see them. They must have sensed the presence of inimical beings, for now and then one would glance over his shoulder nervously, or hitch a gun forward as if he had almost seen—then lower it sheepishly and go on.

The very sight of them fired that strange hunger in Smith's new being, and again he flung back his head and yelled fiercely the long wolf-cry toward the frosty stars. At the sound of it a ripple of alarm went through the unclean, nebulous crowd that dogged the hunters' footsteps. Eyes turned toward the approaching pack, glaring angrily from bodies as unreal as smoke. But as they drew nearer the press began to melt away, the misty shapes wavering off reluctantly into the pallor of the night before the sweep of the wolves.

They skimmed over the grass, flying feet spurning the ground, and with a rush and a shout they swooped down around the hunter, yelling their hunger. The men had huddled into a little knot, backs together and guns bristling outward as the were-pack eddied round them. Three or four men fired at random into the circling pack, the flash and sound of it sending a wavering shudder through the pale things that had drawn back to a safe distance, watching. But the wolf-woman paid no heed.

Then the leader—a tall man in a white fur cap— shouted suddenly in a voice of panic terror. "No use to fire! No use—don't you see? These aren't real wolves. . . ."

Smith had a fleeting realisation that to human eyes they must, then, seem wolf-formed, though all about him in the pale night he saw clearly only white, naked women with flying hair circling the hunters and baying hungrily with wolf-voices as they ran.

The dark hunger was ravaging him as he paced the narrowing circle with short, nervous steps—the human bodies so near, smelling so richly of blood and flesh. Vaguely memories of that blood running sweetly eddied through his mind, and the feel of teeth meeting solidly in flesh; and beyond that a deeper hunger, inexplicably, for something he could not name. Only he felt he would never have peace again until he had sank his teeth into the throat of that man in the white fur cap; felt blood gushing over his face. . . .

"Look!" shouted the man, pointing as his eyes met Smith's ravenous glare. "See—the big one with white eyes, running with the she-wolf . . ." He fumbled for something inside his coat. "The Devil himself—all the rest are green-eyed, but—white eyes—see?"

Something in the sound of his voice lashed that hunger in Smith to the breaking point. It was unbearable. A snarl choked up in his throat and he gathered himself to spring. The man must have seen the flare of it in the pale eyes meeting his, for he gasped, "God in Heaven! . . ." and clawed desperately at his collar. And just as Smith's feet left the ground in a great, steel-muscled spring straight for that tempting throat the man ripped out what he had been groping for and the starlight caught the glint of it upraised—a silver cross dangling from a broken chain.

Something blinding exploded in Smith's innermost brain. Something compounded of thunder and lightning smote him in midair. An agonised howl ripped itself from his throat as he fell back, blinded and deafened and dazed, while his brain rocked to its foundations and long shivers of dazzling force shuddered through the air about him.

Dimly, from a great distance, he heard the agonized howls of the werewomen, the shouts of men, the trample of shod feet on the ground. Behind his closed eyes he could still see that cross upheld, a blinding symbol from which stream-ers of forked lightning blazed away and the air crackled all around.

When the tumult had faded in his ears and the blaze died away and the shocked air shuddered into stillness again, he felt the touch of cold, gentle hands upon him and opened his eyes to the green glare of other eyes bending over him. He pushed her away and struggled to his feet, swaying a little as he stared round the plain. All the white werewoman were gone save the one at his side. The huntsmen were gone. Even the misty denizens of the place were gone. Empty in the grey dimness the wasteland stretched away. Even the thin piping overhead had fallen into shocked silence. All about them the plain lay still, shuddering a little and gathering its forces again after the ordeal.

The werewoman had trotted off a little way and was beckoning to him impatiently over her shoulder. He followed, instinctively anxious to leave the spot of the disaster. Presently they were running again, shoulder to shoulder across the grass, the plain spinning away under their flying feet. The scene of that conflict fell behind them, and strength was flowing again through Smith's light-footed body, and overhead, faintly, the thin, shrill chattering began anew.

With renewed strength the old hunger flooded again through him, compellingly. He tossed up his head to test the wind, and a little whimper of eagerness rippled from his throat. An answering whine from the running woman replied to it. She tossed back her hair and sniffed the wind, hunger flaming in her eyes. So they ran through the pale night, hunter and huntress, while dim shapes wavered from their path and the earth reeled backward under their spurning feet.

It was pleasant to run so, in perfect unison, striding effortlessly with the speed of the wind, arrogantly in the knowledge of their strength, as the dreadful dwellers of the aeon-cursed moor fled from their approach and the very air shuddering when they bayed.

Again the illusion of misty towers and walls wavered in the dimness before Smith's eyes. He seemed to run down marble-paved streets, and felt again the clank of a belted sword and the ripple of rich garments, and saw the skirts of the woman beside him moulded to her limbs as she fled along with streaming, jewel-twined hair. He thought that the buildings rising so nebulously all around were growing higher as they advanced. He caught vague glimpses of arches and columns and great domed temples, and began, somehow uneasily, to sense presences in the streets, unseen but thronging.

Then simultaneously his feet seemed to strike a yielding resistance, as if he had plunged at a stride knee-deep into heavy water, and the woman beside him threw up her arms wildly in a swirl of hair and tossed back her head and screamed hideously, humanly, despairingly—the first human sound he had heard from her lips—and stumbled to her knees on the grass that was somehow a marble pavement.

Smith bent to catch her as she fell, plunging his arms into unseen resistance as he did so. He felt it suck at her as he wrenched the limp body out of those amazing, invisible wavelets that were lapping higher and higher up his legs with incredible swiftness. He swung her up clear of them, feeling the uncontrollable terror that rippled out from her body course in unbroken wavelets through his own, so he shook with nameless panic, not understanding why. The thick tide had risen mufflingly about his thighs when he turned back the way he had come and began to fight his way out of the clinging horror he could not see, the woman a weight of terror in his arms.

It seemed to be a sort of thickness in the air, indescribable, flowing about him in deepening waves that lapped up and up as if some half-solidified jelly were swiftly and relentlessly engulfing him. Yet he could see nothing but the grass underfoot, the dim, dreamlike marble pavement, the night about, the cold stars overhead. He struggled forward, dragging his legs by main force through the invisible thickness. It was worse than trying to run through water, with the retarded motion of nightmares. It sucked at him, draggingly, as he struggled forward through the deeps of it, stumbling, not daring to fall, the woman a dead weight in his arms.

And very slowly he won free. Very slowly he forced his way out of the clinging horror. The little lapping waves of it ceased to mount. He felt the thickness receding downward, past his knees, down about his ankles, until only his feet sucked and stumbled in invisibility, the nameless mass shuddering and quaking. And at long last he broke again, and as his feet touched the clear ground he leaped forward wildly, like an arrow from a bow, into the delightful freedom of the open air. It felt like pure flying after that dreadful struggle through the unseen. Muscles exulting at the release, he fled over the grass like a winged thing while the dim buildings reeled away behind him and the woman stirred a little in his arms, an inconsidered weight in the joy of freedom.

Presently she whimpered a little, and he paused by a stunted tree to set her down again. She glanced round wildly. He saw from the look on her bone-white face that the danger was not yet past, and glanced round himself, seeing nothing but the dim moor with wraith-like figures wavering here and there and the stars shining down coldly. Overhead the thin shrilling went by changelessly in the wind. All this was familiar. Yet the werewoman stood poised for instant flight, seeming unsure in just what direction danger lay, and her eyes glared panic into the dimness. He knew then that dreadful though the were-pack was, a more terrible thing haunted the wasteland—invisibly, frightfully indeed to wake in the wolf-woman's eyes that staring horror. Then something touched his foot.

He leaped like the wild thing he was, for he knew that feel—even in so short a time he knew that feel. It was flowing round his foot, sucking at his ankle even as he poised for flight. He seized the woman's wrist and twisted round, wrenching his foot from the invisible grip, leaping forward arrow-swift into the pale darkness. He heard her catch her breath in a sobbing gasp, eloquent of terror, as she fell into stride beside him.

So they fled, invisibility ravening at their heels. He knew, somehow, that it followed. The thick, clutching waves of it were lapping faster and faster just short of his flying feet, and he strained to the utmost, skimming over the grass like something winged and terror-stricken, the sobbing breath of the woman keeping time to his stride. What he fled he could not even guess. It had no form in any image he could conjure up. Yet he felt dimly that it was nothing alien, but rather something too horribly akin to him . . . and the deadly danger he did not understand spurred on his flying feet.

The plain whirled by blurrily in their speed. Dim things with eyes fluttered away in panic as they neared, clearing a terror-stricken way for the dreadful were-people who fled in such blind horror of something more dreadful yet.

For eternities they ran. Misty towers and walls fell away behind them. In his terror-dimmed mind it seemed to him in flashes that he was that other runner clad in rich garments and belted with the sword, running beside that other fleeing woman from another horror whose nature he did not know. He scarcely felt the ground underfoot. He ran blindly, knowing only that he must run and run until he dropped, that something far more dreadful than any death he could die was lapping hungrily at his heels, threatening him with an unnameable, incomprehensible horror—that he must run and run and run . . .

And so, very slowly, the panic cleared. Very gradually sanity returned to him. He ran still, not daring to stop, for he knew the invisible hunger lapped yet not far behind—knew it surely without understanding how—but his mind had cleared enough for him to think, and his thoughts told curious things, half-realised things that formed images in his brain unbidden, drawn from some far source beyond his understanding. He knew, for instance, that the thing at their heels was unescapable. He knew that it would never cease its relentless pursuit, silent, invisible, remorseless, until the thick waves of it had swallowed up its quarry, and what followed that—what unimaginable horror—he somehow knew, but could not form even into thought-pictures. It was something too far outside any experience for the mind to grasp it.

The horror he felt instinctively was entirely within himself. He could see nothing pursuing him, feel nothing, hear nothing. No tremor of menace reached toward him from the following nothingness. But within him horror swelled and swelled balloon-like, a curious horror akin to something that was part of him, so it was as if he fled in terror of himself, and with no more hope of ever escaping than if indeed he fled his own shadow.

The panic had passed. He no longer ran blindly, but he knew now that he must run and run forever, hopelessly . . . but his mind refused to picture the end. He thought the woman's panic had abated, too. Her breathing was evener, not the frantic gasping of that first frenzy, and he no longer felt the shaking waves of pure terror beating out from her against the ephemeral substance that was himself.

And now, as the grey landscape slid past changelessly and the thin shapes still wavered from their path and the piping went by overhead, he became conscious as he ran of a changing in the revulsion that spurred him on. There were little moments when the horror behind drew him curiously, tightening its hold on that part of his being so strangely akin to it. As a man might stare over a precipice-edge and feel the mounting urge to fling himself over, even in the face of his horror of falling, so Smith felt the strong pull of the thing that followed, if thing it might be called. Without abatement in his horror the curious desire grew to turn and face it, let it come lapping over him, steep himself in the thick invisibility —even though his whole being shuddered violently from the very thought.

Without realising it, his pace slackened. But the woman knew, and gripped his hand fiercely, a frantic appeal rippling through him from the contact. At her touch the pull abated for a while and he ran on in an access of revulsion, very conscious of the invisibility lapping at their heels.

While the access was at its height he felt the grip of her hand loosen a little and knew that the strange tugging at something within was reaching out for her. His hand tightened over hers and he felt the little shake she gave to free herself of that blind pull.

So they fled, the strength in each bearing the other up. Behind them relentlessly the Something followed. Twice a forward lapping wave of it brushed Smith's heel. And stronger and stronger grew the blind urge within him to turn, to plunge into the heavy flow of what followed, to steep himself in invisibility until—until— He could form no picture of that ultimate, but each time he reached the point of picturing it a shudder went over him and blankness clouded his mind.

And ever within him that thing akin to the Follower strengthened and grew, a blind urge from his innermost being. It grew so strong that only the grip of the werewoman's hand held him from turning, and the plain faded from about him like a grey dream and he ran through a curving void—a void that he somehow knew was bending back upon itself so that he must eventually, if he ran on, come round behind his pursuer and overtake it, wade head-on into the thick deeps of invisibility . . . yet he dared not slacken his running, for then it would catch him from behind. So he spun in the treadmill, terror ahead, terror behind, with no choice but to run and no hope for all his running.

When he saw the plain at all it was in dim flashes, unaccountably blurred and not always at the correct angles. It tilted without reason. Once he saw a dark pool of water slanting before him like a door, and once a whole section of landscape hung mirage-like above his head. Sometimes he panted up steep inclines, sometimes he skimmed fleetly down steeper slopes—yet he knew the plain in reality lay flat and featureless from edge to edge.

And now, though he had long ago left those misty towers and walls far behind, he began to be aware that his flight had somehow twisted and they loomed once more, shadowily; overhead. With a sickening sense of futility he fled again down the dream-vague marble pavements between rows of cloudy palaces.

Through all these dizzy metamorphoses the pursuer flowed relentlessly behind, lapping at his heels when he slowed. He began to realise, very dimly, that it might have overtaken him with ease, but that he was being spurred on thus for some vast, cloudy purpose—perhaps so that he might complete the circle he was so vaguely aware of and plunge of his own effort headlong into the very thing from which he fled. But he was not fleeing now, he was being driven.

The dim shapes of buildings reeled past. The woman running at his side had become something cloudy and vague too, a panting presence flying from the same peril—into the same peril—but unreal as a dream. He felt himself unreal too, a phantom fleeing hand in hand with another phantom through the streets of a phantom city. And all reality was melting away save the unreal, invisible thing that pursued him, and only it had reality while everything else faded to shapes of nothingness. Like driven ghosts they fled.

And as reality melted about them, the shadowy city took firmer shape. In the reversal everything real became cloudy, grass and trees and pools dimming like some forgotten dream, while the unstable outlines of the towers loomed up more and more clearly in the pale dark, colours flushing them as if reviving blood ran through the stones. Now the city stood firm and actual around them, and vague trees thrust themselves mistily through unbroken masonry, shadows of grass waved over firm marble pavements. Superimposed upon the unreal, the real world seemed vague as a mirage.

It was a curious architecture that rose around them now, so old and so forgotten that the very shapes of it were fantastic to Smith's eyes. Men in silk and steel moved down the streets, wading to their greave-clad knees in shadowy grass they did not seem to see. Women, too, brushed by in mail as fine-linked and shining as gowns of silver tissue, belted with swords like the men. Their faces were set in a strained stare, and though they hurried they gave an impression of aimlessness, as if moved by some outer compulsion they did not understand.

And through the hurrying crowd, past the strange coloured towers, over the grass-shadowed streets, were-woman and wolf-man fled like the shadows they had become, pale wraiths blowing through the crowds unseen, the invisible follower lapping at their feet when they faltered. That force within which had urged them to turn and meet the pursuer now commanded them irresistibly to flee—to flee toward that same ending, for they knew now that they ran toward what they fled, roundaboutly; yet dared not stop running for deadly fear of what flowed along behind.

Yet in the end they did turn. The werewoman ran now in blind submission, all the strength dissolved that at first had carried her on. She was like a ghost blowing along on a gale, unresisting, unquestioning, hopeless. But in Smith a stouter spirit dwelt. And something strong and insistent was urging him to turn—an insistence that had no relation to the other urge to wait. It may have been a very human revolt against being driven, it may have been a deeply ingrained dislike of running from anything, or of allowing death to overtake him from behind. It had been bred in him to face danger when he could not escape it, and the old urge that every fighting thing knows—even a cornered rat will turn—drove him at last to face what followed him and die resisting—not in flight. For he felt that the end must be very near now. Some instinct stronger than the force that harried them told him that.

And so, ignoring the armoured crowd that eddied round them, he gripped the werewoman's wrist hard and slackened his speed, fighting against the urge that would have driven him on, choking down the panic that rose involuntarily as he waited for the thick waves to begin their surging round his feet. Presently he saw the shadow of a tree leaning through the smooth stone of a building, and instinctively he chose that misty thing he knew to be real for a bulwark to set his back against, rather than the unreal wall that looked so solid to his eyes. He braced his shoulders, holding a firm grip on the woman's wrist as she struggled and whimpered and moaned in her wolf-voice, straining to break the hold and run on. About, the mail-clad crowd hurried by heedlessly.

And very soon he felt it—the lapping wavelets touching his toes. He shuddered through all his unreal body at the feel, but he stood steady, gripping the struggling wolf-woman in a resolute hold, feeling the thick waves flowing around his feet, creeping up to his ankles, lapping higher and higher round his legs.

For a while he stood at bay, feeling terror choke up and up in his throat as the waves rose round him, scarcely heeding the woman's struggles to be free. And then a further rebellion began to stir. If die he must, let it be neither in headlong flight nor in dazed and terrified quiescence, but violently, fighting against it, taking some toll, if he could, to pay for the life he was to lose. He gasped a deep breath and plunged forward into the quaking, unseen mass that had risen almost to his waist. Behind him at arm's length the werewoman stumbled unwillingly.

He lurched forward. Very swiftly the unseen rose about him, until arms and shoulders were muffled in thickness, until the heavy invisibility brushed his chin, his closed mouth, sealed his nostrils . . . closed over his head.

Through the clear deeps he forged on, moving like a man in a nightmare of retarded motion. Every step was an immense effort against that flow, dragged through resisting depths of jelly-like nothingness. He had all but forgotten the woman he dragged along behind. He had wholly forgotten the coloured city and the shining, armoured people hurrying past. Blinded to everything but the deep-rooted instinct to keep moving, he forced his slow way onward against the flow. And indescribably he felt it begin to permeate him, seeping in slowly through the atoms of his ephemeral being. He felt it, and felt a curious change coming over him by degrees, yet could not define it or understand what was happening. Something urged him fiercely to go on, to struggle ahead, not to surrender—and so he fought, his mind whirling and the strange stuff of the thing that engulfed him soaking slowly through his being.

Presently the invisibility took on a faint body, a sort of clear opaqueness, so that the things outside were streaked and blurred a little and the splendid dream city with its steel-robed throngs wavered through the walls of what had swallowed him up. Everything was shaking and blurring and somehow changing. Even his body no longer obeyed him completely, as if it trembled on the verge of transition into something different and unknown. Only the driving instinct to fight on held clear in his dazed mind. He struggled forward.

And now the towered city was fading again, its mailed people losing their outlines and melting into the greyness. But the fading was not a reversal—the shadow-grass and trees grew more shadowy still. It was as if by successive steps he was leaving all matter behind. Reality had faded almost to nothing, even the cloudy unreality of the city was going now, and nothing but a grey blankness remained, a blankness through which he forged stubbornly against the all-engulfing flow that steeped him in nothingness.

Sometimes in flashes he ceased to exist—joined the grey nothing as part of it. The sensation was not that of unconsciousness. Somehow utter nirvana swallowed him up and freed him again, and between the moments of blank he fought on, feeling the transition of his body taking place very slowly, very surely, into something that even now he could not understand.

For grey eternities he struggled ahead through the clogging resistance, through darknesses of non-existence, through flashes of near-normality, feeling somehow that the path led in wild loops and whorls through spaces without name. His time-sense had stopped. He could hear and see nothing, he could feel nothing but the immense effort of dragging his limbs through the stuff that enfolded him, and the effort was so great that he welcomed those spaces of blankness when he did not exist even as an unconsciousness. Yet stubbornly, unceasingly, the blind instinct drove him on.

There was a while when the flashes of non-existence crowded closer and closer, and the metamorphosis of his body was all but complete, and only during brief winks of consciousness did he realise himself as an independent being. Then in some unaccountable way the tension slackened. For a long moment without interludes he knew himself a real being struggling upstream through invisibility and dragging a half-fainting woman by the wrist. The clarity of it startled him. For a while he could not understand—then it dawned upon him that his head and shoulders were free—free! What had happened he could not imagine, but he was free of it.

The hideous grey nothingness had gone—he looked out over a plain dotted with low trees and low, white, columned villas like no architecture he had ever seen before. A little way ahead a stone slab no higher than himself leaned against a great boulder in a hollow fringed with trees. Upon the slab an indescribable symbol was incised. It was like no symbol of any writing he had ever seen before. It was so different from all the written characters men make that it scarcely seemed akin to writing at all, nor traced by any human hand. Yet there was a curious familiarity about it that did not even puzzle him. He accepted it without question. He was somehow akin to it.

And between him and the engraved slab the air writhed and undulated. Streamers of invisibility flowed toward him, mounting as they flowed. He struggled forward, exultation surging within him, for—he knew, now. And as he advanced the thick resistance fell away from him, sliding down his shoulders, ebbing lower and lower about his struggling body. He knew that whatever the invisibility was, its origin lay in that symbol on the stone. From that it flowed. Half-visibly, he could see it. And toward that stone he made his way, a dim purpose forming in his brain.

He heard a little gasp and quickened breathing behind him, and turned his head to see the werewoman, moon-white in the undulating, almost-visible flow, staring about with wakened eyes and incomprehension clouding her face. He saw that she did not remember anything of what had happened. Her green-glowing eyes were empty as if they had just opened from deep slumber.

He forged on swiftly now through the waves that lapped futilely around his waist. He had won. Against what he did not yet know, nor from what cloudy terror he had saved himself and her, but he was not afraid now. He knew what he must do, and he struggled on eagerly toward the slab.

He was still waist-deep in the resisting flow when he reached it, and for a dizzy instant he thought he could not stop; that he must wade on into the very substance of that unnameable carving out of which came the engulfing nothingness. But with an effort he wrenched round and waded cross-stream, and after a while of desperate struggle he broke free into the open air.

It was like a cessation of gravity. In the release from that dragging weight he felt he must scarcely be touching the ground, but there was no time now to exult in his freedom. He turned purposefully toward the slab.

The werewoman was just floundering clear of the stream when she saw what he intended, and she flung up her hands with a shriek of protest that startled Smith into a sidewise leap, as if some new terror were coming upon him. Then he saw what it was, and gave her an amazed stare as he turned again to the stone, lifting his arms to grapple with it. She reeled forward and seized him in a cold, desperate embrace, dragging backward with all her might. Smith glared at her and shook his shoulders impatiently. He had felt the rock give a little. But when she saw that, she screamed again piercingly, and her arms twined like snakes as she struggled to drag him away.

She was very strong. He paused to unwind the fierce clasp, and she fought savagely to prevent it. He needed all his strength to break her grip, and he pushed her from him then with a heavy shove that sent her reeling. The pale eyes followed her, puzzling why, though she had fled in such a frenzy of terror from what flowed out of the stone, she still strove to prevent him from destroying it. For he was quite sure, without understanding why, that if the slab were broken and the symbol destroyed that stream would cease to flow. He could not understand her. He shook his shoulders impatiently and turned again to the stone.

This time she was on him with an animal spring, snarling low in her throat and clawing with frantic hands. Her fangs snapped just clear of his throat. Smith wrenched free with a great effort, for she was steel-strong and very desperate, and gripped her by the shoulder, swinging her away. Then he set his teeth and drove a heavy fist into her face, smashing against the fangs. She yelped, short and sharply, and collapsed under his hand, sinking to the grass in a huddle of whiteness and wild black hair.

He turned to the stone again. This time he got a firm grip on it, braced his legs wide, heaved. And he felt it give. He heaved again. And very slowly, very painfully, he uprooted its base from the bed where for ages it must have lain. Rock ground protestingly against rock. One edge rose a little, then settled. And the slab tilted. He heaved again, and very deliberately he felt it slipping from his hands. He stood back, breathing heavily, and watched.

Majestically the great slab tottered. The stream flowing invisibly from its incised symbol twisted in a streaked path through the air, long whorls of opacity blurring the landscape beyond. Smith thought he felt a stirring in the air, a shiver, as of warning. All the white villas dimly seen through the dark wavered a little before his eyes, and something hummed through the air like a thin, high wailing too sharp to be heard save as a pain to the ears. The chattering overhead quickened suddenly. All this in the slow instant while the slab tottered.

Then it fell. Deliberately slow, it leaned outward and down. It struck the ground with a rush and a splintering crash. He saw the long cracks appear miraculously upon its surface as the great, fantastic symbol broke into fragments. The opacity that had flowed outward from it writhed like a dragon in pain, flung itself high-arching into the shivering air—and ceased. In that moment of cessation the world collapsed around him. A mighty wind swooped down in a deafening roar, blurring the landscape. He thought he saw the white villas melting like dreams, and he knew the werewoman on the grass must have recovered consciousness, for he heard a wolf-yell of utter agony from behind him. Then the great wind blotted out all other things, and he was whirling through space in a dizzy flight.

In that flight understanding overtook him. In a burst of illumination he knew quite suddenly what had happened and what would happen now—realised without surprise, as if he had always known it, that the denizens of this wasteland had dwelt here under the protection of that mighty curse laid upon the land in the long-past century when the city fell. And he realised that it must have been a very powerful curse, laid down by skill and knowledge that had long since vanished even from the legends of man, for in all the ages since, this accursed moor had been safe haven for all the half-real beings that haunt mankind, akin to the evil that lay like a blanket over the moor.

And he knew that the curse had its origin in the nameless symbol which some sorcerer of forgotten times had inscribed upon the stone, a writing from some language which can have no faintest kinship with man. He knew that the force flowing out from it was a force of utter evil, spreading like a river over the whole salt waste. The stream of it lapped to and fro in changing courses over the land, and when it neared some dweller of the place, the evil that burnt for a life-force in that dweller acted as a magnet to the pure evil which was the stream. So, evil answering to evil, the two fused into one, the unfortunate dweller swallowed up into a nirvana of non-existence in the heart of that slow-flowing stream.

It must have worked strange changes in them. That city whose shapes of shadow still haunted the place assumed reality, taking on substance and becoming more and more actual as the reality of the captive waned and melted into the power of the stream.

He thought, remembering those hurrying throngs with their strained, pale faces, that the spirits of the people who had died in the lost city must be bound tenuously to the spot of their death. He remembered that young, richly garmented warrior he had been one with in fleeting moments, running golden-sandaled through the streets of the forgotten city in a panic of terror from something too long past to be remembered—the jewelled woman in her coloured sandals and rippling robes running at his side—and wondered in the space of a second what their story had been so many ages ago. He thought that curse must somehow have included the dwellers in the city, chaining them in earth-bound misery for centuries. But of this he was not sure.

Much of all this was not clear to him, and more he realised without understanding, but he knew that the instinct which guided him to turn up-stream had not been a false one—that something human and alien in him had been a talisman to lead his staggering feet back toward the source of his destroyer. And he knew that with the breaking up of the symbol that was a curse, the curse ceased to be, and the warm, sweet, life-giving air that humanity breathes swept in a flood across the barrens, blowing away all the shadowy, unclean creatures to whom it had been haven for so long. He knew—he knew. . . .

Greyness swooped round him, and all knowledge faded from his mind and the wind roared mightily in his ears. Somewhere in that roaring flight oblivion overtook him.

When he opened his eyes again he could not for an instant imagine where he lay or what had happened. Weight pressed upon his entire body suffocatingly, pain shot through it as jagged flashes. His shoulder ached deeply. And the night was dark, dark about him. Something muffling and heavy had closed over his senses, for no longer could he hear the tiny, sharp sounds of the plain or scent those tingling odours that once blew along the wind. Even the chattering overhead had fallen still. The place did not even smell the same. He thought he could catch from afar the odour of smoke, and somehow the air, as nearly as he could tell with his deadened senses, no longer breathed of desolation and loneliness. The smell of life was in the wind, very faintly. Little pleasant odours of flower-scent and kitchen smoke seemed to tinge it.

"—wolves must have gone," someone was saying above him. "They stopped howling a few minutes ago—notice?— first time since we came into this damned place. Listen."

With a painful effort Smith rolled his head sidewise and stared. A little group of men was gathered around him, their eyes lifted just now to the dark horizon. In the new density of the night he could not see them clearly, and he blinked in irritation, striving to regain that old, keen, clarity he had lost. But they looked familiar. One wore a white fur cap on his head. Someone said, indicating something beyond Smith's limited range of vision,

"Fellow here must have had quite a tussle. See the dead she-wolf with her throat torn out? And look—all the wolf-tracks everywhere in the dust. Hundreds of them. I wonder. . . ."

"Bad luck to talk about them," broke in the fur-capped leader. "Werewolves, I tell you—I've been in this place before, and I know. But I never saw or heard tell of a thing like what we saw tonight—that big white-eyed one running with the she-wolves. God! I'll never forget those eyes."

Smith moved his head and groaned. The men turned quickly.

"Look, he's coming to," said someone, and Smith was vaguely conscious of an arm under his head and some liquid, hot and strong, forced between his lips. He opened his eyes and looked up. The fur-capped man was bending over him. Their eyes met. In the starlight Smith's were colourless as pale steel.

The man choked something inarticulate and leaped back so suddenly that the flask spilled its contents half over Smith's chest. He crossed himself frankly with a hand that shook.

"Who—who are you?" he demanded unsteadily.

Smith grinned wearily and closed his eyes.

FOREWORD

by Sam Moskowitz

"**S**ong in a Minor Key" by
C. L. Moore first appeared in the second anniversary issue of
the fan magazine *Scienti-Snaps* dated February 1940 and
mimeographed with extraordinary neatness and clarity by a
very large man with an artistic bent named Walter E.
Marconette. That issue also featured a variety of material by
Don A. Stuart (John W. Campbell), August Derleth, Donald
Wandrei, Clark Ashton Smith, Henry Kuttner, Ross
Rocklynne, Lee Gregor (Milton A. Rothman), and Charles R.
Tanner. Responsible for the banner assembly was an active
Cleveland fan and columnist Jack Chapman Miske, whose
aggressive solicitation begun with the August 1939 number
had elevated the magazine into a high-powered leader on the
basis of the quality of its contents.

Henry Kuttner who was an avid fan and had been a
frequent contributor of humor to the fan magazines in the
past undoubtedly influenced his wife C. L. Moore to contrib-
ute. There seems little doubt that both contributions were
written especially for the issue considering Moore's letter in
the same issue which read: "The two *Scienti-Snaps* containing

the Merritt articles arrived yesterday, and I've enjoyed all of both numbers very much. I've seen a lot of fan publications, and the percentage of interesting articles in them isn't terribly high as a rule. There are exceptions, and I think yours is one of them. The art work is the best I've seen. Most drawings in such magazines are not very good to begin with, and suffer badly in reproduction. I adored Tanner's parody on 'Father William.' A parodist usually wrecks the metre for the sake of the text, but this is one case in which the text was very skillfully and amusingly altered without sacrificing metre or rhythm. I'm looking forward to the anniversary issue."

For the curious, Kuttner's article in the issue titled "Newts in Science Fiction" was a humorously done bid for more mature sex in science fiction.

SONG IN A MINOR KEY

by C. L. Moore

"Dreams that might have been, dreams woven with dust. Northwest Smith comes home . . ."

Beneath him the clovered hill-slope was warm in the sun. Northwest Smith moved his shoulders against the earth and closed his eyes, breathing so deeply that the gun holstered upon his chest drew tight against its strap as he drank the fragrance of Earth and clover warm in the sun. Here in the hollow of the hills, willow-shaded, pillowed upon clover and the lap of Earth, he let his breath run out in a long sigh and drew one palm across the grass in a caress like a lover's.

He had been promising himself this moment for how long—how many months and years on alien worlds? He would not think of it now. He would not remember the dark spaceways or the red slag of Martian drylands or the pearl-gray days on Venus when he had dreamed of the Earth that had outlawed him. So he lay, with his eyes closed and the sunlight drenching him through, no sound in his ears but the passage of a breeze through the grass and a creaking of some insect nearby—the violent, blood-smelling years behind him might never have been. Except for the gun pressed into his ribs between his chest and the clovered earth, he might be a boy again, years upon years ago, long before he had broken his first law or killed his first man.

No one else alive now knew who that boy had been. Not even the all-knowing Patrol. Not even Venusian Yarol, who had been his closest friend for so many riotous years. No one would ever know—now. Not his name (which had not always been Smith) or his native land or the home that had bred him, or the first violent deed that had sent him down the devious paths which led here—here to the clover hollow in the hills of an Earth that had forbidden him ever to set foot again upon her soil.

He unclasped the hands behind his head and rolled over to lay a scarred cheek on his arm, smiling to himself. Well, here was Earth beneath him. No longer a green star high in alien skies, but warm soil, new clover so near his face he could see all the little stems and trefoil leaves, moist earth granular at their roots. An ant ran by with waving antennae close beside his cheek. He closed his eyes and drew another deep breath. Better not even to look; better to lie here like an animal, absorbing the sun and the feel of Earth blindly, wordlessly.

Now he was not Northwest Smith, scarred outlaw of the spaceways. Now he was a boy again with all his life before him. There would be a white-columned house just over the hill, with shaded porches and white curtains blowing in the breeze and the sound of sweet, familiar voices indoors. There would be a girl with hair like poured honey hesitating just inside the door, lifting her eyes to him. Tears in the eyes. He lay very still, remembering.

Curious how vividly it all came back, though the house had been ashes for nearly twenty years, and the girl—the girl. . . . He rolled over violently, opening his eyes. No use remembering her. There had been that fatal flaw in him from the very first, he knew now. If he were the boy again knowing all he knew today, still the flaw would be there and sooner or later the same thing must have happened that had happened twenty years ago. He had been born for a wilder age, when men took what they wanted and held what they could without respect for law. Obedience was not in him, and so—

As vividly as on that day it happened he felt the same old surge of anger and despair twenty years old now, felt the ray-gun bucking hard against his unaccustomed fist, heard the hiss of its deadly charge ravening into a face he hated. He could not be sorry, even now, for that first man he had killed. But in the smoke of that killing had gone up the columned house and the future he might have had, the boy himself— lost as Atlantis now—and the girl with the honey-colored hair and much, much else besides. It had to happen, he knew. He being the boy he was, it had to happen. Even if he could go back and start all over, the tale would be the same.

And it was all long past now, anyhow; and nobody remembered any more at all, except himself. A man would be a fool to lie here thinking about it any longer.

Smith grunted and sat up, shrugging the gun into place against his ribs.

III.

LEIGH BRACKETT
AND
RAY BRADBURY

INTRODUCTION

"**L**orelei of the Red Mist" is an unusual novella—one which is in some aspects unique. While collaborations are not all that uncommon, it isn't often that an established writer simply turns a half-finished novella over to a talented newcomer and asks him to complete it. But then, neither established professional Leigh Brackett nor rising star Ray Bradbury can be considered your basic common-garden-variety writer.

Born in Los Angeles, California on December 7, 1915, Leigh Brackett was already the uncrowned queen of space opera by the time she married fellow science fiction writer Edmond Hamilton in 1946. From her first published science fiction story, "Martian Quest" (*Astounding Science Fiction,* February 1940), to her final work, the screenplay for *The Empire Strikes Back* (1980), Brackett maintained her flair for science fiction high adventure. As C. L. Moore had done a few years earlier, Brackett captured the spirit of science-fantasy with a blend of swordplay and super-science set on exotic planets. Never mind that Brackett's Mars and Venus are the worlds envisioned by Edgar Rice Burroughs rather than the planets revealed by NASA probes. Brackett's worlds of canals and ruined cities, steaming swamps and red deserts, are far more interesting than telemetered realities. Many of Brackett's stories appeared in that quintessential space opera pulp, *Planet Stories,* where every planet in the solar system was a likely spot for derring-do. An example of *Planet Stories'* editorial approach: Brackett had sold them a story, "The Dragon-Queen of Venus." However, the Summer 1941 issue in which it was to appear already had a story set in the steaming swamps of Venus, so the editors changed her title to "The Dragon-Queen of Jupiter" and set it in the steaming swamps of Jupiter—occasionally forgetting to change "Venus" to "Jupiter" in the published version.

But onward to Ray Bradbury. Born in Waukegan, Illinois on August 22, 1920, in 1934 the young Bradbury moved out to Los Angeles where he attended high school. As an avid science fiction fan, The Kid became a close friend of Old Pros Edmond Hamilton and Leigh Brackett. Emerging from the ranks of fandom, Bradbury gained his first professional publication with "Pendulum" in *Super Science Stories* for November 1941. Bradbury's literate, non-formula prose smashed the barriers separating science fiction, fantasy, and mainstream, and The Kid rapidly became the Boy Wonder of the pulp field. By 1947 Bradbury's early fiction had been collected in the landmark Arkham House edition, *Dark Carnival* (partially incorporated in *The October Country,* 1955).

Back to "Lorelei of the Red Mist," which first appeared in the Summer 1946 issue of *Planet Stories.* By 1945 Leigh Brackett had begun writing screenplays. In the middle of writing "Lorelei of the Red Mist," she was given the assignment to co-author with William Faulkner the screenplay of the 1946 film classic, *The Big Sleep.* Not a chance to pass up, even for *Planet Stories.* To save the situation, Brackett asked an eager Ray Bradbury to complete the novella. Bradbury did so—simply by picking up where Brackett had left off and writing the second half all on his own. That's right: no conferences, no mutual revisions, no notes or outlines. The most amazing part is that for years no one has really been able to distinguish for certain where Brackett left off and Bradbury began.

The secret can now be told. Leigh kept meaning to find the transition point for me, but her untimely death on March 24, 1978 brought an end to our four years of friendship. Fortunately Ray still well remembers the spot where he took over, as he wrote to me on July 9, 1987:

"I don't have a copy of LORELEI with me, but the place where I take over occurs in the middle of the story, undersea, where the golden hounds coming swimming/drifting in the tides. I'm sure with a bit of searching you'll find that paragraph. I took over right there! And the fusion is fine, isn't it? When Leigh read what I had done she cried, 'Son of a bitch! Goddamn! You're *me!*' 'Yep,' I said, blushing and ducking my head. Let me know if you find the paragraph!'"

The reader can easily find this paragraph here in *Echoes of Valor II* from Bradbury's hint. For all of you out there with a Summer 1946 *Planet Stories* on hand, I'll make it easy for you: It's at the bottom of the first column on page 21 of the magazine.

Brackett went on to write more screenplays and more space operas—as well as mysteries and westerns. Her other major screenplays include *Rio Bravo* (1959), *El Dorado* (1967), *Rio Lobo* (1970), and *The Long Goodbye* (1973). Shortly after "Lorelei of the Red Mist" was published, she began writing a series of stories and novels about her best-known character, Eric John Stark—a tough, lean space rogue much in the mold of C. L. Moore's Northwest Smith. Clearly Brackett's favorite of her creations, Eric John Stark would later depart our solar system to reappear as an interstellar adventurer in three of her last novels—*The Ginger Star* (1974), *The Hounds of Skaith* (1974), and *The Reavers of Skaith* (1976).

Bradbury went on to overwhelm the science fiction/fantasy field of the late 1940s and 1950s, moving in the 1960s beyond the confines of genre fiction into areas of creativity as elusive and indefinable as his writing. His best-known books are classics and include *The Martian Chronicles* (1950), *The Illustrated Man* (1951), *The Golden*

Apples of the Sun (1953), *Fahrenheit 451* (1953), *Dandelion Wine* (1957), *A Medicine for Melancholy* (1959), and *Something Wicked This Way Comes* (1963). A complete bibliography of Bradbury's work actually does fill one entire book (now in need of considerable updating), and while The Kid now is silver of hair, his enormous talent remains unblunted and unchecked.

Read then, "Lorelei of the Red Mist"—an intriguing fusion of two of the genre's great dreamers. You'll encounter one Hugh Starke, a prototype of Eric John Stark, and one Conan, who does not hail from Cimmeria.

LORELEI OF THE RED MIST

by Leigh Brackett and Ray Bradbury

The Company dicks were good. They were plenty good. Hugh Starke began to think maybe this time he wasn't going to get away with it.

His small stringy body hunched over the control bank, nursing the last ounce of power out of the Kallman. The hot night sky of Venus fled past the ports in tattered veils of indigo. Starke wasn't sure where he was anymore. Venus was a frontier planet, and still mostly a big X, except to the Venusians—who weren't sending out any maps. He did know that he was getting dangerously close to the Mountains of White Cloud. The backbone of the planet, towering far into the stratosphere, magnetic trap, with God knew what beyond. Maybe even God wasn't sure.

But it looked like over the mountains or out. Death under the guns of the Terro-Venus Mines, Incorporated, Special Police, or back to the Luna cell blocks for life as an habitual felon.

Starke decided he would go over.

Whatever happened, he'd pulled off the biggest lone-wolf caper in history. The T-V Mines payroll ship, for close to a million credits. He cuddled the metal strongbox between his feet and grinned. It would be a long time before anybody equaled that.

His mass indicators began to jitter. Vaguely, a dim purple shadow in the sky ahead, the Mountains of White Cloud stood like a wall against him. Starke checked the positions of the pursuing ships. There was no way through them. He said flatly, "All right, damn you," and sent the Kallman angling up into the thick blue sky.

He had no very clear memories after that. Crazy magnetic vagaries, always a hazard on Venus, made his instruments useless. He flew by the seat of his pants and he got over, and the T-V men didn't. He was free, with a million credits in his kick.

Far below in the virgin darkness he saw a sullen crimson smear on the night, as though someone had rubbed it with a bloody thumb. The Kallman dipped toward it. The control bank flickered with blue flame, the jet timers blew, and then there was just the screaming of air against the falling ball.

Hugh Starke sat still and waited . . .

He knew, before he opened his eyes, that he was dying. He didn't feel any pain, he didn't feel anything, but he knew just the same. Part of him was cut loose. He was still there, but not attached anymore.

He raised his eyelids. There was a ceiling. It was a long way off. It was black stone veined with smoky reds and ambers. He had never seen it before.

His head was tilted toward the right. He let his gaze move down that way. There were dim tapestries, more of the black stone, and three tall archways giving onto a balcony. Beyond the balcony was a sky veiled and clouded with red mist. Under the mist, spreading away from a murky line of cliffs, was an ocean. It wasn't water and it didn't have any waves on it, but there was nothing else to call it. It burned, deep down inside itself, breathing up the red fog. Little angry bursts of flame coiled up under the flat surface, sending circles of sparks flaring out like ripples from a dropped stone.

He closed his eyes and frowned and moved his head restively. There was the texture of fur against his skin. Through the cracks of his eyelids he saw that he lay on a high bed piled with silks and soft tanned pelts. His body was covered. He was rather glad he couldn't see it. It didn't matter because he wouldn't be using it anymore anyway, and it hadn't been such a hell of a body to begin with. But he was used to it, and he didn't want to see it now, the way he knew it would have to look.

He looked along over the foot of the bed, and he saw the woman.

She sat watching him from a massive carved chair softened with a single huge white pelt like a drift of snow. She smiled, and let him look. A pulse began to beat under his jaw, very feebly.

She was tall and sleek and insolently curved. She wore a sort of tabard of pale grey spider-silk, held to her body by a jeweled girdle, but it was just a nice piece of ornamentation. Her face was narrow, finely cut, secret, faintly amused. Her lips, her eyes, and her flowing silken hair were all the same pale cool shade of aquamarine.

Her skin was white, with no hint of rose. Her shoulders, her forearms, the long flat curve of her thighs, the pale-green tips of her breasts, were dusted with tiny particles that glistened like powdered diamond. She sparkled softly like a fairy thing against the snowy fur, a creature of foam and moonlight and clear shallow water. Her eyes never left his, and they were not human, but he knew that they would have done things to him if he had had any feeling below the neck.

He started to speak. He had no strength to move his tongue. The woman leaned forward, and as though her movement were a signal four men rose from the tapestried shadows by the wall. They were like her. Their eyes were pale and strange like hers.

She said, in liquid High Venusian, "You're dying, in this body. But *you* will not die. You will sleep now, and wake in a strange body, in a strange place. Don't be afraid.

My mind will be with yours, I'll guide you, don't be afraid. I can't explain now, there isn't time, but don't be afraid."

He drew back his thin lips baring his teeth in what might have been a smile. If it was, it was wolfish and bitter, like his face.

The woman's eyes began to pour coolness into his skull. They were like two little rivers running through the channels of his own eyes, spreading in silver-green quiet across the tortured surface of his brain. His brain relaxed. It lay floating on the water, and then the twin streams became one broad flowing stream, and his mind, or ego, the thing that was intimately himself, vanished along it.

It took him a long, long time to regain consciousness. He felt as though he'd been shaken until pieces of him were scattered all over inside. Also, he had an instinctive premonition that the minute he woke up he would be sorry he had. He took it easy, putting himself together.

He remembered his name, Hugh Starke. He remembered the mining asteroid where he was born. He remembered the Luna cell blocks where he had once come near dying. There wasn't much to choose between them. He remembered his face decorating half the bulletin boards between Mercury and The Belt. He remembered hearing about himself over the telecasts, stuff to frighten babies with, and he thought of himself committing his first crime—a stunted scrawny kid of eighteen swinging a spanner on a grown man who was trying to steal his food.

The rest of it came fast, then. The T-V Mines job, the getaway that didn't get, the Mountains of White Cloud. The crash . . .

The woman.

That did it. His brain leaped shatteringly. Light, feeling, a naked sense of reality swept over him. He lay perfectly still with his eyes shut, and his mind clawed at the picture of the shining woman with sea-green hair and the sound of her voice saying, *You will not die, you will wake in a strange body, don't be afraid . . .*

He was afraid. His skin pricked and ran cold with it. His stomach knotted with it. His skin, his stomach, and yet somehow they didn't feel just right, like a new coat that hasn't shaped to you . . .

He opened his eyes, a cautious crack.

He saw a body sprawled on its side in dirty straw. The body belonged to him, because he could feel the straw pricking it, and the itch of little things that crawled and ate and crawled again.

It was a powerful body, rangy and flat-muscled, much bigger than his old one. It had obviously not been starved the first twenty-some years of its life. It was stark naked. Weather and violence had written history on it, wealed white marks on leathery bronze, but nothing seemed to be missing. There was black hair on its chest and thighs and forearms, and its hands were lean and sinewy for killing.

It was a human body. That was something. There were so many other things it might have been that his racial snobbery wouldn't call human. Like the nameless shimmering creature who smiled with strange pale lips.

Starke shut his eyes again.

He lay, the intangible self that was Hugh Starke, bellied down in the darkness of the alien shell, quiet, indrawn, waiting. Panic crept up on its soft black paws. It walked around the crouching ego and sniffed and patted and nuzzled, whining, and then struck with its raking claws. After a while it went away, empty.

The lips that were now Starke's lips twitched in a thin, cruel smile. He had done six months once in the Luna solitary crypts. If a man could do that, and come out sane and on his two feet, he could stand anything. Even this.

It came to him then, rather deflatingly, that the woman and her four companions had probably softened the shock by hypnotic suggestion. His subconscious understood and accepted the change. It was only his conscious mind that was superficially scared to death.

Hugh Starke cursed the woman with great thoroughness, in seven languages and some odd dialects. He became healthily enraged that any dame should play around with him like that. Then he thought, *What the hell, I'm alive. And it looks like I got the best of the trade-in!*

He opened his eyes again, secretly, on his new world.

He lay at one end of a square stone hall, good sized, with two straight lines of pillars cut from some dark Venusian wood. There were long crude benches and tables. Fires had been burning on round brick hearths spaced between the pillars. They were embers now. The smoke climbed up, tarnishing the gold and bronze of shields hung on the walls and pediments, dulling the blades of longswords, the spears, the tapestries and hides and trophies.

It was very quiet in the hall. Somewhere outside of it there was fighting going on. Heavy, vicious fighting. The noise of it didn't touch the silence, except to make it deeper.

There were two men besides Starke in the hall.

They were close to him, on a low dais. One of them sat in a carved high seat, not moving, his big scarred hands flat on the table in front of him. The other crouched on the floor by his feet. His head was bent forward so that his mop of lint-white hair hid his face and the harp between his thighs. He was a little man, a swamp-edger from his albino coloring. Starke looked back at the man in the chair.

The man spoke harshly. "Why doesn't she send word?"

The harp gave out a sudden bitter chord. That was all.

Starke hardly noticed. His whole attention was drawn to the speaker. His heart began to pound. His muscles coiled and lay ready. There was a bitter taste in his mouth. He recognized it. It was hate.

He had never seen the man before, but his hands switched with the urge to kill.

He was big, nearly seven feet, and muscled like a draft horse. But his body, naked above a gold-bossed leather kilt, was lithe and quick as a greyhound in spite of its weight. His face was square, strong-boned, weathered, and still young. It was a face that had laughed a lot once, and liked wine and pretty girls. It had forgotten those things now, except maybe the wine. It was drawn and cruel with pain, a look as of something in a cage. Starke had seen that look before, in the

Luna blocks. There was a thick white scar across the man's forehead. Under it his blue eyes were sunken and dark behind half-closed lids. The man was blind.

Outside, in the distance, men screamed and died.

Starke had been increasingly aware of a soreness and stricture around his neck. He raised a hand, careful not to rustle the straw. His fingers found a long tangled beard, felt under it, and touched a band of metal.

Starke's new body wore a collar, like a vicious dog.

There was a chain attached to the collar. Starke couldn't find any fastening. The business had been welded on for keeps. His body didn't seem to have liked it much. The neck was galled and chafed.

The blood began to crawl up hot into Starke's head. He'd worn chains before. He didn't like them. Especially around the neck.

A door opened suddenly at the far end of the hall. Fog and red daylight spilled in across the black stone floor. A man came in. He was big, half naked, blond, and bloody. His long blade trailed harshly on the flags. His chest was laid open to the bone and he held the wound together with his free hand.

"Word from Beudag," he said. "They've driven us back into the city, but so far we're holding the Gate."

No one spoke. The little man nodded his white head. The man with the slashed chest turned and went out again, closing the door.

A peculiar change came over Starke at the mention of the name Beudag. He had never heard it before, but it hung in his mind like a spear point, barbed with strange emotion. He couldn't identify the feeling, but it brushed the blind man aside. The hot simple hatred cooled. Starke relaxed in a sort of icy quiet, deceptively calm as a sleeping cobra. He didn't question this. He waited, for Beudag.

The blind man struck his hands down suddenly on the table and stood up. "Romna," he said, "give me my sword."

The little man looked at him. He had milk-blue eyes and a face like a friendly bulldog. He said, "Don't be a fool, Faolan."

Faolan said softly, "Damn you. Give me my sword."

Men were dying outside the hall, and not dying silently. Faolan's skin was greasy with sweat. He made a sudden, darting grab toward Romna.

Romna dodged him. There were tears in his pale eyes. He said brutally, "You'd only be in the way. Sit down."

"I can find the point," Faolan said, "to fall on it."

Romna's voice went up to a harsh scream. "Shut up. Shut up and sit down."

Faolan caught the edge of the table and bent over it. He shivered and closed his eyes, and the tears ran out hot under the lids. The bard turned away, and his harp cried out like a woman.

Faolan drew a long sighing breath. He straightened slowly, came round the carved high seat, and walked steadily toward Starke.

"You're very quiet, Conan," he said. "What's the matter? You ought to be happy, Conan. You ought to laugh and rattle your chain. You're going to get what you wanted. Are you sad because you haven't a mind anymore, to understand that with?"

He stopped and felt with one sandaled foot across the straw until he touched Starke's thigh. Starke lay motionless.

"Conan," said the blind man gently, pressing Starke's belly with his foot. "Conan the dog, the betrayer, the butcher, the knife in the back. Remember what you did at Falga, Conan? No, you don't remember now. I've been a little rough with you, and you don't remember anymore. But I remember, Conan. As long as I live in darkness, I'll remember."

Romna stroked the harp strings and they wept, savage tears for strong men dead of treachery. Low music, distant but not soft. Faolan began to tremble, a shallow animal twitching of the muscles. The flesh of his face was drawn, iron shaping under the hammer. Quite suddenly he went down on his knees. His hands struck Starke's shoulders, slid inward to the throat, and locked there.

Outside, the sound of fighting had died away.

Starke moved, very quickly. As though he had seen it and knew it was there, his hand swept out and gathered in the slack of the heavy chain and swung it.

It started out to be a killing blow. Starke wanted with all his heart to beat Faolan's brains out. But at the last second he pulled it, slapping the big man with exquisite judgment across the back of the head. Faolan grunted and fell sideways, and by that time Romna had come up. He had dropped his harp and drawn a knife. His eyes were startled.

Starke sprang up. He backed off, swinging the slack of the chain warningly. His new body moved magnificently. Outside everything was fine, but inside his psychoneural setup had exploded into civil war. He was furious with himself for not having killed Faolan. He was furious with himself for losing control enough to want to kill a man without reason. He hated Faolan. He did not hate Faolan because he didn't know him well enough. Starke's trained, calculating, unemotional brain was at grips with a tidal wave of baseless emotion.

He hadn't realized it was baseless until his mental monitor, conditioned through years of bitter control, had stopped him from killing. Now he remembered the woman's voice saying, *My mind will be with yours, I'll guide you . . .*

Catspaw, huh? Just a hired hand, paid off with a new body in return for two lives. Yeah, two. This Beudag, whoever he was. Starke knew now what that cold alien emotion had been leading up to.

"Hold it," said Starke hoarsely. "Hold everything." *Catspaw! You green-eyed she-devil! You picked the wrong guy this time.*"

Just for a fleeting instant he saw her again, leaning forward with her hair like running water across the soft foam-sparkle of her shoulders. Her sea-pale eyes were full of mocking laughter, and a direct, provocative admiration. Starke heard her quite plainly:

"You may not have any choice, Hugh Starke. They know Conan, even if you don't. Besides, it's of no great importance. The end will be the same for them—it's just a matter of time. You can save your new body or not, as you wish." She smiled. "I'd like it if you did. It's a good body. I knew it, before Conan's mind broke and left it empty."

A sudden thought came to Starke. "My box, the million credits."

"Come and get them." She was gone. Starke's mind was clear, with no alien will tramping around in it. Faolan crouched on the floor, holding his head. He said:

"Who spoke?"

Romna the bard stood staring. His lips moved, but no sound came out.

Starke said, "I spoke. Me, Hugh Starke. I'm not Conan, and I never heard of Falga, and I'll brain the first guy that comes near me."

Faolan stayed motionless, his face blank, his breath sobbing in his throat. Romna began to curse, very softly, not as though he were thinking about it. Starke watched them.

Down the hall the doors burst open. The heavy reddish mist coiled in with the daylight across the flags, and with them a press of bodies hot from battle, bringing a smell of blood.

Starke felt the heart contract in the hairy breast of the body named Conan, watching the single figure that led the pack.

Romna called out, "Beudag!"

She was tall. She was built and muscled like a lioness, and she walked with a flat-hipped arrogance, and her hair was like coiled flame. Her eyes were blue, hot and bright, as Faolan's might have been once. She looked like Faolan. She was dressed like him, in a leather kilt and sandals, her magnificent body bare above the waist. She carried a longsword slung across her back, the hilt standing above the left shoulder. She had been using it. Her skin was smeared with blood and grime. There was a long cut on her thigh and another across her flat belly, and bitter weariness lay on her like a burden in spite of her denial of it.

"We've stopped them, Faolan," she said. "They can't breach the Gate, and we can hold Crom Dhu as long as we have food. And the sea feeds us." She laughed, but there was a hollow sound to it. "Gods, I'm tired!"

She halted then, below the dais. Her flame-blue gaze swept across Faolan, across Romna, and rose to meet Hugh Starke's, and stayed there.

The pulse began to beat under Starke's jaw again, and this time his body was strong, and the pulse was like a drum throbbing.

Romna said, "His mind has come back."

There was a long, hard silence. No one in the hall moved. Then the men back of Beudag, big brawny kilted warriors, began to close in on the dais, talking in low snarling undertones that rose toward a mob howl. Faolan rose up and faced them, and bellowed them to quiet.

"He's mine to take! Let him alone."

Beudag sprang up onto the dais, one beautiful flowing movement. "It isn't possible," she said. "His mind broke under torture. He's been a drooling idiot with barely the sense to feed himself. And now, suddenly, you say he's normal again?"

Starke said, "You know I'm normal. You can see it in my eyes."

"Yes."

He didn't like the way she said that. "Listen, my name is Hugh Starke. I'm an Earthman. This isn't Conan's brain come back. This is a new deal. I got shoved into this body. What it did before I got it I don't know, and I'm not responsible."

Faolan said, "He doesn't remember Falga. He doesn't remember the longships at the bottom of the sea." Faolan laughed.

Romna said quietly, "He didn't kill you, though. He could have, easily. Would Conan have spared you?"

Beudag said, "Yes, if he had a better plan. Conan's mind was like a snake. It crawled in the dark, and you never knew where it was going to strike."

Starke began to tell them how it happened, the chain swinging idly in his hand. While he was talking he saw a face reflected in a polished shield hung on a pillar. Mostly it was just a tangled black mass of hair, mounted on a frame of long, harsh, jutting bone. The mouth was sensuous, with a dark sort of laughter on it. The eyes were yellow. The cruel, brilliant yellow of a killer hawk.

Starke realized with a shock that the face belonged to him.

"A woman with pale green hair," said Beudag softly. "Rann," said Faolan, and Romna's harp made a sound like a high-priest's curse.

"Her people have that power," Romna said. "They can think a man's soul into a spider, and step on it."

"They have many powers. Maybe Rann followed Conan's mind, wherever it went, and told it what to say, and brought it back again."

"Listen," said Starke angrily. "I didn't ask . . ."

Suddenly, without warning, Romna drew Beudag's sword and threw it at Starke.

Starke dodged it. He looked at Romna with ugly yellow eyes. "That's fine. Chain me up so I can't fight and kill me from a distance." He did not pick up the sword. He'd never used one. The chain felt better, not being too different from a heavy belt or a length of cable, or the other chains he's swung on occasion.

Romna said, "Is that Conan?"

Faolan snarled, "What happened?"

"Romna threw my sword at Conan. He dodged it, and left it on the ground." Beudag's eyes were narrowed. "Conan could catch a flying sword by the hilt, and he was the best fighter on the Red Sea, barring you, Faolan."

"He's trying to trick us. Rann guides him."

"The hell with Rann!" Starke clashed his chain. "She wants me to kill the both of you, I still don't know why. All right. I could have killed Faolan, easy. But I'm not a killer. I never put down anyone except to save my own neck. So I didn't kill him in spite of Rann. And I don't want any part of you, or Rann either. All I want is to get the hell out of here!"

Beudag said, "His accent isn't Conan's. And the look in his eyes is different, too." Her voice had an odd note in it.

Romna glanced at her. He fingered a few rippling chords on his harp, and said:

"There's one way you could tell for sure."

A sullen flush began to burn on Beudag's cheekbones. Romna slid unobtrusively out of reach. His eyes danced with malicious laughter.

Beudag smiled, the smile of an angry cat, all teeth and no humor. Suddenly she walked toward Starke, her head erect, her hands swinging loose and empty at her sides. Starke tensed warily, but the blood leaped pleasantly in his borrowed veins.

Beudag kissed him.

Starke dropped the chain. He had something better to do with his hands.

After a while he raised his head for breath, and she stepped back, and whispered wonderingly,

"It isn't Conan."

The hall had been cleared. Starke had washed and shaved himself. His new face wasn't bad. Not bad at all. In fact, it was pretty damn good. And it wasn't known around the System. It was a face that could own a million credits and no questions asked. It was a face that could have a lot of fun on a million credits.

All he had to figure out now was a way to save the neck the face was mounted on, and get his million credits back from that beautiful she-devil named Rann.

He was still chained, but the straw had been cleaned up and he wore a leather kilt and a pair of sandals. Faolan sat in his high seat nursing a flagon of wine. Beudag sprawled wearily on a fur rug beside him. Romna sat cross-legged, his eyes veiled sleepily, stroking soft wandering music out of his harp. He looked fey. Starke knew his swamp-edgers. He wasn't surprised.

"This man is telling the truth," Romna said. "But there's another mind touching his. Rann's, I think. Don't trust him."

Faolan growled, "I couldn't trust a god in Conan's body."

Starke said, "What's the setup? All the fighting out there, and this Rann dame trying to plant a killer on the inside. And what happened at Falga? I never heard of this whole damn ocean, let alone a place called Falga."

The bard swept his hand across the strings. "I'll tell you, Hugh Starke. And maybe you won't want to stay in that body any longer."

Starke grinned. He glanced at Beudag. She was watching him with a queer intensity from under lowered lids. Starke's grin changed. He began to sweat. Get rid of this body, hell! It was really a body. His own stringy little carcass had never felt like this.

The bard said, "In the beginning, in the Red Sea, was a race of people having still their fins and scales. They were amphibious, but after a while part of this race wanted to remain entirely on land. There was a quarrel, and a battle, and some of the people left the sea forever. They settled along the shore. They lost their fins and most of their scales. They had great mental powers and they loved ruling. They subjugated the human peoples and kept them almost in slavery. They hated their brothers who still lived in the sea, and their brothers hated them.

"After a time a third people came to the Red Sea. They were rovers from the North. They raided and rieved and wore no man's collar. They made a settlement on Crom Dhu, the Black Rock, and built longships, and took toll of the coastal towns.

"But the slave people didn't want to fight against the rovers. They wanted to fight with them and destroy the sea-folk. The rovers were human, and blood calls to blood. And the rovers like to rule, too, and this is a rich country. Also, the time had come in their tribal development when they were ready to change from nomadic warriors to builders in their own country.

"So the rovers, and the sea-folk, and the slave people who are caught between the two of them, began their struggle for the land."

The bard's fingers thrummed against the strings so that they beat like angry hearts. Starke saw that Beudag was still watching him, weighing every change of expression on his face. Romna went on:

"There was a woman named Rann, who had green hair and great beauty, and ruled the sea-folk. There was a man called Faolan of the Ships, and his sister Beudag, which means Dagger-in-the-Sheath, and they two ruled the outland rovers. And there was the man called Conan."

The harp crashed out like a sword-blade striking.

"Conan was a great fighter and a great lover. He was next under Faolan of the Ships, and Beudag loved him, and they were plighted. Then Conan was taken prisoner by the sea-folk during a skirmish, and Rann saw him—and Conan saw Rann."

Hugh Starke had a fleeting memory of Rann's face smiling, and her low voice saying, *It's a good body. I knew it, before* . . .

Beudag's eyes were two stones of blue vitriol under her narrow lids.

"Conan stayed a long time at Falga with Rann of the Red Sea. Then he came back to Crom Dhu, and said that he had escaped, and had discovered a way to take the longships into the harbor of Falga, at the back of Rann's fleet, and from there it would be easy to take the city, and Rann with it. And Conan and Beudag were married."

Starke's yellow hawk eyes slid over Beudag, sprawled like a young lioness in power and beauty. A muscle began to twitch under his cheekbone. Beudag flushed, a slow deep color. Her gaze did not waver.

"So the longships went out from Crom Dhu, across the Red Sea. And Conan led them into a trap at Falga, and more than half of them were sunk. Conan thought his ship was free, that he had Rann and all she'd promised him, but Faolan saw what had happened and went after him. They fought, and Conan laid his sword across Faolan's brow and blinded him; but Conan lost the fight. Beudag brought them home.

"Conan was chained naked in the market place. The people were careful not to kill him. From time to time other things were done to him. After a while his mind broke, and Faolan had him chained here in the hall, where he could hear him babble and play with his chain. It made the darkness easier to bear.

"But since Falga, things have gone badly from Crom Dhu. Too many men were lost, too many ships. Now Rann's people have us bottled up here. They can't break in, we can't break out. And so we stay, until . . ." The harp cried out a bitter question, and was still.

After a minute or two Starke said slowly, "Yeah, I get it. Stalemate for both of you. And Rann figured if I could kill off the leaders, your people might give up." He began to curse. "What a lousy, dirty, sneaking trick! And who told her she could use me . . ." He paused. After all, he'd be dead now. After all, a new body, and a cool million credits. Ah, the hell with Rann. He hadn't asked her to do it. And he was nobody's hired killer. Where did she get off, sneaking around his mind, trying to make him do things he didn't even know about? Especially to someone like Beudag.

Still, Rann herself was nobody's crud.

And just where was Hugh Starke supposed to cut in on this deal? Cut was right. Probably with a longsword, right through the belly. Swell spot he was in, and a good three strikes on him already.

He was beginning to wish he'd never seen the T-V Mines payroll ship, because then he might never have seen the Mountains of White Cloud.

He said, because everybody seemed to be waiting for him to say something, "Usually when there's a deadlock like this, somebody calls in a third party. Isn't there somebody you can yell for?"

Faolan shook his rough red head. "The slave people might rise, but they haven't arms and they're not used to fighting. They'd only get massacred, and it wouldn't help us any."

"What about those other—uh—people that live in the sea? And just what is that sea, anyhow? Some radiation from it wrecked my ship and got me into this bloody mess."

Beudag said lazily, "I don't know what it is. The seas our forefathers sailed on were water, but this is different. It will float a ship, if you know how to build the hull—very thin, of a white metal we mine from the foothills. But when you swim in it, it's like being in a cloud of bubbles. It tingles, and the farther down you go in it the stranger it gets, dark and full of fire. I stay down for hours sometimes, hunting the beasts that live there."

Starke said, "For hours? You have diving suits, then."

"What are they?" Starke told her. She shook her head, laughing. "Why weigh yourself down that way? There's no trouble to breathe in this ocean."

"For cripesake," said Starke. "Well I'll be damned. Must be a heavy gas, then, radioactive, surface tension under atmospheric pressure, enough to float a light hull, and high oxygen content without any dangerous mixture. Well, well. Okay, why doesn't somebody go down and see if the sea-people will help? They don't like Rann's branch of the family, you said."

"They don't like us, either," said Faolan. "We stay out of the southern part of the sea. They wreck our ships, sometimes." His bitter mouth twisted in a smile. "Did you want to go to them for help?"

Starke didn't quite like the way Faolan sounded. "It was just a suggestion," he said.

Beudag rose, stretching, wincing as the stiffened wounds pulled her flesh. "Come on, Faolan. Let's sleep."

He rose and laid his hand on her shoulder. Romna's harpstrings breathed a subtle little mockery of sound. The bard's eyes were veiled and sleepy. Beudag did not look at Starke, called Conan.

Starke said, "What about me?"

"You stay chained," said Faolan. "There's plenty of time to think. As long as we have food—and the sea feeds us."

He followed Beudag through a curtained entrance to the left. Romna got up, slowly, slinging the harp over one white shoulder. He stood looking steadily into Starke's eyes in the dying light of the fires.

"I don't know," he murmured.

Starke waited, not speaking. His face was without expression.

"Conan we knew. Starke we don't know. Perhaps it

would have been better if Conan had come back." He ran his
thumb absently over the hilt of the knife in his girdle. "I
don't know. Perhaps it would have been better for all of us if
I'd cut your throat before Beudag came in."

Starke's mouth twitched. It was not exactly a smile.

"You see," said the bard seriously, "to you, from
Outside, none of this is important, except as it touches you.
But we live in this little world. We die in it. To us, it's
important."

The knife was in his hand now. It leaped up glittering
into the dregs of the firelight, and fell, and leaped again.

"You fight for yourself, Hugh Starke. Rann also fights
through you. I don't know."

Starke's gaze did not waver.

Romna shrugged and put away the knife. "It is written
of the gods," he said, sighing. "I hope they haven't done a
bad job of the writing."

He went out. Starke began to shiver slightly. It was
completely quiet in the hall. He examined his collar, the
rivets, every separate link of the chain, the staple to which it
was fixed. Then he sat down on the fur rug provided for him
in place of the straw. He put his face in his hands and cursed,
steadily, for several minutes, and then struck his fists down
hard on the floor. After that he lay down and was quiet. He
thought Rann would speak to him. She did not.

The silent black hours that walked across his heart were
worse than any he had spent in the Luna crypts.

She came soft-shod, bearing a candle. Beudag, the
Dagger-in-the-Sheath. Starke was not asleep. He rose and
stood waiting. She set the candle on the table and came, not
quite to him, and stopped. She wore a length of thin white
cloth twisted loosely at the waist and dropping to her ankles.
Her body rose out of it straight and lovely, touched mystical-
ly with shadows in the little wavering light.

"Who are you?" she whispered. "What are you?"

"A man. Not Conan. Maybe not Hugh Starke anymore.
Just a man."

"I loved the man called Conan, until . . . ." She caught

her breath, and moved closer. She put her hand on Starke's arm. The touch went through him like white fire. The warm clean healthy fragrance of her tasted sweet in his throat. Her eyes searched his.

"If Rann has such great powers, couldn't it be that Conan was forced to do what he did? Couldn't it be that Rann took his mind and moulded it her way, perhaps without his knowing it?"

"It could be."

"Conan was hot-tempered and quarrelsome, but he . . ."

Starke said slowly, "I don't think you could have loved him if he hadn't been straight."

Her hand lay still on his forearm. She stood looking at him, and then her hand began to tremble, and in a moment she was crying, making no noise about it. Starke drew her gently to him. His eyes blazed yellowly in the candlelight.

"Woman's tears," she said impatiently, after a bit. She tried to draw away. "I've been fighting too long, and losing, and I'm tired."

He let her step back, not far. "Do all the women of Crom Dhu fight like men?"

"If they want to. There have always been shield-maidens. And since Falga, I would have had to fight anyway, to keep from thinking." She touched the collar on Starke's neck. "And from seeing."

He thought of Conan in the market square, and Conan shaking his chain and gibbering in Faolan's hall, and Beudag watching it. Starke's fingers tightened. He slid his palms upward along the smooth muscles of her arms, across the straight, broad planes of her shoulders, onto her neck, the proud strength of it pulsing under his hands. Her hair fell loose. He could feel the redness of it burning him.

She whispered, "You don't love me."

"No."

"You're an honest man, Hugh Starke."

"You want me to kiss you."

"Yes."

"You're an honest woman, Beudag."

Her lips were hungry, passionate, touched with the bitterness of tears. After a while Starke blew out the candle . . .

"I could love you, Beudag."

"Not the way I mean."

"The way you mean. I've never said that to any woman before. But you're not like any woman before. And—I'm a different man."

"Strange—so strange. Conan, and yet not Conan."

"I could love you, Beudag—if I lived."

Harpstrings gave a thrumming sigh in the darkness, the faintest whisper of sound. Beudag started, sighed, and rose from the fur rug. In a minute she had found flint and steel and got the candle lighted. Romna the bard stood in the curtained doorway, watching them.

Presently he said, "You're going to let him go."

Beudag said, "Yes."

Romna nodded. He did not seem surprised. He walked across the dais, laying his harp on the table, and went into another room. He came back almost at once with a hacksaw.

"Bend your neck," he said to Starke.

The metal of the collar was soft. When it was cut through Starke got his fingers under it and bent the ends outward, without trouble. His old body could never have done that. His old body could never have done a lot of things. He figured Rann hadn't cheated him. Not much.

He got up, looking at Beudag. Beudag's head was dropped forward, her face veiled behind shining hair.

"There's only one possible way out of Crom Dhu," she said. There was no emotion in her voice. "There's a passage leading down through the rock to a secret harbor, just large enough to moor a skiff or two. Perhaps, with the night and the fog, you can slip through Rann's blockade. Or you can go aboard one of her ships, for Falga." She picked up the candle. "I'll take you down."

"Wait," Starke said. "What about you?"

She glanced a him, surprised. "I'll stay, of course."

He looked into her eyes. "It's going to be hard to know each other that way."

"You can't stay here, Hugh Starke. The people would tear you to pieces the moment you went into the street. They may even storm the hall, to take you. Look here." She set the candle down and led him to a narrow window, drawing back the hide that covered it.

Starke saw narrow twisting streets dropping steeply toward the sullen sea. The longships were broken and sunk in the harbor. Out beyond, riding lights flickering in the red fog, were other ships. Rann's ships.

"Over there," said Beudag, "is the mainland. Crom Dhu is connected to it by a tongue of rock. The sea-folk hold the land beyond it, but we can hold the rock bridge as long as we live. We have enough water, enough food from the sea. But there's no soil nor game on Crom Dhu. We'll be naked after a while, without leather or flax, and we'll have scurvy without grain and fruit. We're beaten, unless the gods send us a miracle. And we're beaten because of what was done at Falga. You can see how the people feel."

Starke looked at the dark streets and the silent houses leaning on each other's shoulders, and the mocking lights out in the fog. "Yeah," he said. "I can see."

"Besides, there's Faolan. I don't know whether he believes your story. I don't know whether it would matter."

Starke nodded. "But you won't come with me?"

She turned away sharply and picked up the candle again. "Are you coming, Romna?"

The bard nodded. He slung his harp over his shoulder. Beudag held back the curtain of a small doorway far to the side. Starke went through it and Romna followed, and Beudag went ahead with the candle. No one spoke.

They went along a narrow passage, past store rooms and armories. They paused once while Starke chose a knife, and Romna whispered: "Wait!" He listened intently. Starke and Beudag strained their ears along with him. There was no sound in the sleeping dun. Romna shrugged. "I thought I heard sandals scraping stone," he said. They went on.

The passage lay behind a wooden door. It led downward steeply through the rock, a single narrow way without side

galleries or branches. In some places there were winding
steps. It ended, finally, in a flat ledge low to the surface of the
cove, which was a small cavern closed in with the black rock.
Beudag set the candle down.

There were two little skiffs built of some light metal
moored to rings in the ledge. Two long sweeps leaned against
the cave wall. They were of a different metal, oddly vaned.
Beudag laid one across the thwarts of the nearest boat. Then
she turned to Starke. Romna hung back in the shadows by the
tunnel mouth.

Beudag said quietly, "Goodbye, man without a name."

"It has to be goodbye."

"I'm leader now, in Faolan's place. Besides, these are my
people." Her fingers tightened on his wrists. "If you
could . . ." Her eyes held a brief blaze of hope. Then she
dropped her head and said, "I keep forgetting you're not one
of us. Goodbye."

"Goodbye, Beudag."

Starke put his arms around her. He found her mouth,
almost cruelly. Her arms were tight about him, her eyes half
closed and dreaming. Starke's hands slipped upward, toward
her throat, and locked on it.

She bent back, her body like a steel bow. Her eyes got fire
in them, looking into Starke's but only for a moment. His
fingers pressed expertly on the nerve centers. Beudag's head
fell forward limply, and then Romna was on Starke's back and
his knife was pricking Starke's throat.

Starke caught his wrist and turned the blade away. Blood
ran onto his chest, but the cut was not into the artery. He
threw himself backward onto the stone. Romna couldn't get
clear in time. The breath went out of him in a rushing gasp.
He didn't let go of the knife. Starke rolled over. The little
man didn't have a chance with him. He was tough and quick,
but Starke's sheer size smothered him. Starke could remember when Romna would not have seemed small to him. He
hit the bard's jaw with his fist. Romna's head cracked hard
against the stone. He let go of the knife. He seemed to be
through fighting. Starke got up. He was sweating, breathing

heavily, not because of his exertion. His mouth was glistening and eager, like a dog's. His muscles twitched, his belly was hot and knotted with excitement. His yellow eyes had a strange look.

He went back to Beudag.

She lay on the black rock, on her back. Candlelight ran pale gold across her brown skin, skirting the sharp strong hollows between her breasts and under the arching rim of her ribcage. Starke knelt, across her body, his weight pressed down against her harsh breathing. He stared at her. Sweat stood out on his face. He took her throat between his hands again.

He watched the blood grow dark in her cheeks. He watched the veins coil on her forehead. He watched the redness blacken in her lips. She fought a little, very vaguely, like someone moving in a dream. Starke breathed hoarsely, animal-like, through an open mouth.

Then, gradually his body became rigid. His hands froze, not releasing pressure, but not adding any. His yellow eyes widened. It was as though he were trying to see Beudag's face and it was hidden in dense clouds.

Back of him, back in the tunnel, was the soft, faint whisper of sandals on uneven rock. Sandals, walking slowly. Starke did not hear. Beudag's face glimmered deep in a heavy mist below him, a blasphemy of a face, distorted, blackened.

Starke's hands began to open.

They opened slowly. Muscles stood like coiled ropes in his arms and shoulders, as though he moved them against heavy weights. His lips peeled back from his teeth. He bent his neck, and sweat dropped from his face and glittered on Beudag's breast.

Starke was now barely touching Beudag's neck. She began to breathe again, painfully.

Starke began to laugh. It was not nice laughter. "Rann," he whispered. "Rann, you she-devil." He half fell away from Beudag and stood up, holding himself against the wall. He was shaking violently. "I wouldn't use your hate for killing, so you tried to use my passion." He cursed her in a flat sibilant whisper. He had never in his profane life really cursed anyone before.

He heard an echo of laughter dancing in his brain.

Starke turned. Faolan of the Ships stood in the tunnel mouth. His head was bent, listening, his blind dark eyes fixed on Starke as though he saw him.

Faolan said softly, "I hear you, Starke. I hear the others breathing, but they don't speak."

"They're all right. I didn't mean to do . . ."

Faolan smiled. He stepped out on the narrow ledge. He knew where he was going, and his smile was not pleasant.

"I heard your steps in the passage beyond my room. I knew Beudag was leading you, and where, and why. I would have been here sooner, but it's a slow way in the dark."

The candle lay in his path. He felt the heat of it close to his leg, and stopped and felt for it, and ground it out. It was dark, then. Very dark, except for a faint smudgy glow from the scrap of ocean that lay along the cave floor.

"It doesn't matter," Faolan said, "as long as I came in time."

Starke shifted his weight warily. "Faolan . . ."

"I wanted you alone. On this night of all nights I wanted you alone. Beudag fights in my place now, Conan. My manhood needs proving."

Starke strained his in the gloom, measuring the ledge, measuring the place where the skiff was moored. He didn't want to fight Faolan. In Faolan's place he would have felt the same. Starke understood perfectly. He didn't hate Faolan, he didn't want to kill him, and he was afraid of Rann's power over him when his emotions got control. You couldn't keep a determined man from killing you and still be uninvolved emotionally. Starke would be damned if he'd kill anyone to suit Rann.

He moved, silently, trying to slip past Faolan on the outside and get into the skiff. Faolan gave no sign of hearing him. Starke did not breathe. His sandals came down lighter than snowflakes. Faolan did not swerve. He would pass Starke with a foot to spare. They came abreast.

Faolan's hand shot out and caught in Starke's long black hair. The blind man laughed softly and closed in.

Starke swung one from the floor. Do it the quickest way and get clear. But Faolan was fast. He came in so swiftly that Starke's fist jarred harmlessly along his ribs. He was bigger than Starke, and heavier, and the darkness didn't bother him.

Starke bared his teeth. Do it quick, brother, and clear out! Or that green-eyed she-cat . . . Faolan's brute bulk weighed him down. Faolan's arm crushed his neck. Faolan's fist was knocking his guts loose. Starke got moving.

He'd fought in a lot of places. He'd learned from stokers and tramps, Martian Low-Canalers, red-eyed Nahali in the running gutters of Lhi. He didn't use his knife. He used his knees and feet and elbows and his hands, fist and flat. It was a good fight. Faolan was a good fighter, but Starke knew more tricks.

One more, Starke thought. One more and he's out. He drew back for it, and his heel struck Romna, lying on the rock. He staggered, and Faolan caught him with a clean swinging blow. Starke fell backward against the cave wall. His head cracked the rock. Light flooded crimson across his brain and then paled and grew cooler, a wash of clear silver-green like water. He sank under it . . .

He was tired, desperately tired. His head ached. He wanted to rest, but he could feel that he was sitting up, doing something that had to be done. He opened his eyes.

He sat in the stern of a skiff. The long sweep was laid into its crutch, held like a tiller bar against his body. The blade of the sweep trailed astern in the red sea, and where the metal touched there was a spurt of silver fire and a swirling of brilliant motes. The skiff moved rapidly through the sullen fog, through a mist of blood in the hot Venusian night.

Beudag crouched in the bow, facing Starke. She was bound securely with strips of the white cloth she had worn. Bruises showed dark on her throat. She was watching Starke with the intent, unwinking, perfectly expressionless gaze of a tigress.

Starke looked away, down at himself. There was blood

on his kilt, a brown smear of it across his chest. It was not his blood. He drew the knife slowly out of its sheath. The blade was dull and crusted, still a little wet.

Starke looked at Beudag. His lips were stiff, swollen. He moistened them and said hoarsely, "What happened?"

She shook her head, slowly, not speaking. Her eyes did not waver.

A black, cold rage took hold of Starke and shook him. Rann! He rose and went forward, letting the sweep go where it would. He began to untie Beudag's wrists.

A shape swam toward them out of the red mist. A longship with two heavy sweeps bursting fire astern and a slender figurehead shaped like a woman. A woman with hair and eyes of aquamarine. It came alongside the skiff.

A rope ladder snaked down. Men lined the low rail. Slender men with skin that glistened white like powdered snow, and hair the color of distant shallows.

One of them said, "Come aboard, Hugh Starke."

Starke went back to the sweep. It bit into the sea, sending the skiff in a swift arc away from Rann's ship.

Grapnels flew, hooking the skiff at thwart and gunwale. Bows appeared in the hands of the men, wicked curving things with barbed metal shafts on the string. The man said again, politely, "Come aboard."

Hugh Starke finished untying Beudag. He didn't speak. There seemed to be nothing to say. He stood back while she climbed the ladder and then followed. The skiff was cast loose. The longship veered away, gathering speed.

Starke said, "Where are we going?"

The man smiled. "To Falga."

Starke nodded. He went below with Beudag into a cabin with soft couches covered with spider-silk and panels of dark wood beautifully painted, dim fantastic scenes from the past of Rann's people. They sat opposite each other. They still did not speak.

They raised Falga in the opal dawn—a citadel of basalt cliffs rising sheer from the burning sea, with a long arm holding a harbor full of ships. There were green fields inland,

and beyond, cloaked in the eternal mists of Venus, the Mountains of White Cloud lifted spaceward. Starke wished that he had never seen the Mountains of White Cloud. Then, looking at his hands, lean and strong on his long thighs, he wasn't so sure. He thought of Rann waiting for him. Anger, excitement, a confused violence of emotion, set him pacing nervously.

Beudag sat quietly, withdrawn, waiting.

The longship threaded the crowded moorings and slid into place alongside a stone quay. Men rushed to make fast. They were human men, as Starke judged humans, like Beudag and himself. They had the shimmering silver hair and fair skin of the plateau peoples, the fine-cut faces and straight bodies. They wore leather collars with metal tags and they went naked like beasts, and they were gaunt and bowed with labor. Here and there a man with pale blue-green hair and resplendent harness stood godlike above the swarming masses.

Starke and Beudag went ashore. They might have been prisoners or honored guests, surrounded by their escort from the ship. Streets ran back from the harbor, twisting and climbing crazily up the cliffs. Houses climbed on each other's backs. It had begun to rain, the heavy steaming downpour of Venus, and the moist heat brought out the choking stench of people, too many people.

They climbed, ankle deep in water sweeping down the streets that were half stairway. Thin naked children peered out of the houses, out of narrow alleys. Twice they passed through market squares where women with the blank faces of defeat drew back from stalls of coarse food to let the party through.

There was something wrong. After a while Starke realized it was the silence. In all that horde of humanity no one laughed, or sang, or shouted. Even the children never spoke above a whisper. Starke began to feel a little sick. Their eyes had a look in them . . .

He glanced at Beudag, and away again.

The waterfront streets ended in a sheer basalt face honeycombed with galleries. Starke's party entered them, still climbing. They passed level after level of huge caverns, open to the sea. There was the same crowding, the same stench, the same silence. Eyes glinted in the half-light, bare feet moved furtively on stone. Somewhere a baby cried thinly, and was hushed at once.

They came out on the cliff top, into the clean high air. There was a city here. Broad streets, lined with trees, low rambling villas of the black rock set in walled gardens, drowned in brilliant vines and giant ferns and flowers. Naked men and women worked in the gardens, or hauled carts of rubbish through the alleys, or hurried on errands, slipping furtively across the main streets where they intersected the mews.

The party turned away from the sea, heading toward an ebon palace that sat like a crown above the city. The steaming rain beat on Starke's bare body, and up here you could get the smell of the rain, even through the heavy perfume of the flowers. You could smell Venus in the rain—musky and primitive and savagely alive, a fecund giantess with passion flowers in her outstretched hands. Starke set his feet down like a panther and his eyes burned a smoky amber.

They entered the palace of Rann. . . .

She received them in the same apartment where Starke had come to after the crash. Through a broad archway he could see the high bed where his old body had lain before the life went out of it. The red sea steamed under the rain outside, the rusty fog coiling languidly through the open arches of the gallery. Rann watched them lazily from a raised couch set massively into the wall. Her long sparkling legs sprawled arrogantly across the black spider-silk draperies. This time her tabard was a pale yellow. Her eyes were still the color of shoal-water, still amused, still secret, still dangerous.

Starke said, "So you made me do it after all."

"And you're angry." She laughed, her teeth showing white and pointed as bone needles. Her gaze held Starke's. There was nothing casual about it. Starke's hawk eyes turned molten yellow, like hot gold, and did not waver.

Beudag stood like a bronze spear, her forearms crossed beneath her bare sharp breasts. Two of Rann's palace guards stood behind her.

Starke began to walk toward Rann.

She watched him come. She let him get close enough to reach out and touch her, and then she said slyly, "It's a good body, isn't it?"

Starke looked at her for a moment. Then he laughed. He threw back his head and roared, and struck the great corded muscles of his belly with his fist. Presently he looked straight into Rann's eyes and said:

"I know you."

She nodded. "We know each other. Sit down, Hugh Starke." She swung her long legs over to make room, half erect now, looking at Beudag. Starke sat down. He did not look at Beudag.

Rann said, "Will your people surrender now?"

Beudag did not move, not even her eyelids. "If Faolan is dead—yes."

"And if he's not?"

Beudag stiffened. Starke did too.

"Then," said Beudag quietly, "they'll wait."

"Until he is?"

"Or until they must surrender."

Rann nodded. To the guards she said, "See that this woman is well fed and well treated."

Beudag and her escort had turned to go when Starke said, "Wait." The guards looked at Rann, who nodded, and glanced quizzically at Starke. Starke said:

"Is Faolan dead?"

Rann hesitated. Then she smiled. "No. You have the most damnably tough mind, Starke. You struck deep, but not deep enough. He may still die, but . . . No, he's not dead." She turned to Beudag and said with easy mockery, "You needn't hold anger against Starke. I'm the one who should be angry." Her eyes came back to Starke. They didn't look angry.

Starke said, "There's something else. Conan—the Conan that used to be, before Falga."

"Beudag's Conan."

"Yeah. Why did he betray his people?"

Rann studied him. Her strange pale lips curved, her sharp white teeth glistening wickedly with barbed humor. Then she turned to Beudag. Beudag was still standing like a carved image, but her smooth muscles were ridged with tension, and her eyes were not the eyes of an image.

"Conan or Starke," said Rann, "she's still Beudag, isn't she? All right, I'll tell you. Conan betrayed his people because I put it into his mind to do it. He fought me. He made a good fight of it. But he wasn't quite as tough as you are, Starke."

There was a silence. For the first time since entering the room, Hugh Starke looked at Beudag. After a moment she sighed and lifted her chin and smiled, a deep, faint smile. The guards walked out beside her, but she was more erect and lighter of step than either of them.

"Well," said Rann, when they were gone, "and what about you, Hugh-Starke-Called-Conan."

"Have I any choice?"

"I always keep my bargains."

"Then give me my dough and let me clear the hell out of here."

"Sure that's what you want?"

"That's what I want."

"You could stay awhile, you know."

"With you."

Rann lifted her frosty-white shoulders. "I'm not promising half my kingdom, or even part of it. But you might be amused."

"I got no sense of humor."

"Don't you even want to see what happens to Crom Dhu?"

Starke got up. He said savagely, "The hell with Crom Dhu."

"And Beudag."

"And Beudag." He stopped, then fixed Rann with

uncompromising yellow eyes. "No. Not Beudag. What are you going to do to her?"

"Nothing."

"Don't give me that."

"I say again, nothing. Whatever is done, her own people will do."

"What do you mean?"

"I mean that little Dagger-in-the-Sheath will be rested, cared for, and fattened, for a few days. Then I shall take her aboard my own ship and join the fleet before Crom Dhu. Beudag will be made quite comfortable at the masthead, where her people can see her plainly. She will stay there until the Rock surrenders. It depends on her own people how long she stays. She'll be given water. Not much, but enough."

Starke stared at her. He stared at her a long time. Then he spat deliberately on the floor and said in a perfectly flat voice: "How soon can I get out of here?"

Rann laughed, a small casual chuckle. "Humans," she said, "are so damned queer. I don't think I'll ever understand them." She reached out and struck a gong that stood in a carved frame beside the couch. The soft deep shimmering note had a sad quality of nostalgia. Rann lay back against the silken cushions and sighed.

"Goodbye, Hugh Starke."

A pause. Then, regretfully:

"Goodbye—Conan!"

They had made good time along the rim of the Red Sea. One of Rann's galleys had taken them to the edge of the Southern Ocean and left them on a narrow shingle beach under the cliffs. From there they had climbed to the rimrock and gone on foot—Hugh-Starke-Called-Conan and four of Rann's arrogant shining men. They were supposed to be guide and escort. They were courteous, and they kept pace uncomplainingly though Starke marched as though the devil were pricking his heels. But they were armed, and Starke was not.

Sometimes, very faintly, Starke was aware of Rann's

mind touching his with the velvet delicacy of a cat's paw. Sometimes he started out of his sleep with her image sharp in his mind, her lips touched with the mocking, secret smile. He didn't like that. He didn't like it at all.

But he liked even less the picture that stayed with him waking or sleeping. The picture he wouldn't look at. The picture of a tall woman with hair like loose fire on her neck, walking on light proud feet between her guards.

She'll be given water, Rann said. Not much, but enough.

Starke gripped the solid squareness of the box that held his million credits and set the miles reeling backward from under his sandals.

On the fifth night one of Rann's men spoke quietly across the campfire. "Tomorrow," he said, "we'll reach the pass."

Starke got up and went away by himself, to the edge of the rimrock that fell sheer to the burning sea. He sat down. The red fog wrapped him like a mist of blood. He thought of the blood on Beudag's breast the first time he saw her. He thought of the blood on his knife, crusted and dried. He thought of the blood poured rank and smoking into the gutters of Crom Dhu. The fog has to be red, he thought. Of all the goddam colors in the universe, it has to be red. Red like Beudag's hair.

He held out his hands and looked at them, because he could still feel the silken warmth of that hair against his skin. There was nothing there now but the old white scars of another man's battles.

He set his fists against his temples and wished for his old body back again—the little stunted abortion that had clawed and scratched its way to survival through sheer force of mind. A most damnably tough mind, Rann had said. Yeah. It had had to be tough. But a mind was a mind. It didn't have emotions. It just figured out something coldly and then went ahead and never questioned, and it controlled the body utterly, because the body was only the worthless machinery that carried the mind around. Worthless. Yeah. The few women he'd ever looked at had told him that—and he hadn't even minded much. The old body hadn't given him any trouble.

He was having trouble now.

Starke got up and walked.

Tomorrow we reach the pass.

Tomorrow we go away from the Red Sea. There are nine planets and the whole damn Belt. There are women on all of them. All shapes, colors, and sizes, human, semi-human, and God knows what. With a million credits a guy could buy half of them, and with Conan's body he could buy the rest. What's a woman, anyway? Only a . . .

Water. She'll be given water. Not much, but enough.

Conan reached out and took hold of a spire of rock, and his muscles stood out like knotted ropes. "Oh God," he whispered, "what's the matter with me?"

"Love."

It wasn't God who answered. It was Rann. He saw her plainly in his mind, heard her voice like a silver bell.

"Conan was a man, Hugh Starke. He was whole, body and heart and brain. He knew how to love, and with him it wasn't women, but one woman—and her name was Beudag. I broke him, but it wasn't easy. I can't break you."

Starke stood for a long, long time. He did not move, except that he trembled. Then he took from his belt the box containing his million credits and threw it out as far as he could over the cliff edge. The red mist swallowed it up. He did not hear it strike the surface of the sea. Perhaps in that sea there was no splashing. He did not wait to find out.

He turned back along the rimrock, toward a place where he remembered a cleft, or chimney, leading down. And the four shining men who wore Rann's harness came silently out of the heavy luminous night and ringed him in. Their swordpoints caught sharp red glimmers from the sky.

Starke had nothing on him but a kilt and sandals, and a cloak of tight-woven spider-silk that shed the rain.

"Rann sent you?" he said.

The men nodded.

"To kill me?"

Again they nodded. The blood drained out of Starke's face, leaving it grey and stony under the bronze. His hand went to his throat, over the gold fastening of his cloak.

The four men closed in like dancers.

Starke loosed his cloak and swung it like a whip across their faces. It confused them for a second, for a heartbeat— no more, but long enough. Starke left two of them to tangle their blades in the heavy fabric and leaped aside. A sharp edge slipped and turned along his ribs, and then he had reached in low and caught a man around the ankles, and used the thrashing body for a flail.

The body was strangely light, as though the bones in it were no more than rigid membrane, like a fish.

If he had stayed to fight, they would have finished him in seconds. They were fighting men, and quick. But Starke didn't stay. He gained his moment's grace and used it. They were hard on his heels, their points all but pricking his back as he ran, but he made it. Along the rimrock, out along a narrow tongue that jutted over the sea, and then outward, far outward, into red fog and dim fire that rolled around his plummeting body.

Oh God, he thought, if I guessed wrong and there *is* a beach . . .

The breath tore out of his lungs. His ears cracked, went dead. He held his arms out beyond his head, the thumbs locked together, his neck braced forward against the terrific upward push. He struck the surface of the sea.

There was no splash.

Dim coiling fire that drifted with infinite laziness around him, caressing his body with slow, tingling sparks. A feeling of lightness, as though his flesh had become one with the drifting fire. A sense of suffocation that had no basis in fact and gave way gradually to a strange exhilaration. There was no shock of impact, no crushing pressure. Merely a cushioning softness, like dropping into a bed of compressed air. Starke felt himself turning end over end, pinwheel fashion, and then that stopped, so that he sank quietly and without haste to the bottom.

Or rather, into the crystalline upper reaches of what seemed to be a forest.

He could see it spreading away along the downward-sloping floor of the ocean, into the vague red shadows of distance. Slender fantastic trunks upholding a maze of delicate shining branches, without leaves or fruit. They were like trees exquisitely molded from ice, transparent, holding the lambent shifting fire of the strange sea. Starke didn't think they were, or ever had been, alive. More like coral, he thought, or some vagary of mineral deposit. Beautiful, though. Like something you'd see in a dream. Beautiful, silent, and somehow deadly.

He couldn't explain that feeling of deadliness. Nothing moved in the red drifts between the trunks. It was nothing about the trees themselves. It was just something he sensed.

He began to move among the upper branches, following the downward drop of the slope.

He found that he could swim quite easily. Or perhaps it was more like flying. The dense gas buoyed him up, almost balancing the weight of his body, so that it was easy to swoop along, catching a crystal branch and using it as a lever to throw himself forward to the next one.

He went deeper and deeper into the heart of the forbidden Southern Ocean. Nothing stirred. The fairy forest stretched limitless ahead. And Starke was afraid.

Rann came into his mind abruptly. Her face, clearly outlined, was full of mockery.

"I'm going to watch you die, Hugh-Starke-Called-Conan. But before you die, I'll show you something. Look."

Her face dimmed, and in its place was Crom Dhu rising bleak into the red fog, the longships broken and sunk in the harbor, and Rann's fleet around it in a shining circle.

One ship in particular. The flagship. The vision in Starke's mind rushed toward it, narrowed down to the masthead platform. To the woman who stood there, naked, erect, her body lashed tight with thin cruel cords.

A woman with red hair blowing in the slow wind, and

blue eyes that looked straight ahead like a falcon's, at Crom Dhu.

Beudag.

Rann's laughter ran across the picture and blurred it like a ripple of ice-cold water.

"You'd have done better," she said, "to take the clean steel when I offered it to you."

She was gone, and Starke's mind was as empty and cold as the mind of a corpse. He found that he was standing still, clinging to a branch, his face upturned as though by some blind instinct, his sight blurred.

He had never cried before in all his life, nor prayed.

There was no such thing as time, down there in the smoky shadows of the sea bottom. It might have been minutes or hours later that Hugh Starke discovered he was being hunted.

There were three of them, slipping easily among the shining branches. They were pale golden, almost phosphorescent, about the size of large hounds. Their eyes were huge, jewel-like in their slim, sharp faces. They possessed four members that might have been legs and arms, retracted now against their arrowing bodies. Golden membranes spread wing-like from head to flank, and they moved like wings, balancing expertly the thrust of the flat, powerful tails.

They could have closed in on him easily, but they didn't seem to be in any hurry. Starke had sense enough not to wear himself out trying to get away. He kept on going, watching them. He discovered that the crystal branches could be broken, and he selected himself one with a sharp forked tip, shoving it swordwise under his belt. He didn't suppose it would do much good, but it made him feel better.

He wondered why the things didn't jump him and get it over with. They looked hungry enough, the way they were showing him their teeth. But they kept about the same distance away, in a sort of crescent formation, and every so often the ones on the outside would make a tentative dart at him, then fall back as he swerved away. It wasn't like being hunted so much as . . .

Starke's eyes narrowed. He began suddenly to feel much more afraid than he had before, and he wouldn't have believed that possible.

The things weren't hunting him at all. They were herding him.

There was nothing he could do about it. He tried stopping, and they swooped in and snapped at him, working expertly together so that while he was trying to stab one of them with his clumsy weapon, the others were worrying his heels like sheepdogs at a recalcitrant wether.

Starke, like the wether, bowed to the inevitable and went where he was driven. The golden hounds showed their teeth in animal laughter and sniffed hungrily at the thread of blood he left behind him in the slow red coils of fire.

After a while he heard the music.

It seemed to be some sort of a harp, with a strange quality of vibration in the notes. It wasn't like anything he'd ever heard before. Perhaps the gas of which the sea was composed was an extraordinarily good conductor of sound, with a property of diffusion that made the music seem to come from everywhere at once—softly at first, like something touched upon in a dream, and then, as he drew closer to the source, swelling into a racing, rippling flood of melody that wrapped itself around his nerves with a demoniac shiver of ecstasy.

The golden hounds began to fret with excitement, spreading their shining wings, driving him impatiently faster through the crystal branches.

Starke could feel the vibration growing in him—the very fibres of his muscles shuddering in sympathy with the unearthly harp. He guessed there was a lot of the music he couldn't hear. Too high, too low for his ears to register. But he could feel it.

He began to go faster, not because of the hounds, but because he wanted to. The deep quivering in his flesh excited him. He began to breathe harder, partly because of increased exertion, and some chemical quality of the mixture he breathed made him slightly drunk.

The thrumming harp-song stroked and stung him,

waking a deeper, darker music, and suddenly he saw Beudag clearly—half-veiled and mystic in the candle light at Faolan's dun; smooth curving bronze, her hair loose fire about her throat. A great stab of agony went through him. He called her name, once, and the harp-song swept it up and away, and then suddenly there was no music anymore, and no forest, and nothing but cold embers in Starke's heart.

He could see everything quite clearly in the time it took him to float from the top of the last tree to the floor of the plain. He had no idea how long a time that was. It didn't matter. It was one of those moments when time doesn't have any meaning.

The rim of the forest fell away in a long curve that melted glistening into the spark-shot sea. From it the plain stretched out, a level glassy floor of black obsidian, the spew of some long-dead volcano. Or was it dead? It seemed to Starke that the light here was redder, more vital, as though he were close to the source from which it sprang.

As he looked farther over the plain, the light seemed to coalesce into a shimmering curtain that wavered like the heat veils that dance along the Mercurian Twilight Belt at high noon. For one brief instant he glimpsed a picture on the curtain—a city, black, shining, fantastically turreted, the gigantic reflection of a Titan's dream. Then it was gone, and the immediate menace of the foreground took all of Starke's attention.

He saw the flock, herded by more of the golden hounds. And he saw the shepherd, with the harp held silent between his hands.

The flock moved sluggishly, phosphorescently.

One hundred, two hundred silent, limply floating warriors drifting down the red dimness. In pairs, singly, or in pallid clusters they came. The golden hounds winged silently, leisurely around them, channeling them in tides that sluiced toward the fantastic ebon city.

The shepherd stood, a crop of obsidian, turning his shark-pale face. His sharp, aquamarine eyes found Starke. His silvery hand leaped beckoning over hard-threads, striking them a blow. Reverberations ran out, seized Starke, shook him. He dropped his crystal dagger.

Hot screens of fire exploded in his eyes, bubbles whirled and danced in his eardrums. He lost all muscular control. His dark head fell forward against the thick blackness of hair on his chest; his golden eyes dissolved into weak, inane yellow, and his mouth loosened. He wanted to fight, but it was useless. This shepherd was one of the sea-people he had come to see, and one way or another he would see him.

Dark blood filled his aching eyes. He felt himself led, nudged, forced first this way, then that. A golden hound slipped by, gave him a pressure which roiled him over into a current of sea-blood. It ran down past where the shepherd stood with only a harp for a weapon.

Starke wondered dimly whether these other warriors in the flock, drifting, were dead or alive like himself. He had another surprise coming.

They were all Rann's men. Men of Falga. Silver men with burning green hair. Rann's men. One of them, a huge warrior colored like powdered salt, wandered aimlessly by on another tide, his green eyes dull. He looked dead.

What business had the sea-people with the dead warriors of Falga? Why the hounds and the shepherd's harp? Questions eddied like lifted silt in Starke's tired, hanging head. Eddied and settled flat.

Starke joined the pilgrimage.

The hounds with deft flickerings of wings ushered him into the midst of the flock. Bodies brushed against him. *Cold* bodies. He wanted to cry out. The cords of his neck constricted. In his mind the cry went forward:

"Are you alive, men of Falga?"

No answer; but the drift of scarred, pale bodies. The eyes in them knew nothing. They had forgotten Falga. They had forgotten Rann for whom they had lifted blade. Their tongues lolling in mouths asked nothing but sleep. They were getting it.

A hundred, two hundred strong they made a strange human river slipping toward the gigantic city wall. Starke-

Called-Conan and his bitter enemies going together. From the corners of his eyes, Starke saw the shepherd move. The shepherd was like Rann and her people who had years ago abandoned the sea to live on land. The shepherd seemed colder, more fish-like, though. There were small translucent webs between the thin fingers and spanning the long-toed feet. Thin, scar-like gills in the shadow of his tapered chin lifted and sealed in the current, eating, taking sustenance from the blood-colored sea.

The harp spoke and the golden hounds obeyed. The harp spoke and the bodies twisted uneasily, as in a troubled sleep. A triple chord of it came straight at Starke. His fingers clenched.

"—and the dead shall walk again—"

Another ironic ripple of music.

"—and Rann's men will rise again, this time against her—"

Starke had time to feel a brief, bewildered shivering before the current hurled him forward. Clamoring drunkenly, witlessly, all about him, the dead, muscleless warriors of Falga tried to crush past him, all of them at once . . .

Long ago some vast sea Titan had dreamed of avenues struck from black stone. Each stone the size of three men tall. There had been a dream of walls going up and up until they dissolved into scarlet mist. There had been another dream of sea-gardens in which fish hung like erotic flowers, on tendrils of sensitive film-tissue. Whole beds of fish clung to garden base, like colonies of flowers aglow with sunlight. And on occasion a black amoebic presence filtered by, playing the gardener, weeding out an amber flower here, an ameythystine bloom there.

And the sea Titan had dreamed of endless balustrades and battlements, of windowless turrets where creatures swayed like radium-skinned phantoms, carrying their green plumes of hair in their lifted palms and looked down with curious, insolent eyes from on high. Women with shimmering bodies like some incredible coral harvested and kept high over these black stone streets, each in its archway.

Starke was alone. Falga's warriors had gone off along a dim subterranean vent, vanished. Now the faint beckoning of harp and the golden hounds behind him turned him down a passage that opened out into a large circular stone room, one end of which opened out into a hall. Around the ebon ceiling, slender schools of fish swam. It was their bright effulgence that gave light to the room. They had been there, breeding, eating, dying, a thousand years, giving light to the place, and they would be there, breeding and dying, a thousand more.

The harp faded until it was only a murmur.

Starke found his feet. Strength returned to him. He was able to see the man in the center of the room well. Too well.

The man hung in the fire tide. Chains of wrought bronze held his thin fleshless ankles so he couldn't escape. His body desired it. It floated up.

It had been dead a long time. It was gaseous with decomposition and it wanted to rise to the surface of the Red Sea. The chains prevented this. Its arms weaved like white scarves before a sunken white face. Black hair trembled on end.

He was one of Faolan's men. One of the Rovers. One of those who had gone down at Falga because of Conan.

His name was Geil.

Starke remembered.

The part of him that was Conan remembered the name.

The dead lips moved.

"Conan. What luck is this! Conan. I make you welcome."

The words were cruel, the lips around them loose and dead. It seemed to Starke an anger and embittered wrath lay deep in those hollow eyes. The lips twitched again.

"I went down at Falga for you and Rann, Conan. Remember?"

Part of Starke remembered and twisted in agony.

"We're all here, Conan. All of us. Clev and Mannt and Bron and Aesur. Remember Aesur, who could shape metal over his spine, prying it with his fingers? Aesur is here, big as a sea-monster, waiting in a niche, cold and loose as string. The sea-shepherds collected us. Collected us for a purpose of irony. Look!"

The boneless fingers hung out, as in a wind, pointing.

Starke turned slowly, and his heart pounded an uneven, shattering drum beat. His jaw clinched and his eyes blurred. That part of him that was Conan cried out. Conan was so much of him and he so much of Conan it was impossible for a cleavage. They'd grown together like pearl material around sand-specule, layer on layer. Starke cried out.

In the hall which this circular room overlooked stood a thousand men.

In lines of fifty across, shoulder to shoulder, the men of Crom Dhu stared unseeingly up at Starke. Here and there a face became shockingly familiar. Old memory cried their names.

"Bron! Clev! Mannt! Aesur!"

The collected decomposition of their bodily fluids raised them, drifted them above the flaggings. Each of them was chained, like Geil.

Geil whispered: "We have made a union with the men of Falga!"

Starke pulled back.

"Falga!"

"In death, all men are equals." He took his time with it. He was in no hurry. Dead bodies under-sea are never in a hurry. They sort of bump and drift and bide their time. "The dead serve those who give them a semblance of life. Tomorrow we march against Crom Dhu."

"You're crazy! Crom Dhu is *your* home! It's the place of Beudag and Faolan—"

"And—" interrupted the hanging corpse, quietly, "Conan? Eh?" He laughed. A crystal dribble of bubbles ran up from the slack mouth. "Especially Conan. Conan who sank us at Falga . . ."

Starke moved swiftly. Nobody stopped him. He had the corpse's short blade in an instant. Geil's chest made a cold, silent sheath for it. The blade went like a fork through butter.

Coldly, without noticing this, Geil's voice spoke out:

"Stab me, cut me. You can't kill me any deader. Make sections of me. Play butcher. A flank, a hand, a heart! And while you're at it, I'll tell you the plan."

Snarling, Starke seized the blade out again. With blind violence he gave sharp blow after blow at the body, cursing bitterly, and the body took each blow, rocking in the red tide a little, and said with a matter-of-fact tone:

"We'll march out of the sea to Crom Dhu's gates. Romna and the others, looking down, recognizing us, will have the gates thrown wide to welcome us." The head tilted lazily, the lips peeled wide and folded down languidly over the words. "Think of the elation, Conan! The moment when Bron and Mannt and Aesur and I and yourself, yes, even yourself, Conan, return to Crom Dhu!"

Starke saw it, vividly. Saw it like a tapestry woven for him. He stood back, gasping for breath, his nostrils flaring, seeing what his blade had done to Geil's body, and seeing the great stone gates of Crom Dhu crashing open. The deliberation. The happiness, the elation to Faolan and Romna to see old friends returned. Old Rovers, long thought dead. Alive again, come to help! It made a picture!

With great deliberation, Starke struck flat across before him.

Geil's head, severed from its lazy body, began, with infinite tiredness, to float toward the ceiling. As it traveled upward, now facing, now bobbling the back of its skull toward Starke, it finished its nightmare speaking:

"And then, once inside the gates, what then, Conan? Can you guess? Can you guess what we'll do, Conan?"

Starke stared at nothingness, the sword trembling in his fist. From far away he heard Geil's voice:

"—we will kill Faolan in his hall. He will die with surprised lips. Romna's harp will lie in his disemboweled stomach. His heart with its last pulsings will sound the strings. And as for Beudag—"

Starke tried to push the thoughts away, raging and helpless. Geil's body was no longer anything to look at. He had done all he could to it. Starke's face was bleached white and scraped down to the insane bone of it, "You'd kill your own people!"

Geil's separated head lingered at the ceiling, light-fish illuminating its ghastly features. "Our people? But we have no people? We're another race now. The dead. We do the biddings of the sea-shepherds."

Starke looked out into the hall, then he looked at the circular wall.

"Okay," he said, without tone in his voice. "Come out. Wherever you're hiding and using this voice-throwing act. Come on out and talk straight."

In answer, an entire section of ebon stones fell back on silent hingework. Starke saw a long slender black marble table. Six people sat behind it in carven midnight thrones.

They were all men. Naked except for film-like garments about their loins. They looked at Starke with no particular hatred or curiosity. One of them cradled a harp. It was the shepherd who'd drawn Starke through the gate. Amusedly, his webbed fingers lay on the strings, now and then bringing out a clear sound from one of the two hundred strands.

The shepherd stopped Starke's rush forward with a cry of that harp!

The blade in his hand was red hot. He dropped it.

The shepherd put a head on the story. "And then? And then we will march Rann's dead warriors all the way to Falga. There, Rann's people, seeing the warriors, will be overjoyed, hysterical to find their friends and relatives returned. They, too, will fling wide Falga's defenses. And death will walk in, disguised as resurrection."

Starke nodded, slowly, wiping his hand across his cheek. "Back on Earth we call that psychology. *Good* psychology. But will it fool Rann?"

"Rann will be with her ships at Crom Dhu. While she's gone, the innocent population will let in their lost warriors gladly." The shepherd had amused green eyes. He looked like a youth of some seventeen years. Deceptively young. If Starke guessed right, the youth was nearer to two centuries old. That's how you lived and looked when you were under the

Red Sea. Something about the emanations of it kept part of you young.

Starke lidded his yellow hawks' eyes thoughtfully. "You've got all aces. You'll win. But what's Crom Dhu to you? Why not just Rann? She's one of you, you hate her more than you do the Rovers. Her ancestors came up on land, you never got over hating them for that—"

The shepherd shrugged. "Toward Crom Dhu we have little actual hatred. Except that they are by nature land-men, even if they do rove by boat, and pillagers. One day they might try their luck on the sunken devices of this city."

Starke put a hand out. "We're fighting Rann, too. Don't forget, we're on your side!"

"Whereas we are on no one's," retorted the green-haired youth, "except our own. Welcome to the army which will attack Crom Dhu."

"Me! By the gods, over my dead body!"

"That," said the youth, amusedly, "is what we intend. We've worked many years, you see, to perfect the plan. We're not much good out on land. We needed bodies that could do the work for us. So, every time Faolan lost a ship or Rann lost a ship, we were there, with our golden hounds, waiting. Collecting. Saving. Waiting until we had enough of each side's warriors. They'll do the fighting for us. Oh, not for long, of course. The Source energy will give them a semblance of life, a momentary electrical ability of walk and combat, but once out of water they'll last only half an hour. But that should be time enough once the gates of Crom Dhu and Falga are open."

Starke said, "Rann will find some way around you. Get her first. Attack Crom Dhu the following day."

The youth deliberated. "You're stalling. But there's sense in it. Rann is most important. We'll get Falga first, then. You'll have a bit of time in which to raise false hopes."

Starke began to get sick again. The room swam.

Very quietly, very easily, Rann came into his mind again. He felt her glide in like the merest touch of a sea fern weaving in a tide pool.

He closed his mind down, but not before she snatched at a shred of thought. Her aquamarine eyes reflected desire and inquiry.

"Hugh Starke, you're with the sea-people?"

Her voice was soft. He shook his head.

"Tell me, Hugh Starke. How are you plotting against Falga?"

He said nothing. He thought nothing. He shut his eyes.

Her fingernails glittered, raking at his mind. "Tell me!"

His thoughts rolled tightly into a metal sphere which nothing could dent.

Rann laughed unpleasantly and leaned forward until she filled every dark horizon of his skull with her shimmering body. "All right. I *gave* you Conan's body. Now I'll take it away."

She struck him a combined blow of her eyes, her writhing lips, her bone-sharp teeth. "Go back to your old body, go back to your old body, Hugh Starke," she hissed. "Go back! Leave Conan to his idiocy. Go back to your old body!"

Fear had him. He fell down upon his face, quivering and jerking. You could fight a man with a sword. But how could you fight this thing in your brain? He began to suck sobbing breaths through his lips. He was screaming. He could not hear himself. Her voice rushed in from the dim outer red universe, destroying him.

"Hugh Starke! Go back to your old body!"

His old body was—dead!

And she was sending him back into it.

Part of him shot endwise through red fog.

He lay on a mountain plateau overlooking the harbor of Falga.

Red fog coiled and snaked around him. Flame birds dived eerily down at his staring, blind eyes.

His old body held him.

Putrefaction stuffed his nostrils. The flesh sagged and slipped greasily on his loosened structure. He felt small again and ugly. Flame birds nibbled, picking, choosing between his ribs. Pain gorged him. Cold, blackness, nothingness, filled him. Back in his old body. Forever.

He didn't want that.

The plateau, the red fog, vanished. The flame birds, too. He lay once more on the floor of the sea-shepherds, struggling.

"That was just a start," Rann told him. "Next time, I'll leave you up there on the plateau in that body. *Now*, will you tell the plans of the sea-people? And go on living in Conan? He's yours, if you tell." She smirked. "You don't want to be dead."

Starke tried to reason it out. Any way he turned was the wrong way. He grunted out a breath. "If I tell, you'll still kill Beudag."

"Her life in exchange for what you know, Hugh Starke."

Her answer was too swift. It had the sound of treachery. Starke did not believe. He would die. That would solve it. Then, at last, Rann would die when the sea-people carried out their strategy. That much revenge, at least, damn it.

Then he got the idea.

He coughed out a laugh, raised his weak head to look at the startled sea-shepherd. His little dialogue with Rann had taken about ten seconds, actually, but it had seemed a century. The sea-shepherd stepped forward.

Starke tried to get to his feet. "Got—got a proposition for you. You with the harp. Rann's inside me. *Now*. Unless you guarantee Crom Dhu's and Beudag's safety, I'll tell her some things she might want to be in on!"

The sea-shepherd drew a knife.

Starke shook his head, coldly. "Put it away. Even if you get me I'll give the whole damned strategy to Rann."

The shepherd dropped his hand. He was no fool.

Rann tore at Starke's brain. "Tell me! Tell me their plan!"

He felt like a guy in a revolving door. Starke got the sea men in focus. He saw that they were afraid now, doubtful and nervous. "I'll be dead in a minute," said Starke. "Promise me the safety of Crom Dhu and I'll die without telling Rann a thing."

The sea-shepherd hesitated, then raised his palm upward. "I promise," he said. "Crom Dhu will go untouched."

Starke sighed. He let his head fall forward until it hit the floor. Then he rolled over, put his hands over his eyes. "It's a deal. Go give Rann hell for me, will you, boys? Give her hell!"

As he drifted into mind darkness, Rann waited for him. Feebly, he told her: "Okay, duchess. You'd kill me even if I'd told you the idea. I'm ready. Try your god-awfullest to shove me back into that stinking body of mine. I'll fight you all the way there!"

Rann screamed. It was a pretty frustrated scream. Then the pains began. She did a lot of work on his mind in the next minute.

That part of him that was Conan held on like a clam holding to its precious contents.

The odor of putrid flesh returned. The blood mist returned. The flame birds fell down at him in spirals of sparks and blistering smoke, to winnow his naked ribs.

Starke spoke one last word before the blackness took him.

"Beudag."

He never expected to awaken again.

He awoke just the same.

There was red sea all around him. He lay on a kind of stone bed, and the young sea-shepherd sat beside him, looking down at him, smiling delicately.

Starke did not dare move for a while. He was afraid his head might fall off and whirl away like a big fish, using its ears as propellers. "Lord," he muttered, barely turning his head.

The sea creature stirred. "You won. You fought Rann, and won."

Starke groaned. "I feel like something passed through a wild-cat's intestines. She's gone. Rann's gone." He laughed. "That makes me sad. Somebody cheer me up. Rann's gone." He felt of his big, flat-muscled body. "She was bluffing. Trying to drive me batty. She knew she couldn't really tuck me back into that carcass, but she didn't want me to know. It was like a baby's nightmare before it's born. Or maybe you haven't got a memory like me." He rolled over, stretching. "She won't ever get in my head again. I've locked the gate and swallowed the key." His eyes dilated. "What's *your* name?"

"Linnl," said the man with the harp. "You didn't tell Rann our strategy?"

"What do *you* think?"

Linnl smiled sincerely. "I think I like you, man of Crom Dhu. I think I like your hatred for Rann. I think I like the way you handled the entire matter, wanted to kill Rann and save Crom Dhu, and being so willing to die to accomplish either."

"That's a lot of thinking. Yeah, and what about that promise you made?"

"It will be kept."

Starke gave him a hand. "Linnl, you're okay. If I ever get back to Earth, so help me, I'll never bait a hook again and drop it in the sea." It was lost to Linnl. Starke forgot it, and went on, laughing. There was an edge of hysteria to it. Relief. You got booted around for days, people milled in and out of your mind like it was a bargain basement counter, pawing over the treads and convolutions, yelling and fighting; the woman you loved was starved on a ship masthead, and as a climax a lady with green eyes tried to make you a filling for an accident-mangled body. And now you had an ally.

And you couldn't believe it.

He laughed in little starts and stops, his eyes shut.

"Will you let me take care of Rann when the time comes?"

His fingers groped hungrily upward, closed on an imaginary figure of her, pressed, tightened, choked.

Linnl said, "She's yours. I'd like the pleasure, but you have as much if not more of a revenge to take. Come along. We start now. You've been asleep for one entire period."

Starke let himself down gingerly. He didn't want to break a leg off. He felt if someone touched him he might disintegrate.

He managed to let the tide handle him, do all the work. He swam carefully after Linnl down three passageways where an occasional silver inhabitant of the city slid by.

Drifting below them in a vast square hall, each gravitating but imprisoned by leg-shackles, the warriors of Falga looked up with pale cold eyes at Starke and Linnl. Occasional discharges of light-fish from interstices in the walls passed luminous, fleeting glows over the warriors. The light-fish flirted briefly in a long shining rope that tied knots around the dead faces and as quickly untied them. Then the light-fish pulsed away and the red color of the sea took over.

Bathed in wine, thought Starke, without humor. He leaned forward.

"Men of Falga!"

Linnl plucked a series of harp-threads.

"Aye." A deep suggestion of sound issued from a thousand dead lips.

"We go to sack Rann's citadel!"

"Rann!" came the muffled thunder of voices.

At the sound of another tune, the golden hounds appeared. They touched the chains. The men of Falga, released, danced through the red sea substance.

Siphoned into a valve mouth, they were drawn out into a great volcanic courtyard. Starke went close after. He stared down into a black ravine, at the bottom of which was a blazing caldera.

This was the Source Life of the Red Sea. Here it had begun a millennium ago. Here the savage cyclones of sparks and fire energy belched up, shaking titanic black garden walls, causing currents and whirlpools that threatened to suck you forward and shoot you violently up to the surface, in cannulas of force, thrust, in capillaries of ignited mist, in chutes of color that threatened to cremate but only exhilarated you, gave you a seething rebirth!

He braced his legs and fought the suction. An unbelievable sinew of fire sprang up from out of the ravine, crackling and roaring.

The men of Falga did not fight the attraction.

They moved forward in their silence and hung over the incandescence.

The vitality of the Source grew upward in them. It

seemed to touch their sandaled toes first, and then by a process of shining osmosis climb up the limbs, into the loins, into the vitals, delineating their strong bone structure as mercury delineates the glass thermometer with a rise of temperature. The bones flickered like carved polished ivory through the momentarily film-like flesh. The ribs of a thousand men expanded like silvered spider legs, clenched, then expanded again. Their spines straightened, their shoulders flattened back. Their eyes, the last to take the fire, now were ignited and glowed like candles in refurbished sepulchers. The chins snapped up, the entire outer skins of their bodies broke into silver brilliance.

Swimming through the storm of energy like nightmare figments, entering cold, they reached the far side of the ravine resembling smelted metal from blast furnaces. When they brushed into one another, purple sparks sizzled, jumped from head to head, from hand to hand.

Linnl touched Starke's arm. "You're next."

"No thank you."

"Afraid?" laughed the harp-shepherd. "You're tired. It will give you new life. You're next."

Starke hesitated only a moment. Then he let the tide drift him rapidly out. He was afraid. Damned afraid. A belch of fire caught him as he arrived in the core of the ravine. He was wrapped in layers of ecstasy. Beudag pressed against him. It was her consuming hair that netted him and branded him. It was her warmth that crept up his body into his chest and into his head. Somebody yelled somewhere in animal delight and unbearable passion. Somebody danced and threw out his hands and crushed that solar warmth deeper into his huge body. Somebody felt all tiredness, oldness, flumed away, a whole new feeling of warmth and strength inserted.

That somebody was Starke.

Waiting on the other side of the ravine were a thousand men of Falga. What sounded like a thousand harps began playing now, and as Starke reached the other side, the harps began marching, and the warriors marched with them. They were still dead, but you would never know it. There were no minds inside those bodies. The bodies were being activated from outside. But you would never know it.

They left the city behind. In embering ranks, the soldier-fighters were led by golden hounds and distant harps to a place where a huge intra-coastal tide swept by.

They got on the tide for a free ride. Linnl beside him, using his harp, Starke felt himself sucked down through a deep where strange monsters sprawled. They looked at Starke with hungry eyes. But the harp wall swept them back.

Starke glanced about at the men. They don't know what they're doing, he thought. Going home to kill their parents and their children, to set the flame to Falga, and they don't know it. Their alive-but-dead faces tilted up, always upward, as though visions of Rann's citadel were there.

Rann. Starke let the warmth simmer in him. He let it cool. Then it was cold. Rann hadn't bothered him now for hours. Was there a chance she'd read his thought in the midst of that fighting nightmare? Did she know this plan for Falga? Was that an explanation for her silence now?

He sent his mind ahead, subtly. *Rann. Rann.* The only answer was the move of silver bodies through the fiery deeps.

Just before dawn they broke the surface of the sea.

Falga drowsed in the red-smeared fog silence. Its slave streets were empty and dew-covered. High up, the first light was bathing Rann's gardens and setting her citadel aglow.

Linnl lay in the shallows beside Starke. They both were smiling half-cruel smiles. They had waited long for this.

Linnl nodded. "This is the day of the carnival. Fruit, wine, and love will be offered the returned soldiers of Rann. In the streets there'll be dancing."

Far over to the right lay a rise of mountain. At its blunt peak—Starke stared at it intently—rested a body of a little, scrawny Earthman, with flame birds clustered on it. He'd climb that mountain later. When it was over and there was time.

"What are you searching for?" asked Linnl.

Starke's voice was distant. "Someone I used to know."

Filing out on the stone quays, their rustling sandals

eroded by time, the men stood clean and bright. Starke paced, a caged animal, at their center, so his dark body would pass unnoticed.

They were seen.

The cliff guard looked down over the dirty slave dwellings, from their arrow galleries, and set up a cry. Hands waved, pointed frosty white in the dawn. More guards loped down the ramps and galleries, meeting, joining others and coming on.

Linnl, in the sea by the quay, suggested a theme on the harp. The other harps took it up. The shuddering music lifted from the water and with a gentle firmness set the dead feet marching down the quays, upward through the narrow, stifling alleys of the slaves, to meet the guard.

Slave people peered out at them tiredly from their choked quarters. The passing of warriors was old to them, of no significance.

These warriors carried no weapons. Starke didn't like that part of it. A length of chain even, he wanted. But this emptiness of the hands. His teeth ached from too long a time of clenching his jaws tight. The muscles of his arms were feverish and nervous.

At the edge of the slave community, at the cliff base, the guard confronted them. Running down off the galleries, swords naked, they ran to intercept what they took to be an enemy.

The guards stopped in blank confusion.

A little laugh escaped Starke's lips. It was a dream. With fog over, under, and in between its parts. It wasn't real to the guard, who couldn't believe it. It wasn't real to these dead men either, who were walking around. He felt alone. He was the only live one. He didn't like walking with dead men.

The captain of the guard came down warily, his green eyes suspicious. The suspicion faded. His face fell apart. He had lain on his fur pelts for months thinking of his son who had died to defend Falga.

Now his son stood before him. Alive.

The captain forgot he was captain. He forgot everything.

His sandals scraped over stones. You could hear the air go out of his lungs and come back in in a numbed prayer.

"My son! In Rann's name. They said you were slain by Faolan's men one hundred darknesses ago. My son!"

A harp tinkled somewhere.

The son stepped forward, smiling.

They embraced. The son said nothing. He couldn't speak.

This was the signal for the others. The whole guard, shocked and surprised, put away their swords and sought out old friends, brothers, fathers, uncles, sons!

They moved up the galleries, the guard and the returned warriors, Starke in their midst. Threading up the cliff, through passage after passage, all talking at once. Or so it seemed. The guards did the talking. None of the dead warriors replied. They only *seemed* to. Starke heard the music strong and clear everywhere.

They reached the green gardens atop the cliff. By this time the entire city was awake. Women came running, bare-breasted and sobbing, and throwing themselves forward into the ranks of their lovers. Flowers showered over them.

"So this is war," muttered Starke, uneasily.

They stopped in the center of the great gardens. The crowd milled happily, not yet aware of the strange silence from their men. They were too happy to notice.

"Now," cried Starke to himself. "Now's the time. Now!"

As if in answer, a wild skirling of harps out of the sky.

The crowd stopped laughing only when the returned warriors of Falga swept forward, their hands lifted and groping before them . . .

The crying in the streets was like a far siren wailing. Metal made a harsh clangor that was sheathed in silence at the same moment metal found flesh to lie in. A vicious panto-mime was concluded in the green moist gardens.

Starke watched from Rann's empty citadel. Fog plumes strolled by the archways and a thick rain fell. It came like a blood squall and washed the garden below until you could not tell rain from blood.

The returned warriors had gotten their swords by now. First they killed those nearest them in the celebration. Then they took the weapons from the victims. It was very simple and very unpleasant.

The slaves had joined battle now. Swarming up from the slave town, plucking up fallen daggers and short swords, they circled the gardens, happening upon the arrogant shining warriors of Rann who had so far escaped the quiet, deadly killing of the alive-but-dead men.

Dead father killed startled, alive son. Dead brother garroted unbelieving brother. Carnival indeed in Falga.

An old man waited alone. Starke saw him. The old man had a weapon, but refused to use it. A young warrior of Falga, harped on by Linnl's harp, walked quietly up to the old man. The old man cried out. His mouth formed words. "Son! What *is* this?" He flung down his blade and made to plead with his boy.

The son stabbed him with silent efficiency, and without a glance at the body walked onward to find another.

Starke turned away, sick and cold.

A thousand such scenes were being finished.

He set fire to the black spider-silk tapestries. They whispered and talked with flame. The stone echoed his feet as he searched room after room. Rann had gone, probably last night. That meant that Crom Dhu was on the verge of falling. Was Faolan dead? Had the people of Crom Dhu, seeing Beudag's suffering, given in? Falga's harbor was completely devoid of ships, except for small fishing skiffs.

The fog awaited him when he returned to the garden. Rain found his face.

The citadel of Rann was fire-encrusted and smoke shrouded as he looked up at it.

A silence lay in the garden. The fight was over.

The men of Falga, still shining with Source Life, hung their blades from uncomprehending fingers, the light beginning to leave their green eyes. Their skin looked dirty and dull.

Starke wasted no time getting down the galleries,

through the slave quarter, and to the quays again.

Linnl awaited him, gently petting the obedient harp.

"It's over. The slaves will own what's left. They'll be our allies, since we've freed them."

Starke didn't hear. He was squinting off over the Red Sea.

Linnl understood. He plucked two tones from the harp, which pronounced the two words uppermost in Starke's thought.

"Crom Dhu."

"If we're not too late." Starke leaned forward. "If Faolan lives. If Beudag still stands at the masthead."

Like a blind man he walked straight ahead, until he fell into the sea.

It was not quite a million miles to Crom Dhu. It only seemed that far.

A sweep of tide picked them up just off shore from Falga and siphoned them rapidly, through deeps along coastal latitudes, through crystal forests. He cursed every mile of the way.

He cursed the time it took to pause at the Titan's city to gather fresh men. To gather Clev and Mannt and Aesur and Brucc. Impatiently, Starke watched the whole drama of the Source Fire and the bodies again. This time it was the bodies of Crom Dhu men, hung like beasts on slow-turned spits, their limbs and vitals soaking through and through, their skins taking bronze color, their eyes holding flint-sparks. And then the harps wove a garment around each, and the garment moved the men instead of the men the garment.

In the tidal basilic now, Starke twisted. Coursing behind him were the new bodies of Clev and Aesur! The current elevated them, poked them through obsidian needle-eyes like spider-silk threads.

There was good irony in this. Crom Dhu's men, fallen at Falga under Conan's treachery, returned now under Conan, to exonerate that treachery.

Suddenly they were in Crom Dhu's outer basin. Shadows swept over them. The long dark falling shadows of Falga's longboats lying in that harbor. Shadows like black culling-nets let down. The school of men cleaved the shadow nets. The tide ceased here, eddied and distilled them.

Starke glared up at the immense silver bottom of a Falgian ship. He felt his face stiffen and his throat tighten. Then, flexing knees, he rammed upward, night air broke dark red around his head.

The harbor held flare torches on the rims of long ships. On the neck of land that led from Crom Dhu to the mainland the continuing battle sounded. Faint cries and clashing made their way through the fog veils. They sounded like echoes of past dreams.

Linnl let Starke have the leash. Starke felt something pressed into his fist. A coil of slender green woven reeds, a rope with hooked weights on the end of it. He knew how to use it without asking. But he wished for a knife, now, even though he realized carrying a knife in the sea was all but impossible if you wanted to move fast.

He saw the sleek naked figurehead of Rann's best ship a hundred yards away, a floating silhouette, its torches hanging fire like Beudag's hair.

He swam toward it, breathing quietly. When at last the silvered figurehead with the mocking green eyes and the flag of shoal-shallow hair hung over him, he felt the cool white ship metal kiss his fingers.

The smell of torch-smoke lingered. A rise of faint shouts from the land told of another rush upon the Gate. Behind him—a ripple. Then—a thousand ripples.

The resurrected men of Crom Dhu rose in dents and stirrings of sparkling wine. They stared at Crom Dhu and maybe they knew what it was and maybe they didn't. For one moment, Starke felt apprehension. Suppose Linnl was playing a game. Suppose, once these men had won the battle, they went on into Crom Dhu, to rupture Romna's harp and make Faolan the blinder? He shook the thought away. That would have to be handled in time. On either side of him Clev and Mannt appeared. They looked at Crom Dhu, their lips shut. Maybe they saw Faolan's eyrie and heard a harp that was more

than these harps that sang them to blade and plunder—
Romna's instrument telling bard-tales of the Rovers and the
coastal wars and the old living days. Their eyes looked and
looked at Crom Dhu, but saw nothing.

The sea-shepherds appeared now; the followers of Linnl,
each with his harp, and the harp music began, high. So high
you couldn't hear it. It wove a tension on the air.

Silently, with a grim certainty, the dead-but-not-dead
gathered in a bronze circle about Rann's ship. The very
silence of their encirclement made your skin crawl and sweat
break cold on your cheeks.

A dozen ropes went raveling, looping over the ship side.
They caught, held, grapnelled, hooked.

Starke had thrown his, felt it bite and hold. Now he
scrambled swiftly, cursing, up its length, kicking and slipping
at the silver hull.

He reached the top.

Beudag was there.

Half over the low rail he hesitated, just looking at her.

Torchlight limned her, shadowed her. She was still erect;
her head was tired and her eyes were closed, her face thinned
and less brown, but she was still alive. She was coming out of
a deep stupor now, at the whistle of ropes and the grate of
metal hooks on the deck.

She saw Starke and her lips parted. She did not look away
from him. His breath came out of him, choking.

It almost cost him his life, his standing there, looking at
her.

A guard, with flesh like new snow, shafted his bow from
the turret and let it loose. A chain lay on deck. Thankfully,
Starke took it.

Clev came over the rail beside Starke. His chest took the
arrow. The shaft burst half through and stopped, held. Clev
kept going after the man who had shot it. He caught up with
him.

Beudag cried out: "Behind you, Conan!"

Conan! In her excitement, she gave the old name.

Conan he *was*. Whirling, he confronted a wiry little
fellow, chained him brutally across the face, seized the man's

falling sword, used it on him. Then he walked in, got the man's jaw, unbalanced him over into the sea.

The ship was awake now. Most of the men had been down below, resting from the battles. Now they came pouring up, in a silver spate. Their yelling was in strange contrast to the calm silence of Crom Dhu's men. Starke found himself busy.

Conan had been a healthy animal, with great recuperative powers. Now his muscles responded to every trick asked of them. Starke leaped cleanly across the deck, watching for Rann, but she was nowhere to be seen. He engaged two blades, dispatched one of them. More ropes raveled high and snaked him. Every ship in the harbor was exploding with violence. More men swarmed over the rail behind Starke, silently.

Above the shouting, Beudag's voice came, at sight of the fighting men. "Clev! Mannt! Aesur!"

Starke was a god, anything he wanted he could have. A man's head? He could have it. It meant acting the guillotine with knife and wrist and lunged body. Like—*this!* His eyes were smoking amber and there were deep lines of grim pleasure tugging at his lips. An enemy cannot fight without hands. One man, facing Starke, suddenly displayed violent stumps before his face, not believing them.

Are you watching, Faolan, cried Starke inside himself, delivering blows. Look here, Faolan! God, no, you're blind. *Listen* then! Hear the ring of steel on steel. Does the smell of hot blood and hot bodies reach you? Oh, if you could see this tonight, Faolan. Falga would be forgotten. This is Conan, out of idiocy, with a guy named Starke wearing him and telling him where to go!

It was not safe on deck. Starke hadn't particularly noticed before, but the warriors of Crom Dhu didn't care whom they attacked now. They were beginning to do surgery to one another. They excised one another's shoulders, severed limbs in blind instantaneous obedience. This was no place for Beudag and himself.

He cut her free of the masthead, drew her quickly to the rail.

Beudag was laughing. She could do nothing but laugh. Her eyes were shocked. She saw dead men alive again, lashing out with weapons; she had been starved and made to stand night and day, and now she could only laugh.

Starke shook her.

She did not stop laughing.

"Beudag! You're all right. You're free."

She stared at nothing. "I'll—I'll be all right in a minute."

He had to ward off a blow from one of his own men. He parried the thrust, then got in and pushed the man off the deck, over into the sea. That was the only thing to do. You couldn't kill them.

Beudag stared down at the tumbling body.

"Where's Rann?" Starke's yellow eyes narrowed, searching.

"She *was* here." Beudag trembled.

Rann looked out of her eyes. Out of the tired numbness of Beudag, an echo of Rann. Rann was nearby, and this was her doing.

Instinctively, Starke raised his eyes.

Rann appeared at the masthead, like a flurry of snow. Her green-tipped breasts were rising and falling with emotion. Pure hatred lay in her eyes. Starke licked his lips and readied his sword.

Rann snapped a glance at Beudag. Stooping, as in a dream, Beudag picked up a dagger and held it to her own breast.

Starke froze.

Rann nodded, with satisfaction. "Well, Starke? How will it be? Will you come at me and have Beudag die? Or will you let me go free?"

Starke's palms felt sweaty and greasy. "There's no place for you to go. Falga's taken. I can't guarantee your freedom. If you want to go over the side, into the sea, that's your chance. You might make shore and your own men."

"Swimming? With the sea-*beasts* waiting?" She accented the *beasts* heavily. She was one of the sea-*people*. They, Linnl and his men, were sea-*beasts*. "No, Hugh Starke. I'll take a skiff. Put Beudag at the rail where I can watch her all the way. Guarantee my passage to shore and my own men there, and Beudag lives."

Starke waved his sword. "Get going."

He didn't want to let her go. He had other plans, good plans for her. He shouted the deal down at Linnl. Linnl nodded back, with much reluctance.

Rann, in a small silver skiff, headed toward land. She handled the boat and looked back at Beudag all the while. She passed through the sea-beasts and touched the shore. She lifted her hand and brought it smashing down.

Whirling, Starke swung his fist against Beudag's jaw. Her hand was already striking the blade into her breast. Her head flopped back. His fist carried through. She fell. The blade clattered. He kicked it overboard. Then he lifted Beudag. She was warm and good to hold. The blade had only pricked her breast. A small rivulet of blood ran.

On the shore, Rann vanished upward on the rocks, hurrying to find her men.

In the harbor the harp music paused. The ships were taken. Their crews lay filling the decks. Crom Dhu's men stopped fighting as quickly as they'd started. Some of the bright shining had dulled from the bronze of their arms and bare torsos. The ships began to sink.

Linnl swam below, looking up at Starke. Starke looked back at him and nodded at the beach. "Swell. Now, let's go get that she-devil," he said.

Faolan waited on his great stone balcony, overlooking Crom Dhu. Behind him the fires blazed high and their eating sound of flame on wood filled the pillared gloom with sound and furious light.

Faolan leaned against the rim, his chest swathed in bandage and healing ointment, his blind eyes flickering, looking down again and again with a fixed intensity, his head tilted to listen.

Romna stood beside him, filled and refilled the cup that

Faolan emptied into his thirsty mouth, and told him what happened. Told of the men pouring out of the sea, and Rann appearing on the rocky shore. Sometimes Faolan leaned to one side, weakly, toward Romna's words. Sometimes he twisted to hear the thing itself, the thing that happened down beyond the Gate of besieged Falga.

Romna's harp lay untouched. He didn't play it. He didn't need to. From below, a great echoing of harps, more liquid than his, like a waterfall drenched the city, making the fog sob down red tears.

"Are those harps?" cried Faolan.

"Yes, harps!"

"What was that?" Faolan listened, breathing harshly, clutching for support.

"A skirmish," said Romna.

"Who won?"

"*We* won."

"And *that?*" Faolan's blind eyes tried to see until they watered.

"The enemy falling back from the Gate!"

"And that sound, and that sound!" Faolan went on and on, feverishly, turning this way and that, the lines of his face agonized and attentive to each eddy and current and change of tide. The rhythm of swords through fog and body was a complicated music whose themes he must recognize. "Another fell! I heard him cry. And another of Rann's men!"

"Yes," said Romna.

"But why do our warriors fight so quietly? I've heard nothing from their lips. So quiet."

Romna scowled. "Quiet. Yes—quiet."

"And where did they come from? All our men are in the city?"

"Aye." Romna shifted. He hesitated, squinting. He rubbed his bulldog jaw. "Except those that died at—Falga."

Faolan stood there a moment. Then he rapped his empty cup.

"More wine, bard. More wine."

He turned to the battle again.

"Oh, gods, if I could see it, if I could only see it!"

Below, a ringing crash. A silence. A shouting, a pouring of noise.

"The Gate!" Faolan was stricken with fear. "We've lost! My sword!"

"Stay, Faolan!" Romna laughed. Then he sighed. It was a sigh that did not believe. "In the name of ten thousand mighty gods. Would that I were blind now, or could see better."

Faolan's hand caught, held him. "What *is* it? Tell!"

"Clev! And Tlan! And Conan! And Brucc! And Mannt! Standing in the gate, like wine visions! Swords in their hands!"

Faolan's hand relaxed, then tightened. "Speak their names again, and speak them slowly. And tell the truth." His skin shivered like that of a nervous animal. "You said—Clev? Mannt? Brucc?"

"And Tlan! And Conan! Back from Falga. They've opened the Gate and the battle's won. It's over, Faolan. Crom Dhu will sleep tonight."

Faolan let him go. A sob broke from his lips. "I will get drunk. Drunker than ever in my life. Gloriously drunk. Gods, but if I could have seen it. Been in it. Tell me again of it, Romna . . ."

Faolan sat in the great hall, on his carved high-seat, waiting.

The pad of sandals on stone, outside, the jangle of chains.

A door flung wide, red fog sluiced in, and in the sluice, people walking. Faolan started up. "Clev? Mannt? Aesur!"

Starke came forward into the fire-light. He pressed his right hand to the open wound on his thigh. "No, Faolan. Myself and two others."

"Beudag?"

"Yes." And Beudag came wearily to him.

Faolan stared. "Who's the other? It walks light. It's a woman."

Starke nodded. "Rann."

Faolan rose carefully from his seat. He thought the name

over. He took a short sword from a place beside the high-seat. He stepped down. He walked toward Starke. "You brought Rann alive to me?"

Starke pulled the chain that bound Rann. She ran forward in little steps, her white face down, her eyes slitted with animal fury.

"Faolan's blind," said Starke. "I let you live for one damned good reason, Rann. Okay, go ahead."

Faolan stopped walking, curious. He waited.

Rann did nothing.

Starke took her hand and wrenched it behind her back. "I said 'go ahead.' Maybe you didn't hear me."

"I will," she gasped, in pain.

Starke released her. "Tell me what happens, Faolan."

Rann gazed steadily at Faolan's tall figure there in the light.

Faolan suddenly threw his hands to his eyes and choked.

Beudag cried out, seized his arm.

"I can see!" Faolan staggered, as if jolted. "I can see!" First he shouted it, then he whispered it. *"I can see."*

Starke's eyes blurred. He whispered to Rann, tightly. "Make him see it, Rann, or you die now. Make him see it!" To Faolan: "What do you see?"

Faolan was bewildered, he swayed. He put out his hands to shape the vision. "I—I see Crom Dhu. It's a good sight. I see the ships of Rann. Sinking!" He laughed a broken laugh. "I—see the fight beyond the Gate!"

Silence swam in the room, over their heads.

Faolan's voice went alone, and hypnotized, into that silence.

He put out his big fists, shook them, opened them. "I see Mannt, and Aesur and Clev! Fighting as they always fought. I see Conan as he was. I see Beudag wielding steel again, on the shore! I see the enemy killed! I see men pouring out of the sea with brown skins and dark hair. Men I knew a long darkness ago. Men that roved the sea with me. *I see Rann captured!*" He began to sob with it, his lungs filling and releasing it, sucking in on it, blowing it out. Tears ran down from his vacant, blazing eyes. "I see Crom Dhu as it was and is and shall be! *I see, I see, I see!*"

Starke felt the chill on the back of his neck.

"I see Rann captured and held, and her men dead around her on the land before the Gate. I see the Gate thrown open—" Faolan halted. He looked at Starke. "Where are Clev and Mannt? Where are Brucc and Aesur?"

Starke let the fires burn on the hearths a long moment. Then he replied.

"They went back into the sea, Faolan."

Faolan's fingers fell emptily. "Yes," he said, heavily. "They had to go back, didn't they? They couldn't stay, could they? Not even for one night of food on the table, and wine in the mouth, and women in the deep warm furs before the hearth. Not even for one toast." He turned. "A drink, Romna. A drink for everyone."

Romna gave him a full cup. He dropped it, fell down to his knees, clawed at his breasts. "My heart!"

"Rann, you sea-devil!"

Starke held her instantly by the throat. He put pressure on the small raging pulses on either side of her snow-white neck. "Let him go, Rann!" More pressure, *"Let him go!"* Faolan grunted. Starke held her until her white face was dirty and strange with death.

It seemed like an hour later when he released her. She fell softly and did not move. She wouldn't move again.

Starke turned slowly to look at Faolan.

"You saw, didn't you, Faolan?" he said.

Faolan nodded blindly, weakly. He roused himself from the floor, groping. "I saw. For a moment, I saw everything. And Gods! but it made good seeing! Here, Hugh-Starke-Called-Conan, give this other side of me something to lean on."

Beudag and Starke climbed the mountain above Falga the next day. Starke went ahead a little way, and with his coming the flame birds scattered, glittering away.

He dug the shallow grave and did what had to be done

with the body he found there, and then when the grave was covered with thick grey stones he went back for Beudag. They stood together over it. He had never expected to stand over a part of himself, but here he was, and Beudag's hand gripped his.

He looked suddenly a million years old standing there. He thought of Earth and the Belt and Jupiter, of the joy streets in the Jekkara Low Canals of Mars. He thought of space and the ships going through it, and himself inside them. He thought of the million credits he had taken in that last job. He laughed ironically.

"Tomorrow, I'll have the sea creatures hunt for a little metal box full of credits." He nodded solemnly at the grave. "He wanted that. Or at least he thought. He killed himself getting it. So if the sea-people find it, I'll send it up here to the mountain and bury it down under the rocks in his fingers. I guess that's the best place."

Beudag drew him away. They walked down the mountain toward Falga's harbor where a ship waited them. Walking, Starke lifted his face. Beudag was with him, and the sails of the ship were rising to take the wind, and the Red Sea waited for them to travel it. What lay on its far side was something for Beudag and Faolan-of-the-Ships and Romna and Hugh-Starke-Called-Conan to discover. He felt damned good about it. He walked on steadily, holding Beudag near.

And on the mountain, as the ship sailed, the flame birds soared down fitfully and frustratedly to beat at the stone mound; ceased, and mourning shrilly, flew away.

IV.

MANLY WADE WELLMAN

INTRODUCTION

Manly Wade Wellman is best remembered for his haunting fantasies of the Southern Appalachians—particularly those stories concerning his unique character, John, a wandering balladeer who encountered and conquered supernatural evil with the aid of his native wit and a guitar with silver strings. A versatile and prolific author with more than eighty books and over three hundred short stories, Wellman wrote in almost every field—science fiction, Civil War biography, mystery, young adult novels, fantasy, regional histories, mainstream novels, folklore—and won awards in many of these genres. It will nonetheless come as a surprise to most of his fans to learn that Wellman also had a lifelong interest in writing heroic fantasy.

Born May 21, 1903 in the village of Kamundongo in Portuguese West Africa, it is not surprising that Wellman's first published story was a tale of African adventure, "When the Lion Roared," which appeared in the May 1927 issue of *Thrilling Tales* (where he was billed as "The King of Jungle Fiction"). From childhood on Wellman had a fondness for tales of rousing adventure in exotic locales, as well as a fascination with stories and studies of prehistoric mankind. This interest carried through when he became a full-time writer in the early 1930's, at which time Wellman tried unsuccessfully to market two heroic fantasy series.

One of these centered about a likeable rogue named Kardios, the sole survivor (and hapless instigator) of the sinking of Atlantis. While Wellman devoted considerable energy to organizing this series, it was rejected by *Weird Tales* editor, Farnsworth Wright, on the basis that a young writer named Robert E. Howard was already writing as much of this sort of thing as the magazine needed. Wellman abandoned Kardios, but never forgot him, and the series was at last published beginning in 1977 in Andrew J. Offutt's *Swords Against Darkness* series and in other such original anthologies of heroic fantasy.

The other series concerned Hok, a mighty Stone Age warrior who would defeat the Neanderthal hordes, invent the bow, forge the first iron sword, visit Atlantis, and have many other adventures in the Dawn Age. Wellman portrayed Hok as the basis of the legends of Hercules, arguing that a super-strong, skin-clad barbarian whose chief weapon was a club hardly fit in with the usual heroes of Greek mythology. Hok was, therefore, mankind's first great hero—his legend preserved but imperfectly remembered and adapted to suit later myth cycles.

Wellman's first Hok story was a fumbling attempt entitled "The Love of Oloana." In 1935 this story enjoyed the dubious distinction of being rejected by the likes of *Spicy-Adventure Stories,* after which it remained dormant in Wellman's files until after his death. The story at last saw print in 1986 in Robert M. Price's pulp-oriented fanzine, *Pulse Pounding Adventure Stories.* Wellman, however, had faith in his creation, and a few years later Hok and his mate Oloana were to triumph in more polished adventures in one of the major science fiction magazines of the day.

Hok's real debut was in the January 1939 issue of *Amazing Stories* with "Battle in the Dawn," in which Hok banded together the Stone Age tribes to battle Neanderthal man for ultimate supremacy on the planet. The series was well received in *Amazing Stories* and was followed by "Hok Goes to Atlantis" (December 1939), "Hok Draws the Bow" (May 1940), and "Hok and the Gift of Heaven" (March 1941). A final Hok story, "Hok Visits the Land of Legends," appeared in the April 1942 issue of *Amazing Stories'* companion magazine, *Fantastic Adventures.*

While the Hok stories suffer today from Wellman's naive characterizations and pulp-formula plotting, they retain the gusto and energy with which they were written. Wellman was then in his vigorous thirties, writing prolifically for most pulp markets, and Hok was a creative outlet for his keen interest in prehistoric man. This last can be seen in the "editorial" footnotes with which Wellman embellished the Hok stories. As *Amazing Stories* was a science fiction pulp, this was an attempt to infuse a certain scientific verisimilitude, although the result instead adds a distinctly campy charm.

Wellman always maintained that the 1940 film, *One Million B.C.,* with Victor Mature and Carole Landis as the Stone Age lovers, was stolen from his Hok stories. A reading of the pre-film stories and a viewing of the film, however, simply will not bear this out beyond a few circumstantial similarities. The film was remade in 1966 as *One Million Years B.C.,* with John Richardson and Raquel Welch as the stars. Recent major films dealing with Stone Age mankind run the gamut from *Caveman* to *Quest for Fire* to *The Clan of the Cave Bear.*

While such films and novels reflect our continued fascination with prehistoric man, the Hok stories have faded from memory. Four were reprinted in *Fantastic* between 1967 and 1970—without authorization or payment. In the early 1970s an equally honest amateur publisher planned to collect the stories as a book, but the project was abandoned.

But Wellman still had another tale to spin about Hok. In the last few months of his active life, he talked frequently about plans for a new Hok story—one in which Hok was to hunt a mysterious white mammoth. Shortly after completing what was to be his final story (a John tale entitled "Where Did She Wander?"), Wellman began work on the Hok story.

He typed the first page, penned in a few revisions, then inserted the second page into his typewriter. He typed in the numeral 2, then left his desk never to return. A crippling fall that day and a seemingly endless series of horrid medical complications in the months to follow finally ended Wellman's life on April 5, 1986.

So here's Hok in his prime from the Golden Age of the pulps. And here's the untitled fragment of what was to have been a new Hok story.

Writers die. Heroes die. Legends live on.

HOK VISITS THE LAND OF LEGENDS

by *Manly Wade Wellman*

Only Hok could have done it—only Hok the Mighty, strongest and wisest and bravest of the Flint Folk whose chief he was. For Gragru the mammoth was in those days the noblest of all beasts hunted by man—to bring one down was an enterprise for the combined hunter-strength of a tribe. Save for Hok, no man would even think of killing Gragru single-handed.

But Hok had so thought. And for Hok, to think was to do. When winter's heaviest snow had choked the meadows and woods that Hok's people had won by battle from the half-beastly Gnorrls, he put his plan into action.

Not that food was scarce. A late flight of geese had dropped floundering on the frozen river before the village of mud huts, and Hok's sturdy young son Ptao had led the other children to seize them. Hok's brother Zhik had traced a herd of elk to their stamped-out clearing in a willow thicket, and was planning a raid thither. But Hok's big blond head far distances of the spirit. Already he thought of such game as trivial.

On a cloudy gray day, not too cold, he spoke from his cave-door in the bluff above the huts. "I go on a lone hunt," he told the tribe. "It will be several days, perhaps, before I return. In my absence, Zhik is your chief." Then he gave his handsome wife Oloana a rib-buckling hug, and told young Ptao to grow in his absence. He departed along the river trail, heading south for mammoth country.

His big, tall body was dressed in fur from throat to toe. His long shanks wore tight-wound wolfskin leggings, fur inside. His moccasins, of twofold bison leather, had tops reaching almost to his knees, and were plentifully tallowed against wet. His body was wrapped in the pelt of a cave-lion, arms fitting inside the neatly skinned forelegs, mane muffling his neck and chest. Fox-fur gloves protected his hands. All openings and laps were drawn snug by leather laces. Only his great head, with golden clouds of hair and beard, was defiantly bare to winter.

Leaving the village, Hok paused to strap his feet into rough snowshoes.* The Flint Folk had developed such things by watching how nature made broad the feet of hare, ptarmigan and lynx to glide on top of the snow. Hok's weapons were a big bow of yew, a quiver of arrows, a big keen axe of blue flint. At his side hung a sizable deerskin pouch, full of hunter's gear and provisions.

Away he tramped, his blue eyes scanning the horizon. Far off was a black bison, snow-swamped, with wolves closing in. Nearer, gaunt ravens sawed over a frost-killed deer. Winter was the hungry season—eat or be eaten was its byword. Hok's people would eat plentifully of Gragru's carcass . . . Hok journeyed west and south, to where he had once noted a grove of pine and juniper.

It was all of a morning and part of the afternoon before Hok reached the grove. He smiled over nearby mammoth tracks, large enough for him to curl up in. The prey had been there. It would return. He began preparations.

---

*Professor Katherine E. Dopp and others have pointed out the absolute necessity for the invention of snowshoes by Stone Age hunters of Hok's time.—Ed.

He set up headquarters in the center of the grove, scooping out a den in the snow and laying branches above it for roof. His bow and arrows he hung to a big pine trunk, away from damp. Then, axe in hand, he sought out a springy red cedar, felled it and trimmed away the branches. Dragging it to his camp, Hok laboriously hewed and whittled it into a great bow-stave, twice as long as himself and thicker at the midpoint than his brawny calf, with the two ends properly tapered.

Bending the bow was a task for even Hok. From his bag he took a great coil of rawhide rope, several strands thick. With a length of this he lashed the bow horizontally to the big pine. To each end he fastened a second line, making this fast to a tree behind. After that, he toiled to bend one arm, then the other, using all his braced strength and weight and shortening each lashing. The stout cedar bent little by little into a considerable curve.

Next Hok affixed his bowstring of rawhide, first soaking it in slush. When it was as tight as he could make it, he lighted a row of fires near it. As the string dried and shrank in the heat, the bow bent still more.

Meanwhile, Hok was cutting an arrow to fit that bow, a pine sapling thrice the length of his leg. From his pouch he produced a flint point longer than his foot, flaked to a narrow, sharp apex. This he lashed into the split tip, and with his axe chopped a notch in the opposite butt. The finished arrow he laid across his big bow.

"My weapon is ready to draw for killing," he said with satisfaction, and put himself to new toil. A lashing of rope held the arrow notched on the string, and Hok carried the end of this new lashing backward, around a stump directly to the rear. With braced feet, swelling muscles, panting chest, he heaved and slaved and outdid himself until the bow was drawn to the fullest and his pull-rope hitched firmly to the anchorage. He stepped back and proudly surveyed the finished work. "Good!" he approved himself.

He had made and drawn a bow for such a giant as his old mother had spoken of, long ago in his childhood. The big pine to which the bow was bound stood for the archer's rigid gripping hand. The back-stretched rope from the arrow's notch was the drawing hand. All that was needed would be a target in front of it.

And Hok arranged for that.

He cut young, green juniper boughs and made two heaps, three strides apart, so that the arrow pointed midway between them. Then he hacked away branches and bushes that might interfere with the shaft's flight. It was evening by now. He built up his fire behind the drawn bow, toasted a bit of meat from his pouch, and finally slept.

At dawn he woke. Snow was falling. Hok rose and gazed along the little lane in front of the arrow.

There came the prey he hoped for.

Gragru the mammoth, tremendous beyond imagination, marched with heavy dignity to the enticing breakfast Hok had set him. A hillock of red-black hair, more than twice Hok's height at the shoulder,* he sprouted great spiral tusks of creamy ivory, each a weight for several men. His head, a hairy boulder, had a high cranium and small, wise eyes. His long, clever trunk sniffed at one stack of juniper, and began to convey it to his mouth.**

Hok drew his keen dagger of reindeer horn. The mammoth gobbled on, finished the first stack, then swung across to the second.

Hok squinted a last time along the arrow. It aimed at the exact point he had hoped—the hair-thatched flank of the beast. Hok set his knife to the draw-rope—sliced the strands—

Honng! With a whoop of freed strength, the bow hurled its shaft. A heavy thud rang back, and Gragru trumpeted in startled pain.

"You are my meat!" yelled Hok.

---

*This was a specimen of the Imperial Mammoth, which stood some 14 feet high. Partial remains of such a giant can be seen at the National Museum of Natural History in New York City.—Ed.

**Examination of the stomachs of frozen mammoth remains has enabled scientists to decide on juniper as a favorite article of their winter diet.—Ed.

Gragru wheeled and charged the voice. Hok caught his bow and arrows from their hanging place, gathered the snowshoes under his arm, and danced nimbly aside. "I shot you!" he cried again. "I, Hok!"

Blundering through the brush, Gragru looked right and left for his enemy; but Hok had sagely trotted around behind him. A savage exploration of the thicket, to no avail—then Gragru sought the open again. His blood streamed from wounds on either side where the pine-shaft transfixed him, but he still stood steady on his great tree-stump feet.

Hok came to the fringe of the junipers. "You shall not escape!" he yelled at the mammoth. "Hok will eat you!"

This time Gragru did not charge. He knew that death had smitten through hair and hide and bone, to the center of his lungs. No time left for combat or revenge—time only for one thing, the thing that every mammoth must do in his last hour . . .

He turned and struggled away southward through the snow.

Hok watched. He remembered the stories of his fathers.

"Gragru seeks the dying place of the mammoth, the tomb of his people, that no man has ever seen or found.* I shall follow him to that place—learn the secret and mystery of where the mammoth goes to die!"

Quickly he bound on his snowshoes, gained the top of the drifts, and forged away after Gragru, now a diminishing brown blotch in the middle distance.

---

*A similar legend is told about modern elephants and their "graveyard"— it is a fact that bodies of naturally dead elephants are seldom seen. The great beds of mammoth fossils in Russia, from which as much as 100,000 pounds of ivory was gleaned annually in pre-Soviet times, may bear out Hok's belief.—Ed.

CHAPTER II

Where Gragru Died

Even the elephant, degenerate modern nephew of Gragru's race, can outrun a good horse on a sprint or a day's march; and the beast Hok now followed was among the largest and most enduring of his kind. Despite the wound, the shaft in his body, and the deep snow, Gragru ploughed ahead faster than Hok's best pace.

The tall chieftain, however, had a plain trail to follow—a deep rut in the snow, with splotches and spatters of blood. "Gragru shall not escape," he promised himself, and mended his stride. The rising wind, bearing more snowflakes, blew at his wide shoulders and helped him along. Ahead was a ravine, its central watercourse many men's height deep under old snows. Gragru sagely churned along one slope, into country more than a day's journey from Hok's village. Hok had hunted there only a few times.

They travelled thus, hunter and hunted, all morning and all afternoon. Evening came, and Hok did not pause for a campfire, but gnawed a strip of dried meat as he marched. His longest pause was to melt snow between his ungloved hands for drink. Then on into the dusk. The clouds broke a little, and the light of a half-moon showed him the trail of Gragru.

With the coming of night he heard the howl of winter-famished wolves behind. They were hunting him, of course.* The safety of a tree, or at least a rock-face to defend his back,

*Hok's people were contemporary with *Cyon alpinis fossilis*, a species of wolf larger and stronger, and probably fiercer, than modern types. Such hunting animals must have had to pursue and drag down the powerful game of the age, and would not have shrunk too much from combat with man. At least once among the remarkable art-works of Stone Age man is included a painting of a wolf—a lifelike polychrome on the wall of the cavern at Font-de-Gaume, once the home and art studio of a community of the magnificent Cro-Magnons, Hok's race.—Ed.

was the dictate of discretion; but Hok very seldom was discreet. He paused only long enough to cut a straight shoot of ash, rather longer than himself. Then, resuming his journey, he whittled it to a point with his deerhorn knife. This improvised stabbing spear he carried in his right hand, point backward.

The howling chorus of the wolves came nearer, stronger. It rose to a fiendish din as they sighted Hok. He judged that there were five or six, lean and savage. Without slacking his pace, he kept a watch from the tail of his eye. As they drew close to his heels, several gray forms slackened pace cautiously. Not so the leader—he dashed full upon Hok and sprang.

Hok had waited for that. Back darted his reversed spear. The tough ash pike met the wolf's breast in midair, the very force of the leap helped to impale the brute. There rose one wild scream of agony, and Hok let go of the weapon, tramping along. Behind rose a greedy hubbub—as he had foreseen, the other wolves had stopped and were devouring their fallen leader.

"The bravest often die like that," philosophized Hok, lengthening his stride to make up for lost time.

The long ravine came to a head in a frozen lake. Across this, to the south, brush-clad hills. Gragru's wallowing trail showed how hard he found those hills to climb, and Hok made up some of the distance he had lost on the levels. As the moon sank before morning, Hok caught up. Gragru had paused to rest, a great hunched hillock in a shaggy pelt. Hok yelled in triumph and Gragru, galvanizing into motion, slogged away southward as before.

Another day—second of pursuit, third of absence from home. Even Hok's magnificently trained legs must begin to suffer from so much snowshoeing; even Gragru's teeming reservoir of strength must run lower from pain and labor. Given a chance to idle and nurse himself, he could let the air clot and congeal the wounds, but the shaft still stuck through him, working and shifting to begin fresh bleedings. The trail

now led through impeding thickets, and after a brief spurt by
Gragru, Hok had a new advantage, that of using the mammoth's lane through the heavy drift-choked growth. By
afternoon more snow fell, almost a blizzard. Lest he lose the
trail entirely, Hok tramped in Gragru's very tracks instead of
on the firmer drifts beside.

"He weakens," Hok told himself, eyeing new blood
blotches. "At this point he rested on his knees. Yonder he fell
on his side. Brave beast, to get up again! Will he reach the
dying place?"

Full of admiration for Gragru, Hok half-wished the
animal would triumph, but he did not slow down. Hok was
weary, but warm from his exertions and far from falter-
ing.

Night again. During the darkness Hok again kept up a
dogged march. Up ahead somewhere, Gragru was forced to
make a halt of it. His wound was doing its grim best to heal.
Once or twice the mammoth's trunk reached back and
investigated that lodged shaft. But there was too much
wisdom in that high crag of a skull to permit tugging out the
painful thing—that would mean bleeding to death on the
spot. Once again, as the deepest dark heralded the dawn,
Hok drew nigh to his massive quarry. Once again Gragru
stirred to motion, breaking trail for the third day of the
chase.

The mighty stumpy feet were shaking and stumbling by
now. Gragru fell again and again. He rose with difficulty after
each fall, groaning and puffing but stubborn. A fresh hunter
might have caught up—but Hok, however much he would
not admit it, was himself close to the end of endurance. His
deep chest panted like a bullfrog's. He breathed through his
mouth, and the moisture made icicles in his golden beard.
Frost tried to bite his face, and he rubbed it away with snow.
Only his conscious wisdom kept him from tossing aside his
furs as too much weight. By noon he made his first rest-stop.
Knowing better than to sit down and grow stiff, he leaned
his back to a boulder and gulped air into his laboring lungs.
After he had paused thus, and eaten a mouthful of meat, he

was no more than able to resume the pursuit, at a stubborn walk.

"Gragru," he addressed the fugitive up ahead, "you are strong and brave. Any man but Hok would say you had conquered. But I have not given up."

The afternoon's journey led over a great flat plain, rimmed afar by white wrapped mountains and bearing no trees or watercourses that showed above the snow. Almost on its far side was a gentle slope to a ridge, with a peculiar length of shadow behind. Hok saw Gragru ahead of him. The mammoth could barely crawl through the drifts, sagging and trembling with weakness. Hok drew on his own last reserves of strength, stirred his aching feet to swifter snowshoeing. He actually gained.

Narrower grew the distance between them. Hok drew the axe from his belt, balanced it in his gloved right hand. Coming close, he told himself, he would hack the tendon of Gragru's hind leg, bring him down to stay. After that, get close enough to wrench out the piercing shaft, so that a final loss of blood would finish the beast. Then—but Hok could wish only for camp, a fire, sleep.

He toiled close. Closer. Gragru was only fifty paces ahead, tottering to that ridge of the slope. At its top he made a slow, clumsy half-turn. His head quivered between his big tussocked shoulders, his ears and trunk hung limply. His eyes, red and pained, fixed upon Hok's like the eyes of a warrior who sees death upon him. Hok lifted his axe in salute.

"Gragru, I am honored by this adventure," he wheezed. "Eating your heart will give me strength and wit and courage beyond all I have known. You will live again in me. Now, to make an end."

He kicked off the snowshoes, so as to run more swiftly at Gragru's sagging hindquarters. But, before he moved, Gragru acted on his own part. He stretched his trunk backward to the shaft in his wound.

Hok relaxed, smiling. "What, you would die of your

own will? So be it! I yield you the honor of killing Gragru!"

The mammoth's trunk surged with all the strength it had left. Fastening on the head of the lance, it drew, dragged, pulled the shaft clear through and away. A flip of the trunk, and the red-caked weapon flew out of sight beyond the ridge. Then, blood fountaining forth on both sides, Gragru dragged himself after the shaft. He seemed to collapse beyond the ridge.

"He is mine," muttered Hok into the icicles on his beard, and lifted his axe. He ran in pursuit. So swift was he that he did not see what was on the other side of the ridge until too late.

There was no other side, really. Ground shelved straight down from that highest snow-clad point, into a vast, deep valley. There was a drop of eight or ten paces, then the beginning of a steep muddy slope. Hok felt a beating-up of damp warmth, like the rush of air from a cave heated with many fires. He saw thick, distant greenery below him, with a blue mist over it as of rain-clouds seen from a mountain top. All this in one moment.

Then his moccasins slid from under him on the brink, and he fell hard.

Striking the top of the slope all sprawling, he rolled over and then slid like an otter on a riverbank. Perhaps something struck his head. Perhaps he only closed his eyes as he slid.

In any case, Hok dropped into sleep as into warm water. He never even felt himself strike a solid obstruction and halt his downward slide.

CHAPTER III

The Jungle Beneath the Snow

Hok stretched, yawned, opened his eyes. "Where have I fallen?" he inquired of the world, and looked about to answer his own question.

He had plumped into a great bushy thicket of evergreen

scrub, and had lain there as comfortably as in a hammock. By chance or instinct, he still clutched his big flint axe. Above him was the steep slope, and above that the perpendicular cliff with a crowning of snow. But all about him was a springlike warmth, with no snow at all—only dampness.

Hok wriggled out of his branchy bed, examining himself. His tumble had covered his garments with muck. "Pah!" he condemned the mess, and used his gloves to wipe his face, hair and weapons. A look at the sky told him it was morning—he had slept away his fourth night from home.

Then he gazed downward. The valley seemed to throb and steam. He made out rich leafage and tall tree-summits far below. One or two bright birds flitted in the mists. Hok grimaced.

"Summer must sleep through the cold, like a cave-bear," he decided. "I will go down, and look for Gragru's body."

There were shoots and shrubs and hummocks for him to catch with hands and feet, or he would have gone sliding again. The deeper he journeyed, the warmer it became. Now and then he hacked a big slash on a larger tree, to keep his upward trail again. Those trees, he observed, were often summer trees, lusher and greener than any he had ever seen.

"Is this the Ancient Land of safe and easy life?"* he mused.

He threw off leggins and gloves and the muddy lionskin cloak, tying these into a bundle to carry. Further descent into even more tropical temperature, and he hung the superfluous garments in a forked branch of a ferny thicket. "I will get them when I return," he decided, and went on down, clad only in clout and moccasins. Bow, quiver and pouch he slung from his shoulders. The deerhorn dagger rode in his leather

---

*Johannes V. Jensen, Danish poet and scholar, predicates his celebrated "Long Journey" saga on the race-old myth of a warm Lost Country—the memory among Ice-Age men of the tropical surroundings among which the earliest human beings developed, and which were banished by the glaciers.—Ed.

girdle. His big axe he kept ready in his right hand, for what might challenge him.

The first challenger came, not up from the valley, but down from the misty air. Hok saw gray-green pinions, four times wider than his own arm-spread, and borne between them something like an evil dream of a stork. The wings rustled as they flapped—he saw, as they settled upon him, that they were unfeathered membranes like a bat's—and two scaly rear talons slashed at him.*

"*Khaa!*" cried Hok, revolted, and set himself for defense. He parried the rush with his axe. The side, not the edge, of the flint struck that monster's chest, blocking it off. Down darted the long lean neck, and the sharp-toothed beak fastened in Hok's hair. A moment later the clutching lizardy feet closed on the axe-haft. Hok found himself carried shakily aloft.

There was a struggle for the axe. The thing could barely sustain Hok's weight clear of the ground, and it tried to kill, not capture. A long tail belabored him like a club, hideous handlike claws on the wing-elbows scratched and scrabbled at his chest and throat. Hok, dangling in midair, found himself able to voice a savage laugh.

"*Ahai!* You think to eat Hok, you nightmare? Others have found him a tough morsel!" Quitting hold of the axe with one hand, he whipped the dagger from his belt. Thrusting upward, he pierced the scaly throat to the bone.

The jaws let go his hair, and emitted a startled screech. Snaky-smelling blood drenched Hok, and the two fell. The wings, though out of control, partially broke the tumble, and Hok had the wit and strength to turn his enemy under and fall upon it. They struck the slope some paces lower than where the fight began. Hok pinned the still struggling nightmare with his foot, and cleft it almost in two with his axe. Then he stepped clear, nose wrinkled in disgust.

"*Khaa!*" he snorted again, mopping away the ill-scented

---

*The race of pterodactyls, of which this specimen was a survivor, had wing-spreads as wide as twenty-five feet, with beaks four feet long.—Ed.

gore with handfuls of fern. "I'd have doubly died if that bird-snake had eaten me. Are there others?"

His question was answered on the instant. Dry flappings, shrill screams—Hok sheltered in a thicket, and watched a dozen more bird-snakes swoop down to rend and devour their slain brother. It was a sight to turn the stomach of a Gnorrl. Hok slipped away down slope.

Now he came to a gentler incline and larger trees. He journeyed on without mishap for the rest of the morning. Hungry, he ate several strange fruits from vine or tree at which he saw birds pecking. Once, too, a strange thing like a tiny tailed man* scolded him in a harsh high voice and flung down a big husk-fibered nut. Hok dodged the missile, split it and enjoyed both the white flesh and the milky juice.

"Thanks, little brother!" he cried up at the impish nut-thrower.

When noon was past, Hok had come to where he could spy the floor of the valley.

With difficulty he spied it, for it was dusky dark. From it rose fumes, mist-clouds, earthy odors. It was a swamp, from which sprouted upward the tallest and biggest trees Hok had ever seen. They grew thickly, interlaced with the root-ends and butts of vines and creepers, hummocked around with dank clumps of fungi, rimmed with filthy pools. Swarms of biting insects rose, and Hok retreated, cursing.

"I see nothing of Gragru down there," he said. "I'll go sidewise."

Nicking a tree to mark the turnoff, he travelled directly along the slope. Nor had he far to go before he saw Gragru.

Here was the place where mammoths were entombed.

---

*In Europe, where Hok lived, no remains of native monkeys or apes more recent than Pliocene times have been discovered; but, as the paleontologist Osborn reminds us, the tree-dwelling habits of such beasts might have made the remains difficult to keep whole.—Ed.

Above, extending up the valley's slope, was a tunnel through trees and thickets, kept open by so many falling, rolling masses of dead or dying mammoth-meat. At the bottom of the chute rose a stinking stack of remains. Hok could not have counted them—there must be thousands of desiccated and rotted carcasses, the bones gray and curling tusks white. On top lay the freshest of these, Gragru his quarry. And beside it was one that had beaten Hok to the kill.

"First bird-snakes," grumbled Hok. "Now elephant-pigs."

For the thing was bigger than an elephant and grosser than a hog. Its monstrous bulk, clad in scant-bristled hide of slate gray, stooped above the carcass. Its shallow, broad-snouted skull bent down, and powerful fangs tore the hairy hide from Gragru's flesh, exposing the tender meat. That head lifted as Hok came into view, a head larger than that of a hippopotamus. Two small hooded eyes, cold and pale as a lizard's, stared. The mouth sucked and chewed bloody shreds, and Hok saw down-protruding tusks, sharp as daggers. Upon the undeveloped brow, the swell of the muzzle, and the tip of the snout were hornlike knobs—three pairs of them.*

Fixing Hok with that lizardlike stare, the big brute set its elephantine forefeet upon Gragru's bulk and hitched itself nearer. Its bloody, fang-fringed jaws seemed to grin in anticipation of different meat.

"Thing," Hok addressed the monster, "you came unbidden to eat my prey. You yourself shall be my meat, to replace that which I killed."

He lifted his bow, which was ready strung, and reached over his shoulder for an arrow. Just then the elephant-pig moved toward him.

Dinoceras ingens, one of the largest and ugliest of the Dinocerata, flourished in Eocene times and may have lived later. It partook of the natures of rhinoceros and swine, and its teeth suggest it ate both animal and vegetable food. Its many head-bumps may have been primitive horns. Specimens have been found that were twelve feet long and eight feet tall at the shoulders.—Ed.

For all its unwieldy bulk, it came at antelope speed, that great toothed maw open to seize and rend. Hok swiftly drew his long arrow to the head and sent it full at the long protruding tongue. The monster stopped dead, emitting a shrill gargling squeal, and lifted one horn-toed foot to paw at the wound. Hok retired into a bushy thicket, setting another arrow to string.

That thicket would have shielded him from the charge of a buffalo or lion; but the bulk of the present enemy was to buffalo or lion as a fox to rabbits. It charged among the brush, breaking off stout stems like reeds. Hok, lighter, had difficulty getting aside from its first blind rush. He gained the open, and so did the elephant-pig. It spied, wheeled to charge again.

He discharged a second arrow, full at one of those dead eyes. The six-knobbed head twitched at that moment, and the shaft skewered a nostril instead. Again a horrid yell of angry pain. Hok sprang away from under its very feet as it tried to run him down, found himself heading into the swampy bottom. There was a great cylindrical mass among the trees, a trunk which even this hideous monster could not teemed with great thoughts, his blue eyes seemed to gaze on tear down. Hok ran to it, seeking to climb the rough lappings of bark.

"You cannot climb quickly enough," said a voice from within the tree. "Come inside, where I can look at you."

CHAPTER IV

The Man Inside the Tree

It is often like that, even with a hunter as wise and sharp-eyed as Hok. Not until the voice spoke to him, in the language of men,* was he aware that near him in the great trunk was a gaping hole, big enough for him to slide through, and full of blackness.

The tree itself was not a tree. For trees are straight upward shoots of vegetable growth—this seemed a high-built, close-packed spiral, as if someone had coiled a rope, or a worm had made a great casting. Between two woody curves, one upon the other, showed the hole.

"Make haste," bade the voice inside.

Hok saw that the elephant-pig, after a momentary questing to spy and smell him out, was ponderously wheeling to charge. He waited for no third invitation, but dived into the space, head first. A struggle and a kick, and he was inside, among comforting dimness that bespoke solid protection all around. A moment later the huge beast struck outside, with a force that shook every fiber of the strange stout growth within which Hok had taken refuge.

"He cannot break through to us," assured the voice, very near. "This vine is stronger even than Rmanth, the slayer."

Hok made out a dark shape, slender and quiet. "Vine?" he echoed. "But this is a tree, a dead hollow tree."

"The tree that once stood here is not only dead, but gone," he was quietly informed. "If there were light, you would see."

*The old legend, mentioned in the book of Genesis and elsewhere, that once "all men were of one speech" may well be founded on fact—witness similarities of certain key words among races so far scattered as Welsh, Persian, and Mandan Indian. Even in the Stone Age there seems to have been commerce and alliance, which means that men must have understood each other. Languages were simple then. Only with widely divergent races, as the beastlike Gnorrls or Neanderthal men, would there be a definitely separate tongue, hard to pronounce and harder to understand because of differences in jaw structure, brain, and mode of life.—Ed.

Momentary silence, while Hok pondered this statement. Outside the elephant-pig, which seemed to be named Rmanth, sniffed at the orifice like a jackal at a rat-burrow.

"You don't sound like a mocker," was Hok's final judgment aloud. "And it is true that this is a strange growth around us. As for light, why not build a fire?"

"Fire?" repeated the other uncertainly. "What is that?"

Hok could not but chuckle. "You do not know? Fire lights and warms you."

"For warmth, it is never cold here. And for light—I do not like too much."

"There is need of light in this darkness," decided Hok weightily. "If you truly do not know fire, I can show better than I can tell."

He groped with his hands on the floor of the cavern into which he had come. It seemed earthy, with much rubbish. He found some bits of punky wood, then larger pieces, and cleared a hearth-space. From his pouch he brought needful things—a flat chip of pine, one edge notched; a straight, pointed stick of hard wood; a tuft of dry moss.

"Thus," lectured Hok, "is fire made."

Working in the dark, he twirled the stick between his palms. Its point, in the notch of the chip, rubbed and heated. Within moments Hok smelled scorching, then smoke. A faint glow peeped through the gloom. Lifting away the chip, Hok held his moss-tinder to the little coal of glowing wood-meal. The rising blaze he fed with splinters, then larger pieces. The fire rose. "There!" cried Hok, and had time and illumination to look up.

His first glance showed him the refuge—a circular cavity, twice a man's height in diameter, and walled snugly with those close-packed woody spirals. High above the space extended, with what looked like a gleaming white star at some distant apex. The floor was of well-trampled loam and mold, littered with ancient wood chips. His second glance showed him his companion.

Here was a body slimmer and shorter than the average man of the Flint People. The shoulders sloped, the muscles were stringy rather than swelling, there were no hips or calves. Around the slender waist was a clout rudely woven of plant fiber, its girdle supporting a queerly made little axe and what seemed to be a knife. The feet, outthrust toward Hok, looked like hands—the great toe was set well back, and plainly could take independent grasp. On the chest—quite deep in proportion to the slimness—and on the outer arms and legs grew long, sparse hair of red-brown color. Hok could not see the face, for the man crouched and buried his head in his long arms.

"Don't," came his muffled plea. "Don't . . ."

"It will not hurt," Hok replied, puzzled.

"I cannot look, it burns my eyes. Once the forest was eaten by such stuff, that struck down from heaven—"

"Lightning," guessed Hok. "Oh, yes, fire can be terrible when big. But we keep it small, feeding it only sparingly. Then it is good. See, I do not fear. I promise it will not hurt you."

His tone reassured the man, who finally looked up, albeit apprehensively. Hok studied his face.

Long loose lips, a nose both small and flattish, and no chin at all beneath a scraggle of brown beard. From the wide mouth protruded teeth—Hok saw businesslike canines above and below, capable of inflicting a terrible bite. This much was plainly of animal fashion, unpleasantly Gnorrlish. But neither the fangs nor the shallow jaw could detract from the manifest intelligence of the upper face.

For here were large dark eyes, set very well under smooth brows. The forehead, though not high, was fairly broad and smooth, and the cranium looked as if it might house intelligence and good temper.

"Don't be afraid," persisted Hok. "You were friendly enough to call me into this shelter. I am grateful, and I will show it."

Rmanth, the monster outside, sniffed and scraped at the entrance. He seemed baffled. Hok leaned against the wall. "What is your name?" he asked.

The other peered timidly. Hok saw the size and brilliance of those eyes, and guessed that this man could see, at least somewhat in the dark. "Soko," came the reply. "And you?"

"Hok the Mighty." That was spoken with honest pride. "I came here from snowy country up above. I had wounded a mammoth, and followed him down here."

"Mammoths always come here," Soko told him. "Rmanth and his people before him—for he is the last of a mighty race—ate their flesh and flourished. If we dare descend the trees, Rmanth kills and eats us, too. In the high branches—the Stymphs!"

"Stymphs?" echoed Hok. "What are those?"

Soko had his turn at being surprised at such ignorance. "They fly like birds, but are bigger and hungrier—with teeth in their long jaws—man cannot prevail against them—"

"Oh, the bird-snakes! One attacked me as I came down. I killed it, and descended before its friends came."

"You were climbing downward," Soko reminded. "There was cover below. But if you leave the cover to climb upward, you will be slain in the open, by many Stymphs. Not even Rmanth ventures above the thickets."

"As to your elephant-pig, Rmanth," continued Hok, "he has tasted my arrows."

That was another new word for Soko, and Hok passed his bow and quiver across for examination. "One shaft I feathered in his tongue," he continued, "and another in his nostril."

"But were forced to take shelter here. Meanwhile, those wounds will make him the thirstier for your blood. He will never forget your appearance or smell. If you venture out, he will follow you to the finish. Between him and the Stymphs above, what chance have you?"

"What chance have I?" repeated Hok, his voice ringing. "Chance for combat! For adventure! For Victory!" He laughed for joy, anticipating these things. "I'm glad I came—these dangers are worth traveling far to meet . . . but tell me of another wonder. This tree, which is not a tree, but shelters us in its heart—"

"Oh, simple enough," rejoined Soko. He was beginning to enjoy the comradeship by the glowing fire. Sitting opposite Hok, slender hands clasped around his knobby knees, he smiled. "A true tree grew here once, tall and strong. At its root sprang up a vine, which coiled tightly around like a snake. In time that vine grew to the very top. Its hugging coils, and its sap-drinking suckers, slew the tree, which rotted and died in the grip. But the vine held the shape to which it had grown, and when we tree-folk dug out the rotten wood, little by little, it made a safe tube by which we could descend to the valley's floor."*

"That must have taken much labor," observed Hok.

"And much time. My father's father barely remembered when it was begun, that digging."

"You speak as if you live up above here," said Hok.

"We do," Soko told him. "Come, kill the fire lest it burn the forest, and I will take you to the home of my people."

He rose and began climbing upward.

CHAPTER V

The World in the Branches

Hok quickly stamped out the fire.

Its dying light showed him a sort of rough ladder—pegs and stubs of hard wood, wedged into the spaces between the coils of that amazing vine. Soko was swarming well above ground level already. Slinging his weapons to girdle and shoulder-thongs, Hok followed.

Hok had always been a bold and active climber, able to outdistance any of his tribe-fellows, in trees or up cliffs. But Soko kept ahead of him, like a squirrel ahead of a bear. The tree-man fairly scampered up the ladder-way.

"This is another way in which Soko's people are different from the Gnorrls,"** muttered Hok.

*Several types of big tropical vine, both in Africa and South America, create this curious growth-pattern by killing the trees they climb and remaining erect in the same place.—Ed.

**The Neanderthal men were of massive, clumsy build—obviously poor climbers.—Ed.

The climbing-sticks had been meant for bodies of Soko's modest weight, and once or twice they creaked dangerously beneath the heavier Hok. He obviated the danger of a fall by keeping each hand and foot on a different hold, dividing the strain four ways. Meanwhile, the light above grew stronger, waxing and waning as Soko's nimble body cut this way and that across its beam. Finally, noise and bustle, and a new voice:

"Soko! You went down to see what was happening with Rmanth. What—"

"A man," Soko answered. "A strange man, like none you ever saw."

Hok took that as a compliment. He was considered something of a unique specimen, even among his own kind.

"He is master of the Hot Hunger," Soko went on, and Hok guessed that he meant fire. "He has killed one Stymph, he says, and has hurt Rmanth."

A chatter of several agitated voices above. Then, "Will he kill us?"

"I think not," said Soko, and drew himself through some sort of gap above. "Come on out, Hok," he called back. "My friends are eager to see you."

Hok came to the opening in turn. It was narrow for his big body, and he had difficulty in wriggling through. Standing on some crossed and interwoven boughs, he looked at Soko's people.

All the way up, he had thought of Soko as fragile and small; now he realized, as often before, that fragility and smallness is but comparative. Soko, who was a head shorter than himself and slim in proportion, would be considered sturdy and tall among the tree folk—almost a giant. He was the biggest of all who were present. Hok smiled to himself. While he had been pegging Soko as a timid lurker in a hollow, these dwellers of the branches must have thrilled to the courage of their strong brother, venturing so close to the mucky domain of the ravenous Rmanth.

As Hok came fully into view, the gathering—there may have been twenty or thirty of Soko's kind, men, women and children—fell back on all sides with little gasps and squeaks of fearful amazement. With difficulty the chief of the Flint People refrained from most unmannerly laughter. If Soko was a strapping champion among them, Hok must seem a vast horror, strangely shaped, colored and equipped. He smiled his kindliest, and sat down among the woven branches.

"Soko speaks truth," he announced. "I have no desire to fight or kill anyone who comes in peace."

They still stood off from him, balancing among the leafage. He was aware that they moved so swiftly and surely because they got a grip on the branches with their feet. He was able, also, to make a quick, interested study of the world they lived in.

Though Soko had led him upward in a climb of more than twenty times a man's height, the upper hole in the in the vine spiral was by no means the top of the forest. Leafage shut away the sky above, the swampy ground below. Here, in the middle branches of the close-set mighty trees, appeared something of a lofty floor—the boughs and connecting vines, naturally woven and matted together into a vast bridge of platform, swaying but strong. Layers of leafmold, mixed with blown dust, moss and the rotted meal of dead wood, overspread parts of this fabric. The aerial earthiness bore patches of grass and weeds, bright-flowering plants, as richly as though it were based upon the rock instead of the winds. Birds picked at seeds. Hok heard the hum of bees around trumpet-shaped blooms. It was a great wonder.*

"I wondered how you tree-men could possibly live off the ground," he said, with honest admiration. "Now I wonder how you can live anywhere else but here." A deep-chested sigh. "Of such fair places our old men tell us, in the legends of the Ancient Land."

That friendly speech brought the tree-dwellers closer to this big stranger. A half-grown lad was boldest, coming

---

*This description is no fancy. The author himself, and many others, have seen such sky-gardens among the branches of modern rain-forests in West Africa.—Ed.

straight to Hok and fingering his leather moccasins. Hok's first thought was how swiftly young Ptao, at home by the frozen river, could thrash and conquer such a youth—his second was a hope that Ptao would be forebearing and gentle to so harmless a specimen. The others gathered around reassured. They began asking questions. It was strange to all that a human being could kill large beasts for food and fur, and the men were particularly fascinated by Hok's flint weapons.

"We have our own stories of old times, when our fathers made stone things," volunteered Soko. "Now we satisfy ourselves with what bones we can raid from that great pile of mammoths, when Rmanth is not there gorging himself." He produced his own dagger, smaller than Hok's reindeer-horn weapon, but well worked from a bone fragment. "After all, we need not fight monsters, like you."

"If you did fight like me, all together, and with wisdom and courage, Rmanth would not have you treed," said Hok bluntly. "Perhaps I can help you with him. But first, tell me more of yourselves. You think it strange that I wear skins. What are these weavings you wear?"

"The forest taught us," said Soko sententiously. "As the branches weave and grow together, so we cross and twine little tough strings and threads drawn from leaves and grasses. They give us covering, and places to carry possessions. Is it so marvelous? Birds do as much with their nests."

"Nests?" repeated Hok. "And how do you people nest?"

"Like the birds—in woven beds of branches, lined with soft leaves and fiber. A roof overhead, of course, to shed the rain." Soko pointed to a little cluster of such shelters, not far away in an adjoining tree.*

"You do nothing but sleep and play?"

"We gather fruits and nuts," spoke up another of the tree-men. "That takes time and work, for a man who has gathered much must feed his friends who may have gathered little."

"It is so with my people, when one hunter kills much

*The great apes make such nests, roofs and all.—Ed.

meat and others return empty-handed," nodded Hok. "What else, then?"

"A great labor is the mending of this floor," replied Soko, patting with his foot the woven platform. "Branches rot and break. We look for such places, through which our children might fall at play, and weave in new strong pieces, or tie and lace across with stout vines."

Once again Hok glanced upward. "And what is there?"

A shudder all around. "Stymphs," muttered Soko, in a soft voice, as if he feared to summon a flock of the bird-snakes.

"Ugly things," said Hok. "I may do something about them, too. But I am hungry just now—"

Before he could finish, the whole community dashed away like so many squirrels through the boughs, to bring back fistfuls of nuts, pawpaws and grapes. Hok accepted all he could possibly eat, and thanked his new friends heartily.

"I did not mean that you must feed me," he told them. "You should wait for me to finish my talk. But since you bring these fruits, I will make my meal of them. You may take my provision."

From his pouch he rummaged the remainder of his dried meat. It was one more new thing to the tree people, who nibbled and discussed and argued over it. Flesh they had occasionally—small climbers, fledgling birds, even insects—but nothing of larger game, and both cooking and drying of food was beyond their understanding. Hok chuckled over their naivete.

"A promise!" he cried. "I'll give you Rmanth himself for a feast, and I shall roast him on a fire, that which you call the Hot Hunger. But let Soko sit here by me. I want to hear of how you came to this place to live."

Soko perched on a tangle of vines. "Who can tell that? It was so long ago. Cold weather drove us from the upper world," and he pointed northward. "Those who stayed behind were slain by it. Our old men tell tales and sing songs of how the remnants of the fleeing tribe blundered in here and gave themselves up as trapped."

"Why did the ice not follow you in?" asked Hok.

"Ask that of the gods, who drove it to right and left of our valley. In any case, we were sheltered here, though there were many fierce creatures. But the cold was fiercer—we could not face it—and here we stay."*

"Treed by Rmanth and harried by those Stymph bird-snakes," summed up Hok. "You are happy, but you could make yourselves much happier by some good planning and fighting. Who is your chief?"

"I am their chief," growled someone behind him, "and you had better explain—quickly—why you seek to make my people dissatisfied."

CHAPTER VI

A Chief Passes Sentence

There was a sudden gasping and cowering among all the tree-folk, even as concerned the relatively sturdy Soko. Hok turned toward the speaker, expecting to come face to face with a fearsome challenger.

Around the spiral vine-column a little grizzled form was making its way. This tree-man was old and ill-favored, with almost pure white whiskers on his chinless jaw. He wheezed and snorted, as though the exertion were too much for him. Perhaps this was due to his weight, for he was the fattest Hok had yet seen among those dwellers of the trees. His belly protruded like a wallet, his jowls hung like dewlaps. But there was nothing old or infirm about the power in his big, close-set brilliant eyes.

Gaining the side of the nearest tree-man to him, the oldster put out a confident hand and snatched away a sizable

*The Piltdown Race seems to have flourished in the Third Interglacial Epoch, a warm age when even northern Europe was as pleasant and temperate as Italy. Such African-Asiatic fauna as hippopotami and tigers flourished side by side with these forerunners of human beings. When the Fourth Glaciation brought ice and snow to cover Europe, the robust Neanderthals and the later, greater true men of Hok's race could survive and adapt themselves; but a less rugged prehuman type like the Piltdown must flee or perish.—Ed.

slice of the dried meat Hok had distributed. Though the victim of this plunder was an active young man, he did not resist or even question, but drew diffidently away. The old man took a bite—his teeth, too, were young-seeming and rather larger and sharper than ordinary—and grunted approval. Then his eyes fastened Hok's, in a calculated stare of hostility.

But Hok had met the gaze of the world's fiercest beasts and men, and his were not the first eyes to falter. The old tree-chief finally glanced away. Hok smiled in good-humored contempt.

"Well?" challenged the oldster at last. "Do you know how to act before your betters?"

Hok was puzzled. The simple truth was that Hok had never recognized anyone as his better from his youth upwards.

Years before, when a big boy not yet fully mature, the slaying of his father by Gnorrls had made him chief of his clan. His young manhood had barely come to him before he had driven those same beastly Gnorrls from their rich hunting-empire of meadows and woods, and founded in their stead an alliance of several tribes, with himself as head chief. The mighty nation of Tlanis was sunken under the sea because of him. The Fishers in their seaside pile-villages had changed their worship from water-god to sun-god out of sadly learned respect for Hok. If ever he had been subordinate, even only the second greatest individual in any gathering, he had had plenty of time to forget it.

Just now he spat idly, through a gap in the woven branches.

"Show me my betters," he requested with an air of patience. "I know none, on two legs or four."

"I am Krol!" squeaked the other, and smote his gray-tufted chest with a fat fist. "Be afraid, you hulking yellow-haired stranger!"

"Men of the trees," Hok addressed those who listened, "is it your custom to keep fools to make game for you? This man has white hair, he should be quiet and dignified. He is a bad example to the young."

It was plainly blasphemy. Soko and the others drew further away from Hok, as though they feared to be involved in some terrible fate about to overwhelm him. The chief who called himself Krol fumbled in his girdle of twisted fiber, and drew forth an axe of mammoth ivory set in a hard-wood handle. Whirling it around his head, he cast it at Hok.

Hok lifted a big knowing hand, with such assurance that the movement seemed languid. The axe drove straight at his face, but he picked it out of the air as a frog's tongue picks a flying insect. Without pausing he whirled it in his own turn and sent it sailing back. It struck with a sharp *chock,* deep into a big branch just above Krol's head.

"Try again," bade Hok, as though he were instructing a child in how to throw axes.

Krol's big fangs gnashed, and foam sprang out in flecks upon his lips and beard. He waved his fists at his people.

"On him!" he screamed. "Seize him, beat him, bind fast his arms!"

Hok rose from where he sat, bracing himself erect. He looked with solemnity upon the half-dozen or so biggest men who moved to obey.

"Come at me, and you will think Rmanth himself has climbed up among you," he warned. "I do not like to be handled."

Krol yelped a further order, backing it by a threat. The men rushed unwillingly.

Hok laughed, like an athlete playing with children. Indeed, the tree-men were childlike in comparison with him. He pushed the first two in the face with his palms, upsetting them and almost dropping them through the branchy fabric. A third attacker he caught and lifted overhead, wedging him in a fork of the boughs. The others retreated fearfully before such effortless strength. Hok laughed again, watching.

But he should have watched Krol as well. The plump old despot had stolen close unobserved. In one hand he clutched a big fiber husked nut, of the milky kind Hok had enjoyed earlier in the day. A swinging buffet on the skull, and Hok staggered, partially stunned. At once the tree-men rushed back, and before Hok could clear his brain and fight them off, he was swamped. They looped his wrists, ankles and body with quickly-plucked vine tendrils, tough and limber as leather straps.

Krol found time to take some fruit from a child, and husk it with his teeth. "Now, stranger," he sniggered, "you will learn that I am chief here."

Hok had recovered from that stroke. He did not waste strength or dignity by striving against his stout bonds.

"A chief who plays tricks and lets other men do the fighting," he replied. "A chief who strikes his enemies foully, from behind."

Krol had repossessed his ivory axe. He lifted it angrily, as though to smite it into Hok's skull. But then he lowered it, and grinned nastily.

"I heard you blustering when I came up," he said. "Something about fighting. What do you think to fight?"

"I spoke of Rmanth, the elephant-pig," replied Hok. "Yes, and the Stymphs. Your people fear them. I do not."

"Mmmm!" Krol glanced downward, then up. "They are only little pests to mighty warriors like you, huh? You do not fear them? Hok—that is your name, I think you said—I will do you a favor. You shall have closer acquaintanceship with the Stymphs."

Mention of the dread bird-snakes made the tree-folk shiver, and Krol sneered at them with a row of grinning fangs.

"You cowards!" he scolded. "You disgrace me before this boastful stranger. Yet you know that Stymphs must eat, if they are to live and let us alone. Hoist this prey up to them."

"Bound and helpless?" demanded Hok. "That is a part of your own cowardice, Krol. You shall howl for it."

"But you shall howl first, and loudest," promised Krol. "You biggest men, come and carry him up. Yes, high!"

That last was to quicken the unwilling limbs of his fellows, who seemed to like Hok and not to like the prospect of mounting into the upper branches.

Thus driven to obedience, four of the biggest men nimbly rove more vines around the captive, fashioning a sort of hammock to hold him and his weapons. Soko, stooping to tie a knot, gazed intently into Hok's face. One of Soko's big bright eyes closed for a moment—the ancient and universal wink of alliance, warning, and promise.

The four scrambled up and up, bearing Hok among them. Now the sky came into view, dullish and damp but warm. Apparently the valley was always wreathed, at least partially, in light mists. Into a tall treetop the big captive was hoisted, and made fast there like a dangling cocoon. Krol panted fatly as he clambered alongside. The others departed at his nod. Krol, passing Hok, jostled the big bound wrists. Hok felt something pressed against his palm, and closed his fingers upon it.

The hilt of Soko's bone knife! With difficulty he fought back a smile of triumph . . .

Then he was alone in the treetop with Krol.

"Look up, you scoffer," bade Krol. "In the mists—do you see anything?"

"Very dimly, I make out flying shapes," replied Hok quietly. "Two—three—no, many."

"They can see you, and plainly," Krol informed him. "Like my people, the Stymphs have ability to see far on dull days, or dark holes, or even at night. They have cunning sense of smell, too. Probably they scent some prey close at hand now, and wonder if I have hung something up for them."

"You hang food for the Stymphs?" demanded Hok.

"Yes, such men as displease me—don't stare and wonder. I am chief of my tribe. I must keep an alliance with other powers."

Krol squinted upward, where the Stymphs hovered in the mist-wreaths. Opening his wide mouth, he emitted a piercing cry, half howl and half whistle. The bird-snakes began to flap as if in response.

"They know my voice, they will come," announced Krol. With the evillest of grins, he swung down to the safety of the foliage below.

No sooner was he gone than Hok began to ply that bone knife Soko had smuggled to him. It was difficult work, but he pressed the well-sharpened edge strongly against the vine loops around his wrist. They separated partially, enough to allow him to strain and snap them. Even as the boldest Stymph lowered clear of the mists and began to angle downward, Hok won his arms free. A few mighty hacks, and he cleared away the rest of his hammocky bonds.

The tree-folk had bound his unfamiliar weapons in with him. Drawing himself astride of a big horizontal branch, Hok strung the big bow and tweaked an arrow out of his quiver.

"I have a feeling," he said aloud to this strange land at large, "that I was sent here—by gods or spirits or by chance—to face and destroy these Stymphs."*

CHAPTER VII

The Stymphs

So confident was Hok of his ability to deal with the situation that he actually waited, arrow on string, for a closer mark. After all, he had killed one such bird-snake with a single quick thrust of his dagger. Why should he fear many, when he had arrows, an axe, and two knives? A big Stymph tilted in the mist and slid down as if it were an otter on a mud-bank. Its long triangular head, like the nightmare of a stork, drooped low on the snaky neck. Its jag-toothed bill opened.

Hok let it come so close that his flaring nostrils caught the reptilian odor; then, drawing his shaft to its barbed head of sandstone, he loosed full at the scaly breast. Hok's bow was the strongest among all men of his time, and a close-delivered arrow from it struck with all the impact of a war-club. The flint point tore through the body, flesh, scales and bone, and

*Readers who know the mythology of ancient Greece will already have seen some connection between the surviving pterodactyls called Stymphs and the Stymphalides, described as "great birds" who ate men. The ancient Greeks said that the Stymphalides had plumage of metal, which sounds very much like reptilian scaliness. Hercules, the Grecian memory of Hok, is credited with destroying these monsters as one of his twelve heaven-assigned labors.—Ed.

protruded behind. The swoop of the Stymph was arrested as though it had blundered against a rock in midair. It whirled head over lizard tail, then fell flopping and screeching toward the great mass of foliage below.

"*Ahai!*" Hok voiced his war-shout, and thundered mocking laughter at the other Stymphs. "Thus Hok serves those who face him. Send me another of your champions!"

Several of the abominations had flown a little way after their falling friend. But, before they could get their cannibal beaks into the stricken body, it had lost itself among the branches, and they came up again to center on the more exposed meat in the treetop. Two advanced at once, and from widely separate angles.

Hok had notched another arrow, and sped it into the chest of one. Before he could seize a third shaft, the other Stymph was upon him. Its talons made a clutch, scraping long furrows in his shoulder. He cursed it, and struck a mighty whipping blow with his bow-stave that staggered it in mid-flight. Clutching the supporting branch with his legs, he tore his axe from its lashing at his girdle, and got it up just in time to meet the recovering drive of the brute. Badly gashed across the narrow, evil face, the Stymph reeled downward, trying in vain to get control of its wings and rise again.

More Stymphs circled this third victim of Hok, and tore several bloody mouthfuls from it. A loud clamor rose over Hok's head—the smell of gore was maddening the flock. Slipping his right hand through the thong on his axe handle, he looked up.

The sky was filling with Stymphs. Though never a man to recognize danger with much respect, Hok was forced to recognize it now. Where he had thought to meet a dozen or score of the monsters, here they were mustered in numbers like a flock of swallows—his system of counting, based on tens and tens of tens, would not permit him to be sure of their strength, even if he had time.

For they had dropped all over him, all of them at once.

A toothy jaw closed on his left elbow. Before it could bite to the bone, he whipped his axe across and smashed the shallow skull with the flat of the blade. Back-handing, he brought the axe round to smite and knock down another attacker. Axe and bow-stave swept right and left, and every blow found and felled a Stymph. The stricken ones were attacked and rended by their ravenous fellows, which made a hurly-burly of confusion and perhaps saved Hok from instant annihilation by the pack. As it was, he knew that the Stymphs were far too many for him.

The end of this furious struggle in the open top of the jungle came with an abrupt climax that Hok never liked to remember afterward. He had ducked low on his limb to avoid the sweeping rush of a big Stymph, and for a moment loosened the straddle-clutch of his legs. At the same moment another of the creatures dropped heavily upon his shoulders, sinking its claws into his flesh. Its weight dislodged him. Hok lost all holds, and fell hurtling into the leafy depths below.

His right hand quitted its hold on the big axe, which remained fast to his wrist by the looped thong. Reaching up and back as he fell, he seized the Stymph by its snaky throat and with a single powerful jerk freed it from its grasp upon his ribs and brought it under him. Its striving wings were slowing the fall somewhat, though it could not rise with his weight. A moment afterward, the two of them crashed into the mass of twigs and leaves, hit an outthrust bough heavily.

The Stymph, underneath, took most of that shock. Its ribs must have been shattered. At the instant of impact, Hok had presence of mind to quit his grip upon its neck, and managed to fling his arm around the branch. He clung there, feet kicking in space, while the Stymph fell shrieking into the middle branches.

Again he was momentarily safe. He looked up. The Stymphs, where they were visible through sprays of greenery, were questing and circling to find him, like fish-hawks above the water's surface.

"Ahai! Here I am, you bird-snakes!" he roared his challenge, and climbed along the branch to a broader fork, where he could stand erect without holding on. And here he found shelter, even from those ravenous beaks and claws.

A great parasitic growth, allied to giant dodder or

perhaps mistletoe, made a great golden-leafed mat above him, circular in form and wider across than the height of two tall men. It could be seen through, but its tough tendrils and shoots could hold back heavier attacks than the Stymph swarm might manage.

"Come on and fight!" he taunted again. "I have killed many of you, and still I live! Ahai, I am Hok the Mighty, whose sport it is to kill Stymphs and worse things than Stymphs!"

The flattened, darkling brains of the Stymphs understood the tone, if not the words of that defiance. They began to drop down on winnowing scaly wings, peering and questing for him. "Here, just below!" he cried to guide them. Then he slung his bow behind him, and poised his axe, spitting between hand and haft for a better grip.

They settled quickly toward him, wriggling and forcing their way through the upper layers of small twigs. He laughed once again, and one of the Stymphs spied him through the tangled matting. It alighted, clutching the strands with its talons, and with a single lancing stroke of its tight-shut beak drove through a weak spot in the shield. Hok stared into its great cold eyes, and shifted his position to avoid its snap.

"Meet Hok, meet death," he said to it, and chopped off that ugly head with his axe. The body flopped and wriggled beyond his jumble of defending vegetation, and three of the other Stymphs came down all together to feast upon it.

That was what Hok wanted. "So many guests come to dine with Hok?" he jibed. "Then the host must provide more meat."

He laid his longest arrow across the bow-stave. For a moment the three fluttering bird-snakes huddled close together above the prey, almost within touch of him. Setting the head of his arrow to an opening among the whorls and tangles, he loosed it at just the right moment.

A triple shrillness of pained screaming beat up, and Hok was spattered with rank-smelling blood. Skewered together like bits of venison on a toasting-stick, the three Stymphs floundered, somersaulted and fell, still held in an agony of conjunction by Hok's arrow. For the first time, unhurt Stymphs drew back as in fear. Hok made bold to show himself, climbing up on top of his protecting mat.

"Do you go?" he demanded. "Am I as unappetizing as all that?"

They came yet again, and he dodged nimbly back into safety. More arrows—he had a dozen left. These he produced, thrusting them through broad leaves around him so as to be more quickly seized and sped. Then, as the Stymphs blundered heavily against his shield of natural wickerwork, he began to kill them.

Close-packed as they were, and within touch of him, he could not miss. By twos and threes his arrows fetched them down. Even the small reptile-minds of the flying monsters could not but register danger. Survivors began to flop upward, struggle into the open air above the branches, retreat into the mist. Hok hurled imprecations and insults after them, and once more mounted the mat to kill wounded wretches with his axe, and to drag his arrows from the mass of bodies.

Well-mannered as always, he took time to thank the curious tangled growth that had been his bulwark. "My gratitude to you, who made me a shield from behind which I won this victory," he addressed it. "You were sent from the Shining One, whom I worship. He knew I needed help, down here in the mists beyond the reach of his rays. My children shall never forget this kindness."*

From below came an awkward scrambling, and Krol, the chief of the tree-folk, mounted upward into view.

"Greetings," Hok chuckled at him. "See what sport I have made with your friends, the bird-snakes."

Krol might have feared the huge, blood-smeared chief of the Flint People, had he not been so concerned with the retreat of the Stymphs overhead.

"They will go," he chattered. "They will never come back, because they fear you. If I had known—"

---

*The surviving myth tells how Hercules (Hok) was sheltered from the Stymphalides by the buckler of Pallas Athene, so that he was able to win victory at leisure.—Ed.

"If you had known, you would not have hung me up for them to eat," Hok finished for him. "As it is, I have driven off your ugly allies, by fear of which you ruled your people. That fear will be gone hereafter. So, I think, will you."

Hok swung down to a branch above Krol and feinted a brain-dashing blow with his axe. Then he laughed as the tree-chief let go all holds, dropping six times his own length through emptiness. He caught a branch below.

"You and I are enemies!" he snarled upward. "Though you have beaten my Stymphs, there remain other things — even Rmanth! I shall see you dead, and your body rended by the tusks of Rmanth, Hok the Meddler!"

And then, though Hok began climbing swiftly downward, old Krol was swifter and surer. They both descended through thickening layers of foliage, to the woven living-place of the tree-people.

CHAPTER VIII

The Dethroning of Krol

$\mathbf{B}$y the time the slower-climbing Hok had come down to that mighty hammocklike footing, Krol had had precious minutes to gather his followers and howl orders and accusations into their ears.

"Ah, here he comes to mock us, the overgrown invader!" Krol yelled, and shook a furious finger toward the approaching Hok. "He has slain the Stymphs, who protected us!"

"I have slain the Stymphs, who feasted on any tree-man daring to climb as high as the open air above the forest," rejoined Hok, with a lofty manner as of one setting Krol's statement right. "I have helped you, not injured you."

Krol glared with a fury that seemed to hurl a rain of sparks upon Hok. "You biggest men," he addressed the other tree-folk out of the side of his broad, loose mouth, "seize him and bind him a second time."

Hok set his shoulder-blades to the main stem of a tree.

He looked at the tree-men. They seemed a trifle embarrassed, like boys stealing from a larder. Soko, the biggest among them, was plainly the most uneasy as well. Hok decided to profit by their indecision.

"You caught me once because I was playful among you," he said. "Hok never makes the same mistake twice. Standing thus, I cannot be knocked down from behind. Meanwhile," and he quickly strung his bow, notching an arrow, "I shall not only strike my attackers, I shall strike them dead."

"Obey me!" blustered Krol, and one of the men lifted a heavy milk-nut to throw. Hok shot the missile neatly out of the hand that held it.

"No throwing," he warned. "Charge me if you will, but make it a fight at close quarters. Those who survive will have a fine tale to tell forever." He glanced sideways, to a gap in the matting. "But the first man to come within my reach I shall cast down there. Krol, is your other ally, Rmanth, hungry?"

The half-formed attack stood still, despite Krol's now hysterical commands to rush Hok. When the old tree-chief had paused, panting for breath, Hok addressed the gathering once again:

"You cannot hope to fight me, you slender ones. The Stymphs, who have held you frightened for so long, fell dead before me like flies in the frost. Of us two—Hok or Krol—who is greatest?"

"Hok is greatest," announced Soko suddenly.

It was plain that none had dared suggest rebellion against Krol since the beginning of time. Krol was as taken aback as other hearers. Soko turned toward Krol, and the old chief actually shrank back.

"He admits killing the Stymphs, he admits it!" jabbered Krol, flapping a nervous paw at Hok. "If they are gone, how shall strangers be kept out of this land of ours?"

Hok guessed that this was an ancient and accepted argument. The tree-folk naturally feared invasion, must have been taught to think of the Stymphs as their guardians against such a danger. He snorted with scornful amusement.

"The old liar speaks of 'this land of yours,'" he repeated.

"How is it your land, men of the trees, when you can neither tread its soil nor look into its sky—when bird-snakes prey on you above, and an elephant-pig prowls below, so that you must dwell forever in this middle-part like tree frogs?" He paused, and judged that his question had struck pretty close to where those folk did their thinking. "I have been your benefactor," he summed up. "The open air is now yours, for Krol says the Stymphs have fled from it. The next step is—"

"To kill Rmanth?" suggested someone, a bolder spirit among the hearers.

"The next step," finished Hok, "is to get rid of that tyrant Krol."

Krol had drawn back into a sort of tangle of branches and vines, which would serve as a partial screen against any rush. He snarled, and hefted his ivory-bladed axe in one hand.

"You speak truth, Hok," put in Soko, more boldly than before. "Go ahead and kill Krol."

But Hok shook his golden shock-head. "No. I could have done that minutes ago, with a quick arrow, or a flick of my axe. But I have left him for you yourselves to destroy. He is your calamity, your shame. He should be your victim."

Krol made play with his axe. "I will hew you all into little shreds!" he threatened in a high, choked voice. Soko was the first to see how frightened the old despot was. He addressed his fellows:

"Men of my people, if I kill Krol, will I be your chief?" he asked. "Such is custom."

Several made gestures of assent, and Soko was satisfied.

"Then I challenge him now." With no wait for further ceremony, Soko put out one lean, knowing hand and borrowed a weapon from the woven girdle of a neighbor. It was a sort of pick, a heavy, sharp piece of bone lashed crosswise in the cleft of a long, springy rod. He approached Krol's position.

"Come and be killed," Soko bade his chief, in a sort of chant. "Come and be killed. Come and—"

Krol came, for he was evidently not too afraid of anything like an even battle. Hok, a giant and a stranger, had

terrified him. The repudiation of the whole tribe had un-
manned him. But if Soko was alone a challenger, Krol
intended to take care of his end.

There was still pith in his pudgy old arm as he swung the
ivory axe at Soko. The younger warrior parried the blow
within a span's distance of his face, missed a return stroke
with the pick. A moment later they were fencing furiously
and quite skillfully, skipping to and fro on the shaky footing.
Hok, who had a fighting man's appreciation of duelling
tactics, watched with interest.

"Well battled!" he voiced his applause. "Strike lower,
Soko, his guard is high! Protect your head! Don't stumble
or—Hai! Now he is yours!"

Indeed, it seemed so. Krol had feinted Soko into a
downward sweep with the pick, and had slipped away from
the danger. With Soko momentarily off balance, Krol struck
with his axe; but a quick upward jerk of Soko's weapon-butt
struck his wrist, numbing it. The axe fell among the trampled
leaf-mold on the branchy mat. Krol was left unarmed before
Soko.

Now despair made the challenged chief truly dangerous.
Krol sprang before Soko could land a last and fatal stroke. He
threw his arms around Soko's body, and sank his sharp fangs
into Soko's flesh at juncture of neck and shoulder. The two
scrambled, fell, and rolled over and over, perilously close to a
terrible fall. The chattering onlookers danced and gesticu-
lated in pleased excitement.

Hok, whose own teeth were far too even for use as
weapons, was about to remark that biting seemed grossly
unfair, when the issue was decided. Soko tore loose from the
grip of Krol's jaws and turned the old man underneath. Krol
doubled a leg and strove to rip Soko's abdomen open with
the nails of his strong, flexible toes, but a moment later Soko
had hooked his own thumbs into Krol's mouth corners. He
forced his enemy's head back and back, until the neck was on
the point of breaking. With a coughing whine, Krol let go all
holds, jerked himself free, and next moment ran for his life.

At once the spectators gave a fierce shout, and joined the
chase. Hok, following over the swaying mass of boughs,

could hear a hundred execrations being hurled at once. Apparently every man and woman, and most of the children, among the tree-folk had a heavy score to settle with the fierce old fraud who had ruled them. Soko, leading the pack, almost caught up with Krol. But Krol avoided his grasp, and disappeared into something.

Hok came up, pushing in among the yelling tree-men. He saw a new curiosity—Krol's fortress.

It was made like the nest of a mud-wasp, a great egg-shaped structure of clay among the heavier branches of a tall tree. Apparently Krol had spent considerable time and thought on his refuge, against just such an emergency as this. Hok judged that within was a baskety plaiting of chosen branches, with the clay built and worked on the outside thickly and smoothly. The whole rondure was twice Krol's height from top to bottom, and almost the same distance through. It was strongly lodged among several stout forks, and had but one orifice. This was a dark doorway, just large enough for Krol to slip through and perhaps a thought too narrow for shoulders the width of Soko's.

"Krol's nest is well made," Hok pronounced, with frank admiration. "My own tribesmen sometimes make their huts like this, of branches with an outer layer of earth. Why are not all your homes so built?"

The yelling had died down. Soko, his big eyes watching the doorway to the mud-nest, made reply: "Only Krol could fetch clay. We dare not go to the valley's floor after it."

"No," rejoined a grumble from inside. "Nor do you dare go after—*water!*"

That reminder plainly frightened every hearer. They drew back from the den of Krol, looked at each other and at Soko.

"What does he mean?" demanded Hok. "Water does he say? When it comes to that, where do you get water?"

Soko pointed to the opening. "He gets it. Krol." Soko's throat, still torn and chewed from the battle, worked and gulped. "We should have thought of that. Without Krol, we can get nothing to drink."

One or two of his hearers made moaning sounds and

licked their mouths, as if already dry and thirsty. Hok questioned Soko further. It developed that the tree-folk had big dry gourd-vessels, fashioned from the fruit of lofty vines, and these they let down on cords of fiber. Krol, the single individual who would venture to the ground level, scooped up water from a stream there, and the others would draw it up for their own use. Hok nodded, praising in his heart the wisdom of Krol.

"It is yet another way in which he kept his rule over you," he commented. "Yet Krol must die some day. How would you drink then?"

"When I die, you all die," pronounced Krol from his fastness. "I declare you all in danger. Without me to guide your gourds into that stream, thirst will claim you one by one."

Silence. Then a wretched little man attempted a different question:

"What is your will, mighty Krol?"

Krol kept majestic silence for a moment. Finally:

"You will all swear to obey my rules and my thoughts, even unspoken wishes. You will range far to pluck all the fruits I like, and bring them to me. You will yield Soko up as a victim—"

"Wait, you tree-people!" burst out Hok in disgust. "I see you wavering! Do you truly mean to let that murderer destroy Soko, who is the best man among you?"

Nobody answered. Hok saw them stare sickly. Krol went on:

"I have not finished. Soko as a victim, I say. And also this troublesome stranger, Hok. Their blood will increase my walls."

CHAPTER IX

The Hot Hunger Obliges

For a moment Hok had an overpowering sense of having guessed wrong.

He had spoken the truth when he announced that the killing of Krol was the tree-men's responsibility, not his. Violent death was no novelty in his life, and he had inflicted enough of it on large, strong foes to be hesitant about attacking weak, unworthy ones. Too, he had no wish to take on the rule of Krol's people as an additional chore. If Soko, who seemed a fair chieftainly type, did the killing, then Soko would confirm himself as leader. Hok could depart from this Ancient Land with a clear conscience.

But just now his half-languid forbearance was shunting him into another nasty situation. Three or four of the men were murmuring together, and there was a stealthy movement of the clan's whole fighting strength in the direction of Soko. At once Hok pushed forward at and among them. Quick flicks of his open hands scattered them like shavings in the wind.

"Fools!" he scolded them. "Weak of wit! You deserve no better than a life roosting in these trees. Soko and I have brought you to the edge of freedom, and you cannot take advantage!"

"That is good talk," seconded Soko, with considerable stoutness. "Krol has fled before me. Since he will not fight, I am chief. Let any one man among you come and strive with me if he thinks otherwise."

The half-formed uprising was quelled. One or two men fidgeted. Said one: "But who will fetch us water?"

"Who but Krol?" chimed in the old rascal from behind his mud walls. "I make no more offers until you come to me with thirsty throats, begging."

The speaker glanced sidelong at Hok. He half-whispered: "Krol wants the blood of Soko and the stranger—"

"He shall have blood enough and to spare, if you even think of fighting," Hok cut him off roughly. "Krol spoke of using it 'for the thickness of his walls.' What did he mean?"

Soko pointed to the den. "He mixes earth with blood, and it turns into stone."

Hok came toward the big egg of clay, and saw that Soko

spoke truth. The texture of that fortress was more than simple dried mud. Hok prodded it with his finger, then a dagger-point, finally swung his axe against it. He made no more than a dint. Even his strength and weapons could not strip that husk from Krol.*

"Hai, the old coward has built strongly," he granted. "Well, the front door is open. Shall I fetch him out?"

Soko nodded eagerly, and Hok cut a long straight shoot from a nearby branch. This he poked in through the entrance hole. It encountered softness, and Hok grinned at the howl that came back. Then the end of the stick was seized inside, and he grinned more widely.

"Do you think to match pulls with Hok?" he queried. "A single twitch, and you come out among us."

Suiting action to word, he gave his end a sharp tug. Krol let go, and Hok almost fell over backward as the stick came into view.

But upon it was something that made the tree-folk scream with one voice of horror, while Hok himself felt a cold chill of dismay.

Krol had clung to the end of the stick only long enough to attach a peculiar and unpleasant weapon of his own—a small, frantic snake banded in black and orange. This creature came spiralling along the pole toward Hok, plainly angry and looking for trouble. Hok dropped the pole, grabbing for his bow. Fallen upon the woven floor, the snake turned from him to Soko, who was nearest at the moment. Soko scrambled away, bellowing in fear.

But then Hok had sent an arrow at it, and spiked it to a lichen-covered stub of bough that thrust into view from the platform. The ugly little creature lashed to and fro like a worm on a fish-hook. Its flat head, heavily jowled with poison sacs, struck again and again at the shaft that pierced it.

---

*Blood and earth, mixed into a primitive cement, dates back to long before the dawn of history. It is fairly universal among the simple races of the world, and is used to make durable hut-floors in both Africa and South America. The blending calls for considerable judgment and labor; the author has seen samples, and has tried to imitate them for himself, but with only indifferent success.—Ed.

"Wagh!" cried Hok, and spat in disgust. "The touch of that fang is death. Does Krol live with such friends?"

"Snakes do not bite Krol," volunteered Soko, returning shakily.

"I do not blame them," rejoined Hok. "Well, he seems prepared for any assault. Siege is the alternative."

"I am thirsty," piped up a child from behind its watching mother. Hok ordered a search for milk-nuts, and half the tribe went swinging away through the boughs to bring them. Soko lingered at Hok's elbow.

"Hok! Only the death of Krol will save us. There are some in the tribe who will slay us if we sleep, if we relax watch even—"

"And your blood will plaster my walls afresh," promised Krol, overhearing.

Hok made another close inspection of Krol's defenses, keeping sharp lookout lest Krol turn more snakes upon him. He hacked experimentally at several of the branches that supported the structure, but they were tough and thick, would take days to sever. After a moment, inspiration came to him. He began to prune at nearby twigs and sticks, paying especial attention to dry, dead wood. Soon he had cleared most of the small branches from around the den, and stacked his cuttings carefully to one side.

"What will you do to force him out?" asked Soko.

"It is not I who will force him out," replied Hok cryptically. "It is my friend, the Hot Hunger."

"The Hot Hunger!" repeated Krol and his voice sounded hollow.

As the nut-gatherers returned, Hok gave them another errand, the collection of small faggots of dry branches. They obeyed readily, for Krol voiced no more threats, and Soko was acting the part of a chief. As the little stores of fuel came in, Hok began to peg and tie them to the outside of the clay den. Finally, while all watched in round-eyed wonder, he fished forth his firemaking apparatus.

Upon a thick carpet of green leaves he kindled the smallest of fires. All but Soko, who had seen fire-building once before, whimpered and drew away. Hok was all the more glad, for he wanted no crowding and bough-shaking to set the treetops ablaze. Having found and kindled a torch to his liking, he stamped out the rest of the fire with his moccasin heel and returned to the fuel-festooned den of Krol.

He ignited the broken, splintery end of a twig. It flared up, and other pieces of wood likewise. Hok nodded approval of his work.

"See, it will soon be night," he announced. "Will someone bring me a little food? I shall watch here."

"Watch what?" asked one of the tree-folk.

"Krol's embarrassment. Where are some of those milk-nuts?"

Twilight was coming on, with dusk to follow. Most of the tree-men led their families to distant nests, peering back in worried wonder. Soko remained with Hok.

"You are going to burn Krol," guessed Soko, but Hok shook his head in the firelight, and pegged more sticks to the blood-mingled clay.

"Help me to spread thick, moist leaves to catch any fire that falls, Soko. No, Krol will not wait long enough to be burned. Eventually he will come forth to face us."

From within the den came a strange sound, half wheeze and half snarl.

"You are a devil, Hok," Krol was mumbling. "It grows hot in here."

Soko was encouraged. "Come and be killed," he set up his chant of challenge. "Come and be killed. Come and be killed."

Krol wheeze-snarled again, and fell silent. Hok fed his fire judiciously. The blood-clay cement was scorching hot to his fingertips. Dusk swiftly became night.

"Hok, listen," ventured Krol after a time. "You and I are reasonable men. Perhaps I was wrong to make an enemy of you. You are wrong to remain an enemy of mine. I have it in mind that you and I could do great things. Your strength, with my wits—"

"This talk is not for bargaining, but to throw us off guard," Hok remarked sagely to Soko.

Soko peered into the dark opening of the den. "Come and be killed," he invited Krol.

Krol wheezed again, this time with a sort of sob as obligato.

"Your hearts are as hard as ivory," he accused shakily. "I am old and feeble. The things I did may have been mistakes, but I was trying to help my people. Now I must die horribly, of the Hot Hunger, because a big yellow-haired stranger has no mercy."

Hok lashed a handful of fresh fuel together with a green vine and tied it to a peg he had worked into the clay, setting this new wood afire.

"I judge that Krol is at his most dangerous now," he told Soko. "Beware of those who seek to make you sorrow for them. Tears bedim the eyes."

"Come and be killed," repeated Soko.

He had come quite close to the opening, and Krol made his last bid for victory and safety.

He dived forth, swift and deadly as the little coral snake he had attempted to use against Hok. The impact of his pudgy old body was enough to bowl over the unready Soko.

Winding his legs and one arm around the body of his younger rival, he plied with his free hand a long bone dagger.

Hok, on the other side of the fiery den, hurried around just in time to see two grappled bodies roll over, and then fall through a gap in the broad mat. Two yells beat up through the night—Soko's voice raised in startled pain, Krol's in fierce triumph. Then, as Hok reached the gap, there was only one voice:

"There, Soko, hang like a beetle on a thorn! You shall have time to think of my power before you die! I, Krol, depart for Rmanth, my only friend, whom I shall feed fat with the corpses of my rebellious people!"

CHAPTER X

Hok Accepts a Challenge

In the complete darkness, climbing might have been a dire danger; but the fire that still burned around the abandoned fortress of Krol shed light below. Hok was able to find footing among the branches, and to descend with something of speed.

At a distance of some twenty paces below the matted mid-floor of the jungle, he found Soko. His friend seemed to dangle half across a swaying branch-tip, struggling vaguely with ineffectual flaps of arms and legs. Of Krol there was no glimpse or sound.

"Soko, you still live!" cried Hok. "Come with me, we will hunt for Krol together!"

"But I cannot come," wheezed Soko, pain in his voice.

A sudden up-blazing of the fire overhead gave them more light, and Hok saw the plight that Soko was in.

Evidently Krol and Soko had fallen upon the branch, Soko underneath. As earlier in the day with Hok and the Stymph, so in this case the lower figure in the impact had been momentarily stunned. Krol, above, had taken that moment to strike downward with the big bone dagger, pouring all his strength into the effort.

That dagger had pierced Soko's body on the left side, coming out beyond and driving deep into the wood of the branch. As Krol himself had put it, Soko was like a beetle on a thorn. "I cannot come," he moaned again, making shift to cling to the branch with both hands, to ease the drag on hs wound.

Hok balanced himself on the bough, and began to work his way out toward the unhappy tree-man. There was no nearby branch by which to hold on or to share Hok's weight. The single outward shoot swayed and crackled beneath him. He drew back to safer footing.

"I must find another way to him," muttered Hok,

tugging his golden beard. Then he thought of such a way, and began to climb upward again.

"Don't leave me," pleaded Soko wretchedly.

"Courage," Hok replied, and searched among branches for what he needed. He found it almost at once—a clumsy mass of vines, strong and pliable as leather thongs. Quickly he cut several of the sturdiest strands, knotting them together. Then he located a stronger branch which extended above the one where Soko was imprisoned. He slid out along it, and made fast one end of his improvised line.

"I am in pain," Soko gasped, his voice weak and trembling.

"Courage!" Hok exhorted him again. He hung axe, bow, quiver and pouch on a stout stub of the base branch. Then he swung down by the knotted vines, descending hand under hand toward Soko.

He came to a point level with the unfortunate prisoner of the wedged dagger, and almost within reach. By shifting his weight he made the cord swing, and was able to hook a knee over the lower bough. Then, holding on by a hand just above a knot in the vines, he put out his other hand to the knife that transfixed Soko.

Even as he touched it, Soko gave a shudder and went limp. He had fainted.

Hok was more glad than otherwise, and forthwith tugged on the tight-stuck weapon with all his strength. It left its lodgment in the wood, and came easily out of Soko's flesh. With nothing to hold him to his lodgment, Soko dropped into emptiness.

Hok made a quick pincerlike clutch with his legs. He caught Soko between his knees, as in a wrestling hold. His single handhold on the vine was almost stripped away, but he grimly made it support the double weight. The bone dagger he set between his teeth. Then, still holding the senseless Soko by pressure of his knees, he overhanded himself upward again. He achieved a seat on the larger branch, and laid Soko securely upon a broad base of several spreading shoots.

Soko bled, but not too profusely. Krol had struck hastily

for all his vicious intent, and the knife had pierced the
muscles of chest and armpit, just grazing the ribs without
hurting a single vital organ. Hok quickly gathered handfuls
of leaves, laying them upon the double wound and letting the
blood glue them fast for a bandage. In the midst of these
ministrations Soko's wide eyes opened again.

"You saved me, Hok," he said in a voice full of trembling
gratitude. "That makes twice or three times. Krol—"

"He still lives," rejoined Hok grimly, repossessing himself of his weapons. "Perhaps he steals upon us even now."

Soko's brilliant eyes quested here and there in the night.
"I think not," he said. "I have command of myself again.
Shall we go upward?"

His wound was troublesome and he climbed stiffly, but
he was back to the side of the dying fire well before Hok. "I
thirst," he complained.

"Because you have lost blood," Hok told him, and took
a fiery stick to light the inside of Krol's abandoned den.
Among the great quantity of possessions he saw several
gourds. One of these proved to be full of water, warm but
good. He gave it to the thankful Soko.

Soko drank, and passed the gourd to Hok. "How can we
kill Krol now, my friend?" he asked. "Because we must kill
him. You understand that."

Hok nodded, drinking in turn. "You shall do it without
my help, so as to be chief according to custom. My task will
be to destroy Rmanth, and roast him for your people. I made
such a promise."

"Promise?" repeated Soko. "Who can keep a promise
like that?"

"I have never broken a promise in my life, Soko. Here,
help me put out this fire, lest some coals destroy the jungle.
And tell me how we shall find Rmanth."

Soko could not do so. His only ventures to the ground
had been by way of the vine-spiral tube in which Hok had first
found him. He reiterated that Krol, and Krol alone, possessed
the courage and knowledge to face Rmanth and come away
unhurt.

"Well, then, where do you let down gourds for water?"

"Near the hollow tube. Why?"

"Tomorrow all the tree-dwellers shall have fresh water. That is another of Hok's promises. Will you watch while I sleep, Soko? Later waken me, and sleep yourself."

Soko agreed, and Hok stretched out wearily upon ferny leafage. He closed his eyes and drifted off into immediate slumber.

Sleeping, he dreamed.

He thought he saw a marshalling of his old enemies. He himself was apparently arrayed singly against a baleful mob. In the forefront was Kimri, the black-bearded giant from whom he had won the lovely Oloana. There was also Cos, a paunchy, nasty-eyed fellow who had ruled the walled town of Tlanis until Hok adventured thither and changed all that. Over the head of Cos looked Romm, who once made the bad guess that renegading among the Gnorrls would give him victory over Hok's Flint Folk. Djoma the Fisher slunk pretty well to the back, for he was never over-enthusiastic about fighting Hok man to man. It was a delightful throng of menaces.

"I will have the pleasure of slaying you all a second time," Hok greeted them, and rushed. One hand swung his axe, the other jabbed and fenced with a javelin. In his dream, those second killings seemed much easier than had the first. The ancient enemies fell before him like stalks of wild rice before a swamp-buffalo. He mustered the breath in his deep chest to thunder a cry of triumph, when—

They seemed to fade away, and at the same time to mould and compact themselves into yet another form. This one was hairy, pudgy, grizzled, but active. Bestial lips writhed and fluttered, wide eyes that could see in the dark glared.

"So, you big yellow-haired hulk!" choked a voice he knew, beside itself with rage. "I find you unprepared, I kill you *thus!*"

Hok threw himself forward, under the stroke of some half-seen weapon. His hands struck soft flesh, and he heard the threatening words shrill away into a shriek.

Then the dream became reality.

Dawn had come. Soko, wounded and weary, had dozed off during his watch, and Krol had returned to take his vengeance.

Only Hok's sense of danger, shaking him back to wakefulness, had given him the moment of action needed before a blow fell. Krol had poised a big club, a piece of thorn-wood stout enough to break the skull of a horse. This weapon now swished emptily in air, as Hok grappled and held helpless the gray old sinner.

"Soko! Soko!" called Hok loudly.

Soko looked up, washing the sleep from his own eyes. "Eh?" he yawned, then he too was aware of the danger. He sprang up.

"Soko," said Hok, "I swore that you would kill this man and become chieftain in his place. Do so now. Do not let him escape once more."

Soko drew a dagger. Hok let go of Krol.

The deposed ruler of the tree-men made a last effort to break for safety, but Hok blocked his retreat. Then Soko caught Krol by his long hair. The dagger he held—it was the same big bone blade that had spiked Soko to the branch last night—darted into the center of Krol's chest. Blood bubbled out. The old despot collapsed, dying.

The wakening tree-people were hurrying from all sides to stare and question. Hok clapped Soko's unwounded shoulder.

"Obey your new chief," he urged the gathering. "Be afraid of him, follow him, respect him. He is your leader and your father."

Krol looked up, blood on his wide mouth. "What about the water?" he sneered, and with a coughing gobble he died.

There was silence, and Soko, in the first moment of his power, could only look to Hok for guidance.

"People of the trees," said Hok, "I have been challenged. Krol was bad and deserved death. But he spoke the truth when he reminded us that water was not at hand while Rmanth roamed below. In other words, Rmanth must be destroyed. I promised that, did I not?" He balanced his axe in one hand, and nodded to Soko. "Come, chief. We will arrange the matter."

Soko followed him, trying not to seem too laggardly. Hok raised his voice: "Go to the usual place, you others, and let down your gourds. Water shall be yours, now and forever after."

He and Soko came to the tube that gave sheltered descent to the ground level. Hok entered it first, swinging downward by the rough ladder-rungs. Soko for once did not climb faster than he. Hok came to the floor of the cavity, and without hesitation wriggled through the lower opening into the outer air, standing upon the damp earth of the valley bottom. Soko had to be called twice before he followed.

"Look around for that stream of water," directed Hok. "There, isn't that it, showing through the stems below us? Come on, Soko. You are a chief now."

At that word, Soko drew himself up. "Yes, I am a chief," he said sturdily. "I will do what a chief should do, even though Rmanth eats me."

"You shall eat Rmanth instead," Hok said confidently. "But first, the water."

They came to the edge of the stream. Gourds dangled down from above, on lengthy vine strings. Hok and Soko guided them into the water, and tugged for them to be drawn up. Glad cries beat down from the upper branches, as the hoisters felt the comforting weight of the containers.

"The voices will bring Rmanth," Soko said dully.

Hok glanced over his shoulder. "He is already here. Leave him to me. Go on and fill gourds."

He turned from Soko and walked back among the trees, toward the gray bulk with its six knobby horns and hungry tusks.

"I have a feeling that this was planned for both of us," Hok addressed the elephant-pig. "Come then. We will race, play and fight, and it shall end when one of us is dead."

CHAPTER XI

The Termination of Rmanth

Several accounts have descended to us of how Hok raced, played and fought that day.* But names have been changed, some facts have been altered for the sake of ritual or romance. In any case, Hok himself talked little about the business, for such was not his way. The only narrators were the tree-folk, who did not see much of what happened. Which makes the present story valuable as new light on an old, old truth.

Hok saw that Rmanth was at least six times more angry than when they had met last. The arrow in his tongue had evidently broken off or worked its way out, though pink-tinted foam flecked Rmanth's great protruding tusks. The arrow in his nostril still remained, and his ugly snout was swollen and sore. His eyes remained cold and cunning, but as Hok came near they lighted with a pale glow of recognition.

"You know me, then," Hok said. "What have we to say and do to each other?"

Rmanth replied by action, a bolting direct charge.

Tree-thickets sprouted between the two, but Rmanth clove and ploughed among them like a bull among reeds. His

---

*The myth that will rise quickest to the reader's memory is the one concerning Hercules and his conquest of the mighty wild boar of Eurymanthis. It is odd, or not so odd, that Greek myths tell the same story in several forms. Thus Theseus, who may be another memory of Hercules or Hok, destroys such a giant swine in his youthful journey to his father's court. Meleager hunts and kills the Calydonian boar. And one of the Tuscan heroes of Latin Legend, named in "The Lays of Ancient Rome" as an adversary of Horatius, won his fame by killing a boar "that wasted fields and slaughtered men."

Such super-swine are described as unthinkably huge and strong, clumsy but swift, with fierce and voracious natures that made them a menace to whole communities and districts. Not even the European wild boar, wicked fighter though it is, could approximate such character and performance. It becomes increasingly sure that Rmanth, the boar of Eurymanthis, and those others, trace back to tales of the now extinct Dinoceras. —Ed.

explosion into attack was so sudden, so unwarned, so swift, that Hok's sideward leap saved him barely in time. As it was, the bristly flank of the beast touched him lightly as it drove by. Rmanth, missing that first opportunity to finish this maddening enemy, turned as nimbly as a wild horse, head writhed around on the huge shoulders and horrid fangs gaping for a crushing bite.

Hok hurriedly conquered an instinctive urge to spring clear—such a spring would only have mixed him up in the brush, and Rmanth's second pounce would have captured him. The part of wisdom was to come close, and Hok did so. He placed one hand against Rmanth's great quivering haunch, the other hand grasping his bow-stave. As the big brute spun to snap at him, Hok followed the haunches around. Rmanth could not get quite close enough to seize him. As the two of them circled, Hok saw a way into the open, and took it at once. He slipped around and behind a big tree. Rmanth, charging violently after, smote that tree heavily. Hok laughed, then headed toward the slope which he had traveled the day before.

Rmanth's thick head must have buzzed from that impact against the tree. He stood swaying his muzzle experimentally, planting his forefeet widely. Hok had done all his maneuverings with an arrow laid ready across his bow, held in place with his left forefinger. Now he had time to draw it fully and send it singing at Rmanth's face.

As before, he aimed at the eye. This time his aim was not spoiled. The shaft drove deep into one cold, wicked orb, and Rmanth rose suddenly to his massive hind-quarters, an upright colossus, pawing the air and voicing a horrible cry of pain. Such a cry has been imagined only once by modern man, and the imaginer was both a scholar and a master of fantasy.* Hok clinched forever his right to his reputation of stout-heartedness. He laughed a second time.

"An arrow in your other eye, and you'll be at my

---

*". . . something between bellowing and whistling, with a kind of sneeze in the middle . . . and when you've once heard it you'll be *quite* content."
—Lewis Carroll, in *Through the Looking-Glass*—Ed.

mercy!" said he, reaching over his shoulder for another shaft in his quiver.

But there was not another shaft in his quiver.

The battlings with the Stymphs, his knocking of the milk-nut from an assailant's hand, the hurried destruction of Krol's gaudy snake, had used up his store of shafts. If Rmanth was half-blinded, Hok was wholly without missiles. He felt a cold wave of dismay for a moment, but only for a moment.

"Perhaps I was not fair to think of hacking and prodding a helpless enemy to death," he reflected. "This makes a more even battle of it. At any rate, Rmanth has forgotten that Soko will be filling the water gourds. Let me play with him further. Here he comes!"

And here he came, in another of his mighty bursts of power, swift and resistless as an updriving avalanche.

Hok dared wait longer this time, for Rmanth must charge up the hill. He had quickly returned his bow to its shoulder loop, and now took a stout grip on his axe. As the gaping fang-fringed maw, from which lolled that inflamed tongue, was almost upon him, he sprang aside as before and chopped at the remaining good eye of Rmanth. Missing, he struck the gray hide of the cheek. His heavy flint rebounded like a hailstone from a hut-roof. Hok turned and ran, leaping from side to side to confuse his enemy, and paused near the great sloping trail down which dying mammoths were wont to slide themselves. A carrion stench assailed his nostrils, and he remembered his original quarrel with Rmanth.

"You ate my prey," he accused the lumbering hulk, which turned stubbornly to pursue him further. "Gragru I trapped, wounded, and chased. He was mine. He recognized my victory. But you lolled below here and gorged yourself on my hunting. You owe me meat, Rmanth, and I intend to collect the debt."

His voice, as usual, maddened the elephant-pig. When Hok began to scale the slope backward, Rmanth breasted the climb with great driving digs of his massive feet and legs.

But now the advantage was with Hok. Lighter, neater-footed, he could move faster on the ascent than could this mighty murderer. Indeed, he could probably gain the snow-lipped plain above and escape entirely. But he did not forget his promise to Soko's people. Victory, not flight, was what he must achieve.

"Come near, Rmanth," he invited, moving backward and upward. "I want a fair chance at you."

Rmanth complied, surging up the slanting trail with a sudden new muster of energy. Hok braced himself and smote with his axe at Rmanth's nose. Right between the two forward horns his blade struck, and again Rmanth yelled in furious pain. But the blow only bruised that heavy hide, did not lay it fully open. Rmanth faltered, and Hok retreated once more.

"This nightmare cannot be wounded," he reflected aloud. "At least not in the side or head or muzzle, like an honest beast. What then? The neck, as with a bull?"*

But there was no way to get to Rmanth's neck. He did not charge with head down, like a stag or bison or rhinoceros, but with nose up and mouth open, like a beast of prey. Hok wished that he had a spear, stout and long. It might serve his turn. But he had only the axe, and it must not fail him. He continued his retirement, along the trail he remembered from his previous descent.

So for some time, and for considerable rise in altitude. Then, suddenly, Rmanth was not crowding Hok any longer. Hok paused and grimaced his defiance.

"Tired?" he jeered. "Or afraid?"

Plainly it was the latter, but Rmanth's fear was not for Hok. He turned his one good eye this way and that, looking up into the sky that at this point was not very misty. He

---

*The sturdiest of animals can be dealt with by attacking the spine through the nape of the neck. Most familiar of such attacks is probably the sword-thrust of the matador in a Spanish bullfight. The bull is induced to lower his head, bringing into reach a vulnerable spot the size of one's open palm at juncture of neck and shoulders. Elephant and rhinoceros also can be killed by a proper stab there, since the spinal cord is close to the surface, for all the thick, hard hide. Scientists think that the down-pointing front teeth of the sabre-tooth tiger—extinct, or very rare, in Hok's time—were designed by nature for just such a mode of killing.—Ed.

sniffed, and wrinkled a very ugly gray lip that reminded Hok
of Krol.

Then Hok remembered. "Oh, yes, the Stymphs. Krol
told me that you did not venture far enough from the shelter
of the trees for them to reach you. But think no more about
them, Rmanth. I killed most of them. Those who lived have
flown away. Perhaps the snow will destroy them—they seem
to think it a kinder neighbor than Hok."

He moved boldly into an open space on the slope.
Rmanth snorted and wheezed, seeming to wait for sure
doom to overtake the audacious human. Then he squinted
skyward again, was plainly reassured, and finally followed
Hok upward.

"Well done, elephant-pig!" Hok applauded. "This is
between you and me. No Stymph will cheat the conqueror."

More ascent, man and beast toiling into less tropical
belts. Hok found himself backing into a ferny thicket. It was
here that—yes, wadded into a fork was his bundle of winter
clothing.

As he found it, it seemed that he found also a plan, left
here like the clothes against his need. He felt like shouting
out one of his laughs, but smothered it lest Rmanth be placed
on guard. Instead he seized and shook out the big lion skin
that was his main protection against blizzards. Its shaggy
expanse was blond and bright, like his own hair.

"See, Rmanth," he roared, "I run no more! Catch this!"
He flung the pelt right into Rmanth's face.

Next moment those mighty fangs had closed upon the
fur. The horrid head bore its prize to earth, holding it there as
if to worry it. His neck was stooped, the thick skin stretched
taut. . . . Hok hurled himself forward in a charge.

Before Rmanth was aware that the hide in his jaws was
empty, Hok had sprung and planted a moccasin upon his
nose, between those forward horns. Rmanth emitted a
whistling grunt and tossed upward, as a bull tosses. Hok felt
himself flipped into the air, and for a moment he soared over
the necknape, the very position he hoped for.

Down slammed his axe, even as he hurtled. It struck
hard, square, and true across the spine of Rmanth, back of the

shallow skull. Hok's arms tingled with the back-snap of that effort, and his body was flung sidewise by it.

But Rmanth was down, stunned or smashed. He floundered to his knees. Hok ran to him, dagger out. A thrust, a powerful dragging slash, and the thick hide was torn open. Once more the axe rose and fell. The exposed spinal vertebrae broke beneath the impact with a sound like a tree splitting on a frosty night.

Rmanth relaxed, and abruptly rolled down slope, as dead mammoths were wont to roll. Hok saved his last breath, forbearing to shout his usual signal of victory. Snatching up his crumpled lion-skin cloak, he dashed swiftly downward in pursuit of that big lump of flesh he had killed.

CHAPTER XII

The Feast and the Farewell

Those men, women and children who had been Soko's tree-people sat at last on the solid soil, stockaded about with the mighty trees of the jungle, and roofed over with the impenetrable mat of foliage, vines and mould that had once been their floor and footing. They sat in a circle near the brink of the stream, and in the circle's center was a cheerful cooking fire of Hok's making. The air was heavy with the smell of roast meat.

There had been enough of Rmanth for all, and more than enough. Once Hok had found Soko and shown him the carcass, it had been possible, though not easy, to coax the other men down to ground level. And it had taken all the muscle of the tribe, tugging wearily on tough vine-strands, to drag Rmanth to the waterside. After that, it was an additional labor, with much blunting of bone knives, to flay away his great armor of hide. But when the great wealth of red meat was exposed, and Hok had instructed the most apt of the tribe in the cooking thereof—ah, after that it was a fulfillment of the most ancient dreams about paradise and plenty.

Three or four tribesmen were toasting last delectable

morsels on green twigs in the outlying beds of coals. More of them lolled and even slept in heavy surfeit, assured that no great trampling foe would overtake and destroy them. The children, who no amount of gorging could quiet down, were skipping and chattering in the immemorial game of tag. To one side sat Soko, on a boulder that was caught between gnarled roots, and his pose was that of a benevolent ruler.

A comely young woman of his people was applying a fresh dressing of astringent herbs and leaves to the wound Krol had made the night before. Grandly Soko affected not to notice the twinges of pain or the attractions of the attendant. He spoke with becoming gravity to Hok, who lounged near with his back against a tree, his big flint axe cuddled crosswise on his lap.

"There is much more meat than my people will ever finish," Soko observed.

"Build fires of green wood, that will make thick smoke," Hok directed. "In that smoke hang thin slices of the meat that is left. It will be dried and preserved so as to keep for a long time, and make other meals for your tribe."

Soko eyed Hok's bow, which leaned against the tree beside him. "That dart-caster of yours is a wonderful weapon," he observed. "I have drawn two shafts, still good, from Rmanth's body. If I can make a bow like it—"

"Take this one," said Hok generously, and passed it over. "I have many more, as good or better, in my own home village. Study the kind of wood used, how it is shaped and rigged, and copy it carefully. Your men can hunt more meat. A jungle like this must have deer and pig and perhaps cattle. Since your people have tasted roasted flesh, they will want more on which to increase their strength."

"We will keep coals from that cooking fire," said Soko.

"Do more than that," Hok urged. "You have seen my fire-sticks and how I used them. Make some for yourself, that the fire may be brought to you when you need it." He peered around him. "See, Soko, there are outcroppings of hard rock near and far. I see granite, a bit of jasper, and here and there good flints. Use those to make tools and weapons instead of bone or ivory."

The dressing of Soko's wound was completed. Soko dismissed the young woman with a lordly gesture, but watched her appreciatively as she demurely departed. Then he turned back to his guest. His smile took from his face the strange beast-look that clung to the wide loose lips and chinless jaw.

"Hok," he said, "we shall never forget these wonders you have done for us, and which you have taught us to do for ourselves. In future times, when you deign to come again—"

"But I shall not come again," Hok told him.

Soko looked surprised and hurt. Hok continued:

"You and I are friends, Soko. It is our nature to be friendly, unless someone proves himself an enemy. But your people and my people are too different. There would be arguments and difficulties between them, and then fights and trouble. When I leave here, it will be forever. I shall not tell at once what I have seen. What I tell later will be only part of the truth. Because I think you and your kind will be better off untroubled and unknown in this valley."

Soko nodded slowly, his eyes thoughtful. "I had been counting on your help from time to time," he confessed. "Perhaps experience will help me, though. What shall we do here after you are gone?"

"Be full of mystery," said Hok sententiously. "The Stymphs seem to have flown away, but their reputation will linger over your home. I judge that game does not prowl near, and only the mammoth knows the valley—to dive into it and die. If ever a hunter of my sort comes near, it will be the veriest accident."

"Thus you will have the chance to make your people strong and wise. They have regained the full right to walk on the ground and breathe air under open skies, which right was denied by Krol. In times to come, I venture to say, you shall issue forth as a race to be great in the outer world. Meanwhile, stay secret. Your secrecy is safe with me."*

*Again referring to the Greek myths, there is the tale of how Hercules came close to the Garden of the Hesperides, a fruitful paradise guarded by dragons. Now we know the source of that story.—Ed.

He rose, and so did Soko. They shook hands.

"You depart now, at only the beginning of things?" Soko suggested.

"The adventure and the battle, at least, are at an end," Hok reminded him. "I am tormented by a sickness of the mind, Soko, which some call curiosity. It feeds on strife, travel and adventure. And so I go home to the northward, to find if my people do not know of such things to comfort me. Goodbye, Soko. I wish you joy of your Ancient Land."

He picked up his furs and his axe, and strode away toward the trail up the slope. Behind him he heard Soko's people lifting a happy noise that was probably their method of singing.

UNTITLED HOK FRAGMENT

by Manly Wade Wellman

In those days Hok the Mighty was chief of the Flint People, where they lived in their line of caves taken from the fierce, half-human Gnorrls. Mighty he was called, for that was what he was, tall, huge-muscled, tawny-haired and tawny-bearded. His loincloth was a leopard's pelt, his cloak the fur of a black-maned lion. He could wrestle down the next strongest man of the tribe, could throw a javelin farther and truer than anyone. He killed lions and cave bears with a single blow apiece of his great axe of blue stone. He hunted down bison and deer, and fetched back loads of meat as much as two ordinary men could lift.

At dawn he would climb the highest rock above the caves and sing, deep-voiced, to the rising sun that made his hair and beard sparkle. All listened and joined in on Hok's song. The men respected him, would have feared him if he hadn't been so good-tempered. The women smiled their admiration, but Hok smiled back only on Oloana, his lovely wife with hair like the night without stars. He was Hok the Mighty, unchallenged in the world he knew until there came into it the subtle man named Plorr and the giant creature named Guargu, that was as blinding white as snow and seemed impossible for even Hok to kill.

Plorr came among them one spring day when Hok and two others hunted and killed a red deer among grass scattered with flowers. Plorr was dressed in a fitted loincloth and cape of white-tanned doeskin, and on his feet he wore shaggy shoes instead of the moccasins the Flint People had. He was tall and bonily thin, his sharp face was scraped clean of beard, and his long brown hair was braided behind his neck. In his right hand he carried a javelin. He put up an open hand in the peace sign, and he smiled crookedly at Hok.

"Are you the chief here?" he asked, in a language like theirs.

Hok smiled back. "If I'm not the chief, you can tell me about yourself until the chief gets here. We don't see many strangers. What's your name, and what do you want?"

"I'm Plorr."

(fragment ends)